SCATTERED TO THE WIND

FOURTEENTH BOOK IN THE BRIGANDSHAW CHRONICLES

PETER RIMMER

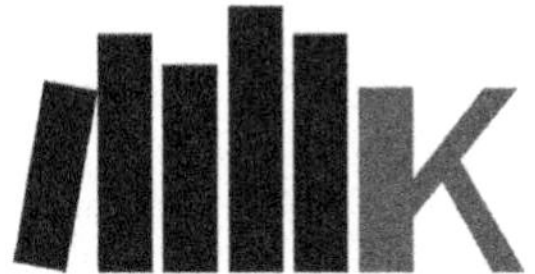

ABOUT PETER RIMMER

Peter Rimmer was born in London, England, and grew up in the south of the city where he went to school. After the Second World War, aged eighteen, he joined the Royal Air Force, reaching the rank of Pilot Officer before he was nineteen. At the end of his National Service, he sailed for Africa to grow tobacco in what was then Rhodesia, now Zimbabwe.

The years went by and Peter found himself in Johannesburg where he established an insurance brokering company. Over 2% of the companies listed on the Johannesburg Stock Exchange were clients of Rimmer Associates. He opened branches in the United States of America, Australia and Hong Kong and travelled extensively between them.

Having lived a reclusive life on his beloved smallholding in Knysna, South Africa, for over 25 years, Peter passed away in July 2018. He has left an enormous legacy of unpublished work for his family to release over the coming years, and not only they but also his readers from around the world will sorely miss him. Peter Rimmer was 81 years old.

To read more about Peter's life, please visit his website: https://www.peterrimmer.com/novelist/author/

ALSO BY PETER RIMMER

The Brigandshaw Chronicles

The Rise and Fall of the Anglo Saxon Empire

Book 1 - Echoes from the Past

Book 2 - Elephant Walk

Book 3 - Mad Dogs and Englishmen

Book 4 - To the Manor Born

Book 5 - On the Brink of Tears

Book 6 - Treason If You Lose

Book 7 - Horns of Dilemma

Book 8 - Lady Come Home

Book 9 - The Best of Times

Book 10 - Full Circle

Book 11 - Leopards Never Change Their Spots

Book 12 - Look Before You Leap

Book 13 - The Game of Life

Book 14 - Scattered to the Wind

Book 15 - When Friends Become Lovers

Great Value Box Sets

The Brigandshaw Chronicles Box Set (Books 1-3)

The Brigandshaw Chronicles Box Set (Books 4-6)

The Brigandshaw Chronicles Box Set (Books 7-9)

The Brigandshaw Chronicles Box Set (Books 10-12)

Standalone Novels

All Our Yesterdays

Cry of the Fish Eagle

Just the Memory of Love

Vultures in the Wind

In the Beginning of the Night

The African Trilogy Box Set including Cry of the Fish Eagle, Vultures in the Wind and Just the Memory of Love)

~

The Asian Sagas

Bend with the Wind (Book 1)

Each to His Own (Book 2)

The Asian Sagas Duet Box Set (Books 1-2)

~

The Pioneers

Morgandale (Book 1)

Carregan's Catch (Book 2)

The Pioneers Duet Box Set (Books 1-2)

~

Novella

Second Beach

SCATTERED TO THE WIND

This novel is entirely a work of fiction. Names, characters, long-standing establishments, places, events and incidents are either the products of the author's imagination or used in a fictitious manner. Any resemblance to actual persons, living or dead, is purely coincidental.

First published in Great Britain in March 2022 by

KAMBA PUBLISHING, United Kingdom

10 9 8 7 6 5 4 3 2 1

PART 1

MARCH TO APRIL 1994 — "WOMEN"

1

Phillip Crookshank arrived home at the end of March, the rains in Zimbabwe almost finished. He was alone. Completely alone. With the new truck parked under a riverine tree, he walked to the ablution block and let himself in. The well-packed tents were stacked in the big room that led to the bathrooms and the toilets. He pulled down a bag with its frame tent packed neatly inside. The bags of poles stood against the opposite wall. It took Phillip an hour to put up his three-compartment tent on the bank above the Zambezi River and make himself comfortable. The river was flowing, the birds singing, the truck full of supplies he had bought in Harare. In a short while, the sun would go down. He made the fire that would keep him safe in the night. From the comfort of a faded chair he looked out over the big river, the joy of being home, away from the crowd, overwhelming. Poor Martha. What would she be thinking? Sometimes, in a fight, it was better to get the hell out of the way. The sun began to set, flooding the sky with colour, a perfect African sunset. A fish eagle flew low in front of him across the water looking for its supper. A buck barked from the other side of the river. The animals were coming down to the water to drink in perfect peace. In half an hour it was dark, the flames from the fire flickering. The new tourist season would open in April. He had time. Alone. Time to think.

"Peace and quiet. What more can a man want?"

The coolbox in the truck, connected to the battery through the socket for the cigarette lighter, had kept the beers cold. On the table, next to the chair, stood a plate of uncooked steak and lamb chops with an open bottle of South African wine. Poor Martha. She would have enjoyed the wine. With the light of day gone, the mosquitoes were Phillip's only problem, making him reposition his canvas chair nearer the smoke of the fire. Having spent most of his life in the African bush he had grown used to the mosquitoes. Every day he would take his anti-malaria pills to prevent any problems. With the cold beer finished, a glass of wine in his hand, and the meat grilling over the campfire, he was content. In a few weeks, when Martha had simmered down, he would think again about what to do about his wife. At the moment in the African bush, America and Kansas City were far away.

When the meat was cooked, Phillip ate his supper. He was tired. The owls were calling, a soft wind rustling the leaves in the trees, the joy of being home overwhelming. With the mosquito net set up over the camp bed in his tent, Phillip slowly drank his wine. When he got up to go to his bed he took the loaded rifle with him. With the gun next to him under the cover of the mosquito net, Phillip lay thinking, thinking about life. All those twists and turns. All those predicaments. Slowly, Phillip drifted into sleep and dreams, all night dreaming of Martha.

For three long, beautiful days Phillip was alone. On the fourth day after his flight from Kansas City, he heard the sound of an engine. When the small safari bus stopped and Phillip's business partner Jacques stepped down, Phillip was smiling.

"Phillip! What the hell are you doing back in Africa? Where's Martha?"

"She threw me out."

"Did she now? How long have you been here? Did you buy a new truck? What's going on, Phillip?"

"Martha lost our baby."

"I'm so sorry. You both so wanted a child... Is the marriage over?"

"I don't know. We only married when she was seven months pregnant. Strange to think that boy was made on the banks of this river. Life plays many games with us. Some good. Some not so good... How are you, Jacques? When do the first tourists arrive? I stocked up with supplies in Harare. Good to see you, partner. Nothing better in life than true old friends. You want a beer? They're cold. I started the generator and charged the batteries."

"A group of six on the second of April. From England. A four-day tour. I'd like a beer. You want to talk about Martha? Are you going back to America?"

"I have no idea. It's so good to be home. You don't have to put up with people."

"The bookings are solid for the whole winter season."

"What happens when you have a business partner doing the marketing in America. When are Munya and Sedgewick due back?"

"Tomorrow or the next day. Another group arrive from America on the third. So that fancy wedding I flew all the way to America for, was a waste of time?"

"Looks like it. We'll have to see. Women, Jacques. They're different to us."

"Tell me that again. All that money down the drain. And your business in America as a venture capitalist?"

"I still own the investments."

"Are they doing any good?"

"You wouldn't believe it. Cheers, old boy. You have no idea how much I have missed Africa."

"Down the hatch. Good to have you back. Not to be sentimental, Phillip, but I've missed you. We all have... Poor Martha."

"She tried to jump off the tenth-floor balcony. The old lady across the way waved. Never did find out her name. She always waved. Lived on her own. Lonely."

"Where is Martha now?"

"Staying with her mother. I told Aggie what she had tried to do. Aggie didn't want Martha to be alone in our apartment. It's far worse for a woman to lose a baby."

"Will she come right?"

"They say so. We hope so. I've told Aggie if Martha wants my help I'll be back on the next plane. Someone said time heals everything."

"Life's a bugger."

"You can say that again. A year ago I didn't even know Martha."

"How it goes with men and women. Especially when you get them pregnant. But life goes on."

"Not for everyone."

"I'm sorry. Wasn't thinking. This is all a surprise."

"You got a girlfriend?"

"You know me. Safety in numbers. There's always some hungry tourist looking for some fun."

"Use a condom."

"Now you're telling me. What's for supper? You shot any game?"

"Not yet. Don't want to break the silence. I'll catch some bream. Just look at that crocodile. Those big, bulging eyes are full of hunger and hope as he looks at me."

"What are you doing?"

"Waving at the crocodile. He's not even blinking. He's a big bugger. Have

Munya or Sedgewick found themselves wives? We can give them jobs. When you attend a tourist seminar in America and they find you know what you're talking about, the travel agents take you seriously. Nothing like one-on-one contact to promote a business. People like to see who you are before they recommend you to their customers. Trust. Not much trust left in our brave new world. In America, they're all after a fast buck... He's off. The bugger's had enough of staring at me."

"They haven't got the *lobola*."

"We can advance them the money. Now that's the way to go. You pay the father for the daughter. How much do they want?"

"Five cows."

"African culture makes far more sense than ours. I've always said I wished I had been born an African."

"Do you have permanent residence in America?"

"Not if Martha divorces me."

"I'd love to live in the States. Are you going to take the boat to go fishing?... No. Maybe I wouldn't. It's just our politics in Zimbabwe that makes me nervous. You never quite know what is happening. Mugabe hates us whites. Says we stole his country."

"Didn't we?"

"We sure made something of it. When Rhodes arrived there were four hundred thousand people living in what is now Zimbabwe. Now there are over eleven million. Must have done something right."

"Want another beer? I can fish tomorrow. I've kept some steaks in the coolbox."

"You got any wine?"

"Plenty. We all drink too much. Why Martha says she lost the baby. Aggie drank when she was pregnant. Told her daughter there wasn't a problem. Who knows? It's all in the lap of the gods. Beer or wine?"

"Beer. Then the wine. What a lovely day. Now the rains are over for six months the valley cools so beautifully. The humidity goes. You still got your cottage in the Vumba?"

"Why sell it? You can't get money out of Zimbabwe even if I needed it. I love that place up in the mountains. At five thousand feet above sea level, you don't feel the heat of an African summer. World's View was three thousand feet above sea level. Dad still says he pines for the farm. All the money in the world can't compensate for life on an African farm. It was given to one of Mugabe's political cronies."

"I know."

"How long have we known each other?"

"Fifteen years. In an hour the sun will go down. Better start the fire. Glad you're home. I'll make myself a bed in your tent. Put up my own tent tomorrow."

"Got three compartments."

"I'm so sorry about you and Martha."

"So am I. Never seen a woman in so much pain."

"It was a boy then?"

"We lost a son. Stiff upper lip. Men don't cry. All that crap. A son would have given both our lives a purpose."

"Can she get pregnant again?"

"Maybe. She thinks not. Two previous marriages and she didn't get herself pregnant. And not for want of trying. At thirty-seven, pushing thirty-eight, she thinks her chances of having a baby are slim."

"Did you two fight?"

"She went crazy. You blame the nearest person for your problems. That was me. I read somewhere two hundred thousand women in England have had abortions. Some want kids. Some don't. Kind of stupid. Ironical. One longs for a child as the most important thing in life, and another kills her baby. In an earlier day, the Church prevented people using contraceptives. Said it defeated God's work. Now there are too many people on the planet and most people have changed their minds. In most countries, abortions are now legal. Man always changes the rules when it suits him. We no longer know the difference between right and wrong. Maybe we never did. I'll open a couple of bottles of red wine and let them breathe. I'll put a match to the fire when we're ready. That giraffe with its legs splayed drinking from the river is so beautiful. Nature. Nature never changes. Just man."

"She'll get over her pain."

"I hope so. For her sake. Living in the depths of depression must be hell on earth. So, what you been up to while I was in America?"

They talked, drank together, and enjoyed each other's company. Two old friends discussing their problems. When the fire burned down Phillip baked the potatoes and cooked the meat. Another day in Phillip's life came and went. In the dark of the night, he woke in the tent to the roars of a lion. It was coming from the Zambian side of the river. He got out from under the mosquito net and went out of the tent to put wood on the fire to frighten away the animals, the rifle firmly in his right hand. The lion's roar had not woken Jacques.

Back in the tent, with the light from the flames of the fire reaching up into the dark of the riverine trees, he tried to go back to sleep. He could see the light of the campfire through the canvas of the tent. Frogs were croaking from the river, the crickets singing. It had all happened so fast: meeting an American tourist on one of his safaris, getting her pregnant. Going to live in America, becoming a venture capitalist by using part of the inheritance from his famous grandfather, getting married, the big reception, and Martha losing their baby. And all in less than a year. From the quiet of the bush to all the people and turmoil of living in an American city. Noise, stress, people's arguments, all foreign to Phillip, everything a constant chase to make money, most of it wasted. Two owls began hooting at each other from the trees, making Phillip smile and drift back into his peace and solitude. Jacques was snoring. They had drunk two bottles of red wine. The Zimbabwe steaks, cooked over an open fire, were the best in the world. In the morning he would go fishing. Lying on his back, Phillip drifted gently back into his dreams.

When he woke with the dawn, his first thought was of Martha. Poor Martha: where they were, deep in the Zambezi Valley, there was no telephone, no way to phone and give her comfort. He got out of bed, filled the big tin kettle with water, and placed it on the hot embers of the fire. When steam poured from the spout of the kettle, Phillip made two mugs of tea and stood up from where he was kneeling next to the fire. Jacques was standing next to him. Phillip handed him a mug of tea. Mugs in hand, they walked down to the water's edge. The bush was alive with small birds twittering, calling, flitting from tree to tree. Phillip breathed in the cool of the morning air, happy to be alive for the first time since Martha had lost his baby. Life had to go on. How it had always been. Down the centuries from generation to generation. Some living, some dying, some happy, and some downright miserable.

After a breakfast of bacon and eggs cooked in the big frying pan with the long handle over the embers of last night's fire, Phillip went fishing. Jacques had gone off to prepare Chewore camp for the onslaught of the tourist season. The small boat with its outboard motor had been stored under a canvas canopy next to the ablution block, the only permanent building on their camp. Without permanent structures, the camp was unlikely to be taken over by the government's indigenisation programme, a programme, like the takeover of white farms, designed to benefit the supporters of the ruling ZANU (PF) party of Robert Mugabe. Indigenisation, a new word in the lexicon. Without Jacques and Phillip, and their contacts overseas, other than a few second-hand tents, the business would have no value. Time would tell. In Africa, everything was politics.

Phillip took the canvas covering off the boat and checked the tyres of the small two-wheel trailer. He backed the truck he had just bought in Harare up to the trailer and joined the two together. In the workshop of the car dealer, he had made them attach a winch to the front of the truck and a tow bar to the back bumper. Carefully, Phillip backed the truck down the sloping bank and into the water of a small cove, detaching the boat from the trailer as it floated. Further out, the river was running powerfully. After three pulls of the cord, the small petrol engine fired. Phillip climbed into the boat and pushed it forward, dropping the propeller into the water before locking the engine to the back of the boat. There were four fishing rods tucked under the seats. With the worms he had dug from the sand in the cove earlier, putting them in a small tin can, Phillip was ready to fish. He took the boat out into the river, his right hand on the rudder. Keeping close to the shore, Phillip put-putted up the river, the sun hot on his face. In the middle of the Zambezi, bits and pieces of broken trees floated down with the flooding water. The rains had been good. As he watched the surface of the river ahead to avoid any surprises, the movement of the air caused by the moving boat cooled the sweat on Phillip's face.

For ten minutes, he ran upriver to his favourite fishing spot, a big cove with tall reeds on either side of the water, where he dropped anchor. Enjoying every moment, Phillip took out one of the rods, baited the hook and cast the line out into the river, slowly winding it in. Within a minute he felt the bite of a fish. Then another. Phillip struck. He had caught his fish. For an hour, Phillip filled the bottom of the small boat with thrashing Zambezi bream, the best-eating fish in the world. When he put-putted back to camp, there were eight fish in the bottom of the boat, a feast for both of them. The sun was getting hot. Leaving the boat pulled half out of the water of the small cove, he packed the fish in the box he had left in the back of his truck and drove up the bank to the camp. Next to his tent was another three-compartment tent. Jacques was sitting under a tree, his arms resting comfortably on the wooden armrests of a canvas chair. Next to him was another chair waiting for Phillip. Between the chairs was the coolbox with the beers.

"How many fish you got?"

"Eight."

"Should be enough. What a perfect day. It's so beautiful in the shade of the trees looking out over the water. Paradise on earth. You want a beer? Silly of me. Must be hot in the sun out on the river. Sit yourself down, partner."

"My pleasure. There is no view in the world more beautiful than that river."

"I'm hungry."

"You're always hungry. Cheers. May our life in Africa go on forever."

"I'll drink to that. Have you ever voted in an election?"

"Don't be bloody stupid. There's only one party when it comes down to it. Whatever they say, we live in a one-party state. Not that two parties make much difference according to my dad. All politicians are after the same thing. Power. And the prestige and money that comes with it. They don't give a damn about the people. Promises, promises. Giving money today for the next generation to pay. No, I never voted. And you?"

"What for? Is the beer cold enough?"

"Just right."

"Let's look at those fish. My, they're big. I'll get a knife and gut them. Fish for brunch. Who cares about politics? If they bugger you up, they bugger you up. No point in permanently worrying. The trick is to get the hell out of the way. A cold beer, fresh fish, the shade of a tree. What more can a man want? I believe in living in the present. Letting tomorrow take care of tomorrow."

"Any women in the first two tours?"

"There are always women, Phillip. Depends what they look like. Depends what they want. This time we'd better be careful. We're a couple of lucky bastards. Never forget it. Why doesn't Martha leave the rat race and come here to live by the river?"

"We tried it for a few weeks, you remember? She likes to work at her high-powered job in advertising. Says it makes life interesting."

"Each to his own. One man's fish is another man's poison. All that crap. Would you like her to come out?"

"Of course I would. She's my wife."

"Do you love her?"

"We were just getting to truly know each other. Love is a word with too many meanings. Did we get on together? Have fun? Laugh together? It was all coming nicely. She's a good woman. A good person. As a family, we would have been happy for the rest of our lives. The only problem was the clash of our cultures. Rural Africa against the great metropolis of America. Living in peace or among the turmoil and excitement of people. She grew up on a farm. City life only came after her father died and her mother sold the farm and moved to the city. In today's world, half the planet now lives in cities. Why I don't know. Money, I suppose. In a hundred years, a life like this will be as rare as hen's teeth. Oh, now look at that. The hippo is coming out of the water. Such luck he can't run up the bank. He's big. He's beautiful. Here comes another one. The whole family. Look at that little one. Dad really is a big bastard. The family are following him down the shoreline of the river. No worry about us. We're part of it. Blend in... Yes, I'd love Martha to join me. We'll just have to wait and see. You can't force people to do what they don't want. She'll have to make up her own mind. Give her time. If she really misses me she'll come. The company she works for wants us to move to New York. They want to open a branch."

"My goodness, can you just imagine living in New York? The nearest I ever get to a city like New York is in a movie."

"You'd live there?"

"Why not? Pretty exciting."

"And give up all this? What would you do for a living?"

"Become a gangster. In every movie there are gangsters."

"Be serious."

"The bad guys are the ones who make money. Ask Mugabe. He's stashed away millions of the country's money in off-shore bank accounts."

"Is he really as bad as that? Do we really know?"

"Rumours. What people say. You think they're wrong?"

"Who the hell knows? Where are you going?"

"To get a knife."

Phillip watched his friend and business partner walk to the small bus and come back with a long hunting knife. Jacques began gutting the fish. A breeze had come up, rustling the leaves in the trees high above Phillip's head. The family of hippo had walked out of sight. There were no more animals, the only movement the constant flow in the middle of the big river. The sun was hot and right overhead, the big trees protecting Jacques and Phillip. If, instead of Martha coming to live by the river he went to New York, would they be happy? Did it matter for what reason he had married her? They were married. Only a horrible divorce would change what they were. And would a divorce make them happier? In New York, there would not be the peace and solitude of Africa, instead, they would have the New York Philharmonic Orchestra. They could watch the music of Mozart being played, not just hear it from a CD player. There would be grand theatre. Musicals. Pop Concerts. Jazz in the nightclubs. All that wonderful New Orleans jazz. Not all the people would want to argue. Many would have talent and stories to tell. He would find another pub like Solly's Saloon he had spent so much time in. It wasn't all bad. Phillip got up, went to the coolbox and took out two beers, handing one to Jacques.

"Why are we never satisfied, Jacques?"

"I don't know. You tell me. Look at that. I'm the best fish gutter in the business. Poor bastards. When the sun came up they were swimming happily in the river. Now look at them."

"Where are you going now?"

"To throw their guts in the river. There was a musical about New York. *42nd Street*. It was an extravaganza set during the Great Depression. Can still see the pictures... Shit, it's hot when you get in the sun."

"You'd really want to leave Africa?"

"Not unless I'm forced to. I'm an Oosthuizen. An Afrikaner. My family have lived in Africa for three hundred years. We aren't going anywhere with luck. But it doesn't hurt to think of other places. The whole world is changing. You take your chances. Go put two of those fish over last night's fire. I'm hungry."

"So you said."

"Nothing wrong with being hungry. Don't cook them too much. I like my fish juicy. Just cooked enough. So the flesh comes off the bone."

"Anything you say, your majesty."

"Well, get on with it. And thanks for the beer."

"Your servant, sir."

Friends, Phillip thought. What would they do without friends? Happy as a pig in shit he carried two gutted fish to the campfire, put them on a log and walked to the ablution block where their equipment was stored. With the griller, he went back to the fish and put them side by side inside the grip of it. With a piece of firewood, he raked the embers. Jacques was whistling a tune down by the water. Beneath the white ash, the embers were hot. With two logs placed either side of the heat, Phillip put the fish over the fire and stepped back into the shade of the trees. Handful by handful, Jacques was throwing the guts of the fish as far as he could out into the river, picking guts out of a bucket he had brought from the bus with his hunting knife. The man was always organised. Why the business worked. Why the tourists went home satisfied.

"You want a salad with the fish, Jacques?"

"Of course I do."

"So sorry, your honour. I'll go pull a lettuce and make a salad dressing. How did the vegetable garden do after the rains?"

"Pretty good."

"Did the pigs get under the wire?"

"Not this time. Luckily, monkeys don't like green vegetables. Anyway, they can't get in the garden."

"You made a good cage."

"One big cage of barbed wire and wire mesh over the strands of wire. Got to feed those tourists properly. What they pay for. A safari deserves five-star food. And don't forget the garlic in the salad dressing."

"When were Munya and Sedgewick last here?"

"A week ago. They'll bring the first batch of tourists from the airport when they return."

"Did you spend the rains in camp?"

"Most of it. There are always things to be done. I fixed the canvas on four of the tents. Everything is perfect for the new season."

"Was it hot by the river?"

"Stifling. I brought fifty new books and read every one of them. You know, reading a book you like is far better than the crap they have on Zimbabwean television. Or watching videos."

"Were there any women to keep you company?"

"Why? Are you jealous?"

"I'm a married man."

"But not too happily. I'm sorry, Phillip. That was uncalled for. I've never had a permanent relationship with all the coming and going. I'll watch the fish. You go make the salad. You make the best damn salad dressing in Africa. Don't forget a table and the chairs. Oh, look at that. Your fish are cooking perfectly. We'd better eat the fish first and then have the salad. Fish, salad, and more fish."

"Did you wash out the bucket?"

Smiling, Phillip put up the folding table in the shade of the trees and went back for the chairs. The fish were cooked. With two cold beers in front of them on the metal table, they ate their lunch, neither of them bothering to talk. For Phillip, the fish was perfect. Absolutely perfect. Leaving the bones of the fish on his plate, and Jacques putting two more bream in the griller, he went to pull the lettuce and make their salad. He was home. At peace. The rush and chaos of living in America as far away as the moon.

Putting the salad bowl on the table, Phillip added the dressing. Jacques brought the griller to the table, opened it up and took out the fish.

"Any word from your sister in England, Jacques? Are they enjoying themselves?"

"Renée's been there six years with her husband. Making money but she hates it."

"What's she been doing?"

"Did a year's course in beauty treatment. She's a beautician making as much money as Godfrey."

"What's he do?"

"Has a degree in mechanical engineering. His friend has started a new business in Perth. Wants them to join him in Australia. Renée's going to start her own business. It's all go. They never stop."

"The modern world."

"She misses Africa."

"Don't we all when we have to go?"

"Just the two of us left. Renée and Jacques. I miss my sister as much as my parents. In the old days, families stayed together in the same places for generations. Now the families are fragmented. No wonder so many people are unhappy with their lives. Far better to create a working farm and pass it on down the family."

"I know the feeling. A father and mother in England. A brother on the Isle of Man. A sister in California. I'll never get to know my nieces and nephews. And it doesn't just stop with families. You make a friend, next minute he's gone. A third of Americans don't live in the states they were born in. The English are all over the world. In the years to come, there'll be more families of English origin in Australia than in England. They say in ten years there will be more foreigners in Birmingham than British. People have lost their roots in pursuit of what they think will be a better life."

"Your family left England for Africa."

"That's my point. Why are so many people dissatisfied with where they were born? One big churning melting pot."

"How long are you going to stay this time, Phillip?"

"Who knows? No one settles down."

"Did you hear that? Guinea fowl. We'll gut a couple and put them in the embers of the fire, feathers and all, and eat them for breakfast. You want another fish?"

"I'm done."

"So am I. I'm going to take a nap under the trees. It's not all bad, my friend."

"You can say that again. I just wish I could stop thinking of my poor Martha. Life in all its turmoil. And I can't even make a phone call."

"In life be grateful for small mercies."

"I'll try. I'll join you under the trees. Shit, it's hot."

2

When Munya and Sedgewick arrived with the second fifteen-seater bus and the six English tourists everything was ready. Phillip watched Jacques smile. One of the girls had caught his eye. Munya walked across and handed Phillip a letter.

"Sent to Manica Travel by an American courier service. It's marked urgent. Manica say we are booked solid from the end of April."

"How are you, Munya? Have you and Sedgewick found yourselves wives? Jacques and I will help with the *lobola*. Jacques tells me that's your problem. We'll be able to give them jobs to give them something to do out here in the bush."

"How's America? Didn't expect you back. I'll show the tourists their tents."

"Any problems at the airport?"

"The plane from London was on time."

With the letter in his hand unopened, Phillip welcomed the guests, smiling, being polite, conducting his business. At the mention of an American courier, Phillip's stomach had flipped, fear stopping him from immediately opening the letter. When the tourists were sitting under the trees, their bags taken to their tents, Phillip walked upriver, keeping under the shade of the trees. Jacques was offering drinks and snacks to the tourists. As he walked away the fear increased, his fingers gripping the letter in panic. It was the middle of the day, the birds quiet, no sign of any wild animals. Under a tree, Phillip sat on a fallen branch and tore open his letter. It was addressed to Phillip Crookshank care of Manica Travel, Harare. The address had been typed. Inside was a one-paragraph letter in Martha's handwriting.

> *Phillip, please, please, please come home. I don't want to kill myself. I'm so sorry, honey. Come home. I can't live without you.*

Phillip's flood of relief was overwhelming. For a long while he sat smiling, his mind so happy he wanted to sing.

"Are you okay, Phillip?" Jacques had left the tourists to Munya and Sedgewick and walked up the river.

"Never better. She wants me back. The letter's from Martha. Can you imagine? Be happy for me, Jacques. I'm going home to my wife."

"When are you leaving?"

"Now."

"That's pretty short notice." Jacques sat himself down on the log next to Phillip. "The tourists like the camp. You shouldn't leave until tomorrow or you'll be driving in the dark."

"I'll leave the new truck and the keys at the airport. I don't want Martha to change her mind or do anything silly."

"You can phone her from Makuti."

"Or walk in on her."

"Munya and Sedgewick want money to buy ten cows."

"Good for them."

"The pretty girl is single. On her own."

"Then everyone is happy."

"Don't you want to think about it, Phillip?"

"There's nothing to think about. She didn't put the letter in the mail. Sent it by fast courier. I want the first plane back to America."

"You want some lunch?"

"All I want to do is go. It worked. Leaving her on her own worked."

"Are you going to bring her back to Africa?"

"Who knows? Who the hell knows? She wants me back, that's what matters. For one terrible moment, I thought the letter was from Aggie telling me Martha had killed herself."

"You mind if we just sit and talk?"

"Of course. What you want to talk about?"

"Martha. I know it's none of my damn business but I'm your friend. Friends try and help each other. You're in a right royal tizzy. Understandable. Don't you need to take a step back and look carefully? From what you said, she threw you out of her apartment without concern for your feelings. In her circumstances what she did was understandable. She wanted to kill herself. Wanted everyone the hell out of the way. The poor girl had been growing that baby in her belly for nine months with a passion. Maybe she's overreacted again. Wrote you that letter on the spur of the moment. If she's been suffering from depression the depression may come back again. Let her stew awhile. Let her realise she can't tell you to get out and expect you to come back the first moment she asks you to. She needs a little of her own medicine. Needs to think of you and not just think of herself. You both lost a baby. Not just Martha."

"What are you suggesting?"

"Munya will be taking these tourists back to the airport in four days' time. Go with them. Leave me with the new truck instead of leaving a valuable asset vulnerable at the airport. There's no certainty you'll get a lock-up garage. Four days will give you time to think rationally. I don't like the idea of my friend driving alone at night in a panic. You're not saying anything. I'm sorry. It's none of my damn business. You do what you think is best."

Phillip looked hard at Jacques and away again. His first instinct had been to tell him to go to hell for interfering in private business. To tell a good friend to go to hell was as stupid as Martha telling her husband to get out of the apartment. The flowing river in front of him began coming back into focus. Two pigeons were calling. A dove made the distinctive call that sounded like 'how's father'. Maybe Jacques was right. Maybe rushing back at the first call would be worse than letting Martha have more time alone to know she really wanted him back again. To realise her letter had not been sent on the spur of a moment. When he left Kansas City, Martha had gone to stay with her mother. Aggie was looking after her, making sure she didn't do anything stupid.

"I could fly with this group to England on the same plane. There's a flight to New York every day from Heathrow. It's that dove. Keeps asking me 'how's father'. Thanks, Jacques."

"What old friends are for. We're going to have a nice *braai* around the campfire tonight. A few drinks. Give you time to reflect on what you have to do when you return to America. Munya's going to take the tour to look at the animals. Sedgwick is going with him to explain everything they're seeing. You and I can prepare the food while having a drink together. Get the surprise of the letter through your system. You know that old cliché, Phillip: 'Fools rush in where angels fear to tread.' In six days when you get back to your Martha, you'll be one of those angels. Come on. We'll walk back. The beers are cold. Your life is on track again. And for the second time, I'll miss you, you old bastard. Why does the world have to be so big? Makes me sad, losing my old friend."

"You too need a wife."

"Probably. Shit, it's hot. I'm going for a skinny dip in the river."

"Mind the crocodiles."

"Coming?"

"Race you to the water."

Throwing their clothes off as they ran Phillip smiled. What would he ever do in life without friends?

"Can they see us?"

"I hope not."

Laughter replaced Phillip's panic. Everything was going to be all right. He had a future. A wife. The hope of a family. He was not going into middle age in a few years' time on his own. By the time they reached their discarded clothes, they were dry, the sun searing their skin. When they reached the camp the bus and the tourists had gone. Phillip opened the wire door to the cage that protected the vegetables from the wild animals, walking upright inside Jacques's fifty foot-square construction with overhead shade-cloth protecting the vegetables from the hot sun. As always, when Jacques did something he did it properly. Phillip picked lettuce, tomatoes and pulled out two onions. He was happy the panic had gone, no more sinking feeling in the pit of his stomach. Jacques had put up the long table under the trees and laid out the cutlery and the plates in preparation for the evening *braai*. The fire was still burning, small whiffs of white smoke rising from the ashes. There was a new pile of wood ready next to the campfire. Phillip washed the lettuce in a bucket and made the salad dressing. With the coolbox full of meat under the long table everything was ready. The first day of the new season at Chewore camp had begun. Jacques handed Phillip a beer.

"What's her name?"

"Who?"

"The pretty one who was flirting with you, Jacques. Cheers."

"Good health. To hell with your wealth. May your life always be content... Tracy. Her name is Tracy."

"What's she doing on safari all on her own?"

"Looking for fun. In those first years of your twenties, that's what you are looking for. Again, to your health old friend, to hell with your wealth. Money never bought no one happiness."

For two hours, alone in the African bush, the sun going down, the birds beginning to sing, the first of the animals coming down to the river to drink, Phillip and Jacques reminisced. With the red sunset slashed across the heavens, the tour bus came back to camp, Munya and Sedgwick smiling, the tourists talking about the animals they had seen out on the plain away from the river. Drinks were passed around. The fire was rekindled. Tracy flirted with Jacques. Phillip chuckled to himself. There was nothing wrong with being a safari operator. Later, when the alcohol increased the volume of the conversation around the campfire, Phillip put the meat over the coals. The crickets were loud, the frogs calling from the river, the birds calling to each other from the trees. A perfect evening in Africa. With the smoke from the fire protecting them, there was no sign of any mosquitoes. With the meat, Munya handed out glasses of red wine that Jacques poured from the bottles Phillip had opened earlier. When Phillip went to his tent he was tired, a little drunk, and gloriously hopeful. Through the night he dreamed of Martha. In his dreams both of them were happy.

The dawn chorus of birds woke him early. He got up and went to look for the big tin kettle to put on the fire for the morning tea. There was no sound from the tents of the tourists. He was the first to get up. With the kettle filled with water and resting on the coals of last night's big fire, Phillip went down to the river. Under his trousers, he had put on his bathing costume. Checking the small cove in front of their camp for crocodiles, Phillip went for his morning swim. When he got out, the girl called Tracy was watching him. She was smiling. Phillip put on his shirt and trousers.

"Is it safe to swim?"

"Not really. We don't let the tourists go in the water for fear of the crocodiles and the hippo. Did you sleep well?"

"Like a baby."

"I'm so pleased."

"What's for breakfast?"

"Bacon and eggs."

"That's so British."

"Zimbabwe used to be a British colony. We called it Rhodesia. I put the kettle on for tea."

"So British."

"Yes, I suppose it is."

"Jacques says you are going back to America."

"My wife is American."

"What's America like?"

"Not quite so British."

They laughed and walked together up the steep embankment.

"I'll help you make the tea, Phillip. Only four days. I could spend my life in a place like this."

"I did."

"Why are you leaving?"

"Life goes on. How it happens. They say a good life is a varied life. We'll just have to see."

It was a day in camp like so many other days for Phillip, a day that made him his living, gave him something to do, a purpose in his life. Ever since his grandfather Crossley had died leaving him all that money he had tried to put his inheritance out of his mind. For Phillip, a life spending someone else's money had no purpose. The point of making money was having fun while doing it. The girl Tracy flirted outrageously with Jacques. She wanted fun. Looking at wild animals was a bonus. Jacques and Munya took the tour on the afternoon drive out onto the plain. Left to himself while Sedgewick prepared for the evening meal, Phillip sat under a tree reading a book. When he left the book and looked out over the river he sat thinking. Thinking about life. Thinking about the past and the future. Once again his life was about to be stood on its head. Everything he had known for the first thirty-seven years of his life was going to be lost, the chance of Martha, the advertising executive, wanting to look after a bunch of tourists on the banks of the Zambezi River in faraway Africa, as great as being struck by lightning and attacked by a white shark at the same time. If he wanted Martha, he would have to want America and the life of a venture capitalist in New York City making more money. Was there any fun in making all that money? Phillip wasn't sure. Everything he had ever wanted was right in front of him. Then again, did anything ever last in life? He wasn't sure. Maybe life was all about going forward, not standing still, not sitting in a canvas chair in the shade of a tree and watching the most beautiful river on earth flow past him. Sedgwick came and joined him, bringing his folding chair which he put down next to Phillip and making himself comfortable. For a long while, they sat in companionable silence.

"You don't really give your future father-in-law actual cows?"

"It's the symbol of a very old tradition. If you pay for something you appreciate it more and look after it. In some of the old traditional farmlands, they still give out cows to pay for a bride. Like so many of our wonderful traditions, it's dying. Everything now is money. We say here's five cows and give our future in-law a cheque."

"Will the tradition last? The tradition of *lobola*?"

"Probably not. We've been taken into the modern world. More and more of us. We all get an education. Learn to read and write. Do arithmetic. Learn new skills and live in cities."

"Would you like to live in a city?"

"I'd like to go back to the old days before the modern world arrived to swallow us up. Live life in a *kraal*. Run cattle."

"And have four wives?"

"One good girl will be enough for me."

"I'm going back to America."

"I know. Rural Africa. The old rural Africa. That would be my dream."

"And mine, Sedgwick."

While they sat thinking of themselves the sun began to set. The birds began to sing. Only when they heard the engine of the bus did they get up, fold their chairs and walk back to the camp.

"You'll like having a wife. Just choose the right girl. That's the difficult part, Sedgwick. Finding someone who likes what you like yourself. I'm going to miss Africa. Everything, including all your traditions. Do you like the new modern world that's invaded Africa?"

"Some of it. Better get the fire going. Don't forget your book."

It was all part of the process of evolution. The process of life. Nothing, unless you were lucky, ever stayed the same. After the *braai* and too many drinks, they all went to their tents. All except Tracy. Hoping the rest of the group had not seen her, she sneaked into Jacques's tent next to Phillip's. For an hour Phillip tried to sleep. He hoped Jacques was using a condom. Life, when it came down to it, was so basic. All part of the fun. All part of the memory-making. In years to come, in the cold of an English winter, Tracy, by then a mother with three children, would look back and remember her safari and the nights spent with a safari operator on the banks of the Zambezi River. Sex in a tent with a stranger. No obligations. No complications. Just fun. Smiling to himself at life's luck, Phillip rolled over, blocked his ears with the pillow, and was quickly sound asleep. When an owl calling from the tree above the tent woke him all was quiet in the night. Everyone was sleeping. Phillip got up, went outside and piled wood on the fire. Long, half-trees that would burn through the night making them safe. With the fire burning bright, his loaded rifle in his right hand, Phillip stepped out from under the trees and away from the fire. Above, the night sky was dark, with only the smallest sickle moon. High up in the universe Phillip looked at three layers of stars, some twinkling, all of them bright. The owl was again calling to its mate. In front, the flowing river reflected the stars in the heavens. A gentle, cool breeze brushed the African night.

"There has to be a God to have created so much beauty," Phillip whispered to himself, the emotion so great it made tears come to his eyes. A surge of yearning passed through him. He wanted to thank someone for bringing him into so perfect a night. So perfect a place. It made Phillip wish he was religious. If he'd been religious he would have sunk to his knees and thanked his God. Not sure if an all-powerful God, who had created the heavens in all that beauty, would have bothered to create mankind with its wars and hatred, Phillip walked back to his tent, a sad feeling permeating his body. In his bed, lying on his back, Phillip lay thinking. Wondering. Wondering what it was all about. One lost soul among all the billions of people that made up humanity. A brief touch of life in the great universe. No importance. No consequence. No reason he could think of for having been given his life. And in thirty years, if not sooner, he would die and turn to dust, another life that came and went, a brief, tiny moment of thought in the great unknown of human existence. And when he woke and got up there were people. Normal people. Talking, laughing, sampling the soft light at the start of a new day. Everything normal, practical, few questions of consequence in any of their heads. Lives going forward. Taking it all for granted. Sedgwick came across and handed him a mug of tea.

"What a beautiful day. Thanks for the tea. I think it's my turn to take our guests on the morning run in the bus. You want to come with me? Good. After the run, we'll cook them breakfast. It's just such a beautiful day." The smiles, the chatter, the mug of hot tea had brought him back to normality. He had rejoined the world.

That morning they were lucky. Elephant. A whole herd of elephant. Two giraffes eating the tops of the trees, their long necks pushing their heads towards heaven. Out on the plain away from the thick line of trees along the river, it was mostly grass as high as a man's waist. High up in the sky a pair of hawks were circling, calling their joy at being alive, going higher and higher on the thermals. Phillip pointed out the birds and everyone looked up, everyone but Tracy who had stayed with Jacques. The sun was burning hot. Back in the bus, Phillip drove them to the river. Again there was luck. It was the same family of hippopotamus Phillip had watched earlier, the big animals taking no notice of the tourists' cameras. When Phillip could see they had had enough he drove them back to camp for their breakfast, food and conversation now more important than the hippo. Why the tours were so short. After four days their attention spans would be at their limit, their interest in the wilds of Africa waning, their thoughts going home to their work, their friends, the routine of life in the towns and suburbs they had grown used to. Their holiday, a talking point to show off in all those trivial conversations, the photographs making it all look important. The irony of life, Phillip told himself. The reality. It never failed to amaze him. All the way back, Phillip talking into his small microphone, describing the animals and birds they looked at through the windows. Delivering his product.

Doing his job. Giving his customers value for their money. And the day went on.

"What are we giving them for supper tonight, Jacques?"

"Fish. Tomorrow is wild boar on the spit."

"Who's catching the fish?"

"You are, partner. Our friends want to go out with you on the boat. Everyone but Tracy. She and I are going hunting for tomorrow's pig."

"Ah. The great white hunter. Back to the old days. Did I ever tell you about Sebastian Brigandshaw?"

"Many times, Phillip. And his son Harry. Without the Brigandshaws, so you tell me, your family would never have come to Africa. Your father would not have met your mother. You would never have been made. Something like that. Sebastian was one of the first white hunters. Hunted for ivory in a country sparsely populated by people. He and his friend Tinus Oosthuizen, my distant relative."

"You've got a good memory. I'd forgotten you were related. Wasn't he your great-great-uncle? Something like that."

"You know, I always enjoy your stories. Round the campfire tonight you should tell our new friends the story of the Brigandshaw family. They lived exciting lives in exciting times. Why were things so much more exciting in the past?"

"Stories, probably. Time embellishes them. The trick is to enjoy the life we have. Enjoy now. And if I don't catch a fish?"

"Our guests will go hungry. I'll dig the worms for you. Of course, you'll catch lots of fish. You're the best fisherman on the Zambezi. In these parts anyway."

"I'm the only one."

"That's my point. If the fish aren't biting, we'll have wild boar for supper."

"And tomorrow?"

"You'll get up early and go catch them fish."

With the five tourists in the boat taking their endless photographs, the sundown just below the trees, Phillip went fishing. The group all knew each other from England, Tracy the odd one out. Tracy worked for the travel agent in Birmingham that had booked the tour, a free holiday for her donated by the airline to encourage the agency to use their airline, a tool of marketing that worked. It was the early season when the planes were not fully booked. The boat put-putted upriver to the inlet Phillip always fished. Within a minute of casting his line, he caught a fish, to the delight of the tourists. For an hour of squeals and excitement, Phillip fished out their supper of Zambezi bream. Two tiger fish, caught among the bream, were thrown back into the river. Too many bones, the big fish not edible. In the quiet moments between catching fish, Phillip told them about the English Brigandshaws, keeping the tourists amused. With enough fish thrashing on the bottom of the boat, Phillip started the outboard motor on the first pull and took them back to camp.

AT THE END of the fourth day, with the bags packed ready to start the journey in the morning to Harare airport, Phillip was torn between losing his life in the wilds of Africa and going back to Martha.

"Thanks for your advice, Jacques."

"Look after yourself, old friend. Sedgewick will bring the bus back with the first American tour."

And the game went on. The way it was. The way it had always been for Phillip. Never quite reaching a conclusion. For a long while, away from the others, Phillip looked at the bushveld that had given him so much comfort. The birds and crickets were still singing. The river was flowing, the sun shining.

"Are you ready, Phillip?"

"Coming. Saying my goodbyes to Africa."

"Don't want to be late at the airport. Are you driving?"

"You can drive, Sedgwick. I need time to think."

3

The phone call to Martha echoed for a long while after Phillip put down the phone. She was distant. Distracted. As if there were other things on her mind.

"It's me."

"Oh, Phillip. How nice of you to call. Did you get my letter?"

"They brought it to me in Chewore. No phone, of course."

"Where are you?"

"London."

"That's interesting."

"I can catch a flight to New York and change planes for Kansas City. How are you?"

"Bearing up. Busy. Clients never stop wanting something. Never have time to think for myself."

"That's good, isn't it?"

"I suppose so. Got to run. Franklyn and I are taking a client out to lunch. Never stops. When are you coming over?"

"A few things to do in England. My father and my stepmother."

"Of course. You look after yourself."

"You said you couldn't live without me. Is everything all right between us?"

"We'll have a long chat when you get here, Phillip."

"You sound distracted."

"I am. Lots on my mind, all of it work. Franklyn still wants me to move to

New York and open the branch. Let me know the time of your arrival."

"You will be there?"

"Of course I will. Didn't you read my letter?"

"You sounded desperate."

"I was. I'm better now. It's all work. It never stops. America."

"I'll leave a message with the flight details if you don't pick up. Will you meet me at the airport?"

"I'll try. If I'm not there catch a cab. Got to go. Franklyn's at my door. Oh, and Marcin's doing better than even he imagined. The value of Linguare shares on the private market are going through the roof. Everyone in the know wants a piece of it. See you when you arrive."

When the plane had arrived at Heathrow Airport in London, Phillip had taken a taxi to his father's flat in Chelsea, knocking unannounced on the door.

"Phillip! Goodness gracious me. I thought you were in America. How's Martha? Come in. Bergit went down to the shops. There's one thing in London they are not short of and that's shops. What on earth are you doing in London? Randall's here with Meredith and my grandson. This is a lovely surprise. They all went shopping with your stepmother."

"How are you both?"

"Not so bad, I suppose. Never does any good complaining."

"I went back to Chewore. Martha threw me out after she lost the baby. Now she wants me back."

"Give me that suitcase and come in, son. Well, I'll be blowed. Can't have you standing in the doorway. We were so sad you lost your baby... It's cold in England in April. Most of the year. I miss World's View. Africa was perfect. No point in crying over spilt milk. I'll make us some tea and you can start from the beginning."

"When are they due back?"

"You know women. Shopping. They love shopping."

"What are they shopping for?"

"Don't ask me. Are you going to stay with us for a few days? With Randall and Meredith in town, you'll have to sleep in the lounge. This is so exciting. We can get Craig and Jojo over for supper. All we need is Myra and I'd have all my children under one roof."

"Before I do anything, may I use your phone to call Martha? She will be at work. She says she can't live without me despite our argument."

"That's wonderful. You make your call and I'll make the tea."

Phillip was still standing looking at the phone when his father came back with the tea.

"How's your lovely wife? Milk and one sugar, I seem to remember."

"I'm not sure."

"She must have been happy to hear from you."

"I'm not sure. She was distant. Far away."

"It's difficult to make out what people are thinking when you're speaking to them on the telephone. You can't see that lovely smile. The happiness in their eyes. Now, sit down and tell me what's been happening. Randall's new book is still selling like hotcakes. I wish I could write books. Give me something to do. There's nothing worse in life than boredom. On the farm, I was always on the go. Now all I do is sit and think. Drives poor Bergit crazy. But enough of my problems."

"How are Craig and Jojo getting along in England?"

"They hate the English weather. Otherwise, they seem happy. We all miss Africa."

"Don't tell me. Has Jojo heard from her father?"

"Not a word. Cut her right out of the family for going with the son of an Englishman. The Africans never like their children to marry out of the tribe. Not that they are married yet. There's a whole new world out there that my generation doesn't want to understand. He'll come round to it or he'll never get to know his grandson Harold. Grandchildren. Now that's a whole new thing. You have your kids and have no idea how fast they will multiply."

"Are they going to stay in England?"

"You'll have to ask them. Parents are the last to be told. I've learned not to ask too many questions. Enjoy your tea. What would we English ever have done without our cups of tea?... She was very beautiful, your mother. Livy had that talent to bring a face to life in her portraits. Her paintings are going to last forever. I'd love to have been a creative artist. Write symphonies. Books. Paint pictures like that portrait of your mother you are staring at. Artists through their work will live forever."

"I love ancient music. Haydn's Twenty-Eighth Symphony is our favourite. Martha says the slow movement is the most evocative music she has ever heard. That music makes both of us feel so happy. My poor mother. I would so much have liked to know her. Randall says we missed so much losing our mother. He doesn't even remember her. All we have is Livy Johnson's portrait of her. Bergit was wonderful bringing us up but however you try and think differently you can't replace your own mother and father. Why I so much wanted my son. And it's worse for the mother to lose her baby. Poor Martha. She wanted to jump off the tenth-floor balcony of our apartment building."

"You can always have another baby."

"Can we? She was twice married before I got her pregnant in the Zambezi Valley. She didn't think she would ever fall pregnant. Why she didn't bother with contraception. Anyway, we're married. And thanks, Dad, for flying across the pond to be at my wedding. That was one hell of a party. Who would have ever thought that just a few weeks later Martha would lose the baby, the reason for the big wedding. Anyway, it brought the Crookshank family together. Randall said he enjoyed himself. So did Myra. But life goes on. At least she wants me back again."

"Do you love her?"

"That's the strangest part. We married because we had to for the sake of the baby. Two strangers who had had a fling on a safari in the middle of Africa. But the longer we stayed together, the more we found in common. Our love of music. Love of books. We both understand other people, or maybe we just think we do. So different backgrounds. From different countries. Strangely, I think we were falling in love with each other. Does that sound strange to you, Dad?"

"We all need another person in our lives. You'd better sit down and stop staring at the portrait of your mother."

"Lost in the bush while driving blind drunk, ran out of petrol and killed by a pride of lions. My mother."

"That's how it was. Life has many pitfalls. Alcohol is one of them."

"Was she a drunk?"

"Some would say so."

"My poor mother. Anyway, enough of me and my problems. Tell me about your life in England. Tell me about Bergit. She must be enjoying having a grandson on her doorstep. When are Craig and Jojo getting married?"

"Why don't you ask them? The only way Harold can be a Crookshank, have the surname Crookshank, is for them to be married. Otherwise, he'll be Harold Tafara for the rest of his life. Life is so damn complicated at the end of the twentieth century. Good to see you, Phillip. I miss my kids. All those years bringing you up and then you're all gone. Myra seems to like California. At least that's good. Don't think it's much fun to be married to a celebrity. All that media attention. But all you can do is take life as it comes."

"I just hope Martha really wants me back in her life."

"You'll have to fly over and find out. Face to face, you'll both be able to make the right decision. Only you two can decide your future. I'm so sorry for both of you she lost your baby. But like losing your mother to a pride of lions, life goes on until we die. Let me put on some music. I don't think I have Haydn's Twenty-Eighth Symphony. How does a little Mozart sound to you? Classical music. There's so much beautiful music. Whatever would we do without our music?"

"Mozart would be wonderful. We learn so much from our parents. I owe my love for classical music to you and Bergit. Sitting outside around the swimming pool in the heat of an African evening with classical music flowing from the gramophone in the lounge. How I remember growing up. Despite losing my mother we were all so happy. Mozart flowing out into the African bush. Only the animals to hear. Now that was beauty. I wonder what the young Mozart would have thought if someone would had told him his music would be played through a mechanical player in the middle of the African bush?"

"Maybe he can see us now enjoying his music."

"To have given so many people joy. That must be satisfaction. So many of us in life just come and go, soon forgotten, buried in the ground, or burned to dust and stuffed in an urn."

"You're thinking of your son."

"I just keep wondering what kind of a life he would have had. The chance of life is so slim. He just missed it."

They drank their tea in silence, Phillip watching his father stare at the portrait of Phillip's dead mother. His father sighed and turned back to Phillip.

"You know the strangest part. I wanted to marry Livy but she didn't want to be part of all that African political turmoil. She went back to England. Then I fell in love with your mother. Makes you think, doesn't it? That chance of life. The trick is to enjoy whatever we have... That's the tea done. You want a drink?"

"Thought you'd never ask. Oh, and thanks for being my father."

"Always a pleasure, son. Always a pleasure. Beer or whisky?"

"Let's start with a cold beer."

"Coming up. And all that long journey to Africa and here I am back in good old England. Full circle. Makes you think. We all have a dream, Phillip. She came all that way from America to Africa to find you. Some call it destiny. Some call it luck. Let's hear the rest of the story. Didn't you put some of your grandfather's money into this new computerised technology? Did you lose your shirt?"

"Quite the opposite."

"Bit like me investing in this Chelsea block of flats with Livy when we could still get our money out of Rhodesia. Now that was luck. Or I'd by now be bumming off the state and living in two rooms. You want a glass?"

"Of course. I was brought up to drink properly. Not out of a bottle."

They both laughed. They sat opposite each other in companionable silence listening to Mozart, drinking their beers, the panic of Martha and the distant phone call subsiding in Phillip's stomach. He would have to see what happened back in Kansas City.

When Bergit arrived back with Randall and his family Phillip sat on the sofa grinning at the surprised looks on their faces. Then he got up and hugged his stepmother. They were all smiling and laughing. It was good to be back with his family.

"The bar's open. How was the shopping? How's my little grandson? Give him to me, Meredith."

Turning from Bergit, Phillip put his hand out to his brother. Instead of shaking hands, they gave each other a hug, Phillip smiling at Meredith over Randall's shoulder.

"So what are you doing in London, Phillip?"

"It's a long story."

"I'll bet it is."

"Dad says *Love Song* is still selling well."

"All that publicity and advertising by my publishers, it damn well should be. These days it's all about hyping a new product or a new book."

"How's the Isle of Man?"

"Cold. Quiet. A good place to write. But Meredith thinks we'll have to move out of our isolation if Douglas is to meet other children as he grows up. Life never really stays the same. Thanks. I'll have a beer."

"In the fridge, Randall."

"Sorry, Dad. Bergit, Meredith, what you want to drink? What you want me to do with all these packages? Talk about shopping till you drop. I love women, but how they shop. Why don't I take everyone out to supper? The caretaker's wife can look after Douglas. Nothing wrong with owning one's block of flats. Anyway, the caretaker's wife loves looking after our little boy. Comes with not having any children of her own. The Savoy or the Ritz? Or that little Italian restaurant around the corner? Italian it is."

"What's it about, Randall?"

"What 'what's it about'?"

"Your new book. You are writing a new book?"

"People, Phillip. My books are all about people. *Strangers in the Night*. I stole the title from an old Frank Sinatra song. They say only seven stories have ever been written. We writers tell the same old stories with different backgrounds. People think life is so complicated but it isn't. We all get born, grow up through our childhood, and end up having to make a living one way or the other. All this age of democracy and everyone being nice to each other is a load of crap. We're all animals, with the basic instincts of animals. The seven stories of man. The trick is to tell the stories in a way that keeps the reader captivated, so the reader can leave behind his own daily life making his living. You get the system right and you make all that lovely money man so craves. You and I were lucky, Phillip. We inherited money from Grandfather Crossley. We've never known poverty, so I shouldn't knock money. For most, the pursuit of money is life's eternal chase. I'll go get Mrs Grimshaw and we can all go out to dinner. Consumers, that's what we are. Make money. Spend money. How the economy keeps going around. The faster the velocity of money going around and around the better for everyone."

"Do you enjoy your life, Randall?"

"Of course I do. I'm married. Have a son. Own a little farm away from the turmoil of people."

"But you're thinking of leaving the Isle of Man?"

"Ironical isn't it."

"What's it like to write a bestseller?"

"Like any success, it's about money. Didn't I hear on the grapevine you too were writing a book?"

"I tried to write my memoirs of life in the bush as a safari operator, to escape from the urban life of an American city. Didn't work. I can't write. In the end, I bored myself. Now I'm going back to my wife in America to continue the pursuit of money as a venture capitalist."

"So you are going to carry on then? Why? When you've got a few million dollars already from our grandfather."

"I have no idea. Martha says it's something to do. She says that we all like to show off if we have all that money. As you said, it keeps the world economy going around. As you know, she's in advertising, the great big engine that makes us all want to go on spending. These days most people spend borrowed money, so who the hell knows where we will all end up? In America, it's all about the money. Stupid. Now I'm going back to the money to live in a glorified hutch, ten, twenty, thirty storeys above street level to look out at other human hutches in their skyscrapers."

"Isn't living in a big American city exciting?"

"Parts of it. Friends. Having your own kids. Having a job to do. You're lucky both of you have Douglas. You have a new purpose in life. Martha and I may not be able to have our own children. Where are you going to live if you leave the Isle of Man?"

"Whoever knows?"

"Life goes on. You'd better go get the caretaker's wife. I'm hungry."

"Have you booked your flight to America?"

"Not yet. I wanted to phone Martha. She'd be so envious of Douglas. From generation to generation. All those unknown ancestors in our past, without one of whom we wouldn't be standing here having a drink. All those future descendants we will never know about."

"Have another drink. You're going to make me cry. The trick of life is to enjoy oneself. Let's all go out and enjoy ourselves. It's so good to be back among my family."

"How far have you got with the new book?"

"Three chapters. The first chapter is always a bastard. Then the book begins to run."

The caretaker's wife came up from the basement flat she shared with her husband ten minutes later. The old man had stayed behind watching television. Still chattering, they all went out to dinner. Outside it was raining. Phillip's father had called a taxi. They all piled in. At the Italian restaurant, they were shown to a table big enough for the five of them, the owner pulling out the chair for Bergit. The man gave each of them a menu and stood back wringing his hands in anticipation. One by one they looked up and gave him their order, the man retrieving their menus with a smile. Phillip smiled to himself. Life was all about making money. Phillip looked around the table at his family. He was content, happy, no longer longing for Africa, no longer worrying about Martha. A bottle of Chianti with its bulbous bottom encased by straw was put on the table in front of Phillip's father. The whole family were laughing, enjoying themselves, enjoying each other's company. All around them groups of people were eating their suppers. Background music played from a speaker attached to the top of the far wall. It was warm inside, their coats having been left at the front desk with the owner's wife. The young girl who served them the food was the owner's daughter, the restaurant a family business. She was pretty and smiled at Phillip, the only man at the table without a partner. Life never changed. The eternal chase. Randall and Meredith were talking books, prompted by questions from Bergit. Phillip sat back enjoying himself and listened. Another plate of food was put in front of him by the pretty girl.

"You have a good suntan if you don't mind my saying. Have you been on holiday?"

"I've lived most of my life in Africa."

"That's nice. Enjoy your food."

"I will."

Meredith was looking at him with an unspoken question smiling in her eyes. Phillip looked at the pretty girl and back at Meredith.

"Have you published your children's book, *Talking to the Animals*?"

"Not yet, Phillip. The publishers are still finalising the illustrations. They paid me a fifty thousand dollar advance a year ago. Who knows what they get up to in these big publishing houses? Villiers Publishing is more interested in Randall. Did him a favour by accepting his wife's book."

"Are you writing another book?"

"Not with Douglas. He's a full-time occupation."

"Do you really want to live in a city?"

"He's got to have other kids to play with. We can't let him grow up in isolation staring at the mountain, listening to the sea pounding in the distance."

"Why ever not?"

"He's a boy. Kids need company. How it works."

"How's Randall going to write surrounded by all the noise of a city?"

"We're going to soundproof a room. Right now, Douglas breaks his train of thought. Kids are complicated."

"I wish I knew."

"I'm sorry. I wasn't thinking. I can't imagine losing my baby."

"We all need a family, Phillip." Phillip's father had been listening to their conversation, a sad look on his face.

"I know, Dad."

"Martha will welcome you with open arms. Try again for a son. Never give up. Never giving up is the secret for a happy life. You know the old adage: if you don't first succeed, try, try again. How's the food?"

"Damn perfect. Italians know how to cook."

By ten o'clock, they were all tired and ready to go home. Phillip went to the front desk and asked the owner's wife to phone for a taxi, while Randall paid the bill. Watching Randall and Meredith through the evening, Phillip had seen the tension, an undercurrent playing below the surface of all the jokes and the laughter. For Randall, moving from the peace and quiet of the Isle of Man would be a disaster for his writing. Walking down to the sea, alone on the windswept beach was the time Randall had told Phillip he found his stories. Being cooped up in a soundproof room would make his mind sterile. The problem wasn't Douglas growing up on his own, the problem was Meredith stuck in the middle of nowhere with nothing to do. When he had asked her if she was writing a sequel to her children's book she had said no, the only discord in an otherwise perfect evening. Two people living together wasn't always so easy. For Phillip, Meredith's unspoken problem was a lesson to learn if he wanted his own marriage to go forward harmoniously. Martha loved living in the excitement that came with a big city, and he'd better get used to it.

The couch in the lounge pulled out into a bed, Bergit bringing him a blanket and a duvet. When he was tucked up in bed, she leaned down and kissed Phillip on the forehead. They smiled at each other.

"Thanks, Mum."

"You haven't called me mum since you were a child."

"I was wrong. You are my mother. Thank you for everything. Are Randall and Meredith all right?"

"They will be. She's bored on her own with Randall in his study or walking alone on his plot walks down the beach. She needs company. Why don't you suggest they come and live in New York, if you and Martha are going to live there? You two brothers always enjoy each other's company. If you can't have a child with Martha, you will at least have a nephew. Think about it. His publishers are American. They'd love him to live in New York. Make him do all those interviews with the media to promote his books. There's more to being a successful author than writing a book. They can keep the farm on the Isle of Man and use it for holidays. The poor woman is bored, Phillip. Have a good sleep. See you in the morning. It's lovely to have you back in my home. I so miss Myra. Anyway, that's life. At least I have Craig round the corner."

"I don't think Randall and I know how lucky we were to have you as our stepmother."

"You're going to make me cry."

"Sleep well, Bergit. Sleep well, Mum."

"And you, my son."

PHILLIP BOOKED his flight to Kansas City the next morning. When he phoned Martha all he got was the answering machine. He left a message, giving the flight number and his arrival time at the airport in Kansas City. There was a three-hour wait in New York for the second part of his journey. Travel, it always bugged Phillip.

"When do you go? Did you sleep all right?"

"Like a baby, Randall. You're lucky with that son of yours. He doesn't cry."

"Sleeps and eats. That's my son. Meredith spends half her life spooning food down his throat. She gave up breastfeeding a couple of months ago."

"Why don't you come and live in New York with us?"

"Are you kidding?"

"If you're going to move back among people you might as well go live in the big one. Villiers Publishing would love it. All those talk shows on radio and television. Boost the sales of your books no end."

"I hate that kind of attention."

"You and I would have some laughs. I found a good pub in Kansas City. I miss Solly's Saloon. We'll find another Solly's Saloon in New York. Leave the women at home with Douglas. They'll love all the women talk. Tell each other all their secrets. If Meredith wants to she can find herself a job and put Douglas in a nursery. Women love to talk about themselves to each other. What Meredith misses on your little farm."

"We'll have to find homes for the animals. They won't let us bring cats and a dog to America. I'd have to apply for residence."

"You're a famous author employed by an American publisher. They'll give you a residence permit at the drop of a hat. They'd like nothing better than to turn you into an American author. Something to boast about. All that lovely tax money. How America has done so well over the years. They bring in the best. From top foreign students who attend their universities and stay on afterwards, to bestselling authors. You've got more than enough money to buy yourself a swank apartment. You'll have fun. They'll all want to entertain a celebrity."

"That's the part I really hate. People gushing all over you trying to get a piece of the crap they call fame."

"Everyone wants fame."

"Not when you get it. My joy is in the writing. Not in all the attention."

"Where else are you going to live? The Crookshank brothers on a New York safari."

"There aren't any animals."

"Oh, there are plenty of animals in New York. You got to believe it. In America, they have three bolts on their doors and a security system a mouse can't penetrate. Think about it. She's bored, Randall. Like me with Martha, we can't be selfish. If we want to have wives, we have to think about their lives. Put ourselves in their positions. When you're writing or plot walking what's there to do for Meredith?"

"Not much, Phillip. Good morning. I'd love to live in New York. Can you believe it, Douglas is still fast asleep?" They both looked around sheepishly at Meredith standing in the spare bedroom doorway.

"Did you hear what Phillip was saying, Meredith?"

"Every word of it, darling. Music to my ears. There's nothing better in life than a bit of excitement. Relieves the boredom of the daily routine. Whoops. There he goes. Guess what? My baby's hungry."

PART 2

APRIL 1994 — "IN PURSUIT OF WEALTH!"

1

While Phillip was cooking his family breakfast in England, Martha was dreaming in her sleep in her mother's spare bedroom in Kansas City, the wind outside banging on the window, her dream in turmoil. They were out on a boat, cowering down, and a bird with its wings the width of the small boat was swooping down on them making Phillip and Martha put their hands up to protect their faces. In the water next to the boat a big animal surfaced, opening its jaws, its teeth long, white and menacing. Martha woke screaming. The latch on the window behind the curtains was loose, making a loud rattle. The dream faded quickly, the immediate thought of Phillip coming home on Friday bringing peace and comfort to Martha, calming her down.

"Are you all right?"

"I'm fine, Mother. Go back to your bed. Just had a bad dream. The latch is loose on the window."

"The wind's blowing."

"We were out fishing on the Zambezi River and a hippo came up next to the boat, its jaws wide open. Fortunately, that's when I woke up. I've been lucky all my life. Whenever I have a nightmare I wake up before something terrible happens. Sorry to wake you."

"You know, I slept in this same bed with your father for half my life. You were made in this bed."

"I don't want all the gory details, Mother. Go back to sleep."

"I'm awake. When you get older you don't go back to sleep so easily. Why don't we have a nice little chat together?"

"I'm working tomorrow, Mother."

"You're always working."

"I can't believe he's coming back after what I did. The one person who can help me get over losing my baby and I kick him out of my apartment. All my agony thrown at poor Phillip. You really think he'll come? Won't change his mind? He's stopping over with his family. What if he wants to stay in England? We only married because I got pregnant. I'm so excited he's coming back but if he doesn't arrive what am I going to do? My life's on a knife-edge. Damn that rattling window. Listen to it."

"When does Franklyn want you to relocate to New York?"

"Today, if possible. We have five clients waiting for us to open our New York branch. Marcin Galinski wants to talk about a grand plan to promote his voice recognition software across the whole planet. He's taken on three more engineers this month and that's just the beginning. Wants to corner the market before someone else comes up with a better product. Says you need to improve information technology every six months. Market share. That's what he wants. You get a fifty per cent share of an internet market with all those players and you make so much money it blows your mind."

"Have you sold your apartment?"

"I think so."

With the wind rattling the window, Martha poured out her problems to her mother as they lay in the dark, the old double bed from the farm comfortable and warm. When Martha finished her monologue there was no response from her mother. Martha leaned up in bed and looked down on her sleeping mother, the outside lights from the city just enough to see her mother's face. Gently, Martha kissed her mother on the cheek. Lying back in bed, Martha smiled to herself: whatever would she have done without her mother? When Martha drifted back into her sleep the wind had gone down stopping the window-rattling, her sleep untroubled by bad dreams. In the last of the night, Martha woke briefly, put out her hand to the person sleeping next to her thinking it was Phillip and drifted back into her sleep. When she woke her mother was opening the curtains to the day and Martha felt rested, her mind alert, ready for the coming rush.

It took her an hour to get up, shower, dress, eat her breakfast and commute to Horst and Maples's offices. Franklyn was already sitting at his desk behind the glass window of his small office. Jaz had her head down at her desk in the cubicle next to Martha's. No one looked up to say good morning. Martha sat down and picked up the phone, dialling a client. The rush of day had begun. Concentrating on her work she went about her daily routine. When she looked up to see Franklyn standing in front of her desk she had no idea how long he had been there: deep in her work, time passed quickly.

"When's he arriving?"

"Friday afternoon. He's spending a few days with his father."

"Have you sold the apartment?"

"Had a reasonable offer."

"Take it. I want you in New York on Monday. Marcin just phoned. He says it's urgent. That if we don't pull our finger out he'll appoint another agency to do his work."

"You, me, and especially Phillip, are shareholders in Linguare.com."

"He doesn't care. He's the controlling shareholder. Taking Phillip with you will help. Marcin's prepared to spend as much money as it takes on advertising. He agrees with me that a company's income is in direct proportion to its spend on advertising. The more advertising, the bigger the company's turnover. Provided the ratio of advertising cost is smaller than the profit content of the turnover, the more you advertise, the more money you make. He wants us in New York now. Book your flights."

"What about Phillip?"

"You'll have a weekend to get used to each other again. Screw his brains out. He won't care whether it's Kansas City or New York. A fresh start in a new city will do your marriage more good than staying here to be reminded of why you kicked him out."

"Are you more interested in the client than me, Franklyn?"

"The client always comes first. Business comes first. If you want to be a success in life that's how it works. Oh, and I want Jaz to go with you. She's agreed. She and the boyfriend she lives with are having problems. She fancies Marcin, and with luck, he fancies her. I've seen them together. We don't want to lose a client that's going to be the next Microsoft."

"Isn't there more to life than business?"

"Of all people, you know there isn't."

"Jaz can hear you touting Marcin."

"I hope so. You got to use all the ammunition you've got, Martha. Phone the travel agency and book your flights. Phone your realtor and sell the apartment."

"Yes, sir."

"That's my girl. Oh, and book me a seat on the same flight. We're going in with all our guns blazing. Life never stops. Get on top of it. You blink these days and someone has pinched your best client. It's one constant fight for money."

"What do you do with all your money, Franklyn?"

"Spend most of it. Invest the rest."

"And if someone runs off with your investment?"

"Spread the risk. Keep your money in more than one asset. More than one currency. More than one country. One goes up and another comes down. But you hold on to the value of your money. Spread the risk. When I retire, or they kick me out, I want to live in luxury. A nice little place in the Cayman Islands by the sea. You got to think ahead, Martha. My fifty-thousand-dollar start-up investment in Marcin Galinski's company hasn't been all bad. The rate that young man is building his business I'll be able to retire on that investment alone. When the time looks right, or when our friend floats his company on the New York stock exchange, I'll sell some of my shares in Linguare.com and spread the money round the world. Never stop thinking in life. That's the secret. Here they come. Six of them. All one company. Whatever would our clients do without us?"

Smiling at Jaz in the next cubicle, she watched Franklyn greet his happy clients.

"Did you hear all that, Jaz?"

"He thinks Marcin fancies me."

"Does he?"

"I don't know. We'll have to find out. The best investment for a girl is a rich husband, provided you don't sign a prenuptial contract."

"Would you marry a man just for his money?"

"A lot of people do. Love is fickle. Money, properly invested like our boss Franklyn invests his money, is a lot more lasting. And if you got money you'll always get a man."

"What happened to Noah?"

"I caught him cheating. In my bed. Men! Anyway, that killed that one. One minute you love 'em, the next minute you hate 'em. Plenty more fish in the sea... You want me to book the flights? Where are we going to stay? I know, I'll phone Marcin and ask him to recommend a nice hotel close to his office. Doesn't he sleep on a mattress in his office half the time?"

"That's sneaky, Jaz."

"Got to think. I like Marcin. He's tall and good looking. Forget about his money. Life's all about having fun. A roll in the hay with a young man in his early twenties is just what I need to get over my cheating lover. Friday, Martha. Good luck to you. Nothing better than good sex."

"Stop smirking. We need more staff. This company is expanding as fast as your future boyfriend's company in New York."

"Haven't got him yet."

"You will. Give him a ring. Start the charm cycle. But be careful. He's also a client. The pursuit of men. Why are we never satisfied?"

For a long while, Martha sat at her desk thinking of Phillip. She wanted to be satisfied. To be with a man for the rest of her life. She was tired of all the chasing: two more years and she'd be entering her forties. Taking out her personal phone book she looked for the number of her gynaecologist. With the number staring at her she changed her mind. Sometimes in life it was better not to know. If she wanted to hold Phillip for the rest of her life she would have to get pregnant: give him the child they both so much wanted; the cement that would hold them together. She had done it once with him, she could do it again. Happy in her mind, she went back to her work, the office humming around her, the phones ringing, people talking, business as usual. When the lunch trolley came she bought a packet of sandwiches, eating while she worked. By six o'clock in the evening she had had enough.

"You want to go for a drink, Jaz? Are the flights booked? You know it's my birthday on Friday. I'm not sure Phillip remembers the date of my birthday. Last April I hadn't met him! Can you believe it? All that love, hope and disaster in less than a year. The dreaded forties are approaching. You know what? Let's go visit Solly's Saloon. It's Phillip's favourite drinking hole. It'll make me feel he's close. After a few drinks, I'll cook us all supper in my mother's apartment."

"You still staying with her?"

"Doesn't want me to be on my own. Phillip told her I tried to jump off the balcony. If it weren't for the old lady across the way waving at me I'd have gone. Depression so deep is terrible. You want to die. Kill all the pain inside of you once and for all. Have you ever been depressed, Jaz? It's the worst pain you can imagine. Look at me. I'm talking about myself as usual. Why are we all so selfish? Are you ready?"

"Lead the way. What's for supper?"

"I'll have to look in the fridge. Mother always waits for me to come home before she or I start supper. Did you get hold of Galinski?"

"Oh, yes. Nice hotel a block from his office. I could feel his lust coming down the telephone. He's glad for you Phillip's on his way back. In this world there are no secrets from anyone."

"Does he know I tried to kill myself?"

"I didn't ask him. Not the best way to impress a client. Let's go. A cab to Solly's Saloon. Let's get started."

"Not too many drinks."

"Of course not. I can't work the next day on a hangover."

"Who was he cheating with?"

"Never seen her before until I found her in my bed. Can you believe the cheek of the man?"

"Are you going to nail Marcin Galinski?"

"Of course I am. Whether anything comes out of it we'll just have to see. You look so much better with Phillip coming home. Now you look happy. I was worried about you. We all were. Everything is going to turn out just fine."

"I want to get pregnant again."

"I know you do. Come, Martha. It's time to have fun."

"Don't forget rule eleven. Never talk business in the pub."

"Never break the rules. Does rule nine apply to a client?"

"Not if Franklyn says it doesn't. Just don't start screwing a co-worker. Get you both fired. I like Franklyn's rules. You know where you stand."

"What was rule one again?"

"Work, work, work."

"Of course."

The pub was full of people when they arrived in the happy hour, the drinks priced low to get the customers started. After two drinks the price was no longer so important.

"Martha! Good to see you."

"Good to see you, Solly. And don't be so discreet. Phillip, your best customer, is coming back on Friday. It's also my birthday. I want that nice little table in the corner for two at eight o'clock. This is my co-worker, Jaz. Excuse me, could you move down one barstool so I can sit next to my friend Jaz?"

"Do anything for a pretty lady. Give them both a drink on me, Solly. It's the happy hour. Turn up the music. My name is Jack."

"Jack who?"

"Does it matter?"

"And what do you do for a living, Jack?"

"As little as possible. Fact is, I'm out of work."

"What line were you in?"

"Advertising back in New York. Came to visit my old mother with time on my hands."

"Did you get fired?"

"I want to start my own business. Most of my old clients will follow me. It's the person who looks after them that counts, not so much the agency. What you two drinking? What line of business are you in, lady?"

"Advertising."

"Now isn't that a coincidence?"

"On Monday we are going to New York to open a branch for our agency."

"They say more good business starts in a pub than anywhere else. People contact. That's what it's about."

"Two of Solly's fancy vodka cocktails. My husband says Solly is the best cocktail maker in Kansas City."

"You're married?"

"I hope so."

"You're not wearing a ring."

"It's a long story."

"We got all night Solly. Two of your fancy cocktails for the ladies."

"I'm Martha. This is Jaz."

"Pleased to meet you."

"Are you married?"

"Not at the moment. Monday, you say? I'll write down my phone number in New York. Introduce you to the city."

It made Martha smile. The game never stopped. For an hour she plied Jack with questions before she was satisfied. She would introduce him to Franklyn. When they left to go to her mother's apartment to make themselves supper they had just had enough drink not to have a hangover.

"What you think of Jack, Jasmine?"

"As a man or a future co-worker?"

"You saw where I was going. He's got ten million in new accounts for the picking."

"I was on the other side of you. I'm not so sure about our friend Jack."

"Wasn't he flirting with you? I've got his phone number. If nothing else, a nice coincidence. Let's go eat some food."

"He wants to be his own boss. Have his own company. Only way to make serious money and be in control of his life. I wish I had the guts. Companies use their employees to benefit the company. All the nice talk is when they need you. Why don't we start our own ad agency? Ask Franklyn to join us. He's just an employee like the rest of us. If Marcin is after the three of us more than Horst and Maples we can land his account."

"You're being disloyal to your employer."

"As Jack just said: when it suits 'em they fire you."

"He wasn't fired."

"Got out just in time by the sound of it. Like politics and politicians, employees and company directors are always manoeuvring with each other, to get what they want. Most of the smiles are false. People stab you in the back to get what they want. You're only safe when you own the business. It shouldn't be too difficult to find out if Marcin will go with us."

"Especially if you sleep with him."

"That will help. We all connive, Martha. We just don't admit it. Half the time we don't even admit it to ourselves."

Not sure where Jaz was going, Martha poured themselves a drink, raided the fridge and cooked supper, Jaz taking a cab back to her lonely apartment soon after they had eaten the meal.

"Isn't it wrong to take your employer's clients and start a company on your own?"

"It's stealing in the moral sense of the word. Why? Is my daughter going to start her own business? That's interesting. Your father always said he hated working for other people. Why he had his own farm."

"It'll be in New York."

"I know. Sad, but what can I do? I'm used to being alone. The two boys rarely visit their mother. How it works. You spend all that time and energy bringing up your children and then they go their own way. We all think only of ourselves, Martha. You go do what you have to do. Don't worry about your mother. Now Phillip's on his way back the smile is on your face again. I don't have to worry about you. Let's go to bed. A few more nights of companionship and then it's all gone. Alone, I wake in the night and worry about all three of you."

"Would taking the Linguare account be stealing? Through Phillip's investment as a venture capitalist, I brought them the account."

"That's for your conscience to work out. People bring accounts to their companies to keep their jobs. But who am I to know? I'm just an observer. Aren't you tired?"

"Jaz has got me thinking. Bowden, Poland and Fairbanks has a nice ring to it."

"Aren't you now Martha Crookshank?"

"Then it's Bowden, Crookshank and Fairbanks. If Jack joins us we can add his surname, whatever it is. When Phillip goes back to investing more of his money in start-ups we'll get those accounts as well. Be part of Phillip's package: we'll give you the capital and tell you how to market your product. I love the world of business. You always got to keep thinking. New ideas. New ways of going about your business."

"I'm going to bed. Can't keep up with my children. Where do you get all the ideas from?"

"By thinking, my mother. By thinking. A great philosopher once said, 'most people would rather die than think, and many of them do.'"

"Who was it?"

"How do I know? I remember the quotes, not the name of the person who spouted it. 'To bed, to sleep, perchance to dream.' Now that's Shakespeare."

"I don't know how I borned you."

"Isn't that incorrect English?"

"Come to bed and stop arguing with your mother. I'm going to miss you."

"I'm going to miss you too. Give me a hug. Thanks for looking after me after I lost my baby."

"What mothers are for. Now we're both crying."

"Nothing wrong with a good cry. Nothing wrong with being sentimental. I'll phone you every day."

"Not the same as having my own child in the room next to me."

"I'm not a child. I'm pushing forty."

"You'll always be my child."

"I so want a child of my own."

"I know you do. With luck, you'll get yourself pregnant again."

"I'm scared to see the doctor in case he says I'll never get pregnant again."

"We all hope, Martha. What life's all about. Keeps us going."

"Will he really come back on Friday?"

"Think positive. And turn your light off. Talk to you in the morning. If you don't get a proper night's sleep you won't be able to think clearly in the morning."

2

While Martha was sleeping peacefully next to her mother's room, Jasmine Fairbanks was lying awake in her empty apartment thinking. In future, she was going to use men instead of being used by them. Noah Hughes. What a lovely specimen. All that talk of love and future together was just to get himself off every night in an apartment where she paid half the rent. He'd gone. Out the door. Good riddance to bad rubbish. Seething with jealousy, Jaz could not sleep, her eyes wide open in the semi-dark, her mind chasing itself round and round, her frustration building. At twenty-six, two years older than Marcin the genius, she was going to take her revenge. Take what she wanted. Think of herself. Let other people worry for themselves. And if Franklyn and Martha brought her into a partnership, she wouldn't have to worry about going for the likes of Marcin with all their personal money. She'd have her own. Be independent. A woman with her own money. Thinking of Marcin, she began to calm down. The trick was to seduce him properly. Make him want more. Give him just enough sex so he wanted more. And get his business. If they did the job right for Linguare.com, even if she broke up with young Marcin it would not matter. Seduction. Women's power over men. When a man wanted a woman sexually he'd do anything to keep her. She'd keep him just on the edge. Flirt with other men. Use her power as a woman. The power of sex. The pull. And never suck the lust out of him, that was the trick. On Monday she was going to New York to restart her life and be in control. When Jaz finally fell asleep she had forgotten Noah Hughes, the man no longer important. When she woke in the morning she was raring to go.

"You're a conniving bitch, Jasmine Fairbanks. But I don't give a damn. Thinking of other people did me no good. Let's go get 'em, Jaz. The whole world is out there waiting."

Running across the nice red bedroom carpet towards the bathroom, Jaz gave a skip. She laughed. She was happy. She had a plan. At the age of twenty-six, she finally had a plan.

On the Friday when Martha drove to the airport to hopefully pick up Phillip, Jaz's old life in Kansas City was about to end, her new life in New York about to begin. She had packed up Noah's belongings in boxes, not wanting to see him.

"You've got a key. Pick up your things on Monday evening. I'll be in New York. And get stuffed, Noah. Screwing some bloody woman in my bed."

"But I love you, Jaz."

"Don't talk shit."

"We were getting along fine."

"Until you screwed it up. Literally."

"She came on to me. We'd had a few drinks after work. You were always working half into the night. I'm sorry."

"Screw you, Noah."

With a satisfied look on her face at the thought of her last conversation with Noah, she looked up to see Franklyn leaning over the glass partition of her cubicle.

"What's that grin on your face for, Jaz?"

"There's nothing more satisfying than slamming down a phone. Martha's gone to pick up Phillip, then they are going to Solly's for dinner. You think we could go for a drink? And don't look like that at me, Franklyn, I would never break rule nine. I've something I want to talk to you about. I've been talking to Martha. We have a plan and we'd like you to be part of it. It's business. Strictly business. You can ask your wife to join us. Have her opinion. She's also a woman."

"What are you up to, Jaz? The airport first thing on Monday morning. Have you got all the files together?"

"In my briefcase. Don't worry, I'm organised. You coming for a drink?"

"What's this all about?"

"It's a surprise."

"I hate surprises. Tell me."

"Not in the office."

"How can it be business if you won't discuss it in the office?"

"Are you coming?"

"Let me phone my wife and tell her I'm going to be late. Friday night is family night in the Bowden home. My daughter Tildy is cooking the dinner. She's invited her boyfriend. Boyfriends at sixteen! You know, my son wants to be a rock star. He's now out of school and doesn't want to go to college. Spends all day in his room sleeping and playing his electric guitar."

"You know what Dagwood said: the best thing in life is a nap between naps. Go and phone your lovely wife. We won't be more than an hour."

"YOU WANT us to start our own agency!"

"That about sums it up."

"Are you out of your mind? All three of us have perfectly good jobs that pay us well enough to live good lives. Why do we want to start our own business, Jaz?"

"To give us maximum security. Make certain of our futures. Give us control over our lives."

"Was this idea yours or Martha's?"

"A man called Jack we met in the pub. Linguare's account belongs to you and Martha. With Phillip, you were the start-up investors. Your money went into the business. Had nothing to do with Horst and Maples."

"And Martha wants you as part of it. Why?"

"Because Marcin Galinski is about to become my lover. You saw it yourself. The Crookshank and Bowden money. My seduction."

"It's immoral."

"Probably. But fun. If it doesn't work we don't have to tell anyone and life goes back to normal. Now, here's the rest of it. Jack has ten million in accounts he can bring with him. With Phillip back in town, there are going to be a host of new start-ups to be invested in, all of which will get their money on the condition Bowden, Crookshank and Fairbanks receive the advertising accounts. Jack will be a junior partner until he has proved himself."

"Do you want to join my family for dinner?"

"I'd love to. Is Tildy a good cook?"

"She wants to impress the boyfriend."

"How it goes, Franklyn. How it goes. What's your son's name? I've met your wife but not your son and daughter."

"Clarence. Tildy and Clarence. Joanne's father's name was Clarence. He calls himself Clarry... You really think Marcin will give a new advertising company all his business?"

"Hasn't done too badly as a new company himself. New companies have drive. Lots and lots of drive. It's a whole new world out there. You don't have to be born into a family with a family business and wait for your father to retire before becoming the boss. Young brains know what's coming with all the new technology and can start up on their own when they leave college. They don't need internships to learn. They know the future in business from intuition. They can get rich on their own without having to rely on other people. In my father's day, you would never have found a man of twenty-four who has built from scratch a company the size of Marcin's. Young people understand each other. Why Martha knows I'm important if you want to land the Linguare account. You only get one life, Franklyn. Let's give it a go."

"I've got more to lose than you and Martha. I have a family to support. Kids are expensive. When Clarence finally pulls his finger out and applies to go to college it's going to cost me a fortune. And then there's Tildy. If the new venture crashes I'll be out of a job and no advertising agency will want to employ me. Martha's married to Phillip with all his old and new money. You're young. Who knows, you might hook a Marcin permanently? You have the looks."

"Your investment in Linguare will see you through. When the company goes public you can sell your shares. Nobody got anything in this lovely life without taking a chance. Haven't you saved any money?"

"Some. Not enough. I need a salary to support my family. These young companies with all their new ideas can die as quickly as they blossom. They don't have saleable assets like an oil company with billions of oil still in the ground. They have an idea. Own an idea. But if that idea is trumped by a better idea they are worth nothing. A salary and a pension. That's security. You need enough money to pay the bills. Put your children through college."

"What about having fun? Have confidence in yourself, boss. You're good. People employ Horst and Maples because of you."

"I'll talk to Joanne."

"That's my boss."

"You know I could fire you both for even thinking of going out on your own and taking away company clients?"

"But you won't. I know you, boss. You're a good man. Let's go talk to your wife... Electric guitar. Is he any good at it?"

"Not by the sound coming out of his bedroom. But who am I to know? Most modern music to me is one big noise. One big beat. You can't hear the words they are singing."

"He'll love New York. So will Tildy. It's the place where everything happens."

"The boyfriend won't like it."

"She's sixteen!"

"You're making me think, Jaz."

Without saying another word, Jaz followed her boss out of the bar. She was smiling. She had him hooked. She knew she had him hooked. If his wife could be convinced, they were in business.

"What's it like being married, Franklyn?"

"Complicated. Very complicated. Especially with children."

The first thing that Jasmine heard as they entered Franklyn's nice suburban home was the strumming sound of an electric guitar coming from behind the closed door of a bedroom. Beneath the strident noise was something pleasant: a beat, a rhythm that made Jaz want to dance.

"I've brought Jasmine home for dinner. Can we lay another place at the table? Jaz has an idea she wants your opinion on, Joanne."

"Oh. And what might that be? Come in and sit down. Tildy's in the kitchen. Clarry is in his bedroom... Turn it down, Clarence! We have a guest for dinner. Just listen to him. I've tried shouting until I'm hoarse but it doesn't make any difference. Sleeps all day and plays that damn guitar into the middle of the night... So, what's this idea that is so important?"

"Martha and I want Franklyn to join our new advertising agency as the senior partner. Move to New York. Martha's husband provided the initial start-up money for Linguare.com which I'm sure you are aware of. We think Marcin will give our new company his account. He wants to spread his company across the planet and can't do so without spending large sums of money on advertising. Franklyn is worried about losing his security as an employee. Losing a steady job."

"Clarence, stop that damn music!"

"I like it. It makes me want to dance. Has a catchy rhythm."

"Really? You could have fooled me. Luckily we own this house, not like living in an apartment with communal walls. Thank goodness. He's stopped. Ah, Clarence. Meet Jasmine. She works for your father and is staying for dinner. She wants us to form a new company and move to New York."

"New York! How wonderful. When are we leaving? I can join a band. Everything happens in New York. I'm bored out of my mind in Kansas City. Nothing ever happens here. All my friends want to live in New York. Does Tildy know? Tildy! We're going to live in New York. You'll have a new school. Dad's starting his own business."

"I haven't decided yet."

"But you will. It's so wonderful. Tildy, come out of the kitchen."

"What about James?"

"He hasn't arrived yet."

"But what about him, Clarry?"

"What about him? Aren't you excited about going to New York?"

"When are we leaving? Supper's almost ready. That's the doorbell. Must be James. He can come and visit in the holidays. Are we going to buy a swank apartment in Manhattan? Oh, my goodness. It's awesome... Hello. You must be Jasmine. Is this idea something to do with you?"

"Sort of, Tildy."

"I hope you like roast beef. It's one of our family favourites. For starters, I've done a nice soup. I'll put another place on the table. New York! What a lovely surprise. Kansas City is so boring... Hi, James. Come in. We're moving to New York. This is Jasmine, one of my father's co-workers. Are you hungry? Silly question. You're always hungry."

"When are you going?"

"I don't know. You can visit in the holidays. Don't look so crestfallen. In New York, we'll all have a future. Smile, Jamie boy. Life's got to be fun. When you get out of school who knows where you'll want to be living? Put on some music, Clarry. You've nearly got that last piece. Keep at it. Everything comes with practice. The Bowdens of New York. Has a nice ring to it."

"Do you write your own music, Clarence?"

"Most of it, Jasmine. Nice to meet you... Can I have a drink? It's Friday night. Family night. New York. It might even persuade me to go to college. How about that, Father? Make mine a beer."

"Family!"

"What's wrong with family, Father?"

"You're all incorrigible."

By the end of supper the job was done, her plan in motion, Jasmine not sure whether to call herself a manipulator or a conniving bitch. Clarence drove her home.

"Don't you want me to come up?"

"No, Clarence. You're a little too young for me."

"What's age got to do with it?"

"Thanks for the lift. Drive home carefully."

"Why does my father only let me drink one beer?"

"Because he's a good father and doesn't want you to become an alcoholic. Good night, Clarence. See you in New York."

"You can call me Clarry."

"I'm sure I can."

Leaning across she kissed him on the cheek and got out of the car. Men! The moment they got out of puberty they wanted sex. She walked across the road, up the stairs and let herself into her apartment. The cardboard boxes with Noah's things in them had gone. There wasn't even a note. Shaking her head, she went to bed. As she lay, the name Bowden, Crookshank and Fairbanks kept ringing in her mind, keeping her pleasantly awake. For once, it was nice to feel good. To know where she was going. If the whole venture crashed Franklyn would still find a way to make himself a living. The man had brains. All you needed in life was brains. To the sound of the distant night traffic, Jaz drifted into her sleep, the last picture in her mind that of the tall, good-looking Marcin Galinski, the genius of information technology, the man of her dreams.

WHILE JASMINE WAS DREAMING of Marcin Galinski and unlimited wealth, a few blocks away in her own apartment, Martha Crookshank was lying awake next to Phillip, a soft smile of satisfaction on her face, the satisfaction both mental and physical. The day had gone better than she hoped, from the first sight of each other at the airport and running towards each other, to the passionate lovemaking that had started the moment the door to her apartment closed. Instead of talking they screwed the brains out of each other until they were so exhausted, they fell asleep in the big double bed, their arms wrapped around each other. Sometimes, as Martha told herself as she lay on her back smiling, actions were better than words. After three hours of on and off sex, any bad feelings there might have been had been blown out of the window, the past unimportant, both of them happy with the present. Whether the luck would extend to a pregnancy, Martha could only hope. They were home. Together. That was all that was important. Relief mingled with her satisfaction as she thought of their future, her world again the colour of roses. The sound of the night traffic rumbled up from the surrounding streets of the city, a pleasant background to Martha's thoughts. With her lips still just open, Martha fell back into her sleep, back into her dreams, all her dreams soft with happiness and hope. In the first light of dawn, she was woken by Phillip gently feeling her body. Again they made love, both of them reaching their climax together. Then they got the giggles.

"Thank you for coming home."

"Thank you for asking me. Life, however pleasant the surroundings, is never much fun on your own."

"Are you happy to be back in America?"

"America? Who knows? Does it matter where we are so long as we love each other? Time will only tell where we live."

"You want some tea or coffee?"

"I want you. All of you. Please don't let us fight with each other ever again."

"You like the idea of going to New York?"

"A fresh beginning will hopefully wipe out all the bad memories. Are you working today? You sometimes worked on Saturdays."

"Not in the office. When we've had our breakfast I'm going to phone Jaz and see what happened with Franklyn. Then we can hire a boat and go out on the river if it isn't raining."

"What time do we all fly to New York on Monday?"

"Eleven o'clock at the airport."

"Sometimes the speed of life in America takes the breath out of me. I'll make tea for you and me coffee. America. The great land of dreams. Are people ever satisfied with what they've got? It never stops."

"When you stop, life catches up with you. Going forward is fun. One long, happy adventure. You know, they say the worst thing in life is boredom. Bored we shall not be, Phillip Crookshank."

"We're happy. We've got each other. What more can we want?"

"Fun. Lots and lots of fun. Tea coming up."

"Thank you, my lady. There's no more fun in life than a nice cup of tea or coffee in the perfect company of a husband and wife."

"With a biscuit."

"Of course. With a biscuit."

And the day went on.

3

By the following Friday, after Martha, Franklyn and Jaz had gone off to do their work, Phillip Crookshank, feeling like a lost soul in the towering human jungle of New York, sat in front of the blank television set in their hotel room one block from the offices of Marcin Galinski and his team of software engineers. Flicking the remote for something better to do he found the travel channel and a programme on Africa, again changing the channel, and finally turning off the television. Phillip looked at the four walls, up at the ceiling and back to the blank television before getting up and walking around the room. Outside, through the window, he could see the towering skyline of the great city of New York, and down below, the constant movement of traffic. Trying not to think of Jacques, Munya and Sedgewick going about their day at the Chewore safari camp, he put on his coat and went out. Finding a taxi was easy. The first idea had been to go and see Marcin Galinski except there was nothing to say. What Phillip knew about computers and software technology could be written on the back of a postage stamp. He'd be a nuisance. They'd got his money. What else did they want?

"Where you want to go, mister?"

"You know a bar in this part of Manhattan?"

"All of them."

"A small, intimate bar full of locals."

"Where you from?"

"Does it matter?"

"Not really. You don't need a cab to find a bar."

"But I need you to tell me the right one. Here's twenty dollars. Will that help?"

"You get out my side of the cab. Walk across the street and round the corner. A sign says Harry B's. Give my regards to Harry."

"What's your name?"

"Does it matter? Thanks for the twenty. Enjoy New York."

"I'm trying."

"You better run. It's beginning to rain. The mayor of New York controls everything but the weather."

Dodging the traffic, Phillip followed the cab driver's instructions. And there it was. The entrance at the top of the stairs to Harry B's. Looking at his watch Phillip saw it was just gone eleven o'clock in the morning. Wiping the rain from his face Phillip walked up the stairs and into Harry B's saloon. Looking around made Phillip laugh. The pub didn't look much different to Solly's Saloon. Smiling, already feeling at home, Phillip walked across and sat on a tall stool up at the bar.

"What can I get you?"

"A beer. Any kind of beer. At home I drink Castle. Are you the owner Harry?"

"Harry started this bar back in the thirties I think it was, soon after prohibition. I bought it two years ago. Try a Miller Lite."

"I'm the only customer in your bar."

"You and me. It's early. What brings you here so early?"

"Nothing to do. My wife's working. Forming a new company with her co-workers from her old company. I run a safari business in Africa. Or I did. Now I'm a venture capitalist. Invest in new ventures... Make it a Miller. When did you open the bar?"

"Five minutes ago."

"My wife and I are moving to New York."

"Help yourself to the peanuts. I'm Terry."

"Terry in Harry B's. The cabbie thought you were Harry. What did the B stand for?"

"They never told me."

"I'm Phillip. The nuts are good. Boredom. There's nothing worse in life than boredom. Tell me your story, Terry. There's just the two of us."

"Where do you want me to start?"

"At the beginning. It all starts at the beginning."

"What part of Africa?"

"The banks of the Zambezi River. The beer tastes good. I have shares in a business round the corner. You'll be seeing me again I expect."

"Well, let me think. I grew up in Brooklyn, never lived nowhere but New York. Now look at that. I got another customer. The story will have to wait. Enjoy your beer."

Life in the big city: it was all beginning again. Sipping his beer, Phillip began to enjoy himself. He was going to make some friends. In Phillip's life he had found it was all about making friends. Through the morning they came in one by one. By midday, the barstools up at the long bar were dotted with sitting men. Not one woman. The row of men sat and drank on their own. Like Phillip they had faraway looks on their faces. By lunchtime the drinks had found their tongues. There was conversation. Intermittent laughter. Smiles on all but two of the faces. Between Phillip and a man with a sour face was an empty stool on the other side of him. The chances were the others knew him. There was always one in a bar. A man alone. Trying not to look at him, Phillip stared straight ahead at the bottles on the shelves at the back of Terry's bar.

"You want another one, Phillip? You've been nursing that one for half an hour."

"I'm killing time. I'll be doing a lot of time killing in my future. In the old days back in my father's England the man went out to work, the woman did the housework. How the world has changed."

"She must make a lot of money for you not to have to work."

"Oh, I've got money. Enough for both of us. That isn't the problem. Give me another of those beers."

"Coming up."

"You're getting busy."

"Got to have customers to make money."

"Silly of me."

Which left Phillip thinking: in all his thirty-eight years he had never understood people who made more money than they needed. He could never see the point. Now Martha was off on the pursuit of her own company to make more and more money she would lavish on a lifestyle Phillip was unable to understand. What was the attraction of an apartment halfway up to the sky that cost a hundred million dollars? Going to a big city to earn a basic living, Phillip could understand. That was often necessity. But when a man had an unearned income from his savings, what was better than a nice cottage in the country? A cottage like the one Phillip owned in the mountains of the Vumba he lived in during the heat of the Zimbabwe summer. Could a Manhattan apartment be better than his cottage? He doubted it. But not for his Martha. She wanted the bright lights and the flashy apartment. But what could he do? He wanted Martha. Was overjoyed to be welcomed back by her. And if he wanted a marriage he would have to do what he was told.

"Can't have it both ways, china."

"You talking to me? You mind if I move up a barstool? Nothing worse than drinking on your own."

"Be my guest."

"What's the problem?"

"Women."

"Don't tell me. It's always women. You can't live with them and you can't live without them. You want another of those beers?"

"Why not?"

"How long you been in New York?"

"A few days. I'm with my wife. She's out forming a company with her old co-workers. They're in advertising."

"What do you do for a living?"

"Nothing. Absolutely nothing. That's my problem. What do you do in life when you've got more money than you need?"

"Give some of it to me."

"Why are you alone drinking so early in the morning?"

"I've been looking for a job. I'm a cook. Some make it sound better by calling themselves a chef."

"There must be plenty of jobs."

"There are. That's my problem. I work awhile, save my money and go on a binge. Some would call me an alcoholic. Why the others here avoid me. I'm good company until I'm drunk. Then I get nasty."

"Forewarned is forearmed. I'm Phillip. I've just arrived in America from my home in Africa. My American wife wanted me back again."

"Do you love her?"

"I do. That's the other side of the problem."

"Grant Howard. The best chef in New York."

"What's your speciality?"

"Boiled beef and carrots."

"You're kidding?"

"Of course I am. Food is food. All you got to do is cook it. After twenty years of practice that isn't so difficult. Nice to meet you, Phillip."

"Nice to meet you, Grant."

"Are you in a hurry?"

"Not in the slightest."

As the booze went down Grant changed like a chameleon. At the end, he was dogmatic, argumentative and then aggressive. The man knew everything. He was always right. Never listened to another man's opinion. About to get up and find another companion before it ended in a fight, Phillip paid his bill. Two other men in the bar were watching them, as had been Terry.

"Grant, you've had enough. Please leave my bar."

"That's typical! You take a man's money and then kick him out."

"You've started two fights in my bar. You're lucky I let you in."

"You're a piece of shit, Terry."

"So are you, Grant. Do yourself a favour and go home. You're charming sober and a pain in the butt when you're drunk. Go home to your wife."

"She hates me."

"I'm not surprised, poor girl. Phillip, why don't you move to the other end of the bar. You need to pace your drinking, Grant. Instead of being right all the time take a man's advice and drink slowly. For a while, you two were enjoying your conversation together. Phillip's just arrived in New York. I don't want him to think you're a typical New Yorker."

"Are you kicking me out? You and whose army?"

"Don't be silly, Grant. Half the men at the bar would love to throw you out. Go now without making a scene and I'll forget this when you come back again. Please, Grant. We've had this discussion many times before. You're lucky I let you in. Now be a good boy and go home."

The bar had gone silent as Phillip walked away. When he looked back from the other end of the bar Grant had gone. He found an empty stool and sat down.

"That was rather unpleasant." The man Phillip spoke to had a 'shit never stops' look on his face.

"He's his own worst enemy. Done it to all of us one time or another. Why we all avoid him. I'm a happy drunk like the rest of us. Or most of us. One of the problems of drinking in pubs. Bar fights. One day someone is going to hit Grant so hard they'll knock his teeth out. He should go to AA. Get some help. Can you imagine the life of his poor wife?"

"Have they got kids?"

"One. Left home at eighteen and never went back. Drink's a big problem for some people. Destroys their lives. We were all watching you. Waiting. It's kind of a game in Harry B's. When he moved up to talk to you it was just a question of time."

"Why didn't someone warn me?"

"Part of the initiation. Welcome to Harry B's. You staying in this part of

New York for long? I'm Ollie. Ollie Leftwich. Terry says your name is Phillip. You're from Africa."

"He talked about me?"

"We were all waiting. Taking bets on how long you'd avoid a fight. I said you wouldn't punch him. Now you're part of the club. Welcome. Drink and drugs. Ruins many a life in America. People have too much time on their hands to indulge themselves. The money flows. Life at the end of the twentieth century. Where it will take us, who knows? We're spoilt. There's always a fast buck to be made. Plenty of jobs. All that surplus money to spend on alcohol. Back in the thirties when this bar started a man had to work just to make a living. Really work. Jobs were difficult to come by. A man had to look after himself. No handouts in the thirties. We're going soft. Grant should stop drinking before it ruins his life and the life of his wife. Sometimes she comes into the bar to take him home. Poor woman. Must be a living hell."

"You want a drink, Ollie?"

"Why not? At least we know both of us are happy when we get drunk. So, what can you tell me this Friday afternoon in Harry B's saloon?"

Making friends. It was all about making friends. Feeling sorry for Grant and his wife, Phillip began with an animal story. Everyone liked stories about animals. Even the dangerous ones. Time was passing. Switching from beer to lime juice and soda, the time ticked away. Hopefully, by six o'clock Martha would be back in their hotel room. They would go out to dinner. He would keep off the drink. Grant had taught him a lesson. There was nothing worse in life than a floundering alcoholic, a man out of control. Having told his story with a laugh and a smile he left the bar to go for a walk along the bustling streets of Manhattan.

"What a world," he said to the traffic. He was lucky. It was not raining. Putting his best foot forward Phillip walked as fast as possible in and around the people, trying to get his daily exercise. Phillip hated not being fit. And it pushed the alcohol from Harry B's out of his system. After an hour of good walking, Phillip turned back. When he got to the hotel, Martha was waiting. She was smiling. Both of them were smiling as they chatted about her day.

"Why don't you want to drink?"

Phillip told the story of Grant Howard.

"You must look for some more investment opportunities. Give you something to do, Phillip. Marcin is coming with us. We've been to lawyers to form our new company, Bowden, Crookshank and Fairbanks. All three of us have sent written letters of resignation to Horst and Maples by DHL courier service. We're committed. We're all staying in New York. Now we need to find an office close to Linguare and start working on their advertising campaign. I've sold my apartment."

"You don't waste time."

"What's the point? I'm so happy. Nothing better in life than a challenge. We can start looking for an apartment. Aren't you happy for me, Phillip?"

"I'm delirious."

"Be serious."

"I am. Oh, I am."

"Thanks, honey."

"My pleasure. Sorry about no drinking. That man gave me a fright. Don't you have to go back to Kansas City to tie up all the ends?"

"Once they know you want to leave a company they don't want you anywhere near the place in case you try to steal their accounts. Someone else will pick up where I left off. It's all in the files or on the computer. We'd all secretly cleaned out our desks. There's nothing left that we want and they sure as hell don't want us. Franklyn's talking to his family on the phone right now. Joanne will pack up the house and put it on the market."

"And what's Jaz doing?"

"Seducing Marcin Galinski. They're out to dinner."

"She doesn't waste time either."

"Her apartment is rented. She's given them notice. She's given instructions to the removers to pack up her stuff and put it in storage. Sent them the key. Moving isn't that difficult if you have money. We're going to be flat out the moment we find an office. Before, even. First, we got to find our way around the New York media. Get to know all the new people. Galinski couldn't believe his luck when he saw Jaz. He may be the new powerhouse in the world of information technology but when it comes to women he's a pussycat. She's already got him eating out of her hand."

"Has she slept with him?"

"Don't be silly. She'll play him as long as she can before she gives in. She'll have his hormones dancing on the ceiling before she takes off her panties."

"She's manipulating him."

"Of course she is. We want to prove to him we three are the answer to his advertising so that by the time he's grown bored with Jaz, we'll be firmly in the saddle."

"Will he get bored with her once they've had sex?"

"Happens. Got to be prepared. We want his business."

"How's Linguare.com coming along?"

"You can't believe it. And when we launch our advertising campaign and make Linguare a household name, the value of our shares will have doubled again. You think you're rich now, honey. Just you wait. We're going to need you for the advertising campaign. Have you interviewed on television and radio as the start-up capitalist who invested his money in the best damn new idea of the twentieth century. You'll be pumping Linguare.com and yourself. People will come to you with their new ideas looking for capital. There's nothing better than being famous to attract business. You're going to have your own office at Bowden, Crookshank and Fairbanks. A big sign on the door. Crookshank Investment Inc... Are you going out like that? You'd better change. In New York, everything is about image. You're going to have those cameras pointed at you, Phillip, by the time we're finished. Got to look right. You got to get used to it."

"I don't want cameras."

"Can't have a thriving venture capitalist business without them. All the big names suck up to the media. Fame makes money, Phillip. Now go and change."

"Yes, my lady."

"I'm not kidding."

"I know you're not."

"That man in the pub sounded horrible. Don't ever get yourself into a fight when you're famous or the media will turn it into a circus. We're going to be big in New York. Got to behave ourselves. Wow, what a day. It's all happening."

"Why do I want to be famous?"

"To make lots and lots of money. Over the weekend we're going apartment hunting."

"Who's paying for it?"

"We both are. Even money. With both of us putting in money we'll be able to afford a place that will blow their minds."

"Who?"

"People. Everyone we meet. We'll be recognised as rich people. Part of the new financial elite. Be good for both of our business."

"And make us more money."

"You've got it. Now hurry. Go change. I'm so happy to have you back again. Marcin said without your initial financial help he wouldn't have done what he's done."

"He'd have found another investor."

"Maybe. Maybe not. When it works it looks easy. Hindsight is an exact science."

"It's nice to be appreciated."

"What's that faraway look, honey? Are you dreaming about all those billions of dollars you are going to make with the help of the likes of Marcin Galinski? Now that guy's really smart."

"Not really. I was thinking about my cottage in the Vumba. I'm going to have a shower."

"That's my boy."

Standing under the shower with hot water streaming over him, Phillip reflected on life: when you didn't have it, you wanted it; when you had it, it wasn't quite so much fun as you expected. He had a wife, money and all he did was go to the pub and get himself into an argument. Life didn't make sense. He could still feel the day's alcohol rumbling in his stomach. He had a headache. And tomorrow, what was he going to do? They could go to a concert, go to the theatre, invite their friends out to dinner. And all the time in the back of his mind all he wanted was the peace and solitude of the Zambezi Valley or the Vumba mountains. Money! What was the point of all this money? Shaking his head, he got out of the shower and walked naked into the bedroom.

"You really do have a tan."

"It happens when you spend your life in the sun. Along with skin cancer."

"You don't have skin cancer!"

"I hope not. The sun's rays are more dangerous than they used to be. If you worry about every disease they talk about you'd go crazy."

"Put on some clothes. I'm hungry. Where are we going?"

"Wherever you like."

"Aren't you hungry?"

"Got a headache. Drinking all day is a hobby for fools."

"We'll eat, come home, make love and get a good night's sleep. How does that sound? Are you glad to be home?"

Phillip smiled without answering. His home was in the Zambezi Valley and the Vumba mountains, not in the turmoil of what other people thought of as the most exciting city in the world.

"Do you like New York, Phillip?"

"I love it."

"Give me a kiss."

"My pleasure, my lady."

"Did any of your family have one of those weird English titles?"

"None that I am aware of. Why, do you want to be a Lady Martha? Has a nice ring to it. I'll ask Dad to go see the Queen and get himself a baronetcy. The title is passed down to the eldest son."

"Are you happy, Phillip?"

"Of course I am. I'm with you. I'm married to you. Let's go get ourselves something nice to eat. But no drinking alcohol."

"Not even a nice bottle of wine, honey?"

"Just one."

"Kiss me. You look so lovely naked."

"Careful now."

"We could get them to send up some supper."

"Now you're talking."

"The whole of New York at our beckoning and you want to eat in the room?"

"Make up your mind, Martha."

"Let's go out. New York is so exciting."

Women! thought Phillip. They could change their minds in the blink of an eye. He began to put on his clothes, the smart clothes Martha insisted upon. In the end, it was all about appearances.

At the restaurant, the prices on the elaborate menu blew his mind. A piece of fish he could pull in on the end of a line cost a hundred dollars. With it came bits and pieces with exotic names that most left on the side of their plates.

"This is nice fish but not as good as Zambezi bream cooked over the open fire."

"Just look at everyone. They look so rich."

"All those potential clients."

"It's so nice to be part of it. Makes all the hard work worthwhile. Oh, Phillip, we're going to have so much fun in New York."

The beef course came on a beautiful plate with all the trimmings. The pudding was just as exotic. The twenty per cent tip Martha told him to give the ingratiating waiter was enough to feed two families in Zimbabwe for a month. Phillip gave the man his debit card and tried not to think. Where he came from under the rule of Robert Mugabe, half the population lived on less than a dollar a day.

"You know, they say Mugabe, his family and his political cronies are now worth millions. Not bad for fourteen years in power."

"How did he make all that money?"

"Stole it back from the white man. Land that had stayed bush from the beginning of time had been given a value by the white farmers when they turned it into agricultural land. So he's kicking them out and righteously taking back what was his. Trouble is, most of the land isn't producing anymore."

"Then why do they say Mugabe is so rich?"

"All the money in the country has to go through the central bank controlled by one of his cronies. Next he'll nationalise the mines and white-owned businesses. When he's destroyed everything it won't be his problem. He's old. He's famous. The world loves him as a saviour of his people. Do you think a man like that enjoys his life? People like that never create anything. They only destroy... Where did they go out for dinner?"

"Who?"

"Jaz and Marcin. I thought they might be here."

"Do you like Mugabe as a president?"

"I love him. He stopped the fighting. What's a few tobacco farmers on the garbage heap of history? Africa will have its day. People learn from their mistakes. It's called progress. Can we go? That was the most expensive meal I have ever eaten."

4

While Martha was wondering what was going on in Phillip's head, Jaz was making progress. The restaurant half a block away was even more expensive, Marcin Galinski trying to impress his date. Jaz's seduction had begun when they sat down at the corner table in an alcove perfect for lovers. She had leaned just far enough forward to give him a glimpse of her breasts, the poor boy tripping over his chair as he tried to sit down. If Jaz had been a betting girl she would have laid money on having given the tall good-looking Marcin an erection.

"You look so nice dressed to go out. In the office it's all so casual. Give me your right hand. I want to read your palm. Oh, yes. There it is. It's going to be your year. All the signs are perfect. Your skin is so nice. You don't mind if I stroke it? What a lovely restaurant. We're going to have the perfect evening. You don't have to think of work. You don't have to talk of work. All we will talk about is ourselves. Tell me more about Marcin the man. By the feel of your hand, I can tell you are a sportsman. Men who play lots of sport don't put on weight. Your body is perfect."

"I had a baseball scholarship to Yale. Without baseball, I would not have gone to university. My father is poor. Or rather, he was. I have given them an apartment and looking to buy Dad a grocery store. In a few years, he'll have a chain of stores across America. You need help in life to get started. I need your help, Jaz. Advertising is the key to the success of any business."

"Oh, you'll get all the help a young, good-looking man could ever want."

She had him dangling on the hook, her sexual pull so strong she was mesmerising the genius. Inwardly, it made Jaz smile. Even made her a touch cynical. When it came down to it life was all about sex. Getting control of a man's hormones. Gaining control.

"What are we going to do together this weekend, Marcin?"

"Anything you like."

"Anything? That's interesting. Now let me think. After this beautiful restaurant, you have brought me to we could go to a nightclub. I love dancing to slow music. It's so intimate. Do you like being intimate with a girl, Marcin? Of course you do. You don't have to choke."

With the last pull of her finger across the palm of his hand, Jaz put both of her hands under the table making herself look innocent. She was enjoying herself. She was going to win. She was going to get what she wanted. All the degrees in the world were unable to teach a girl the art of seduction. You had it, or you didn't. You could pull any man you wanted, or you couldn't. For a man, it was all about money. For a girl, it was all about looks.

By the time Marcin came to pay the bill and for them to go to the nightclub she had him as firmly as if she had tied him to a bedpost.

"Are you enjoying yourself, Marcin?"

"It's a perfect evening."

"And it's only just started. Thank you for a lovely supper. Do you know the best bit?"

"Tell me."

"Give me that hand that played baseball for Yale. There's nothing more exciting than the hand of a sportsman."

"Didn't you want to talk about business?"

"What on earth for? We're enjoying ourselves. Having fun. Life's all about having fun."

Hoping she wasn't fooling herself she followed Marcin out of the restaurant. For Franklyn and Martha to include her name in the name of the new company had to do with whether she would be able to control Marcin, her skills in advertising secondary. She had learned that nothing was ever done in life without a reason. They were using her. The way people used each other to suit their own purposes. Nothing in life was what it appeared to be, including the new relationship between Martha and Phillip. Martha wanted a baby before she grew too old. Phillip, Jaz wasn't so sure about. On the surface, he seemed to be happy with all the new arrangements, but under the surface Jaz thought Phillip was uncomfortable living back in America. Too often, when Martha wasn't looking, he had that faraway look on his face. A faraway look that spoke of Africa. Money and wealth were not so important to Phillip. For Martha's sake, she hoped Martha would fall pregnant. Without that first pregnancy, Jaz doubted the two of them would have married. Like Phillip, Jaz was being used, and unless she concentrated she was going to lose the opportunity of a lifetime. She had been lucky once when Phillip and Martha went to live in Africa, taking over most of Martha's clients at Horst and Maples. She had held those clients when Martha returned to Kansas City with Phillip, the idea of permanently living in a safari camp on the banks of the Zambezi River not for Martha. It was always about Martha. Having now resigned from Horst and Maples Jaz's career was in jeopardy without Marcin's business. Not sure whether the first date had gone far enough and with her confidence ebbing, she thought it better to walk to her hotel.

"Are you working in the office tomorrow, Marcin?"

"Of course. We all are. Work is all we do."

"Are some of them still working?"

"Most of them. Getting the product to work is a drug for all of us. Everything we're striving for. Why we sleep most nights on the floor in the office. Gives a whole new meaning to working till you drop."

"Then you better go to them. Forget the nightclub."

"We could go to your hotel room."

"That's naughty. It's a first date. I never have sex on a first date."

"Can't we pretend it's the second?"

"We could but we won't. Walk me the block to my hotel. We don't need a cab. Work comes first. You've said that yourself. We can start again tomorrow evening if you want."

"Of course I want."

"Good. Come round to the hotel tomorrow. I'll be waiting at six o'clock. Give me a call before you come round."

"You don't want to pretend it's the second?"

"Are you horny, Marcin?"

"I'm always horny when you're around."

"Give me a kiss."

"Here in the street?"

"Why ever not? Young lovers. No one will worry. How was that? Poor Marcin. We'd better run. It's beginning to rain. I love New York. It's going to be so much fun."

Breaking into a run, they ran to Jaz's hotel. She kissed him again and went through the swing door into the building. When she looked back he was still standing in the rain.

"You're a bitch, Jaz. A conniving bitch."

"Did you say something, madam?"

"Not to you, Mr Doorman."

"Your friend is still standing in the rain."

Crossing the foyer, Jaz went to the lift, the doorman following and pressing the button.

"Is he still standing in the rain?"

"Don't you want to look?"

"Of course not. It was a first date."

"That explains everything."

For an hour Jaz lay awake in her bed playing the scenes of the evening through her mind. She was playing high stakes poker much like an expensive whore. Or was it all just a game? The fun of life for both of them, the primal force inherent in all of them? Without sex, there would be no people. Hoping there was more to her life in the future than procreation Jaz fell into a troubled sleep.

When she woke in the morning her instant thought was whether she had nailed down Marcin. She got up, showered and phoned Martha.

"You sound perky, Jaz. How did it go?"

"I'm not sure."

"You didn't let him take you to bed?"

"Of course I didn't, stupid. We had an expensive dinner and that was it. He's coming round at six. What's on today's agenda?"

"Nothing for you, Jaz. Concentrate on Marcin."

"What do I do until six?"

"Have a look at New York. Take a ride on the subway. Look for an apartment. Phillip and I are looking to buy. So is Franklyn. Don't lose him, Jaz. We're relying on you. Men can be fickle."

"Is Phillip in the room?"

"He went for a walk."

"How's he enjoying New York?"

"He's already found a bar just around the corner from the hotel. Harry B's... Once I get myself pregnant, we'll be back on track. We love each other."

"What's love, Martha?"

"That's a stupid question."

"Is it? Must I tell Marcin I'm falling in love with him?"

"It would help. Got to go. Phoning all those realtors. Got to have just the right apartment. Concentrate, Jaz. You have an important job on your hands."

With Martha's last words ringing in her head, Jaz stood thinking: one minute you were living with a man, the next you were chasing another one.

When did it ever end? Poor Martha. Two failed marriages and another one dependent on her getting pregnant. What was life all about? Where were they going? Where was she going? Was the endgame just getting rich? There had to be more to life than just money. What was love? Was it a feeling? A nice word for wanting something? A nice word for sex? A word used for getting what you wanted? Love. They all said it was love. And for the life of her Jaz had no idea of the word's true meaning. There was that bar across the road that Martha had mentioned. She had nothing to do. She would walk across the road and visit this Harry B's. Feeling more confident and happy with something to do, Jaz left her room. Downstairs the same doorman was back on duty.

"You work hard. Didn't you get home last night? Where's Harry B's?"

"Across the road. Go over there to that intersection and walk on fifty yards. You'll see the sign at the top of the stairs."

"Thank you kindly."

"Anything for a pretty lady. The sun is shining. Going to be a fine day."

Dodging the traffic, Jaz followed the man's instructions. The bar sign was where the doorman had said it would be. Looking around at the morning traffic she hesitated.

"What the hell? If they think a girl a whore on her own in a bar, who cares?" Her thoughts still racing, Jaz walked up the stairs. The first person she saw was Phillip. He looked forlorn, a man alone sitting up at the bar. Again she hesitated. The last thing she needed to do was pry into Martha's private life. As she turned to go back down the stairs, Phillip turned around. The bar was empty except for Phillip and the barman sitting alone on a barstool away from Phillip. Phillip waved. Caught in the act, Jaz walked across between the tables and chairs to the bar.

"Good morning, Jaz. How was your evening with Marcin?"

"Martha said you had gone for a walk."

"I walked for an hour. Too many people on the pavements. Lovely day. I didn't know where to go. Come and join me for a drink. What brings you to Harry B's?"

"Martha mentioned the place. I was bored. Something to do. I'm seeing Marcin again at six. Do you think my having a relationship with Marcin is important?"

"Martha seems to think so. To me, doing the job right is more important."

"What is my job, Phillip?"

"Advertising, of course."

"I'm only twenty-six. Is that what they really want?"

"How did it go?"

"Made me feel like a whore."

"Life can be complicated. What will you have to drink?"

"You can say that again. I'm not sure if I should be drinking so early in the day."

"It's one of the hazards of living in a city. When you have nothing to do you can sit in a room and watch television or go to a pub. In Africa, I rarely drink. Sometimes with Jacques. Sometimes with the clients. But I never start at this time of the morning."

"Do you want to live in New York?"

"Not really. And Martha doesn't want to be stuck on a safari camp in the middle of nowhere. The silence gets to her. And the heat. She doesn't hear the call of the birds the way I do. There is nothing more beautiful than birdsong. It's never out of tune. Always perfect. Then there are the frogs calling from the side of the river. Crickets singing from the tall grass that stretches for miles away through the bush. New York is all noise and bustle. Never mind. You can't have love and not give up something. Being selfish never helped anyone. This is Terry, the owner of the bar. Harry came and went in the thirties. Terry, meet Jasmine, my wife's business partner. What are you having?"

"I'll join you with one of those beers. I'd love to visit Africa."

"So would I. You can't have everything. Tell me all about Marcin. When I look at it that young man has made me more money than most of my African friends make in ten lifetimes. I should be grateful. A lucky investment. Trouble is, when you have all that money it takes the challenge out of life. I can never understand people who want more and more money... You want me to pour the beer in a glass or do you drink it out of the bottle like my other American friends? Cheers, Jaz. To your health. To hell with our wealth. Sorry, that's an old one from my days at Rhodes University in South Africa."

"Cheers, Phillip. Thanks. What did you read?"

"History. Good old history that goes round and round and never stops repeating itself. One day the world will blow itself to pieces and then it will all stop. All the wars. All the money chasing. All the selfish politics. What are you going to do with your life, Jasmine? Do you fancy Marcin or is it all a cunning plot?"

"I'm not sure. Are we ever sure?"

"Not in my experience. That's part of the fun. You never know what's coming next. Wouldn't it be awful if we knew exactly what was going to happen to us before it happened? Like now. Seeing you come into the bar when I was sitting here on my own was a nice surprise. There's nothing more sad than a man approaching middle age sitting up at a bar drinking on his own. Let's both of us play truant for a while and not tell anyone. What the eye doesn't see, the heart doesn't grieve about."

"Are you worried about Martha?"

"Of course I am. She's a woman. Women get jealous. We both know this is a pleasant coincidence but my wife doesn't. Franklyn, Crookshank and Fairbanks. You're going to be rich, Jaz. That's what's important. You never know. You just might fall in love with Marcin Galinski. He's a very nice young man. And who knows, he might fall in love with you. It's what every man and woman on this planet hope for. Love. Happiness. A family. A lifetime companion: it's nothing too difficult. Life is terribly simple. Modern life tries to make it complicated. Go with your instinct, Jaz. It will all come out in the wash."

"You're kidding."

"Probably. Doesn't hurt to hope. We do a lot of hoping in Africa. In this crazy world, you got to be an optimist. Like Martha. She has to hope for a baby or she'll sink back into her depression."

"Is that why you came back?"

"She wanted to kill herself after she lost our baby. She needs help. My help. All I can do is try and help. You see, I married her. It's my obligation."

"Aren't you doing it for love?"

"I hope so... Smile, Jaz. The world isn't coming to an end. Not just yet, anyway."

"I don't understand men."

"Any more than we understand women. Or anyone for that matter. Including ourselves... You want a packet of peanuts?"

Jaz decided that she might as well go with the flow, and once she started to relax, she began to enjoy herself.

"Why didn't you get married earlier in your life, Phillip?"

"With all the political turmoil and the bush war in Rhodesia, most of the young girls had left the country. There are not too many cross-racial marriages in Zimbabwe. It's frowned on by both sides of the racial divide. My brother Craig is an exception but it forced them to go and live in England away from Jojo's parents. Families and cultures are set in their ways, Rhodesia was the last of the British colonies and only began at the end of the nineteenth century. Lasted less than a hundred years. The young girls from the oldest colonial families could still get ancestral British residency. I never met a girl I liked who wanted to stay in Africa. Many people in the new world are uncertain of their futures. The world is volatile. Financially and politically. And then came Martha. We made love under an African moon and she fell pregnant. Some story. What girl sees a future for herself and her children in Africa? So here I am. What's your story, Jaz? When we meet strangers in bars we ask them their stories."

"I'm not a stranger."

"You're a friend of my wife's, a stranger to me. If you feel uncomfortable we can leave. Wander around the great city on our own. Some even say it's dangerous to be alone on the streets of New York. Especially at night."

"I'm not uncomfortable. Do you think she might come in?"

"She doesn't know where I am. Now, where were we? Do you have brothers and sisters?"

"My father walked out on me and my mother when I was two years old. He says he grew bored of marriage. They were both in their early twenties when I came along. Dad said he wasn't thinking of how it would affect me when he left. We've seen each other every year on holiday but I never got to know him. Mother re-married. I have a stepbrother. We don't get on. But that's a long story. I've been on my own all my life. Has its advantages. I'm self-reliant. Expect nothing from people I don't make for myself. Why this new partnership is so important to me. I want to be independent. Have my own money. I don't want to be beholden to anyone. It's the new age of independent women."

"Don't you want kids?"

"Maybe. Later. First I want to make myself financially independent. I'm using Marcin, Phillip. Do you think that's wrong?"

"I try not to judge other people. Some say business is business. If you all do a good advertising job for Marcin I can't see anything is wrong."

"But using sex to get what you want?"

"Is it any different to using money? I've got far more than I expected from Marcin. It must be sad to be the product of a broken family. My family has always been close. I'm lucky. I shouldn't take it so much for granted."

"Didn't your mother die in an accident?"

"She was killed by a pride of lions. I can blame the lions. Not my parents. Maybe I should blame her for drinking too much alcohol and driving drunk into the bush."

"We all have our problems."

"Want another beer? That one went down quickly."

"Why ever not? How old are you, Phillip?"

"I'll be thirty-eight on the seventeenth of next month. Exactly one month younger than Martha... Did you like your stepfather?"

"I hated him. As my mother grew older and I grew up he had his eye on me more than my mother."

"Did he touch you?"

"Not exactly. Just with his eyes. Creepy. I knew exactly what he was thinking. My stepbrother knew. Why he hated me. Why he hated my mother."

"What happened to your stepbrother's mother?"

"She married three men. All of them rich. All she wanted was money. After the divorce, Felix went to live with his father. Felix is screwed in the head. He drinks too much. Takes drugs. I have nothing to do with any of them."

"And you shouldn't ask your business partner's husband how old he is. Cheers, Jaz. To your success in business."

"What are you going to do for the rest of the day?"

"Go to the hotel and take Martha on a house hunt. Look for the perfect home in a skyscraper. If there is such a thing."

"Many people think so. Africa. Tell me more about Africa."

From eighteen-year-old Clarence to Marcin to Phillip, it didn't seem to make any difference. Every man she had ever met wanted to get into her pants. And finally, Felix had raped her. Put her on her own bed and raped her. Laughed at her. She was sixteen years old.

"Mom. Felix raped me."

"Don't be damn ridiculous. He's your brother. You've grown up together. You're always making up stories to get attention. Your stepfather would never hear of such nonsense."

"You should see the way he looks at me."

"Now what are you inferring? You're a spoilt brat."

"I'm going to tell my father."

"And what's he going to do about it? He walked out on us, remember? Your father is a selfish bastard. All he ever thought of was himself."

"Dad will help me."

"Never has done before."

"Aren't you going to talk to Felix?"

"There's enough trouble in this household without you stirring up shit. Keep your legs together like I should have done with that selfish bastard who is your father."

"And if I'm pregnant?"

"You can have an abortion. Abortions are legal now."

"Would you have aborted me if you could?"

"Probably."

"Thanks, Mom."

"Now stop stirring shit and lay the table for supper. Your stepfather will be home in half an hour. He likes his supper ready on the table."

"He's a bastard."

"Don't you dare say that. He's a good provider. Because of your stepfather we've never wanted for anything. Your father never put in a cent. When I married him pregnant with you he made me sign a prenuptial contract. And when it came to alimony he laughed at me."

"Keep rubbing it in. I'm a burden to you, Mother, and always have been. I wish I'd gone to live with my father."

"You must be joking. Your father has never taken on a responsibility in his whole damn life. His second wife pays for everything. And she didn't want you in her house."

"I can go to the police."

"Jasmine, don't be so damn ridiculous. Where is Felix?"

"Made a bolt for it when I mentioned the police."

"Oh, so that makes sense. You two had sex together but to begin with it was consensual. You only called it rape when you'd got what you wanted. I see how you look at men, Jasmine. You give them the eye. You do that and now you complain. If you're going to have sex, put yourself on the pill. Now lay the table."

"Mother! I am underage! I hate you."

"So you say until it's supper time. Or until you want something. You're a spoilt brat. I've been watching how you look at Felix. If he raped you it's your own damn fault. You asked for it."

"You're a bitch."

"And if that smack in your face isn't hard enough come back and I'll give you another one. Only harder. Don't you dare call your mother a bitch."

As Jaz stared ahead in the bar she could still feel her mother's smack on her face.

"Jaz, where've you gone? You hadn't been listening to a word I'm saying about Africa."

"Sorry, Phillip. I was thinking of something."

"You looked like you were going to puke. I must be boring you."

"I was thinking of my childhood. My teens. Of my mother."

"That must have been nice."

"Not really. How did you get on with your stepmother?"

"I loved her. I owe a great deal to Bergit. She never ever differentiated between me and Randall and her own two kids. Loved us all equally."

"She must be a very unusual woman."

"She is. We'd better go, Jaz. Flat hunting as we call it. Apartment hunting as you Americans call it. Good luck with Marcin tonight. It was fun bumping into you."

"Likewise, Phillip. Likewise. I enjoy talking to you."

"So what were you thinking about when you drifted off?"

"Of being raped at sixteen by my stepbrother."

"Oh, Jaz! That sounds so awful."

"It was."

"What did your mother do about it?"

"Nothing. Absolutely nothing. Next time I'll concentrate on what you were telling me about Africa. I love your stories about Africa. Thanks for the drinks."

With her mind torn between the past and the present, Jaz hurriedly left Harry B's with Phillip following. A few customers had come into the bar making Terry busy. The music was playing. People were talking. It made Jaz feel so alone. Had Felix raped her? To this day she was not sure. Had she unwillingly given him the come-on to make him want what she wasn't going to give him? To get her own back? He was such a pig growing up.

They parted downstairs in the street, Phillip dashing away down the crowded pavement. She would have to be careful with Phillip. Not give him the wrong impression. If Martha had the slightest idea she was flirting with Phillip she'd lose her new job. She walked around the block and back up to Harry B's and sat down again at the bar. Terry raised an eyebrow.

"He's married. Give me a beer."

"Coming up, young lady. Welcome to Harry B's."

"What can you suggest I eat for lunch?"

"Try one of my nice fat hamburgers. What will Phillip do with himself all day?"

"Nothing. That's his problem. Too much easy money and not enough to do. First he inherited from his grandfather. Then he invested in information technology. He's going to buy a place in the vicinity. You'll see a lot of him."

"Must be boring having too much money."

"Not for all of us. Just you watch. I want a nice one-bedroomed apartment close by to rent. Got any suggestions?"

"Max! Come over here. Girl's looking for a rental. Max will help. You can find anything you want in a bar."

"Give me a hamburger, please."

"Coming up."

Jaz waited for the beer and the hamburger. A tall, good-looking man walked over from the other end of the bar."

"How much do you want to pay?"

"As little as possible."

"You could always move in with me."

"Is that a proposition?"

"Not really. Making conversation. I'm the janitor of a high-rise. Fifty-seven floors. They're expensive."

"I can afford a good apartment. I'm a partner in an advertising firm."

"Then you walked into the right saloon. Saw you talking to Phillip."

"His wife is my partner. It's the age of women."

"Always has been."

"Why are you a janitor?"

"Free apartment. Good salary. A job's a job. Don't have no fancy degree. And then there's Harry B's. Best bar in Manhattan. Right, Terry? Let me pay for the hamburger and the beer. My name is Max."

"Mine's Jasmine. You can call me Jaz."

"Mary Sanderson is moving out. Told me this morning. Nice view over Manhattan. All those lights shining at night across the town. One bedroom."

"Sounds perfect. When I've finished my lunch you can show me. I love New York. Everything is so easy."

By the time Jaz walked to Max's block of apartments they had drunk three drinks together, Jaz feeling relaxed. With Max, there would be no repercussions. Mary Sanderson showed them her apartment. It was perfect.

"When can you move in?"

"Tomorrow, I suppose. I'll need to sign a lease. Pay the first month's rent and the deposit."

"If Jaz moves in on Monday will they refund the rest of the month's rent, Max?"

"Probably. Look, I'm just your friendly janitor."

"You're so sweet."

"Just doing my job."

Instead of going back to her hotel as she would have done, Jaz went with Max down to his apartment.

"How many of you run the building? It's big."

"Three of us. The office is next door. Eight-hour shift. There's always something going on. People always want something. Half the apartments have been sold. The rest are rentals. You want to take off your coat? Make yourself comfortable."

"Can I see the bedroom? You have been so helpful. Come here, Max. It's Saturday. Let me show you my appreciation."

With the drinks and the good sex having relaxed them they dozed on the bed, both of them falling asleep. Jaz, remembering her commitment, had left her handbag on the small table next to the bed. Her ringing cell phone woke both of them.

"Hi, Marcin. How are you? Can you make it seven? Lovely boy. See you then."

Smiling, Jaz jumped naked out of Max's bed.

"Got to go, Max. Business calls. When can you get me the lease?"

"Who's Marcin?"

"Business. Just business. Never stops. Lovely to meet you."

"Are we going to do this again?"

"Of course we are. That sex was awesome."

"You're very beautiful naked."

"I know I am. And so are you. You got a body to kill for, Max."

"I know nothing about you."

"That's what's good about it. Sex without complications. And I'm on the pill. See you later, alligator. When are you back on duty?"

"At seven o'clock."

"See? It's perfect. Business at seven."

A good job. A lover. A nice apartment. What more could a girl want, Jaz asked herself. It was all going perfectly for all of them. Even before the new company had been legally formed Franklyn and Martha raised half a million from the bank in an overdraft facility, backed by their shares in Linguare.com and their Kansas City properties. The new company was well funded, Jaz's salary secure. All she had to do was nail down Marcin Galinski and her job would be permanent. On the way back to the hotel, she phoned Martha.

"Got myself a lovely little apartment just around the corner. Moving in on Monday."

"How did you find it so quickly?"

"Had a bit of luck. Met the cutest man. How's the house-hunting going?"

"We've started on the list."

"Galinski's coming round at seven."

"Good luck, Jaz. Concentrate. Don't forget to concentrate."

"When do I get my first month's salary? I have to pay a deposit. Never mind. I've got enough for the moment."

"Just concentrate on Galinski. Leave the rest to me."

Feeling mentally and physically satisfied, Jaz walked the last hundred yards back to her hotel. Life was all about having fun. And making money.

"Good afternoon, miss."

"Good afternoon, Mr Doorman. What a lovely day."

"It's beginning to rain."

"It's still a lovely day."

With her need for sex screwed out of her by Max, her evening with the good-looking genius was going to be a whole lot easier. Jaz showered and washed off the smell of Max. When Marcin phoned up from the hotel foyer Jaz was ready for business, the top two buttons of her dress unbuttoned. As before, she was not wearing a bra.

"There you are, Marcin. Are you ready for a lovely evening?"

First, she smiled at Marcin and then at the doorman. Both men were looking at her chest.

"Can you help me with my coat? It's cold of an evening in a New York spring. Just put it over my shoulders. There we are. Where are we going?"

"To a concert of the New York Philharmonic. Then we go to supper. You said you liked classical music."

"What music are they playing?"

"Beethoven's Seventh Symphony. It's one of my favourites."

"Martha and Phillip love classical music. We're all going to enjoy doing business. There's nothing better than doing business with people who have similar interests. When are you taking me to a baseball game?"

"Do you like baseball?"

"I will if you tell me what the players are doing. I love being told about new things by an expert. There's so much new in life to find out about. A concert. What a perfect start to a Saturday evening in the great city of New York. And I've found myself an apartment close to your offices. I'll be able to concentrate on your advertising programme twenty-four-seven. The three of us will be in your office on Monday morning to explain in detail what we have for you."

"I like your dress, Jaz."

"I thought you would... Thank you, Mr Doorman. Mr Doorman, this is my friend Marcin. Marcin, you go round the other side."

Making the perfect timing, Jaz waited for Marcin to get into the cab before she leaned forward to get in with her overcoat open and flashed him both her breasts. In the weeks and months ahead the poor man had no idea what was coming at him. And all the time with the help of a few Maxes she would keep her distance. It was all about timing. Keeping control. Once the advertising campaign was launched successfully the pressure on Jaz would subside. The outcome of what happened then between her and Marcin would no longer matter. It was all a game. Life was all one big game. And when it came to Max she did not even know the man's surname.

"What are you chuckling about, Jaz?"

"Life. Just life. It's such a wonderful game."

"Is life just a game?"

"Of course it is. You played baseball to get into Yale. You've all made a fun game out of voice recognition software. The trick in life is to enjoy ourselves. The only thing we take seriously is getting the job done right. How was work today?"

"We're finding most of the answers. It's so exciting."

"What excites you most, Marcin?" Smiling, Jaz leaned across and touched the tip of her finger to his lips.

"You, Jaz."

"I hoped you were going to say that."

"Do I excite you, Jaz?"

"Don't be ridiculous." Gently, Jaz licked her lips as she softly smiled at him. Men! They were all so easy when they wanted it.

PART 3

MAY 1994 — "WHERE ARE THE TREES?"

1

On the seventeenth of May, a month after Phillip returned to his wife from Africa, he had his thirty-eighth birthday and a day or two later they had a big party to celebrate. A week earlier they had moved into their new apartment in the same building as Jaz, Max having introduced them directly to the owner, saving them the agent's commission. Phillip suspected Max made a commission on the side but that was the way Americans did business. How the wheels of commerce were greased. How the wheels went round. They both had their fingers crossed: Martha was late with her period. For the first two weeks after his return from the Zambezi Valley, it had been non-stop sex, neither of them able to get enough of each other.

"You better do one of those tests, Martha."

"No. I want to wait. Let nature tell me. Happy birthday, my darling. I love birthdays and Christmas. I'm so happy. Since you came home all those terrible thoughts have gone right out of my head. And now we are going to have a baby. I'm a week late, Phillip. I've never been a week late in my whole damn life except the last time I was pregnant. And this time I am not touching one drop of alcohol. Who's coming tonight?"

"Everyone. Franklyn and his family. Jaz and Marcin. I even invited Max to thank him for finding us this apartment. Your mother is bringing old Mrs Crabshaw. You know she turned ninety-five? Ninety-five and coming to a birthday party even if it is in a wheelchair. What a life that woman has had. I love listening to her stories."

"Does Jaz know you've invited Max?"

"No. Is it important?"

"I hope not. Mind you, there's nothing better than a little competition to keep a man's attention. It's party time. Why do people so love a party?"

"So they can get drunk."

"There's the doorbell. It will be Mom. I can't believe Mrs Crabshaw flew all this way. That woman is amazing. She loves hotels... Hello, Mom. Come in both of you. How are you, Mabel? Let me help. You're the first to arrive. Do you drink alcohol, Mabel?"

"What a silly question. Give the old lady a whisky. How are you, Phillip? Happy birthday. What a lovely new apartment. How are you finding New York? Well, well. A birthday party. Never miss an opportunity. At my age you never know if it will be the last. Give me a hand out of this damn wheelchair and sit me on that sofa. The summer is coming. I love the merry month of May. Give an old lady a kiss. I never miss the opportunity to get a kiss from a good-looking young man. You won't be jealous I hope, Martha. In the old days you wouldn't have stood a chance. All the young men came running... Thank you, dear Phillip. That is so much more comfortable... On the lips, Phillip. Not on the cheek. That's better. Now I'd love a whisky. I love the music you're playing. What is it?"

"Haydn's Twenty-Eighth Symphony. It's Martha's favourite."

"It's just so beautiful."

"When the others come we'll change the music. Tonight is party time. How are you, Aggie? How's my favourite mother-in-law? Thanks for coming all this way for my birthday party. How's the hotel? Good. You're smiling."

"There's nothing better than a free holiday, Phillip. Thank you. From both of us. Now how about a whisky? Can't let Mabel drink on her own. What are you having, Martha?"

"Nothing."

"Oh, my goodness! Are you pregnant?"

"I'm late."

"How late?"

"A week."

"That's good. Have you tested?"

"No. I want to go on hoping."

The main room in the three-bedroom apartment on the forty-ninth floor was the biggest Phillip had lived in, a combination of open-plan lounge and dining room. The ceiling was high for a block of apartments, a round chandelier hanging over the lounge, a focal point of the room. Big windows dominated the one side of the living area. He had space. There was no feeling of the claustrophobia he had felt in their small apartment in Kansas

City. Ever since writing out his cheque for his half of the price, Phillip tried not to think of the money. What they had paid for three bedrooms in Manhattan would have bought half of the Centenary, the farming block where he had grown up in Rhodesia. The furniture from Martha's apartment in Kansas City was sparse, more money to be spent on new furniture. The money needed to live comfortably in Manhattan made Phillip's mind boggle, the extravagance what his stepmother Bergit would have called ridiculous. Phillip, the boy from the farm, was not part of the rich, about to be part of the famous if he followed the publicity trail being laid out for him by Franklyn, Martha and Jaz.

"Are you an advertising agent or a publicist, Martha? This is quite some party. Look at them."

"They're all on the way to getting themselves drunk. More a publicist to answer the question. To advertise your wares you have to get the full attention of the media. Modern power lives with the media. For businessmen and women as much as the politicians. The public is gullible. Easily led. Easily influenced by a man with fame. These days, with all the radio and television that is thrown at everyone, people like what is familiar. They are calling it the cult of celebrity. A publicist makes sure her client never misses an opportunity to exploit the media. What we are determined to do with Marcin, and to some extent with you. Publicity, Phillip. What the new world of commerce and politics is all about. Just putting ads in the newspaper is old hat. A thing of the past. Our way is creative. Look over there at Marcin. All three of those people talking to him are from the media."

"You invited the media to my birthday party?"

"Of course I did. You said I should invite my friends. Come and meet them."

"I'll leave them to the genius."

"Suit yourself. Aren't the lights of New York beautiful now the sun is going down? I love the big window. You can see all the wonderful skyscrapers and that bridge with its moving traffic. It's like being up in heaven looking down on the world. Everything has gone so beautifully for me since you came home. It's all happening so fast. A new company. This apartment. And hopefully I'm pregnant. Thank you for investing in Marcin's business."

"You found him."

"You had the money. It's all about money."

"You can say that again."

Two hours into the party, the guests chatting happily, popular music playing, Phillip stood alone with his back to the guests looking out through the plate-glass window that ran the whole side of the room from the floor to the ceiling, wondering what he was going to do with his life.

"What's the matter, Phillip?"

"Hello, Jaz. Just look at it all. It's beautiful in its own way. The lights of that great city go on forever."

"Have another drink and put a smile on your face. You look sad. Are you still nostalgic for Africa?"

"Of course. Once you've lived in the wilds of Africa it draws you back like a powerful magnet."

"You'll get used to the lights. Grow to love them."

"I hope so."

"Happy birthday. Here comes fun. Max is coming over."

"Careful, Jaz. Martha said I was wrong to invite him. Is something going on?"

"Something is always going on. What makes life exciting. But I'm always careful. Marcin says you should never take your eye off the ball."

"Does he know about Max?"

"Of course he doesn't. Marcin is a baby when it comes to women. He's so naïve it makes me want to giggle."

"Never underestimate the power of jealousy."

"He won't find out. I'm not going to tell him. Neither is Max. There's nothing serious with Max. Just fun to calm my hormones while I tantalise Marcin... Hello, Max. I was just telling Phillip how much I love the lights of New York."

"You want to dance?"

"Not now, Max. Tonight is business."

"Just a dance, Jaz. The others are dancing. What's wrong with a dance?"

Phillip looked from Jaz to Max and across the crowded room to Marcin.

"Jaz, why don't we go talk to the media you and Martha so conveniently invited to my birthday party?"

"Good idea, Phillip. It's all work. Never stops."

"Dad called it World's View."

"What? What did he call World's View?"

"Our tobacco farm in Rhodesia. From the stoep high up on its hill you could see forever. Bush. Nothing but bush. No buildings. No people. The most beautiful view in the world. Far away you could see the mountains. The nearest thing to heaven. Sorry. Excuse us, Max. Business calls. We're in Manhattan. I mustn't forget. Thanks for finding us this apartment. My wife is over the moon."

With Jaz safely talking to Marcin and the tenacious media, Phillip stood back and half-listened to their conversation. The look on Marcin's face said everything. A faint smile played on Phillip's face. The game of sex never ended. No one took any notice of him standing alone, everyone interested in their own conversations. He was a stranger to them, a man from another part of the world, a world in which they had no interest. The word 'outcast' played through Phillip's mind. The party had been thrown for him but it did not matter. With Jaz safe away from Max, Phillip wandered across the room he had half paid for, back to the tall window. Aggie and Martha were bringing the food out from the kitchen and putting the long, oval plates on the oak dining room table. At the top of the table, plates were stacked next to the knives and forks. Clarence, Franklyn's son, was sitting on the arm of the sofa listening intently to one of Mabel Crabshaw's stories. Next to Mabel sat a complacent Jack, the man he and Martha had met in Solly's Saloon, precipitating their move to New York. Like meeting Martha with her safari to Africa, a chance meeting precipitated so much, changed a man's life forever, created a new human being. Were they this time going to have a baby? Phillip could only hope. For both of them. They both needed a purpose in life other than just making money. Max was dancing to the music with young Tildy, Franklyn's precocious sixteen-year-old daughter who loved showing off. Max danced them close to Jaz and Marcin, smiling at Jaz as he passed. Another man Phillip had met in Solly's Saloon walked across: through Phillip, Gordon Blake had found a job as a salesman working for Marcin at Linguare.com.

"When's your brother Randall coming over again to America?"

"How is it going, Gordon?"

"Good. Very good. There's nothing better than having a good product to sell. Happy birthday. My best bit of luck was meeting you on that business trip to Kansas City. One minute you're going one way, the next minute another. How are you, Phillip?"

"Lost. It's difficult to fit in with another culture. No, Randall's not coming. He likes writing books in perfect solitude. Says he can't write with interruptions and anything else in his mind other than his book. They both write. Meredith writes children's stories. Stuck alone with a small child under a mountain on the lonely Isle of Man would not be many people's choice. My brother loves it. A result of our upbringing on the farm in Rhodesia."

"He needs to do more publicity for us promoting our software."

"You got him to endorse your product on the Letterman show once. Be grateful."

"You looked sad standing by the window alone. How are you? Good to have you back in America."

"Nostalgic, not sad, Gordon. You can't have it all. Anyway, with luck Martha is pregnant again and we're going to have a family. How's everything at Linguare.com?"

"Chaotic. Only word for it. Their work ethic is insatiable. In my whole life I have never seen so many excited people absorbed by one challenge. All they do is work and sleep and order in food. It's fun. I'll say that for it... Oh, excuse me. Marcin is waving at me to join him. All that media. Must need my help. Quite a party, Phillip."

Turning his back to the crowded room, Phillip looked out of the window. He was lonely. There was nothing worse than feeling lonely. And talking about Randall had not helped. Through the vision of lights in front of him he could see the arches of the bridge above the moving lights of the traffic. He would get used to it. If he was going to be a father he would have to get used to it: his child was going to be an American. Turning back, Phillip looked across at the food on the dining room table where people were helping themselves. It made him feel hungry. They needed a large painting of an African farm on the wall of the room to calm his nostalgia. Maybe if he wrote to his father's old flame Livy Johnson she would make him a painting. The luck of life. If his father had married Livy instead of her going back to England from Rhodesia he wouldn't have existed; wouldn't be thinking of asking her for a painting. His mind was beginning to wander as he walked across for his supper. Life was all about the present.

With a plate of food Phillip ambled back to the window, eating his food with a fork. No one took any notice of him. Alone, content, he finished his food and put the empty plate on the ledge at his feet that ran the length of the room. Even the music was strange to him. A guest had brought a CD and given it to Martha that blasted out noise. So much modern music was just noise to Phillip. Whatever had happened to the likes of Frank Sinatra and Elvis Presley with their lovely songs full of melody? Now it was all beat. Behind him the pulsing beat of the music, in front the new world: all those people out there who depended on other people for everything. It was all so different from his old life back on the farm where they produced everything they needed for themselves: a log fire in winter, a roast chicken, a glass of milk, their water from the river. Everything under control. As Phillip stared out the window, every light, every moving car, even getting out of the building depended on other people. Total, utter dependency. What happened to everyone when the lights when out? When the pieces of paper called money became worthless? When the food chain shattered and left them with nothing to eat? In a few weeks, they would all starve to death, the whole damn lot of them. The whole brave new world was based on dependency that individuals had no control over. What a world, Phillip thought to himself. It might look pretty now from his forty-ninth floor, halfway up to heaven, but what happened when the lights went out? When all those pulsing shops ran out of food? And did any of the people behind him even think of it? Phillip doubted it. They were too busy working or enjoying a stranger's birthday party. Dependency. What he was looking out at was millions of happy people all dependent upon a commercial system. Out there was life in a city, more than half of humanity. Everything fine when it worked. Not so fine when it didn't. All those piles of money he apparently owned were just entries of pieces of paper: share certificates; bank balances. All depended on other people to give them a value, to give them any worth. A farm was a farm. A share certificate was just a piece of paper. No wonder his father hated living in London. World's View. That was a view to remember. Out there was now total dependency, no one able to fend for themselves. Would it carry on working forever? Only time would tell. The trick, Phillip tried to tell himself, was to enjoy the present and let the future take care of itself.

"What are you thinking about so intensely, Phillip?"

"Hello, Martha. Nothing. Absolutely nothing."

"Marcin is going home with Jaz. Work tomorrow."

"Of course. Everyone but me has a job to do."

"What are you going to do tomorrow when I'm at work, honey?"

"I have no idea. Go to Harry B's. Sit and think. Sit. You know that old saying, 'sometimes I sits and thinks. Sometimes I just sits.'"

"It's a lovely view."

"Yes it is."

"Have another drink."

"What a good idea. Let me join the party. What happens when the lights go out, Martha?"

"Don't be silly, Phillip. The lights of New York will never go out. Jack's coming to a meeting at the new office first thing in the morning. Inviting him to your party has done the trick. He's going to join us. Bring his accounts. Says he's not big enough to do it alone. If he brings all those accounts from his old employer we'll make him a partner."

"What does his old employer think of it? How long did he have a job with them?"

"Ten years. It's just business."

"In a world where everyone trusted each other they might call it something else."

"Competition is competition."

"And swiping part of your employer's business is what? What happened to people's ethics? I'm sorry. I shouldn't be critical about a business I know nothing about."

"He thought they were going to fire him. One of the partners didn't like Jack. They could have fired him on one month's notice if it suited them."

"Why didn't he like Jack?"

"Competition. Employers don't like their employees to become competition."

"This whole new world is nuts."

"Mrs Crabshaw is going back to their hotel with my mother. Come and say goodbye."

"Why don't they stay here?"

"Mabel loves hotels. All part of an old lady's holiday in the great city of New York. She wants to have fun. Not sit around in an apartment."

"Silly of me. I'll escort them down to the lobby and put them in a cab."

"With Jack joining us, tonight has brought us ten million dollars in new billings. Not bad for a birthday party. Come on. They're waiting."

"At your service, my lady. When I come back and they've all gone home I'm going to play a Haydn symphony to get all that noise out of my head."

"Poor Phillip. You'll get used to it, honey."

"I hope so... Mabel, Aggie. Your escort is at your service. It's only forty-nine storeys down to the street."

"Such a lovely party. I do so love a party. Tomorrow, Aggie is going to show me New York. It's all so far from my roots in England and the life Jimmie had planned for us at Hallingham Hall before the Germans killed him at the second battle of the Somme. I can still see his face. From all those years ago. Back then we had an empire. Now the British have nothing. All in one old lady's lifetime."

"You're crying, Mabel."

"Of course I am, Aggie. Thinking of Jimmie always makes me cry. One big heave, Phillip, and I'll be in that damn wheelchair. There we are. Home James and don't spare the horses. This old lady needs to sleep."

"At your service, my lady."

"I would have been you know. Lady Hallingham of Hallingham Hall. Wife of the eighth Baron Hallingham. All that wonderful tradition. And now it's all gone. Thank you all for such a lovely party. England my England. Lost in the wilderness. Gone forever. Never to be seen again. Knights in armour. Men of chivalry. Or was it? Whoever knows?"

With Phillip pushing the wheelchair, Mrs Crabshaw kept talking about snippets from her life, making Phillip smile. He hoped his own future life would be as interesting. After depositing them with the wheelchair in a cab, Phillip stood and looked at the crowds still out on the streets of an evening. Everywhere Phillip looked there were people. No peace and solitude. It was all bustle and noise. A constant flow.

Back in the apartment, a few last guests were still soaking up the alcohol, making Phillip wonder how they were going to work with hangovers the next day. Too much booze the night before froze Phillip's brain. He couldn't think. A good party followed by a bad hangover. What a way to live. Wanting to get to bed with her early meeting with Jack Webber in the morning, Martha persuaded her guests to go home.

"Work tomorrow, everyone. Lovely to have you. Thanks for coming. All sleep well."

Instead of following his wife into the bedroom, Phillip played a Mozart symphony. He sat alone on the sofa listening to the beautiful music, trying to find his peace and solitude. When he went to bed, Martha was fast asleep, a look of peace on her face. He bent over, kissed her softly on the lips, took off all his clothes except his underpants and climbed into bed, not a sound coming from Martha. Phillip turned out the bedside light. Martha had closed the curtains over the windows. The room was almost dark. From outside Phillip could still hear and feel the rumblings of the great city. A door banged from down below. He could hear the beat of distant music, just the beat, not the tune. Phillip turned over and cuddled the pillow, trying to fall asleep. He was thirty-eight years old he told himself, the last thought that passed before his dreams. In his dreams, he was a child playing with a dog. Running with the dog through the veld. He woke once. Martha was still fast asleep. She had not moved. Phillip fell back into his African dreams, a world free of people, a gentle world surrounded by nature.

2

When he woke, Martha had pulled back the curtains. She had opened two of the bedroom windows. Phillip could smell the petrol fumes from the traffic down below, hear the pulse of the great city. Martha was standing beside the bed holding his morning mug of tea.

"Got to go, honey. Have a nice day. See you this evening."

"When?"

"When I come home."

"Thanks for the tea."

"My pleasure."

Phillip went back to sleep. When he woke the tea was cold. A wind was blowing at the curtains. He could hear the loud sound of jet engines flying overhead. And he was thirty-eight years old. Leaning up on one elbow, Phillip drank down his cold tea.

"Now what the hell do I do all day?" he said to the empty apartment. Phillip was bored. However rich and lucky you were there was nothing worse than being bored. Now the chances were his wife was pregnant. Life went on.

Phillip got up, had a shower and put on his tracksuit. Downstairs the sun was shining on the top corner of the building on the other side of the street. Phillip walked down the pavement among the teeming throngs of constantly moving people. If he had run he would have knocked someone over. Walking as fast as was possible, Phillip dodged the rush of people going about their daily business, oblivious of little other than themselves. Some were talking into cell phones. A couple were talking to each other, almost bumping into Phillip. After an hour of struggling to get himself some exercise, he found his way back to the apartment. He would have to join a gym. Sit and pedal a machine. Lift iron bars. Be part of all the city people. He was a New Yorker. He would have to behave like a New Yorker. He made himself some breakfast and ate it in front of the television. Idly, he wondered if Jack Webber had joined their new business. Whether Clarence had applied for a place at New York University. How Tildy was finding her new school. In New York, it was all about people. Lots and lots of people. Turning off the television, Phillip picked up Martha's copy of *Newsweek*. For two hours, Phillip stayed absorbed in the magazine, the music player in the background soothing his nerves with classical music. He put down the magazine and sighed. It was two o'clock in the afternoon. Time to go to Harry B's.

"What else can you do, old cock?"

Muttering to himself he went to the kitchen and made himself a sandwich. If he did not exercise and drank too much beer he would end up fat as a pig like the rest of them. But that was life. His new life. Life in the great city of New York where everything was meant to happen. And he was one of the lucky ones. He had money. Lots and lots of money. Money that Marcin and his friends were working with right now to make him even more money that he had no idea what to do with.

When he reached Harry B's there was no sign of the abusive drunk.

"Give me a beer, Terry."

"Coming up, Phillip. Welcome back to Harry B's."

"Nice to be here."

"The first one is on me."

"You mean it?"

"You're going to be one of my best customers."

"Not much else to do. Thanks, Terry."

"My pleasure. Have a nice day."

And there he was. Thirty-eight years old. Rich, and getting richer. And bored out of his mind. The beer he drank had a hook in it. After a party, the first beer was often difficult. Why he had wanted to go for a run. Exercise pushed the alcohol out of the system, made Phillip feel positive. As usual in a strange bar, no one took any notice of him. It would take months to become as one with the locals. Phillip watched the clock on Terry's wall, trying to drink as slow as possible. After the second beer, the bad taste went away. With his shoulders hunched up at the long bar, Phillip stared at the woodwork, trying to conjure up a future, a vision of his life in the most exciting city in the world. And if Martha did have a baby he'd be the housefather, the househusband or whatever they called it. While his wife went to work to run the family business. Not wanting servants on top of him, Phillip would become the nanny, the cook and chief bottlewasher, not even a cat or a dog to play with the child. Could one lock up a cat up on the forty-ninth floor? Phillip didn't know. Everything was going to be television and little machines for the child to play with, a metallic world far from the real world of trees and grass, the birds and the bees, of sunshine and clouds up in the sky.

"You look like a man about to commit suicide."

"Don't be rude, whoever you are."

"I know the feeling. Been watching you for a couple of hours. Terry says you're from Africa. One of the things I like about this bar is his interest in his customers. Introducing us to each other."

"The more we talk, the longer we stay. All part of his running a profitable business. He only makes money out of the drinks, or a meal or two if he's lucky. You got to work at a business so they tell me."

"What do you do?"

"Nothing, old boy."

"You sound very English."

"We Rhodesians were more English than the English. The very last of the colonials. What do you do for a living?"

"I'm an investment banker. Equities and currencies. When the market is going down we sell short. When it's going up we leverage our capital. You can make two per cent on your money in half an hour."

"Isn't leverage gambling?" What the man was talking about Phillip had no idea. Whether the man himself knew was another question.

"Of course it is. That's the lovely thing about markets. We, investment managers, make money whether the market is going up or down. If we get it wrong all we lose is our bonuses. When the market goes up on a bull run we buy and make big bonuses. When we sell short on a bear market we make big bonuses. It's the only business to be in."

"Gambling with other people's money?"

"I wouldn't put it quite like that. If we get it right our investors in the funds make big money."

"You like big movement in the markets?"

"Something like that. You got any money?"

"My wife calls me a venture capitalist."

"Does she now? You had any good ventures?" The man was now looking bored.

"You heard of Linguare.com?"

"Of course I have. Are you serious? People talk so much crap in bars. Okay. So when did you get in?"

"Right at the start. I was the first."

"Can I buy you a drink?" For the first time, the man was interested in Phillip. Not in himself.

"Why not? You're the first person other than Terry to talk to me all afternoon. My wife works. I sit at home. Marcin Galinski makes me my money. They say he's going to be big in the world of technology. Really big. Save the whole damn American economy now all the manual jobs are going to China."

"You must know a whole lot about technology."

"Not a thing. Like you, it's all about luck."

"I like you. What you having? I'm Spence Meyer. I'm Jewish. You don't have any bias against the Jews?"

"I'm Phillip Crookshank. I'm not sure what I am."

"When's he going public?"

"Why don't you ask him? I can't give you insider information. Isn't that illegal? And no. I don't have any biases. I'm an African."

"You're laughing at me, Phillip. Pulling my leg. You didn't invest in Linguare.com. You read about Galinski in the newspapers. He's getting plenty of publicity."

"Let's talk about something other than business."

"What else is there to talk about at five o'clock in the afternoon? Unless you want to talk about women. I know a nice little club in town but it doesn't get going until late."

"I'm married."

"So am I. Going to the club is just business. Looking after my clients. My wife understands. She's far more interested in my money than she is in me. What good-looking woman fancies a fat man like me? If I got on top I'd suffocate the poor woman."

"Join a gym."

"Are you kidding? Hey, Terry. Give us a drink."

"Coming up, Spence. Coming up."

"You mind if I sit down next to you, Phil?"

"Be my guest. It's a free world. Or so they tell me."

The man eased a backside the size of a small elephant up on the barstool, the stomach flowing under and over the front edge of the bar. Phillip wanted to ask him why he didn't wear a bra but smiled instead.

"Did you really invest in Linguare.com?"

"I did, Spence. My wife and partners are Marcin Galinski's publicists. Why I'm here in New York with a new apartment on the forty-ninth floor. A few months ago I was running my own safari operation with Jacques in the Zambezi Valley. A far cry from New York."

"You can't make money in the Zambezi Valley."

"But you can live. There is nothing better than catching your own fish and cooking it over an open fire."

"You must be kidding. What's wrong with a good restaurant?"

"Thanks for the drink. I'm afraid this will have to be my last one today. I need to go for a walk. Find a nice garden to sit in. Do they have any gardens in New York?"

"It's not all high-rises."

"Thank goodness. I want to see a tree. Look at a flower."

"You can walk down to the water. What's the hurry, Phil? We're just getting acquainted. An investment banker and a venture capitalist. What could be better? Maybe I can find you new opportunities. Have myself a little business on the side. Investment banking is all about information. Scratching people's minds. Finding out what's going on underneath."

"Do you think today's banking system is sustainable? Where, when clients deposit their cash, you use it to gamble with. In the old days in Rhodesia the bank paid the depositor five per cent per annum for money in his savings account and loaned the money to a borrower at ten per cent, backed by the borrower's guarantee: his mortgage, his car, his business. Now you use his deposit to invest in the volatile stock market putting the depositor's money at risk. And doesn't all that leverage you bankers talk about put the whole market in jeopardy?"

"We are all well capitalised. Have money of our own on our balance sheets. We can afford to take the risks."

"We all hope so. But who am I to talk? A man from the bush with a useless degree in history."

"How did you find Galinski?"

"Luck, Spence."

"Where did you get your capital, a man from the African bushveld?"

"From my grandfather's inheritance. Have you heard of the late Hollywood actor Ben Crossley?"

"Of course I have. Everyone has seen a Ben Crossley movie."

"He was my maternal grandfather. As you know as an investment banker, life is about luck. The trick in my life was to choose my parents and my grandparents carefully."

"You're kidding me? You can't choose your parents."

"But it worked. Tell me more about yourself. I love to listen to other people's stories. I find my own boring."

"My grandfather got out of Germany in 1936 with just the shirt on his back. I too was lucky. Or I wouldn't be here talking to you. My grandfather was the only one to survive."

"I'm sorry for your family. I don't understand how people can be so terrible to their own citizens. History is dotted with it. The Spanish Inquisition: that was all about Catholicism. The rise and fall of communism in Russia. Politicians and priests killing people to pursue their own personal agendas. And it never stops. Will the greed of capitalism survive? Who knows? It's been a terrible world with short periods of grace in between. I'm glad your grandfather survived. Tell me more about your family. The only thing we can try and learn from is history."

By the time Phillip and Spence had become friends, both of them were happily drunk, not a care in the world. If it had not been for Phillip's conscience he would have ended up in Spence's nightclub. Instead, he managed to walk himself back to the apartment, back up to the forty-ninth floor.

"Are you home, Martha? Sorry I'm late. Met a man in the pub."

Instead of an answer, there was silence. It was ten o'clock and Martha had still not come home. Phillip went to the bathroom and stood in front of the toilet for a long time relieving himself of the beer. Leaving his clothes on the bathroom floor, Phillip went to bed in his underpants, falling into a drunken sleep. He slept through the night. In the morning his mug of cold tea was beside the bed. Martha had gone to work. He was alone. Thirty-eight years old and alone. The wind was blowing in the curtains, the smell of petrol fumes in the air. On the table beside the bed was a note from Martha.

> *I'm pregnant! Did the test. Have a lovely day, honey. Didn't want to wake you.*

Smiling, Phillip leaned up on one elbow and drank his cold tea. He was going to be a dad. Everything was going to be worth it.

"Let's go cook ourselves one big breakfast, you ungrateful bastard." He was happy. He was going to be a househusband. He had something to do with his future. Something to look forward to. Women! One minute they wanted to wait and let nature tell them with a fat belly if they are pregnant.

The next moment they take the test. Life, in all its glory, was going forward. From generation to generation, 'To the last syllable of recorded time; And all our yesterdays have lighted fools the way to dusty death.'

Breakfast went down well, abating his hangover, his throat no longer feeling like the bottom of a parrot cage. Not wanting another session in the pub, he left the apartment building and went for a walk, not knowing where he was going. The noise, the people, the traffic were much the same. Further away from the office and apartment blocks Phillip broke through the teeming streets and found the waterside. Back from the waterside, he found a small park that was more like a garden. There were trees and flowerbeds, people with dogs on leashes, children in prams, wooden benches for sitting on away from the rush of people. Phillip sat himself down and smiled at the trees. An old man was sitting under one of the trees playing an old violin, Phillip recognising the music of Beethoven. A purring cat got up on the bench and sat next to Phillip, nuzzling his knee. Phillip stroked the cat. An old woman sat down and picked up the cat, taking a cat bowl out of her shopping basket and fed it.

"Is he your cat?"

"They're all my cats. Some call them strays. I call them mine. Would you care for a cup of tea?"

"You have an English accent."

"Never lost it in fifty years. You're English by the sound of it."

"Rhodesian. Or Zimbabwean as they now call us."

"My boyfriend and I tossed up whether to go to America and look for jobs in a city or go to Rhodesia and grow tobacco. Luckily we chose America. A year later we were married but neither of us lost our British accents. It was so sad after the war. Everyone with ambition was leaving England. The empire was collapsing. All there was left was a mundane life in the suburbs, commuting up to the City of London to work. Boring. Why we got out."

"Did you have children? That cat is so hungry."

"Cats love food... Five of them. My Herbert is dead. The kids spread all over the world. Just me and the cats. What brings you to a bench in my favourite little garden?"

"My wife works. I'm going to be a housefather. Or whatever they call a male housewife. Martha's pregnant. It's our second child. She lost the first one."

"You lose all of them in the end. All that work and pressure bringing them up to succeed and the next minute they're gone. They don't even look back at you. I rather like being on my own. I don't have to put up with other people. What did you do in Rhodesia?"

"I'm a safari operator. My father was a tobacco farmer until Mr Mugabe forced us off World's View. Then I met Martha. She was on one of my safaris. She's my wife now."

"Lucky you. What an odd coincidence. I could have been your mother if we hadn't managed to get into the States. Life is so full of chance. At the age of twenty, you only look at the present. What you want today. Never the future. Was it nice living on a tobacco farm?"

"None of us regret my father coming to Rhodesia. It was a life that will stay in my mind forever. And who knows, when Mugabe goes, which happens to all dictators, we might get the farm back."

"Would your American wife like to live on an African farm?"

"Probably not. In life, you have to live and enjoy what you've got. Thank you for the tea. My stepmother says she would never have been able to get through life with four children to bring up without a cup of tea."

"What happened to your mother?"

"She was killed by a pride of lions when Randall and I were little. She too was British."

"How terrible. And if we'd gone tobacco farming that could have been me. Just shows, you never know what's going to happen in life. When's your baby due?"

"In about eight months' time."

"You want a biscuit?"

"I'd love a biscuit. What a strange world."

"Isn't it? And if the cat hadn't made friends with you we would never have spoken. I would never have met the son of a Rhodesian tobacco grower... Aren't those daisies beautiful? I love the trees and the pigeons. Come here every day when the sun is shining."

"Don't you hate all the noise?"

"In the end, you only hear what you want to hear. As a species, we're very good at adapting to our surroundings. Tell me all about Rhodesia. About that life that could so easily have been ours. The life of the last British colonials."

"You're right. We were the last. The very last. The Americans were the first. The Rhodesians the last."

"Such a small little island and we spread ourselves and our culture all over the world. Sad, now, when you look at it."

"All gone."

"Not England. There will always be an England. Just not the England I remember. As we English moved out of the empire, the empire moved into England. With all that new blood and culture, who knows what exciting things will come to Britain? One of my sons has gone to live in London. The world goes round. So do the people. You love animals, I can see."

"Even the lions, despite what they did to my mother. It's such a lovely day."

"You can have another cup of tea if you want. There's still plenty in the flask. It's so nice to talk to someone. What's your name, may I ask?"

"Phillip."

"I'm Mary. My son in England's name is Phillip. I miss my children. But they have their own lives. They phone every now and again. I can't complain. I've had a very good life. We both did. Coming to America. Now it's just me as it was all those years ago when I left home at the age of eighteen to join the Women's Voluntary Service at the end of the Second World War. How I met my husband. How I'm here with you, Phillip, on a park bench in New York. And I expect if we dig back far enough in our English ancestry we'll find we are related. That without one man or woman back there in history, neither of us would be sitting here enjoying our cups of tea."

They sat quietly on the wooden bench drinking their tea, the purring cat between them, a butterfly among the flowers. With the wind blowing from the water the air was clean, perfumed with the smell of the great ocean the British had crossed all those centuries ago, a thought that made Phillip content. In reality, the world was one big place that belonged to all of them whatever nationality they wanted to call themselves. Human life, according to the books, came out of Africa, everyone from the same roots. She was right. The aircraft that flew overhead no longer annoyed Phillip. The old man was again playing his violin, scratching the old strings. Would Beethoven have even imagined his music would still be playing after nearly two centuries? And if he had, would it have mattered to Beethoven, his love for music being in the composing not in the fame. A dog approached with its master, making the cat get down and run to a tree where it climbed up the trunk and sat complacently on a long branch, looking down on Phillip. The dog barked up at the cat, making the owner pull hard on the leash. The dog and the owner walked away, out of the garden, bringing back the peace to himself and the old lady. The barking dog had made the violin player stop playing his music, putting the violin in its case before leaving the garden.

"How big was the farm? World's View. What a lovely name."

"It was six thousand acres."

"It was every Englishman's ambition to own a country estate. Six thousand acres is so big. Why did they force you from your farm?"

"To give it to one of Mr Mugabe's cronies, paid for with government money we couldn't get out of Zimbabwe which made the payment mostly valueless. The man got all my father's hard work and development for nothing. Has no idea how to grow and cure tobacco. So the farm, last time I heard, grows nothing. Dad spent a five-year apprenticeship learning how to grow tobacco. How to farm. Now the man employs no one but house servants. Hundreds of our old employees out of jobs. Dad tries not to think of it. Makes him feel sick. All those families' livelihoods destroyed. Three generations of a family tossed out at the whim of a dictator to keep himself in power. Never mind. How the world goes round. Met a man in the pub last night whose whole family other than his grandfather were killed by the Nazis just because they were Jews. And we Rhodesians thought we had it bad. Sorry Mary, I must be boring you with my family problems. Where will it all end? That's what I ask myself... Oh, good. Here comes the cat. There's nothing more beautiful than a purring cat."

"You're not boring me, Phillip. I love a bit of company every now and again. When I'm dead, what happens won't really matter."

"Hopefully you'll have many more good years feeding the cats."

"I hope so. That's the word, Phillip, we must never forget. Hope. Always hope. Tonight, when I'm at home on my own, maybe one of the kids will give me a ring... What are you going to do with the rest of your day?"

"Nothing, I suppose."

"Do you have money?"

"Too much of it."

"Money never bought happiness."

"But it buys everything else."

"You need a challenge, Phillip."

"Don't we all? Hopefully, bringing up a child will be my challenge."

"And here we are in America. You want a little more tea?"

"Why ever not?"

When the old lady eased her body off the bench to go home to take her medication, Phillip was again on his own. The cat had gone with the old lady, following the slow shuffle past the trees. The day was still young. A man with his back to Phillip was doing his morning exercise standing on the grass, bending his knees, twisting his body to exercise his muscles. Phillip stood up in front of his bench and followed the man's routine. After half an hour the man stopped and turned round. Phillip sat back on the bench. The exercise had made Phillip feel happier with himself. By lunchtime he was feeling hungry. Walking through the gardens checking each of the plants and flowers he went in search of a nice café with tables and chairs open to the sidewalk so he could carry on studying the passing people. All part of his quest to blend in. Ten minutes later he found what he was looking for and sat himself down in the front of a vacant table. A pretty girl brought him the one-page stiff-board menu.

"What do you recommend for lunch?"

"The risotto. We're a family Italian restaurant."

"Are you part of the family?"

"No. I just work here. I'm a student. Have to pay for my room and lodging."

"I'll have the risotto."

Half the tables looking out on the sidewalk were occupied, people eating their lunches, oblivious to Phillip and the passing people. Behind Phillip, with an open sliding door, was the main restaurant. Phillip got up and found the toilet, relieving himself of Mary's tea. He hoped one of her children was thinking of their mother and would give her a ring. The old lady had had so much life and nothing to show for it, no one but her cats interested in an old woman. And if she hadn't fed the cats would they have cared? Everyone wanted something, including the waitress as she put down the food in front of Phillip, smiling her best for a tip. It was tough being a student, and Phillip was reminded of his years at Rhodes University in South Africa when he had plunged into the world of books, absorbed in the great world of history.

"Enjoy your lunch. You want anything else?"

"You can bring me a cup of coffee when I've eaten this risotto. Looks good. I have plenty of time on my hands."

"You're lucky."

"How are the books going? What are you studying?"

"Botany."

"That's lovely. And what are you going to do with a degree in botany?"

"I'll work that out when I get my degree."

"Yes, I'm sure you will."

Eating his lunch, Phillip watched the passing flow of people going up and down the sidewalk on their daily business, most of them in a hurry. To Phillip's surprise, the old man with the violin case walked by, one of the few that was not in a hurry. Botany, the scientific study of plants, the foundation of life on the planet. The old man with the violin waved, recognising Phillip from the garden. Phillip waved him to the table.

"Hello. You want a coffee? I love the classical music. You were playing a string quartet from Beethoven. My favourite symphony is Haydn's number twenty-eight."

The man stood in front of Phillip and waited, staring down at Phillip, making him feel uncomfortable.

"I want money, not coffee. Why I play my music."

"I'm sorry." Phillip dug in his pocket, pulled out his wallet and gave the man a twenty-dollar bill.

"Thanks, mister. Glad you liked my playing. They don't let me sit in the cafés. Don't like beggars."

The man went away as the girl brought Phillip his coffee. Neither said anything about the old man, watching him walk slowly away. It was all part of a day in the life of New York, the rich and the poor, the young and the old, the student looking for a good tip, the beggar desperate for money. It was all part of Phillip's education as he passed his day in New York.

When he left, he gave the girl a twenty-dollar tip.

"Thanks. Many thanks. Were you once a student? What do you do now?"

"Until recently I ran a safari operation in the wilds of Africa."

"You've got to be kidding me. That's just so lovely. Looks like the beggar plays the violin. I love music."

"So do I. Good luck with your studies. Have a good life. He can play Beethoven, you know. At least he can play Beethoven."

Glad he had done some good with his money, Phillip stood up. A beggar and a student. All part of America. Flowers and Ludwig van Beethoven, fumes and noise and all the passing people on the sidewalk, competing with the traffic and the sound of jet engines overhead. It was time to walk to Harry B's. What else was there for him to do? He could eat and drink and end up looking like Spence, obese in the worst extreme. A beautiful sunny afternoon and nothing to do. And his wife was pregnant. He would have to stop missing Africa. Talking about it made him miserable.

"You don't happen to know where I can find a gym?"

"About a ten-minute walk from this restaurant. I'll write it down. Draw you a little map. I appreciate the tip."

"I remember what it was like being a student. That poor man. Does he pass by here often?"

"Every day. He likes sitting on the kerb over there with his back to the lamp post. The owner's wife shoos him away. He's not very good."

"Would be with a better violin. Two of the strings were missing. People only care about themselves and their business. What's your name?"

"Angela. They call me Angie at college... That should find you the gym. I loved sport. Playing tennis was my favourite. Now it's all study and waiting tables."

"I'm Phillip. The risotto was good. I'll be back."

"I hope so."

"Yes, I expect you do. Thanks for the map, Angie."

"Have a nice day."

Trying to convince his thirst for alcohol that he would be better off in the gym, he followed the instructions Angie had written on the piece of paper. All you had to do in New York was ask for what you wanted. The gym was much what he expected: a conveyer belt for running, parallel bars, even a punch bag. A young man with a white towel around his neck and over his shoulder greeted Phillip.

"Do I have to sign up and pay membership?"

"You want to try out? You're wearing a tracksuit and gym shoes. Give you an hour. Then you can decide. Welcome to the gym. Best thing a man can do is keep fit. Prevents a lot of health problems. Eat properly and keep fit, that's my motto in life. You got a suntan. Where you been?"

"I've lived in Africa all my life."

"That explains it. What's your name?"

"Phillip."

"Go for it, Phillip. You can adjust the speed by turning the switch. You new in town?"

"Just arrived."

"Thought so. Call me if you need help."

For the first time in Phillip's life, he was running as fast as he could go and getting nowhere, his position in the gym not moving as he ran against the direction of the conveyor belt. As he grew used to running on a moving platform, he increased the speed making him run faster. He was sweating. After ten minutes he was exhausted and moved to the parallel bars, trying to remember how he did it in boarding school. From there he went to the punch bag and hurt his hands.

"You need boxing gloves. What you think, Phillip? You want to join?"

"I'd better. Yesterday's drinking companion must have weighed more than three hundred pounds. I've tried running in the streets. Too many people. You got to pay to run in New York."

"Everything costs money in a city. There's more to this gym than fitness. You meet new friends. There's a nice snack bar that only serves food that is good for you. You want to join? I'll bring you the forms. You got a credit card in those trousers under your track suit?"

"They're shorts. Sure, I got a debit card. Who hasn't? Can't live in a city without money."

"Welcome to Stigley's gym."

"Is he here?"

"Of course not. He owns the place. Has ten of them. Like everything else in New York, gyms are business."

"Of course. How silly of me."

"How long are you going to be in New York?"

"A month. A year. A lifetime. Who knows? My American wife is pregnant."

"Sign on for a year. It's cheaper. Money well spent. What you spend on a gym will save you a fortune in healthcare. Save your life."

"You're a good salesman."

"Part of my job."

Standing up at the counter, Phillip filled in the application form with all its terms and conditions. The gym was full of people, some of them sweating from their exertions. Music was playing in the background. There were men and women, young and old. When he'd finished, Phillip stood looking at his fellow club members. The man was right. Sitting up at the bar at Harry B's all day was more expensive.

"My name's Volker... That looks fine. All I now need is your debit card and you can stay as long as you like, Phillip."

"Thank you, kind sir."

"All part of the service. I recommend at least two hours in the gym every day. You'll feel a whole lot better after a couple of months. Makes a man enjoy life without drugs or drink. Do you drink, Phillip?"

"Too much."

"Then get fit. Drives the urge for alcohol out of the body. Makes a man look after himself. Your wife can join."

"She's pregnant."

"Even more reason for her being fit. We have a whole routine of exercises for different needs. Even women in the early stages of their pregnancy."

AFTER TWO HOURS, and having unloaded more of his money, his need for a drink and a visit to Harry B's had abated. Phillip walked home to the apartment. An hour after he arrived Martha came home. She was smiling.

"What you been up to? You look flushed."

"Joined a gym. You're home early."

"Now I know I'm pregnant there are going to be no late nights at the office from now on. No stress. No booze."

"You can join my gym. Volker has a routine for pregnant women. Got to be fit to have our baby."

"Aren't you excited by my note beside the bed?"

"Of course I am. Come here."

"Oh, Phillip. Let's just hope it all goes well this time."

"Come and sit down. I'll play some music. Tell you about my day. I found a lovely garden. Just right for a pram and a baby. I'll make some coffee. Sit down, my pregnant wife. It's all going to be just fine. Let's talk about raindrops and roses, whiskers on kittens, bright copper kettles and warm woollen mittens."

"Don't you want to hear about our business? Wasn't that from a song?"

"Not really. I'm sure Max signed up and Marcin is happy with your work. Sit down and relax. Stop thinking of business. Just think of us and our baby. And yes, it was a song. From a musical. Can't remember the name of the musical for the life of me."

"Mom and Mrs Crabshaw are going to the theatre tonight. *Phantom of the Opera* by Andrew Lloyd Webber. Mother and I are going shopping tomorrow. You want to come?"

"Me? Go shopping with two women? Got to be kidding."

"What are you going to do all day?"

"The usual. Now I can go to the gym."

"Wasn't it *The Sound of Music*?"

"Maybe. I have so many bits and pieces in my head. Don't know where half of it comes from. Just part of my life. Today I found a garden with trees and flowers. Did I tell you? When our child is born and you are at work I can take him to the little park in a little pram. I'm going to be a househusband."

"What about venture capitalism?"

"We'll see. Spence took down my phone number."

"Who's Spence?"

"A big man I met yesterday in Harry B's. Must weigh three hundred pounds."

An evening of pleasant trivia at home with his wife, neither of them really listening to each other, most of the talk irrelevant, a pleasant way to pass time in good company away from the rush of life. They drank tea, played their music, had their supper and watched a film on television. In bed, they made love, slow, gentle love knowing they had a baby growing in Martha's womb. A gentle end to their day, both of them sleeping undisturbed right through the night. When Phillip woke the next morning it was Saturday.

"You don't want to come shopping with us?"

"Not really. When are they going back to Kansas City?"

"Tonight."

"Give them both my love. I wonder how she will get to her seat at the theatre?"

"With her walker."

"That old girl is determined."

Left alone, Phillip got out of bed and walked through to the big living room in his underpants. He stood at the big window looking out over Manhattan, his mind a blank, nothing of interest to think about, nothing he wanted to do. It would be another eight months before he would be pushing a pram to the park. From looking at miles of bush to miles of high-rise buildings, stuck up in the sky. What a life. Phillip shook his head. They were going to be shopping all day before Martha went to see them off at the airport. What women got out of shopping was a mystery to Phillip. There was one constructive thing for him to do. He could walk to the gym and run against a conveyor belt staring at a blank wall in front of him, one of a long line of people getting their daily exercise. Phillip bathed, shaved, put on his tracksuit over his shorts and left the apartment, another day in New York begun.

He first walked to the waterside before turning back. In the garden there was no sign of the old lady or the violin player. In the Italian restaurant where he drank a cup of tea it was Angie's day off. At the gym, Volker greeted him. After an hour of exercise he went back to the garden and sat back on his wooden bench. The cat joined him. The cat was purring. The sun was shining on a late spring day in New York. Hopefully, he was getting used to it. Phillip sat, blanking his mind, trying not to think. The cat went off to look for food. There was still no sign of Mary. For a Saturday, the garden was surprisingly empty. Phillip got up and walked home, trying not to think of Harry B's and alcohol. When he got back the apartment was still empty up on the forty-ninth floor. Phillip stared through the plate-glass window. Life at the top. It made him smile. Chuckling, Phillip went to the kitchen and made himself some tea. When Martha let herself in, the kettle was boiling.

"The show was fantastic."

"You want some tea?"

"Make it coffee."

"My goodness. You did do some shopping. Look at all them bags. Did you enjoy your day?"

"Nothing better than shopping. They said goodbye and thank you. They loved the hotel."

"What are we doing tonight?"

"Any suggestions?"

"Not really. You can't drink so that's out. We'll sit and watch television."

"Anything on?"

"You never know until you look at it. What did you buy?"

"Everything."

"Lucky we're rich."

"I don't know what I'd do without money, Phillip."

"We could go and sit under a tree and look at the Zambezi River."

"Don't be silly. That's boring. Anyway, we're in Manhattan."

"Not for me."

"But it is for me. Do you like this new dress?"

"Why don't you put it on? Show me them all. I'll pretend I'm watching a fashion parade."

Phillip watched his wife try on her dresses, praising each one of them, content sitting on the sofa. Two days without booze. He was feeling better. And the day went on, the ordinary day of a married couple, the life so many single people craved. Was he happy, Phillip asked himself? He hoped so. There was nothing else to do with his life except have a family and behave like everyone else.

"You like my new dresses?"

"Of course I do. You have exquisite taste."

"I'm so happy. Take me to your gym. I want to do everything for our baby. And to add to my happiness our new company is going from strength to strength."

"Has she slept with Marcin?"

"Not yet. But she will. She likes him for his body as much as his business. And Marcin can't stop looking at her. Who knows? Our Jaz may become Mrs Galinski."

"What about Max?"

"He's just sex. The Maxes of this world are two a penny for a good-looking gal."

"She's over-sexed."

"Probably. Oh, and Clarence has applied for New York University. And Tildy can't stop talking about Marcin. Poor Franklyn. He's got his hands full. You must come and visit our new offices. Everything has happened so fast; I can't believe it."

"Neither can I."

"Do you really like my dresses?"

"Of course I do."

"Make the tea and coffee. The kettle's boiled."

"Your servant, my lady."

"I never know when you're being serious."

"I've given you a baby. That's serious. Instant coffee. Will that do? I've never been much of a coffee drinker. Sometimes after a good meal. You want some food? I can make us a sandwich."

"I love being married to you, Phillip."

"We're going to be happy together. That's what counts. See our kids grow up. Grow old together. How life is meant to be. I'm glad we won't be drinking. Drink's a problem for a man with too much time on his hands."

"You'll find new start-ups to invest in."

"Probably. Here's your coffee."

3

By Monday morning Phillip was back on his own. Martha was a member of the gym; Volker making her pedal a wheelless bicycle, showing her a routine of exercises, the inveterate salesman playing successfully on the health of the baby. Whether the exercise worked or not, whether the money spent was worth it, only time would tell. Martha had chatted to some of the other girls, telling them about her pregnancy. The best part of the gym for both of them was having something to do together rather than going to a bar or a restaurant or sitting in front of the television. There was sex but how much time was spent on sex in a relationship? Fifteen minutes a day if they were lucky.

Dressed in his tracksuit, his debit card in his wallet in the back pocket of his shorts hidden by his tracksuit, Phillip's daily routine began with a walk to the waterside to smell the clean air blowing from over the water. In the small park the old man was playing his violin, his hat this time visible to Phillip on the grass next to where he was sitting. It made Phillip think where he could find someone to repair the strings of the old violin, or even buy the old man a new one. The cat got up on the bench purring, nuzzling his knee, getting off and wandering away. There was no sign of the old lady. For half an hour, with nothing much to do on a Monday morning, he listened to the old man trying his best to play the violin, the odd passer-by dropping a coin in the upturned hat. Phillip got up and walked across the grass to put a ten-dollar bill in the hat.

"Where can we find someone to fix that violin?"

"Won't work. Need a new violin. Never mind. No one listens to my music."

"Have you played in an orchestra?"

"Of course. The New York Philharmonic. Before my hands contracted arthritis."

"Why don't they look after you?"

"Better things to do, I suppose. I can beg from people but not from my fellow musicians. Too degrading. They forgot about me years ago. Why should the new lot care? I can't play properly so they're not interested in a has-been."

"I can buy you a new violin."

"That would help."

"Do you have an address or a phone number?"

"Of course not. I'm homeless. Sleep in a hospice when I'm lucky. Eat in a soup kitchen. Life in the big city of New York isn't easy when you don't have no money."

"Do you know where to go to buy a violin?"

"Of course I do. Round the corner, there's a second-hand shop that sells musical instruments among other things. Walked around a couple of times. They chased me out."

"Let's go."

"You serious? What's your angle? What you want from me?"

"I love classical music. Can they tune their violins?"

"I can do that myself when I have all the strings. No one in this town does nothing unless they're after something. Are you a newspaper reporter looking for a story? 'One-time member of the best orchestra in the world out on the streets begging with a bust violin.' People love a sob story. Sells newspapers."

"My brother is a novelist. I'm a safari operator."

"What the hell may I ask are you doing in a garden in New York?"

"Passing time. It's a long story."

"They usually are. I had a wife until she walked out on me when I couldn't make a living. Don't blame her. Luckily, we had no children."

"Can the doctors help your hands?"

"Medication is expensive. Anyway, even if I could play like the old days I'd never get a job in an orchestra. Classical music is mostly sponsored. No money in it. People pay to listen to pop. Not to Beethoven."

"Let's go to the shop. What's your name?"

"Does it matter? You're not writing a story. Thanks for the ten bucks."

"My pleasure."

With difficulty, the old man pulled himself up off the ground and put the old violin back in its case. When Phillip turned round to go, Mary was sitting on the bench feeding the cat. With the old man clutching his old violin case, they passed Mary, the cat purring as it ate from Mary's cat bowl.

"We're going to buy a violin, Mary. How are you?"

"The cat's hungry."

"He's always hungry. See you tomorrow. Today is violin day."

"Jonathan. Jonathan Wesley Harnsford Fernsby."

"My goodness."

"We were English aristocrats."

"What happened to the family money?"

"Went down the drain years ago. From a castle in the north of England to begging on the streets of New York. Five hundred years of the Fernsbys. I'm the last of the male line."

"Do you have a title?"

"We haven't used the title since the Seventeenth Earl of Fernsby died in England without a male heir. The American branch of my family weren't going to use an English title in America. And we weren't going back to England. By then the castle was long gone."

"The story gets better and better. Pity I'm not in the media... What happened to the family money?"

"No idea. Probably went to the women. You can inherit money if you are a woman but not the title. The only title a woman can inherit in England is that of the monarch. Queen Victoria. The two Queen Elizabeths."

"Did you ever check what happened to the last earl's money?"

"I was too immersed in my music."

"Did your father check?"

"What for? If they were going to leave us some family money they would have told us about it. Been in the last earl's will."

"He might have died intestate if he had no heirs."

"What's intestate? Sounds like a nasty disease... Here we are. One second-hand shop. Pawnshop. Call it what you like."

"Means he didn't leave a will."

"And what happens to his money?"

"Goes to the state until someone claims it."

"And who can claim it?"

"The heir. His legal descendant. You should tell your father to check."

"He's dead. There's just me. Why you think I sit in a park begging? That's the one I would like."

"Do you mind if I tell my brother Randall your story? He lives on the Isle of Man writing his novels. Randall loves a good story to write about. He'll change all the names of course... How much do you want for that violin?"

"Six hundred dollars."

"I'll take it. Do you take debit cards?"

"Of course."

"There you are, Jonathan Wesley Harnsford Fernsby, Eighteenth Earl of Fernsby. My full name is Phillip Crossley Crookshank."

"You have a good memory for names. Why are you being kind to me?"

"I had the luck in life. You didn't."

"What did he write?"

"*Masters of Vanity* among other books."

"I've read it. The only enjoyment I get from life comes from reading books. The library lends me books. When I've had enough of playing, and no one is passing to give me money, I sit cross-legged on the grass and disappear from my misery into a book. Sometimes for hours. Oblivious to the world. But hang on, he's not your brother if your name is Crookshank. Randall Holiday wrote *Masters of Vanity* about all those vainglorious New York rich bastards who got their comeuppance."

"My brother's name is Randall Crookshank. Holiday is the name he writes under. Villiers Publishing, his publishers, thought the Crookshank name had a bad connotation. People don't like crooks. Can I tell him your story?"

"Of course you can, I owe him. Took me out of my misery. It was a wonderful, captivating story. There's nothing better than good art. Shakespeare, Beethoven and Randall Holiday."

"Is that your way of thanking me for your new violin? Praising my brother?"

"Sort of. Not really. Your brother is good. Just no one is as good as Shakespeare and Beethoven."

"Maybe Mozart and Haydn. Let's go back to the garden where you can tune and play me some Beethoven. That will be your thanks. Was *Masters of Vanity* that good? As his brother, I find it difficult to judge. It's a lovely day. I'll sit back on the bench with Mary and the cat while we listen to you play."

"Suddenly my arthritis doesn't feel so bad. So much is in the mind."

"You can say that again. I wish for the sake of my wife Martha and our child on the way that I could get Africa out of my mind."

"Thank you, Phillip."

"My pleasure. What money is for. Doing some good. Not looking vainglorious."

With a broad smile on his face, Phillip walked across to where Mary was sitting reading a book. There was no better feeling than the satisfaction that came from helping someone. Which made Phillip think, was everything in life selfish?

"Did I do that to feel good or help the poor bastard?... What are you reading, Mary?"

"What did you do? Come and sit down. A book by Angelica Silvers. She also wrote *Rose's Summer*. I love her books. You don't have to think, just float in a perfect world."

"I bought the beggar a new violin. Says he played with the New York Philharmonic. That his ancestors were English aristocrats who lived in a castle. What is it about English titles that fascinate people so much? I know an old lady of ninety-five who says she would have been the wife of a baronet if he hadn't been killed in the First World War. Because she was born in England Mrs Crabshaw wants to live to a hundred and receive a cable on her birthday from the Queen of England. I'm never sure if their stories are fantasy or the truth: an inherent desire to be part of an old aristocracy. Most of the founders of those dynasties were rotten to the core or they wouldn't have got where they did in the first place. A bit like today's politicians. In these old days the politicians, or those who helped the politicians stay in power, were given titles they could pass down the generations with their ill-gotten money. Now political corruption is just about the money."

"He's making a terrible noise. Doubt he played in any orchestra."

"He's just tuning his new violin."

"Scraping a wire by the sound of it. Sets my teeth on edge."

"Oh, well. You can only try."

"It's the thought that counts... Do you mind if I go on reading my book? She has me immersed in a better, more beautiful world where everyone is nice to each other. Where they all love each other. Not a nasty bone in any of their bodies."

"I'm sorry. I'll stop rambling."

Sitting back, not sure if he should have interrupted Mary's reading, Phillip tried not to listen to the discordant sounds coming across the grass from Jonathan. You could only try in life to help people, even if it didn't work. Without realising the cat had climbed onto his knee he stroked the soft fur. Through the leaves of the trees, the sun laid a pattern of light and shade, the pattern moving in the gentle breeze. Phillip let his mind wander back to Africa. With the hot summer over, the tourist season had begun for Jacques at Chewore, the thought making him wonder what he was doing on a park bench in New York stroking a cat. The warmth of the sun and the purr of the cat made Phillip doze, his chin dropping down on his chest. When he woke the cat was still purring, Mary still immersed in her novel, while the sounds coming across from the violin were perfect, every note pure and beautiful. Mary put down her book and began to listen. Across, sitting on the grass holding hands, a young couple were looking towards Jonathan. Instead of being down on the grass next to his begging hat, he was standing up looking proud, his legs splayed. Everyone around him was listening.

"I take it back, Phillip. That man did play with the New York Philharmonic."

"All he needs now is an orchestra. Or the other three members of a string quartet. There's nothing wrong with his hands. Said he had arthritis."

"It comes and goes. My mother had it. My goodness, can he play."

"The world isn't so bad after all. Another day, another world. Best six hundred bucks I ever spent."

"Maybe he is some English aristocrat under all those old clothes."

"With money in England to inherit. I'll ask my father to look into the life and times of the Seventeenth Earl of Fernsby. Give Father something to do."

"Do you know what he's playing?"

"I think it's Mozart. Three hundred or so years old and it's still just as beautiful. I'm sorry. I'm interrupting your reading again."

"Not anymore. I wanted to run away into my book when he was scraping his bow across the strings. New York. They say it's a wonderful town. That you never know what to expect."

"There's nothing better to expect than Mozart. Today was violin day. A day I'll never forget. Just listen to him. He's captivated everyone."

"Makes me feel happy."

"There's nothing nicer than feeling happy, Mary... Jonathan Wesley Harnsford Fernsby."

"Who's he?"

"The man over there playing his violin. Joy, perfect joy. You can keep all your rappers and pop artists. I'll stick with Mozart. Wolfgang Amadeus Mozart, who when he died in his thirties was buried in a pauper's grave but left behind the greatest wealth of all: his music. A short life that will live forever through his beautiful music. I don't know what's making me cry. Mozart or Jonathan, what a day."

"Poor Phillip. You're too old to cry. Let me tell you one of my stories. When I was a girl out of school I met a boy. We were both innocent. We believed in everyone. Trusted everyone. Life had yet to catch up with us. That lovely period in life of innocence when everything and everyone we saw was perfect. Our romance lasted six months. The longest six months of my life. All we did was kiss and hold hands. When another older girl enticed Landers into her bed and seduced him he left me, drawn by the carnal satisfaction of sex. It was the end of innocence for both of us. The start of the other life where people took what they wanted and left. Am I boring you, Phillip?"

"Of course not."

"I'll read my book. Your tears have gone. What were you really crying for?"

"Mozart. Jonathan. The human race... I'd better go. You read your book. The cat's gone. Enjoy the rest of your day."

"You too, Phillip. What are you going to do now?"

"Have a cup of tea in Angie's restaurant. Go home and phone my father in England and ask him to check out the Fernsbys. Have a drink or two in Harry B's. It's been two days without a drop of alcohol. Should be three to let the booze go right out of the system. No, I'll go to the gym and behave myself."

"Go and have a drink."

"You think I should?"

"Enjoy your day, Phillip. You only live once... He's stopped. Listen to that. They're clapping. Putting dollar bills not coins in his hat. That's the first time I have ever seen that old man smile. He's taking a bow. Just look at him."

Smiling to himself, Phillip slipped out of the garden, going straight to Stigley's gym. After two hours of intense exercise, he was ready for a beer. As he walked into Harry B's the first person he saw up at the bar was Spence, the fat backside oozing down on both sides of the round barstool.

"Just the man I was looking for, Phillip. A friend of my son's at New York University has an idea I want to talk to you about. He's twenty-one years old, same age as my son. The best ideas for internet start-ups come from the young. He wants to drop out of university and start a business with two of his varsity friends. You want to listen, Phillip?"

"Not today, Spence. I've done my good deed for the day."

"Maybe tomorrow. We can make money. You said you were a venture capitalist. I checked on you and Marcin Galinski."

"I expect you did. Let's just have a drink and talk a load of rubbish. What brings you here on a Monday afternoon?"

"Looking for you, Phillip. Better than phoning."

"You're after my money."

"The boy is. Not me. I said I might be able to help. Terry, give the man a beer."

Phillip sat back on the barstool next to Spence, mentally shaking his head. He had no self-control. He was back in the pub, just where he shouldn't be, his good intentions thrown to the wind. To make things worse, the beer tasted good. The phone call to his father would have to wait.

"You're sweating, Phillip. What have you been doing?"

"Running in a gym. You should try it."

"You got to be kidding. Just look at me."

"I am. You can start slow. Got to start somewhere."

"Drink your beer and listen to my proposition."

They never stopped. After twenty minutes of barely listening, the first beer drunk, Phillip pricked up his ears.

"You want to go over that again?"

"Oh, good. Now you're listening. Give us another beer, Terry. Nothing like a beer to make a man listen. I do believe I've got his attention. Right. Where was I? The core of the boy's proposition is enabling people across the world to find the books they want to read and not sink into the mire of celebrity advertising and ending up reading a load of self-promoted rubbish, or stories of interplanetary travel, or vampires, or ubiquitous crime novels. We all have our own particular predilections and Perry Mance wants to develop and market a sophisticated application that will enable readers to connect to that vast wealth of books that runs into millions, not the well-marketed few that sit on the shelves of the bookshop chains. He wants everyone to have choice. Have the ability to choose what they want for themselves. In an older world, the reader went into a well-stocked library and asked the librarian to help him, a man or woman with a degree in literature. The reader explained the kind of book he liked to read and the librarian pointed him in the right direction. You didn't have to wander down aisles picking out books by chance and getting home to start reading and find no interest in what you had brought back from the library. The same now applies to bookshop chains where they employ low-cost tellers, who know little or nothing about books, to collect their money. Bookshops are now like supermarkets. You wander around the aisles and pick from the shelves what you want. Which is fine when you know what you want. Perry's application will work like a well-schooled librarian or a bookseller of old who read every book in his shop. There will be no advertising on the application. If there were it would be self-defeating. Readers. Dedicated readers who don't have time to pick a book, read ten pages and throw it away, will pay a small annual fee to download the application. Like buying movies from an online store where you know what you are getting before you sit back on the couch and turn on the television. And yes, if you want, you will be told where to find the book of your choice. In the end, Perry will have the biggest online bookshop in the world. A bookshop crafted to individual likes and cults. It will enable people to go back to reading with satisfaction. And like all good ideas, Phillip, there's a fortune to be made from it, for you, me, Perry and his university friends. If you want a book on your Africa, the application will tell you the book to read."

"And if the book is out of print?"

"They can download a PDF version and read it on their computer."

"That's not so good, reading a book on a computer."

"Not at the moment. But if the demand is there someone will invent a handheld computer you can take to bed. Your brother is a novelist. Ask him what he thinks of Perry's idea. But be quick. We want to get in now so the kids can work on the software."

"How much do they need?"

"Let's liken it to Marcin Galinski's Linguare.com. Half a million dollars."

"You've done your homework, Spence."

"You don't make money sitting on a big fat ass. Well, in this case, maybe you do. Do you want to meet them?"

"Probably."

"Say two-thirty tomorrow afternoon. I'll leave a message on your cell phone with the address where we'll meet."

"You don't waste time."

"Money, Phillip. It's all about making money. To make money you have to move fast or some other bastard will get there first."

"There's a condition if you and I are going into business."

"What's the condition, Phillip? There's always a condition. Why is that?"

"You join my gym. I don't want a business associate with a future health problem. You got to look after yourself."

"Done. I want ten per cent of your shares, my amount of the investment to be re-paid to you out of future dividends."

"So you won't put up any money?"

"I brought the idea. And I have kids to support."

"I must go home and make a phone call to my father. If I'm spending half a million of my dollars tomorrow I'll need a crystal-clear head, without the trace of a hangover."

"I was going home anyway once I'd convinced you to meet Perry."

"Half past two?"

"On the dot. The venue will be on your cell phone. Nice doing business with you, Phillip."

"It's amazing what you pick up in bars."

"It is, isn't it? I picked up my wife in a bar. What with our son, Spence Junior, and his friend Perry, the luck never stops."

"You make your own luck in life, Spence."

"Of course you do."

Back on the forty-ninth floor, Phillip dialled his father's number in London.

"Jeremy Crookshank speaking."

"Phillip Crookshank."

"My goodness."

"How are you, Dad? I need a favour."

"No one makes a phone call without wanting something. Just kidding."

"How are you both?"

"Bored. Nothing to do. You can't communicate with a brick wall the way you can with nature. I miss the peace and solitude of the farm. The call of a dove. Shouldn't complain, I suppose. Some of the Rhodesian farmers ended up with nothing. At least I got out some of my profits to buy this block of flats with Livy. You got to think ahead in life, Phillip. Nothing ever stays the same. Never become complacent."

"Could you ask her to paint me a canvas of the African bush to hang in our New York apartment?"

"Thought you were in Kansas City. What you want, Phillip?"

"For you to investigate the Seventeenth Earl of Fernsby. Find out if he left a will. Whether he left any unclaimed money."

"Shouldn't be too difficult. There can only have been one Seventeenth Earl of Fernsby. Why the interest?"

"I met a beggar in a park playing a violin with two bust strings. Says he's the heir."

"And you believed him?"

"Also said he played in the New York Philharmonic Orchestra. Bought him a new violin."

"Can he play?"

"It was so good it made me cry. The man needs help."

"I'm onto it. Maybe Craig and Jojo can help."

"How's Randall?"

"Writing a book. Not a squeak out of Randall when he's writing."

"Got to go, Dad. Martha's back. I can hear the door. She's pregnant."

"One of these days I'll be able to catch up with my children. No one tells me anything. Bit like old Jolyon in *The Forsyte Saga*. No one told him anything."

"Fernsby. You want me to spell?"

"Not needed. Just give me your new phone number."

Smiling at Martha, home at half past five, Phillip put down the phone.

"How was your day at work?"

"I have a new rule, honey. No talk about my day at work. I want the day's stress to seep out of me to protect our child. I don't even want to think of work once I leave the office. How's your dad?"

"Bored. Missing the farm. Come and sit down. I have a story to tell you about a violin-playing beggar today. Take your mind right off your work. And tomorrow at half past two I'm looking at a new venture with Spence. What are we having for supper?"

"Don't you want to go out?"

"I'd prefer to stay at home and do the cooking."

"First I must go into the bedroom to do Volker's bend and stretch routine of exercises. Did you go to the gym?"

"Two hours. We can go after a light supper, Mrs Fitness-fanatic."

"This time we are going to win. I so want this baby. Life is so hollow without children."

"I know we are. Come and give your husband a kiss."

"You don't still miss Africa, do you Phillip?"

"Of course not. I have a pregnant wife to think about. A new start-up to invest in. On the weekend I'll take you to the park to listen to Jonathan."

"Who's Jonathan?"

"Jonathan Wesley Harnsford Fernsby, heir to the Seventeenth Earl of Fernsby who hopefully left him some money. Don't forget the ten press-ups. Give your stomach muscles the strength to hold our growing baby."

"Do you know anything about giving birth to a baby?"

"Not a thing."

AT HALF PAST two the following afternoon, Phillip walked into Harry B's, the venue on his cell phone no longer surprising. Why not? They both knew where to go. They could sit at a table and talk.

"I'm Phillip Crookshank. Which one of you is Perry Mance? Good afternoon, Spence. First rule of the day, no alcohol until we have conducted our business."

"I'm Perry," the smallest man of the four said with a giggle. The man, more a boy, wore a pair of large glasses that covered the upper part of his face. The giggle petered out as Phillip sat down at the table.

"Tea or coffee. When we have no more business to talk about you can have a drink. Fire away. I'm listening."

Concentrating his mind, not wishing to lose his grandfather's hard-worked-for-legacy, Phillip let them talk, Spence, for once, keeping his mouth shut. They were all so young. Like Mary's story, so innocent. Perry was short in stature and big in the face, the big glasses matched by two big ears. He had an infectious giggle that came every time he mentioned the money he and his two fellow technology students required: there were salaries to be paid, equipment to be bought, much like the cost of Linguare.com; all part of the investment business. After ten minutes, the big round ears and the giggle no longer distracted Phillip. The man looked like a geek but his mind was captivating. After half an hour without a drink order, Terry came across and hovered over the table.

"Sorry, Terry. We're having a business conference. No alcohol until we're finished our business. Then we'll get started."

By four o'clock the presentation was over, everyone looking expectantly at Phillip.

"What do you think, Phillip?" The man-boy gave a nervous giggle.

"I need a week to ask around."

"We can wait a week."

"I hope so. Most importantly, I want to talk to my brother. Ask his opinion on marketing books."

"Spence mentioned him to Spence Junior."

"You want a drink?"

"We don't drink."

"Not even Spence Junior?"

"He drinks. We're fitness fanatics and vegetarians. We all love books. Love the excitement of finding a new author."

"Do you by any chance like classical music?"

"Indeed we do."

"Walk with me to the gardens. I've something to show you. We can chat and get to know each other. In the end, I'm doing business with you, Perry Mance. Not your application, as you call it. I want to know the person in whom I'm investing half a million of my grandfather's dollars before I make a commitment."

"What's in the gardens?"

"A violin player begging for his supper."

"Sounds weird."

"Not as weird as investing half a million dollars in a man you've just met. Spence, you coming?"

"Too far to walk."

"Don't forget you're joining my gym."

"Let me think about it."

"Nothing to think about. We did a deal... Why don't you four want to stay in college and finish your degree?"

"We want to make money."

"Is Spence Junior in the team?"

"No. He's studying finance. All those lovely ways to separate people from their money." The man giggled.

"Aren't you trying to separate me from my money, Perry Mance?"

"Please, no. We want this mind-blowing idea to succeed. In the modern world you need money to set up a business and turn an idea into something tangible. Fulfilling our dream is more important to us three than money."

The man looked at Phillip through the big glasses and giggled.

"Why do you giggle every time you mention or think of money?"

"Money embarrasses me. I had to borrow money from an uncle to go through university."

"Is he rich?"

"Not really. Has a salary. I've promised myself to give Uncle Jim ten per cent of whatever I end up owning in the company."

"Won't he be disappointed in you if you drop out of university?"

"Not if I make him rich."

"You're giggling again."

"Money, Phillip. You don't mind me calling you Phillip?"

"You can call me what you like if you make my money work. No more giggling. Let's go for a walk. I want to know about your family. How you grew up. What you want from your life. The names of your friends. I want you to talk to me."

"Are you going to invest? Spence Junior talks about the need for half a million dollars. Why don't we start with, say, fifty thousand dollars to buy our computers and equipment? We can all work from home. If I explain what I'm doing to Uncle Jim he'll still give me money for my daily needs."

"Or you could stay at university, get your degree and enter the workplace."

"We're scared that if we wait, someone else will pick up on our idea. It all moves so fast in the world of technology."

"What will your friends' parents think of their sons dropping out?

Parents put a lot of time and energy into getting their kids to university. Not to say the cost."

"If we succeed they will give us praise."

"And if we lose?"

"We'll be left on the garbage heap. No future. No dreams. Nothing to achieve in our lives. You don't get far in the jungle without a top degree."

"Have you thought this through?"

"More than you can imagine. Life's a gamble. A short man like me with big ears and glasses needs a whole lot of money to attract the girls. All that running to keep fit doesn't help. They like big men who don't have to wear glasses."

"You like girls?"

"We all do. Trouble is, they don't like us. They want a tall man who plays basketball like Marcin Galinski. Some people get all the luck: the looks, the sporting ability and now that money you helped him make. I'll never be a Marcin Galinski. But I can become rich. And when you count it down it's all about the money."

"Let me go and explain to Terry we're not staying to drink. Are you staying to drink, Spence?"

"Of course we are. Me and Spence Junior are going to get started. Have a nice walk."

"Don't forget about the gym."

"Oh, I will."

Smiling, Phillip led the way. It reminded him of his own days at varsity. Made him happy. Took the years away. The three of them were talking among themselves, pulling each other's legs. The easy chatter of students unaware of anything outside their own insular worlds where everything they had and did was paid for by other people. The years of innocence. It made Phillip envious. Slowly, carefully, Phillip plied them with questions. Were they genuine and honest or not? Life was all about appraising people. Sifting out the sharks. Separating the fools. Looking for the brains under the bullshit.

When they reached the gardens the sun was still shining, the pattern of leaves dappling the grass. Phillip's park bench was empty. There was no sign of Jonathan.

"He may come later. Let's sit on the bench and carry on our conversation. There are two pretty girls over there with a dog."

"They won't even look at us."

"Some girls like a man's mind more than his looks. Let's see what happens... Oh, good. Here comes the cat. Why I brought the doggie bag, except it's for the cat... I'd like to meet your Uncle Jim if that's possible? Bring him into the picture. Does he know what you're up to?"

"Not yet. Do you want to meet my parents?"

"If that is possible."

"I thought it was just about our idea."

"You can invite the family to a dinner party at my new apartment. Martha won't mind. I value my wife's opinion. If what you tell me is true, we are starting something big. We want good foundations. No secrets. Trust. Integrity. After that we can see about the money."

"Who's the weird guy with the guitar coming into the park?"

"Jonathan Wesley Harnsford Fernsby. And it's a violin, not a guitar."

"You're weird."

"I'll take that as a compliment."

Smiling, Phillip waved at Jonathan. The cat was pushing its head at the food. Everything was normal. Phillip put his arms along the back of the bench, his legs pushed out in front of him, Perry Mance seated on his left, the other boys, Larry and Tony, on his right, the cat with its head in the doggy bag in between. The cat was purring. A yellow butterfly of a sort he had not seen before was flitting from flower to flower sucking the nectar in front of him, the flowerbed stretching along the length of the grass. The boys were leaning forward, their elbows on their knees talking to each other across Phillip. The two pretty girls with the dog had turned round once and since ignored them. The violin began to play, making the girls get up from the grass where they were sitting to move closer to the music. The small crossbreed dog followed them with a bark, making the cat stop its purring. The cat pulled its head out of the bag and looked at the dog. The music of Mozart flowed over the green lawn and through the trees in all directions. A pigeon began to call, the sound blending perfectly with the music. The three men-boys kept talking about nothing in particular. The pretty girls sat back on the grass close to Jonathan, the dog in between. People were coming into the gardens attracted by the strains of the music. A couple sat down in front of Jonathan with a picnic basket. Others stood. It was no longer a beggar playing for the odd coin thrown in a hat, more a one-man concert in the park, the birdsong and rustle of the leaves in the trees part of the music. After an hour, the small park was fuller than Phillip had ever seen it. When Jonathan stopped playing and put down his violin the people clapped. Some got up and went across to the upturned hat, putting in dollar notes. Jonathan bowed towards Phillip, making Phillip smile: all a man needed was a new violin and a few banknotes in a hat to make him satisfied. The couple with the picnic basket walked across, the woman offering Jonathan a plastic cup.

Jonathan drank from the cup and smiled up at the couple. He had sat down and was sitting cross-legged on the grass, an open book next to him.

"What are you going to do with a huge amount of money, Perry, when the company succeeds and we have our IPO, floating the company on the New York stock exchange? Apart from attracting women."

"We'll be popular."

"For all the wrong reasons. It won't be you who will be popular. It will be all that money. All the sharks. All the wrong people. You'll never know if they like you or your money. The girls will act like whores. Many women sell their bodies. The more sophisticated money-grabbers deliberately marry to quickly divorce and walk off with millions in a settlement. Big money brings problems for a rich man who can't see through the machinations of women."

"Did your wife marry you for your money?"

"Martha has her own money, fortunately. She married me for the baby which she lost at term soon after we married."

"I'm sorry."

"So was I. She tried to commit suicide. Now she's pregnant again. Be careful about wanting all that money. You three may well find it a curse. The longer you stay at university and study, the more knowledge you will have to develop other ideas. Why the hurry? 'Take it easy greasy,' as an old friend of mine used to say, 'you got a long way to slide.' I have a bad gut-feeling encouraging you to drop your studies. If you haven't told your Uncle Jim, you likely haven't told your parents. Talk to them about your project. Listen to them. All three of you listen to your parents. The lust for money isn't good in a person. Lust brings out the worst in people. Destroys them if they're not careful."

"I said our idea was more important than the money. We just want to have fun."

"But you don't mean it, Perry."

"Don't you want to make another Linguare.com? You're an investor looking to make big bucks. Don't you want more money?"

"All you do is buy a bigger apartment. Doesn't make any difference to your life. You can only sleep in one bed at a time. Look over there. He's enjoying that coffee more than anything money can buy. He played what he loved and they loved what he played. They're laughing. All three of them. Happy people. Better than nervously giggling. Two pretty girls and an old man with a violin. And he doesn't have any money."

"You're not going to give us the money, are you?"

"I'm still thinking. I said a week. We'll see. I just don't want to ruin your lives. Oh, good. Jonathan is going to play again. I thought he was going to read his book."

"We'd better go."

"Do as you wish."

"What do we have to do to convince you?"

"Talk to me. Tell me why today's money is more important than tomorrow's university degree."

"We'll miss a stunning opportunity."

"Maybe... Haydn. I think that is Haydn... Why do you run?"

"After exercise we find our minds are better able to concentrate, better able to think. Why we do it. Exercise clears the mind."

"Now look at that. The whole park has quietened down. People have stopped talking. Music. The perfect sound of music."

"Where's the cat gone?"

"He's finished the food. What people and cats do when they get what they want. They leave. We're all animals, Perry. All with the same instinct... You think Spence Junior will end up as fat as his father?"

"Probably. You know what they say: like father, like son. Must be awful to be burdened by all that excess weight."

"Too much of anything is bad for a person: too much weight, too much power, too much money. People are too often irresponsible and greedy. They should relax, according to my father, and enjoy what they have while it's there: youth, friends, the fun of living. My father says the most difficult thing in life is to hold on to what you have, not make the money or build the farm. He lost everything he owned in Zimbabwe. But he has his memories. You can take away the money but not the memories. In your idea for a business the only end product is money. You can't see your money the way you can see your farm. You can't sit and stare at a share certificate and get enjoyment: it's still a piece of paper. You can buy things to show off, to impress people, to make you feel important, but there's no worth in feeling important. You buy ten houses around the world, an aircraft to ferry you from one to the other; expensive art with names of artists that are famous, the modern art of stuffed animals or piles of chairs a load of crap; everything you do to show off and impress your fellow humans. But all of that materialism is valueless when you compare it to the music flowing over us from the old beggar with the violin. All the money in the world will never compare to Mozart or the violin playing of Jonathan."

For a long while, the four of them sat in silence, Phillip listening to the music of Haydn. Tony and Larry stood up first: Phillip sensed they were bored.

"We're going, Phillip."

"I thought you three loved music? You know my number, Perry, if you wish to bring your parents to dinner. And don't forget Uncle Jim. What you three must decide upon is whether you're looking to have fun like Marcin and his friends, or whether it's all just a lust for money. And don't forget: you want to be happy in life, not rich."

"Are you happy, Phillip?"

"Sometimes. I miss Africa more than you can imagine. I can certainly say my money doesn't make me happy. I was happier in a tent on the banks of the Zambezi River than I am in an apartment forty-nine floors up in the New York sky."

"Why didn't you stay? Why don't you go back?"

"I met Martha. Martha likes the rich life in America you crave for. And we both crave for a baby. Life, Perry. We are never satisfied. Enjoy the rest of your day. And think. Think of what you are really doing, all three of you."

"You're weird."

"As I said before, I'll take that as a compliment. Have a nice day."

"You're not going to give us the money."

"It all depends on you and your parents. And your Uncle Jim. Been interesting talking to you... Now, look at that. Here comes the cat."

As the three walked away down the long path next to the flowerbed, Phillip heard the giggle. They were pointing at the two pretty girls, the girls deliberately ignoring them. Cross-legged, with the book between his knees, Jonathan was far away in the story, oblivious to everything around him. The boys did not look back at Phillip sitting on the bench. The cat got up on his knee. Phillip could feel the purr as well as hear the sound. There was more in the cat's life than just food.

"That went well." The cat took no notice, flexing its claws gently on Phillip's trousers, the sun shining on the cat's fur through the dappling green leaves of the trees. His mind back in Africa, Phillip let himself rest, his eyes closing. In his mind there was peace, his thoughts fading into his dreams. When he woke, the cat was still on his knee fast asleep. Across the lawn, where Jonathan had been reading his book, there was an empty space, no man, no violin, no begging bowl. Gently picking up the cat, Phillip put him down in front of the bench, the cat not wanting to go.

"Time to go home, my pussycat. Thanks for the company."

Slowly, sadly, Phillip walked from the gardens and out onto the teeming streets. Passing Angie's restaurant he impulsively walked inside, the pretty girl smiling at him. Was she pleased to see him or just doing her job of welcoming a customer? Phillip ordered himself a pot of tea. By now Spence and Spence Junior would be happily drunk.

WHEN PHILLIP LET himself into the apartment, he found Martha on the couch reading a woman's magazine.

"Did you finalise the deal?"

"I don't think so."

"Why ever not?"

"It'll ruin their lives. Perry has a giggle. Giggles every time we mentioned the money. I won't ask about your day as you won't tell me. What's on the agenda?"

"Nothing much. Some of these clothes look plain ridiculous."

"They may be coming to dinner."

"Who?"

"Perry Mance's parents and his Uncle Jim. I'd like your opinion. My own instinct tells me they should first get their degrees and then go into business. He's going to phone me if they're coming."

Walking across to the plate-glass window, Phillip looked out over New York, a shudder running through his body. His father was right: it was impossible to communicate with a brick wall or a horizon of skyscrapers. Where were the trees? Out there it was all artificial. With his hands in his pocket, he stood and stared, trying to make sense of a man-made world. After a while, Martha turned on the television, a sitcom where unseen people laughed at the jokes, short bursts of artificial laughter.

"I love this one, Phillip. Come and sit down."

With nothing to do or think, Phillip sat down on the couch next to his wife, taking her hand and giving it a squeeze.

"How's our baby?"

"Our baby is fine. When this is finished we're going to the gym. They're so funny, I love them. There's nothing better than a good sitcom."

4

Perry Mance phoned the next day to say they were coming to dinner, sounding contrite, a man who needed the money more than his ego. Phillip gave him the address, the date and the time. An hour before, Spence had phoned wanting to know whether Phillip was going to invest his money. He too sounded humble: it was amazing to Phillip how far people would sink to make money. Without a yes or a no, the conversation with Spence had been short, the power of money resting with Phillip. He was not enjoying his life as a venture capitalist.

On the Friday he took himself off to the supermarket to prepare for the night's dinner: roast lamb with fresh mint sauce, roast potatoes and four green vegetables, his stepmother's perfect family meal on the farm. By the time Martha came home, the food was prepared, the table laid and the corks removed from two bottles to let the red wine breathe. On the side table stood a large glass bowl full of fruit for dessert. If nothing else, the dinner party had given him something to do. While Martha was having a shower to get herself ready the phone rang. Phillip expected it was Perry Mance cancelling the evening.

"Dad! I thought it was someone else."

"The Seventeenth Earl died without a known relative in England. He was an only child as was his father and grandfather. There was no will. I spent yesterday afternoon at the Home Office with a helpful young girl wading through the records."

"Was there any money?"

"Plenty. All of it held in a trust by the British government waiting for someone to make a claim. The big question is, can your friend prove his ancestry? If he can, he can have the lot: money and title. The fact he's American doesn't make any difference. They'll need birth and marriage certificates going back to when your friend's ancestors first left Britain for America. It was fun. Something to do. St Catherine's House in Kingsway has all the records of births and deaths in England. You'll need to find the equivalent in America. It's been a lovely day. The sun has been shining. Bergit and I took a small boat out on the river. How's New York?"

"Bustling. Full of noise and people. I miss the bush."

"I know the feeling."

"Thanks, Dad. I'll come back. Better go. Throwing a business dinner party looking at a potential investment."

"Be careful, son. It's easier to lose than make. What's he like?"

"Who?"

"Your Fernsby?"

"Old, arthritic and makes a living as a beggar."

"How far the English aristocracy has sunk. The whole of Europe is going down the drain. Oh, how I wish we had been able to stay in Africa. I get letters from friends holding on in Zimbabwe who think the country and Africa will one day come right. Boom, like China is booming at the moment. Eternal optimists. Nothing wrong with it. I just hope you and Martha didn't make a mistake. But that's life. You take your chances. However hard you think, you never know what's ahead when we are all dependent on other people's manipulations."

"Give my love to Bergit."

"I will. Phone me back soon. This has been fun. You can always go back to your cottage in the Vumba."

"Tell that to Martha."

When Martha came out of the bedroom in one of her new dresses it was almost half past seven.

"Tell what to Martha?"

"Dad thinks we should go and live in the cottage in the Vumba next to the lake."

"And twiddle our thumbs. Boring, Phillip... There's the doorbell. I appreciate guests who arrive on time. Everything ready?"

"The lamb's in the oven. After a couple of drinks I'll put on the vegetables."

"Don't forget I don't drink."

"Neither does Perry. Or so he said... Hello, Perry. Please come in. You must be Mrs Mance. I'm Phillip Crookshank and the lady behind is my wife, Martha. Which one of you two gentlemen is Uncle Jim?... Hello. Perry spoke highly of you. Would you care for a drink?"

"I'm Fred, Perry's father. Can't believe a son of mine is at a university. Left school myself at fifteen."

"What do you do, Fred?"

"I'm a trash collector."

"You drive one of those big trucks?"

"Just pick up the bags and empty the cans. Thirty years collecting garbage. Steady job. Not much competition. No one wants to be a garbage collector. Why my wife Tinkerbell and me want our son to succeed. Why we're so pleased you're going to give our Perry the money to get him started. Be first in the family to make money. Can't wait to get my hands on some of it. Don't know where he gets the brains from. Didn't get no brains from his father. Pick it up and sling it in the back of a truck: that's me. Tinkerbell sells ice cream in one of them places. Must be a lost gene that popped back in Perry."

"So you don't mind him not getting his degree?"

"What I want him to do is make money... Wouldn't mind a beer. Is that red wine on the counter? Just look at this place. I can already smell Perry's money. What's for dinner?"

"Roast lamb and all the trimmings."

"It's a whole new world, Perry my boy. A whole new world."

"Your son doesn't drink?"

"Must be that funny gene. Me and Tinkerbell love to get ourselves plastered. Don't we, Jim? Jim's my oldest friend. He left school at sixteen and got a job in an insurance company. Didn't do no moving in thirty years, my brother Jim. Steady job. Didn't get far, like the rest of us Mances. He's a clerk at a desk. What makes me laugh is Perry going to make all that money out of books. Never read no book in my life. Neither has Tinkerbell. Who wants to read a book when you got the television? My, what a view. Like looking over New York from heaven. Never been up this high before. All the garbage is at the bottom... Hello, Martha. I'm Fred. Guess you don't sell ice cream in a parlour. But we're happy. Got jobs. Pay the bills. That's what counts. Fred and Jim and my wife Tinkerbell. And this is what it's all about – my son, Perry. You got no idea how proud we are of Perry. And now he's going to be one of them fancy-pants with all that lovely money. Thanks to your husband. But mark my words. In the end, you'll be thanking Perry and his friends. Thanks, Phillip. Cheers to everyone. This is the start of a lovely friendship if this is how you does business. I can smell that lamb roasting. Give Tinkerbell a gin and Jim a beer."

"What would you like in the gin?"

"Whatever you have."

"Gin and tonic. My English father's favourite. Let's all sit down and get to know each other... Tell me about the life of your family, Fred. So I can get everything into perspective."

"Is his idea good?"

"I spoke to my brother Randall on Wednesday. He thinks so. He's a writer but you don't read books."

"What I want to hear about is Africa. The rest goes over my head. If Perry makes all that money he talks about he's going to give me and his mother a trip to Africa."

Perry let out a giggle, making Phillip smile. The boy was good, knew how to play people. Relaxing with a beer, Phillip let them talk. He would lose Perry his degree, but his own money would be safe in the new venture. They would start small and make them work. Then see what happened. From trash collector to tycoon in two generations in the new, wonderful world of technology that only the youth understood.

"We had an old rule on the farm in Rhodesia, Fred. The guests got the first drink poured for them, and after that, they went up to the bar and poured their own. It was called sundowners, except the drinking went on long after the sun went down. If you drink a little too much tonight it doesn't matter. It's Friday night. We can put you in a taxi and get you home. At the moment Martha isn't drinking as she's expecting our baby, so she and Perry can get to know each other. We'll eat when we're hungry. Sundowners, everyone. Let's get started."

In the past, getting drunk with strangers had always been fun for Phillip. And while Perry's parents and uncle were drinking, Martha would delve deep into the mind of young Perry. In business, as in life, there was nothing better than a second opinion.

By the time Phillip put on the vegetables, the party was well under way. Martha followed Phillip into the kitchen.

"What you think, Martha?"

"He has brains. His mind is sharp. He's also naïve when it comes to money. You'll need to put in a business manager and let the youngsters develop the software."

"Would you put in your own money?"

"Probably. We took a chance with Marcin Galinski. Why not take another one? The lamb looks good. I'm hungry. Wish I could drink with you. There's nothing more boring than being sober surrounded by drunks."

"We're not drunk."

"But you will be. Go back and look after our guests. I'll take over the cooking. They are so different, parents and son. Didn't think such a difference was possible in the same family."

"How's Jaz getting on with Galinski?"

"They're lovers. And I mean lovers. Poor Jaz. All that 'I'm in control' down the toilet. They're talking about living together."

"And your business dealings with Marcin?"

"Everything going to plan. But remember the new rule. No talking business until our baby is born... You weren't serious about the Vumba cottage?"

"Of course not, honey. That was the past. This is the now and the future... Don't forget to make the gravy."

It was all quite fundamental. Martha wanted her baby and the Mances wanted money; each to their own. As Phillip listened to the chatter about the life of a garbage collector – the four of them talking louder and louder as the alcohol went down – Perry watched them through the big glasses with an air of superiority, the superior look and the giggles making Phillip irritated. The young man despised his parents and would have despised Uncle Jim were it not for his uncle's monthly stipend. Worrying about the man losing his degree in exchange for a gamble no longer concerned Phillip. Life on the forty-ninth floor was all about being rich, each making money out of the other. If the venture failed, Phillip would have nothing on his conscience.

Phillip carved the lamb and poured the wine, the vegetable dishes Martha brought from the kitchen passed from one to the other. When the evening came to an end it was Phillip who saw the parents into the taxi, paying the cab driver the fare in advance. An hour before, Perry had excused himself and gone back on the bus to his digs close to the university.

"No one ate the fruit."

"They were more interested in the wine."

"Do you like Perry, Martha?"

"Not particularly. I have had a number of clients over the years I don't like. But it never stopped me doing business with them."

"Did you find out what you wanted?"

"Picked his brains all evening. Go with it, Phillip. Let's go to bed. It's fun drinking together. Not much fun being sober. You were all talking so much rubbish."

"What a party is about. It's a strange old world, Martha. Let's just hope our son doesn't turn out like Perry."

"What's wrong with Perry?"

"He despises his parents."

"And all they want him to do is make money and look after them. The perfect match, if you ask me."

"Shouldn't there be love?"

"Love manifests itself in strange ways. He says he wants your money so he can look after his parents."

"Is he using them to convince me? Anyway. Let's go to bed. Too much booze and I can't think straight. To bed, to sleep, perchance to dream. There's nothing better than a good dream. One thing struck me tonight. That boy is never going to be happy however many millions he makes. He'll always use people, never love them. What a pity. Makes life have no purpose. What's the point of getting yourself rich just to show off your superiority? Life should be about making yourself and other people happy."

"Drink your two pints of water and get some sleep."

"Life in all its facets. The one person I envy is Jonathan Fernsby. He's happy with a violin playing Mozart in a park. He doesn't give a damn about money... Is Jaz after Galinski or his money?"

"Who knows? But I sure as hell would not want to go homeless, Mozart or no Mozart... Why don't we go to a concert tomorrow night?"

"That's the best idea of the evening. The New York Philharmonic. It's not all bad, Martha."

"Whoever said it was? You know, the one joy of not drinking is knowing you won't wake up with a hangover the next morning."

Smiling, trying not to trip over the furniture, Phillip went to the kitchen, forced down two pints of water and took himself off to bed.

PART 4

SEPTEMBER 1994 — "WHAT'S HE REALLY THINKING?"

1

September was Martha's favourite month of the year. The sun was shining, the temperature just right and people had smiles on their faces walking in the streets. It was also the perfect month to go on a holiday.

"Franklyn, I'm taking two weeks' leave. Phillip wants to visit his father and brothers in England... Where's Jasmine? It's ten o'clock in the morning, for goodness sake. At least Jack works his butt off."

"When are you going?"

"Saturday. I've booked the flights."

"Linguare.com is about to launch its final product on the market."

"All the work is done. All the build-up and hype. Jaz has it under control. Ever since she moved in with Marcin Galinski she's been arriving at the office late."

"A girl has to get her priorities straight. The man in her life is more important than the business. Always has been with women. Why women working all day in business find it difficult to maintain a relationship."

"Are you lecturing me?"

"How is Phillip?"

"Bored with nothing much to do. Perry Mance doesn't need his help now he's got the start-up money. All Phillip can do is sit back and see what happens to his new investment. A holiday in Europe will do us both good. Do the baby good. Got to keep the pressure down, Franklyn. Our new company is positively humming. Anyway, I want to ask Randall about books and how best to market them online. Nothing better for running the Mance publicity than picking the brains of a bestselling author. The best idea we had was giving the executives each a separate office. I hated those total open plans. I couldn't concentrate with the constant chatter and noise. This is how to run a successful company. Give the management offices where they can think. Good business is done by thinking before you rush into a project. Why all the new clients are coming to us. Good word of mouth. Product advertising where the buyers can see and understand what they're getting. Not all the bullshit... Ah, there you are, Jaz. Thought you'd forgotten all about us. Work before play, darling."

"We've been in Marcin's office all night. Those guys are so excited it's all finally happening. They know they've got it right this time. The voice recognition software really works."

"You worked all night?"

"We slept for three hours on the floor. Marcin hasn't been home for a week. Neither have the others. Got to work to win, Martha. Did I hear you are going on holiday?"

"I'm pregnant. Priorities, Jaz."

"Of course. I'm sorry."

"How did you hear about my holiday?"

"Franklyn's door was open. I could hear you from reception. Who wants some coffee? I'll be glad when the product launch is over and we can have a normal life. Just one bit of information you'll both be interested in. I'm pregnant. Don't sit there with your mouths open. Look happy for me."

"You're not married."

"Neither were you, Martha, the first time."

"Does he know?"

"Of course he does."

"Are you getting married?"

"Whatever for? Oh, you think I just want his money?"

"Don't you?"

"Money helps. But it isn't everything. We love each other. Can you believe it? Really love each other. I'll go make the coffee."

"Ask Priscilla to make the coffee."

Franklyn looked from Jasmine to Martha, a look of 'what's next' on his face.

"Now I've got two partners who are pregnant! Women. In the old days, the women stayed at home and worked in the kitchen."

"Boring, Franklyn. Nowadays you employ a cleaning company and go out to dinner. Let the cleaners clean the house and the restaurant do the cooking. Two salaries in a household make all the difference. It's the new age for women. Who wants to be a slave to their husband? Freedom. That's what it's all about. A girl wants her freedom."

"And then Phillip sits at home."

"That's his business. My husband has got too much money."

"So has Marcin but it doesn't stop him working all day and night. Oh, dear. Why do I always open my big mouth? Hello, Phillip. Did you hear what we just said?"

"Every word of it. What's the point of working for more money when you have more than you need? Marcin borrowed my money and made a commitment. He still has to make the project work and float his company on the stock exchange. Then you'll see. Have you told them, Martha, that we're going to England on Saturday? I now have every document to support Jonathan's claim. I showed them to him in the gardens. Didn't care."

"Was he playing his violin?"

"Just reading his book. Can I help you, Priscilla, with that coffee machine? I like mine with a little milk and a teaspoonful of sugar... Had a phone call from Beth Hardcastle in Kansas City. Six new staff this year. Reception Perfection Inc is making good money. Event planning's the new big thing in America. Let the professionals do the work to plan your wedding. Willy and Beth send their love, Martha. And it's all happening at Linguare.com."

"Jaz is pregnant."

"My, we have been busy. All part of life. The real part, I suppose. Life is all about reproduction."

"Why have you come to the office, honey?"

"I'm bored."

"Poor Phillip. We'll have a lovely time in England and you won't be bored. So that lawyer traced Jonathan Wesley Fernsby right back to his roots?"

"Every step of the way."

"What are you doing after the coffee?"

"Leaving you to get on with your work. I'll find something to keep myself amused. September. It's a lovely month. At home, it will be the build-up to the start of the rains and the end of the tourist season for Jacques. I worked hard as a safari operator, Jaz. You lot get on with your work. I'll sit with Priscilla at the reception desk and drink my coffee. Congratulations, Jaz. What do you want? A boy or a girl?"

"Doesn't matter."

"Good girl. You two are nice and young to start your family."

"Are we too old, Phillip?"

"Of course not, Martha. It's all about having a family. You know the old saying: 'better late than never'. Beth and Willy are still in their same apartment next to where we lived in Kansas City. One day I'll pay them a visit and go see my old friend Solly in Solly's Saloon. Got to keep up with my three investments. Give me something to do. Off you go, the three of you. Don't let me keep you from your work. Cleaners and cooks. I like that. What I do myself most of the time. And if you didn't have your separate offices I wouldn't be able to eavesdrop so successfully."

Martha, not sure if she had created a problem with Phillip, retreated into her office, closing the door. She could still hear Phillip and Jaz chatting through the closed door, a twinge of jealousy passing through her belly. If Jaz had not got herself pregnant and was living with Marcin, she would have thought the girl was up to something. She walked over and looked out at the buildings, the view not as spectacular as the one from their forty-ninth-floor apartment. She felt her stomach with both hands, hoping everything was well. Once the baby was born her bond to Phillip would be unbreakable. They would be parents. Parents of the same child. Their genes blended forever. After a long think, she heard her husband say goodbye to Jaz and Priscilla, the twenty-one-year-old receptionist. Soon they would be filling up the outer office with more staff as the workload for the four of them increased. In a year or two, they would require the rest of the fourth floor of the building. Smiling at the thought of success, Martha walked back from the window and sat down at her desk. A pile of files left by Gerta, her young assistant, looked at her. Hopefully, like Jaz, Gerta would climb up the corporate ladder and become an executive. Life for Martha was all about being a success.

SMILING to herself at the thought of never again having to worry about money, Jaz walked across into her own office. After the birth she would ask Marcin to set up a trust fund for the baby with her as the sole trustee. If he married her it would be a bonus. A girl had to look after herself. You married them without a prenuptial contract or you had their baby. Either way, if the man was rich enough a girl was set up for the rest of her life. She had told the others they loved each other but did anyone really love another person? People said they loved each other to suit a purpose. And the sex with Marcin was good. What more could a girl want? The top file on her desk placed by Robert her assistant was the current file of Linguare.com, a file in which she had a double interest. As the firm's publicist and the beneficiary of that IPO it was going to make her live-in lover, and the father of her child, as rich as Croesus, the stinking rich king of ancient Lydia. What a world. And it never changed. It was all about making money. And she had tested it. The voice recognition software worked perfectly. That IPO, when it came, would blow their minds.

"You're a lucky little bugger, my child. You are going to have rich parents." Poor Phillip. She felt sorry for him. All the poor man wanted was a child and his Africa. "You can't have both worlds, Phillip. Or maybe you can."

She was still smiling and mumbling to herself as she got down to her work. She had never slept with a much older man like Phillip, the thought making her smile. And the next thing she would have to do was tell Marcin she was pregnant despite what she had told Martha and Franklyn. Life really was a bitch. Was she a bitch? Only life would tell. Whatever the rights and wrongs, a gal had to look after herself. Her own father had walked out on them when she was two years old. Her stepfather had leered at her ever since she had grown breasts. And she had been raped as a girl by her stepbrother Felix, the biggest bastard in the world. Poor Marcin. He had no idea what he was letting himself in for. The pull of sex and the power of money. But now, the first and immediate problem was the success of Marcin's company. Concentrating, Jaz dispelled all other thoughts and sank deep into her work.

WHILE JAZ WAS WORKING on every which way to promote Marcin's company and make it successful, Franklyn was standing at the window in the office next to Martha's, sipping his coffee, contentment written all over his face. There was nothing better in life than being the chief executive officer of his own company. No one to give him orders, no one to fire him, only himself to blame. And if the girls paid more attention to their children than the business so be it. He and Jack Webber would continue to develop the company. At home his wife was looking after the new apartment, Tildy was behaving herself in her new school, and Clarence had at last taken the plunge and enrolled at New York University. Not only did Franklyn have the beginning of a successful company, he had a family. A family that worked. A family that gave purpose to the future success of Bowden, Crookshank and Fairbanks. And if Jack landed the last account from his old company, he would be made a partner, his name included, making it B, C, F and W. And the coffee was just perfect. Putting down the empty coffee cup on the side of his desk, a wooden desk carved on both sides and the front, a joy every time Franklyn looked at it, he sat down behind it in his comfortable chair and picked up the top file left by Hilda his middle-aged assistant, the best old hen in the business. Between Hilda in the office and Joanne at home Franklyn's life was perfect.

Two hours later, having worked his way through the files, he walked out of his big office with its blue carpet and pictures on the walls, crossed the main office where the staff were heads down at their desks, and opened the door to Jack Webber's office without knocking.

"Good morning, Jack."

"You gave me a fright. Writing the final draft of my report for Liberty Soups. The last one to come over to me, Franklyn. What can I do for you, boss? And it's lunchtime, so good afternoon, Franklyn. I've been at this desk since six o'clock this morning and still the work piles up. My phone never stops ringing."

"Do you want any help with Liberty?"

"Will you read my report?"

"Of course."

"I ran the account for my old employer for five years. There's nothing better than fresh eyes. Fresh ideas."

"Be my pleasure, Jack. Joanne wants you to come for dinner on Friday. Bring a girlfriend if you want. Did you hear Jaz is pregnant?"

"So she nailed him."

"Shouldn't look at it like that. She says they love each other."

"Been there before. Got the T-shirt. You're about the only person I have ever met with a successful marriage. All my friends who haven't divorced say they have to work on their marriage twenty-four seven. And even their kids are difficult. Thank Joanne for the invitation. I'll bring Tammy. She's twenty-five, ten years younger than me and gloriously naïve. She still thinks men are nice. Can you believe it?"

"Seven-thirty. Give me what you've done of the report and we'll get our heads together. Ten million dollars in new business if you land Liberty. How's your new South African assistant? She was lucky to get a work permit. Everyone wants to come to America."

"Bamby is good. Where on earth did she get the name Bamby? She says her friends call her Numbi Bamby because of the size of her chest. Here you go. Whatever would we do without computers? I love this office. Martha was right. There's nothing better than having the privacy of one's own office. Here I can think."

"Sorry to barge in."

"You're the boss, Franklyn. You're the boss. How are you and your family finding New York?"

"We love it. They all say it's the best move we ever made. New York. That's where it all happens."

"Is she going to marry him?"

"Who knows? These days the youngsters live together. Too busy getting on with their lives. How the world has changed."

"How old are you, Franklyn, if you don't mind my asking?"

"I'll be fifty in six months' time. Joanne and I married late. When we first met at college we didn't have the money to get married and start a family."

"You've known each other all that time?"

"Only woman I've ever dated. We looked at each other and fell in love."

"And it's lasted all this time."

"And always will."

"You're so damn lucky."

"We know we are. Never had a cross word in our lives. They say that among all the millions out there, there is only one for you. The luck is finding that one. What are the chances? That's the luck. I have no idea what I would do to myself if something happened to Joanne. Thank my lucky stars every day. You should find yourself another wife, Jack. Can't spend all your life on your own."

"Oh, you can when you've had a bad marriage like mine. Sours a person. Makes them cynical, even a little nasty. Friends become more difficult. Could be age. Remember all those friends at school. Cans of soup. Whoever would have thought a company could grow to be worth so many millions of dollars selling soup in cans?"

"People are lazy. Don't have time. You go home, open a can of Liberty Soup you just saw advertised on television, tip it into a pan and you've got your supper. If that isn't enough, open a can of beans. Not everyone can afford restaurants. In the modern world, it's all about time. Unless you are lucky enough to have a wife who prefers to stay at home. A can of soup, a can of beans and a doughnut. Welcome to America... I'll be back when I've read all the details of your marketing strategy. Nice to have you with us, Jack."

"Nice to be here."

Jack watched a smiling Franklyn walk out of the room and close the door behind him. For Jack, the last few months had been traumatic. Leaving his long-time employer; joining the new company that had to prove itself; taking with him his old employer's accounts and feeling guilty; adjusting to new co-workers; employing a new assistant with the biggest breasts he had ever seen in his life, and waiting for the big promotion that would see his name with the others up on the notice board. Instead of going back to finish the Liberty report, Jack got up and walked around the office, the first office he had ever had of his own. Having an office of his own made Jack feel important, no longer a run of the mill drone. For the first time in his life, he was going to be someone, provided Liberty Soups gave him their account. As often happened when he wasn't concentrating on his work he thought of his wife and the old pain of being cheated on came back with a vengeance. Jealousy. There was nothing more painful and worthless than jealousy. Why a man so hated a woman for sleeping with another man was an indigestible puzzle for Jack. People screwed each other and went their separate ways, neither looking back nor barely remembering. But when that one woman was unfaithful all hell was let loose, filling Jack with crunching anger that despite all his screwing of other women would not go away. In his overwhelming mania, Jack understood how a person could kill another person to take away agonising mental pain. Luckily for Jack, he knew he was a coward, the thoughts of revenge never serious. Losing Pippa was all part of his life. All part of his divine providence. Among the mental searching of his constant pain, he hoped she was happy. He needed a drink. He needed another woman in his life, not the worthless moments of sexual satisfaction he found in his brief affairs. He needed to knock some sense into his head and forget the rage that had consumed him when he went home early that terrible day and found his wife being screwed on the living room couch, oblivious to him or the world around her as she screamed out in the final throes of her climax. Standing in that doorway, Jack's life had come to an end. Not even an apology. Just a naughty, mischievous smile.

"Hello, Jack. You're home early. Do you want to join us?"

"We're married, Pippa."

"What's wrong with a bit of fun? After two years you get bored with sex from the same man. We need to add some excitement. If I knew his name, I'd introduce you. I was bored and went to the bar down the road. We've been drinking for hours! Don't look so indignant. It doesn't mean anything. Don't get your balls in a twist. Life's about having fun, not sitting at home all day waiting for your husband to finish work. And getting a job is just as boring. I hate waiting tables. You make a big salary, Jack. What's the point in me working?... Hey, what are you going to do? Put that thing down or get out. If you can't have a bit of fun on the side, this marriage is over. We don't have any kids. What's the bloody point of sitting at home all day on my own? I'm twenty-three. I want a life."

"I love you."

"Don't give me that bullshit. Get your pants off and join in or fuck off. It's a free world. I want a life other than cleaning, and cooking your bloody food.

Get real, Jack. Oh, good. Now you're running away. Why the hell I ever married you in the first place is a mystery. You're a lousy screw. Go and find some other stupid woman to be your slave. Just leave me out of it. And no, I don't want any of your damn money. All I want is some fun in my pathetic little life."

As Jack stood looking at the blank wall it could have been yesterday. Not three years back in his life. Instead of going back to his desk and finishing the report, Jack put on his jacket that was hanging over the back of his chair and walked out of the office.

"Going to see a client, Bamby. Back tomorrow."

Still feeling the rage, Jack walked from the lift through the foyer and out into the street. It was Wednesday but he didn't care. He'd call Bamby the next day and tell her he was sick. He was going on a binge, the kind of binge he normally had on Friday and Saturday. The Liberty report could wait a few more days. He'd done enough already to secure his job. With the rage in his belly increasing, he walked fast down the street and into the bar, a place he never mentioned to anyone in the office. There was a flaw in everyone, he told himself. His flaw was the pain from his wife cheating on him, a pain that only drink in quantity assuaged. When he was drunk, he didn't feel anything. Couldn't remember anything. Past or present. By Friday he would be feeling normal for dinner with the Bowdens, that lucky bastard with a faithful wife.

"What you want, Jack?"

"Double scotch."

"Coming up. Is there something wrong?"

"You don't want to know. Just look after me. I'm in one of my moods."

"I always look after my customers."

"I appreciate it, Dennis."

"So, she's back in your head again?"

"You got it."

"It'll go in the end. Happened to me. Just don't let her ruin your life."

"She's already done that."

"You'll get over it. Time heals. Always does."

"I hope so. And everything in the new office was looking good."

"Get yourself laid."

"Tried that."

"Then do it again. There you go, Jack. I'll have one with you. Down the hatch."

Hearing Franklyn talk about his perfect marriage had started the rot for

Jack. Before that disgusting afternoon, Jack thought Pippa was his one. The only one. The love that would take him through life.

"Down the hatch, Dennis. Why can't I forget the bitch? That's better. Give me another double. Why did they call this bar the Cock and Hen?"

"No idea. Better ask the owner. All I do is run his bar."

"How long you been a barman, Dennis?"

"Thirty years, take a year or two."

"What's it been like?"

"The tips are good. I make friends. Bar friends. It's our own little world away from the traffic of life."

"Do you mind listening to our problems?"

"Not at all. Makes my day interesting. Makes me appreciate what I've got at home and who I am. You don't have to be rich and own your own business to be happy. You just need enough to pay the bills and keep your wife and kids happy. We all have jobs. The kids have been doing part-time jobs since they were ten years old. They put it all in a kitty box and share it with the whole family. We all pull together, Jack."

"Have you saved any money over the years?"

"Sure we have. There'll be enough to retire into the country when I'm too old to work bars. Provided you spend less than you earn, money isn't a problem... Hello, Chris. Same as usual?"

"Thanks, Dennis."

"There we go. One beer. You two enjoy your drinks. Talk to Jack. He's in one of his moods."

"Oh, my goodness. That woman again. Cheer up, Jack. You're the lucky one. You don't have a wife to put up with. Why do you think I spend so much of my time in the Cock and Hen? She never stops moaning at me. Always complaining. Everything is my fault. After fifteen years of marriage, nothing has changed. Let me buy you a drink."

"What's wrong with life?"

"I have no idea. Give him whatever he's having, Dennis. My one happy escape is this bar. There we go. To life, Jack. It's the only one we've got. The only one we are going to get. Enjoy it."

"To life, Chris. Good to see you."

"That's better. Good to see you, Jack. What friends are for. Whatever would we do without the escape of our friendly little bar? Bars. The mix of life. The good, the bad and the ugly. Some prefer to call it the human race. So, what's on today's agenda, or shouldn't I ask seeing you're drinking doubles? Let's talk about baseball. Forget our women. How long have we been drinking together?"

"Three or four months."

"Seems like we've been friends for years."

"You got out of the office early."

"I'm a salesman. Make my own times. Been a good month, September. My commission will be good. Why I like being a commission salesman. When I'm short of money I can work longer hours and earn enough to meet my commitments, and stop my wife whining. There's nothing worse than a perpetually whining wife."

"How long did you say you'd been married?"

"Fifteen years."

"Why do you put up with it?"

"We both put up with each other. Neither of us has an alternative. She has her lady friends she can moan to. I have the Cock and Hen."

"Do you still have sex?"

"Most nights. Not tonight if I'm drunk. Or if I do I won't remember."

"Is the sex good?"

"Sex is sex. Makes you sleep better. With a wife, it's less complicated. We both get what we want."

"You got kids?"

"No kids. We can't have kids. My wife's infertile. Part of why she's always whining. Why she wants sex. Even now she thinks she might get pregnant."

"Maybe it's you. Have you had your sperm checked?"

"There are some things in life, Jack, you just don't want to know."

"You could adopt."

"Are you kidding? Why would I want to pay for someone else's little bastard?"

"Maybe she will get pregnant."

"You think so?"

"Stranger things have happened."

"Let's forget about women. I love this little bar. Dennis, put up the baseball on the television. Here we go. And bring us another round. Make mine a double brandy."

"Coming up, Chris."

"Look at that. He's the best barman in New York. Now we're having fun."

Within an hour the bar was full, everyone drinking and watching the baseball. All thoughts of Pippa had gone out of Jack's head. He was going to land the Liberty Soups account for Franklyn. Life once again was fun. With the ball clouted out of the park, the whole bar stood up. This was America in all its glory.

"Whose round is it, Chris?"

"Who cares? Put 'em up, Dennis. I'm getting nicely pissed."

A bar, a friend, a game of baseball. What more could a man want? An hour later, remembering his responsibilities to Franklyn, Jack left the bar and went home to his small apartment where he opened a can of Liberty Soup and tipped it in the pan. Instead of getting drunk on a Wednesday he would get an early night and work properly in the morning. With the soup warm in the pan, Jack took a spoon and ate his supper. The soup was quite delicious. There was nothing better than promoting a good product. Later in bed, the memory of Pippa out of his head, Jack went to sleep. Outside the traffic was rumbling, the sound of a police siren the last thing Jack remembered as he fell into his sleep. In his dream, children were stuffing a large kitty box with banknotes and coins. When Jack woke it was Thursday morning. The sun was up. Time to shower, get changed and go to his office. His new office where a man could concentrate on his own.

"Good morning, Bamby."

"Good morning, Jack. It's a lovely day. Franklyn wants to see you."

"What about?"

"Your report. I've re-typed everything with Franklyn's additions."

"Is it better?"

"I think so."

"Am I late? Slept like a baby right through the night. Nothing better than a good sleep. We've got to get this last account, Bamby. Got to win. Life's all about winning."

In his own office, Jack sat at his desk and read the corrected report. He was right. Two heads were better than one. Smiling, Jack went to the door of Franklyn's office and knocked.

"Come in, Jack."

"How did you know it was me?"

"A good guess... What you think?"

"Much better. Your English is so much better than mine. The exact right word can make all the difference. Do you think the report is finished? I'm never sure when I've said enough."

"Looks good to me. Let 'em have it, Jack. All you need is the summary. You haven't forgotten tomorrow's dinner party?"

"Seven-thirty on the dot."

"You look chipper today."

"I feel good, Franklyn. Just this one last account."

"And then it will be 'welcome, partner'. Life at the top. What we all want.

Martha says it's all about winning. Go get 'em, Jack. They're ripe for the picking. I always tell my clients the most important part of a successful business is a good advertising agent who is constantly thinking. Constantly thinking of new ideas to promote his client's business. You got to advertise to win."

"Thanks, Franklyn."

"My pleasure. And thanks for knocking."

"My pleasure."

Both of them laughing, Jack returned to his office, closed the door, sat down behind his desk and began writing the summary of the Liberty Soups report. Despite all the problems in his life he was going to get his name up on the notice board in the foyer of the building. He was finally going to arrive. Partner in an advertising and publicity business. Jack Webber, a life of wealth and respect. His final revenge on Pippa, still waiting tables and looking for tips.

2

While Jack Webber was gloating at the prospect of getting his own back on his ex-wife, Martha was working the phone. All morning she had been calling her friends in the media, pumping the launch of voice recognition software.

"Does it work, Martha? Can't print a story about something that doesn't work."

"Contact Linguare and ask them for a publicity pack. It's going to revolutionise the world. No more keyboards and typing. You'll love it."

"Thanks for telling me."

"My pleasure."

After completing her list, repeating the same story all day, she had had enough of the office.

"Can't do anymore. Time to go home."

"Do you always talk to yourself, Martha?"

"Hello, Franklyn. Must have made over two hundred phone calls today right across the country. Nothing better than the personal touch. Direct contact."

"Joanne is having a little dinner party tomorrow. Will you and Phillip come? I've invited Jack and Jasmine. Jack's bringing a girlfriend. You fly off on holiday the next day. A nice little send-off. Jack's presenting his report to Liberty Soups tomorrow morning. Should be told if they are coming across to us. How is Gerta getting on?"

"Just great. If she's anything like Jaz she will be a credit to me... What time tomorrow?"

"Seven-thirty."

"Is Jaz bringing Marcin?"

"We'll all be at the party. Go home to Phillip and get some rest. Never forget your baby."

"It's been wonderful putting the company together."

"All worked perfectly. Tomorrow night will be fun. One big, happy family. What makes for a good business. Harmony in the workplace. That's what I strive for."

Back on the forty-ninth floor of their apartment, Martha stood looking out of the big plate-glass window in the living room, the whole of New York spread out in front of her. There was no sign of Phillip. Instead of going to the gym she made herself coffee and returned to the window to think. The Linguare.com account was safely theirs, Jack had one more to go to reach ten million dollars in annual billings, getmethatbook, the new Perry Mance start-up, was developing nicely, as were a string of new accounts. Despite trying to look on the bright side of life, the fear came back again, a cold, terrible fear running right through her body, making her feel physically sick. Was she again going to lose her baby, her body inherently unable to give birth? A cold sweat broke out on her brow and around her neck. Her hands began to shake, slopping her coffee. Her whole stomach was gripped by contraction. Putting the palm of her free hand to the cold glass of the window, she tried to steady herself. Slowly, the noise of New York came back to her consciousness as her hand slipped down the window and Martha sank to her knees. If she lost the baby this time she would kill herself. This time there would be no old lady across the way to give her a friendly wave and stop her from falling. Despite what she said to Phillip, she knew he wanted to go back to Africa to his life along the banks of the Zambezi River. It was only the thought of having a child that kept Phillip in New York. He hated the life of a venture capitalist, despite all the financial success. He hated living in a city. The life Phillip Crookshank cherished above all others was life in the African bush, the place of his birth, the one true love of his life. Rolling over, sitting on her behind, the coffee spilled along the ledge at the bottom of the window, the cup lying on its side, she stared at the ceiling and down at the oak dining table, crying to herself as the fear subsided and she fought to control herself to protect her baby. After ten minutes sitting numb on the floor, she got up, found a cloth in the kitchen and returned to the big room to clean up the mess, before sitting down on the ledge, her back to New York.

"Don't leave me, darling. I want you so much. Please. Mummy's calling to you. Can you hear? Four more months and we'll see each other."

Only when the key went into the front door letting Phillip into the apartment did Martha get up, brushing down the front of her skirt as she forced a smile on her face.

"Hello, honey. Did my husband have a lovely day?"

"They're all pretty much the same. A walk to the waterfront, a seat in the park with Mary and the cat listening to Jonathan, a pot of tea in the restaurant talking to the waitress, and two hours with Volker in the gym."

"You didn't go to Harry B's?"

"Not today. How are you, Martha? How's our baby?"

"Never felt better. We've been invited to dinner tomorrow. The partners and Jack. A send-off for our trip to Europe."

"Have you started to pack?"

"I'll do it after supper. What do you want to eat?"

"I can't believe Jonathan has not the slightest interest in his ancestral money. Tells me to do what I like in London with all the documents. All he wants is to get back into an orchestra or play his new violin in the park. His arthritis is much better now it's controlled by the drugs I helped him get. He's even composing his own music. I'm going to try and find a string quartet who want a violin player with money. You always say money buys anything. Maybe this time it will buy Jonathan happiness. Anything you've got. I'm not that hungry. September. Your favourite month. What's wrong with the window? Looks like something has spilled."

"I knocked over my coffee looking out the window... Two hundred phone calls today."

"You work too hard and I do nothing. Where are we going to dinner?"

"Franklyn's. His wife's going to cook. She loves throwing a dinner party. And she knows how to cook. Quite a family, the Bowdens. So he's composing music?"

"Funnily enough he's not. Says only Mozart and Haydn can write perfect music for strings. He's writing songs. The music and the words. Weird hearing him sing accompanied by a violin. I'm thinking of buying him a guitar."

"Can he sing?"

"Not very well. But there's nothing wrong with the words and the music."

"You've found a strange life in New York."

"Life in the gardens. Better than staring out of the window. Are you all right, Martha? You look flushed."

"Hot flushes. I'm having a baby."

"Of course. Do you mind if I put on some classical music? It takes me away from all the bricks and mortar... England on Saturday. One flight and Dad will be waiting at the airport with Bergit. So far and yet so near. I'm going to visit my family. Can't wait to see them. You know what we'll talk about?"

"Africa. You always do. Those wonderful years in Africa when the rest of the world passed you by."

"We all remember our dreams. You want tea or coffee?"

"I'm fine. I'm going to start the packing. What kind of songs are they?"

"Love songs. Love songs from his past. There was a girl called Linda."

"That's romantic... Make me some coffee."

In the bedroom, the fear came back again making Martha sit forlornly on the side of the bed, the wardrobe open in front of her. She could hear Phillip whistling a tune as he made the tea and coffee in the kitchen. With both hands gripping the edge of the bed, Martha controlled herself by trying to make out what Phillip was whistling.

"What are you whistling, Phillip? Is it a song I know?"

"Probably not. It's Jonathan's 'Linda'. He calls it 'The Last Time I Heard of Linda'."

"Didn't someone do that before?"

"Everything's been done before. Your voice sounds frightened. Is everything all right?"

"When did he last see Linda?"

"Thirty-five years ago. I asked him. He was twenty years old. Linda was nineteen."

"Were they lovers?"

"He didn't say. Says he can see her face as clear as if it was yesterday. I wish I could play music. I envy artists like my brother. The Isle of Man is going to be beautiful at the end of September. Randall with his books on his little farm with his wife and child. What a life that is. Writing a book in perfect solitude without all the rush and tumble of people. Never mind. There I go again. Nostalgia is boring. The secret of life is to stay in the present and only think of the future. Forget the past. Your coffee is on the table in the lounge. My word, it really is a view. Strange to wonder what everyone out there is thinking. Mostly we only think of ourselves. Bit like one big flock of sheep. Do you think sheep think individually, or just follow the flock? When a dog chases a flock of sheep, the whole lot run round in the same circle."

"What are you talking about, Phillip?"

"I have no idea. My mind is wandering. Can you imagine how much cement and bricks went into building all those skyscrapers? September in New York as the sun goes down and Jonathan thinks of Linda. I wonder what he will do with all that inherited money when I lay claim to it for him? Take months or years to finalise, I suppose. But you never know. In a month or two, my friend the homeless violin player in the park will be as rich as Marcin Galinski."

"Is there that much money in the estate?"

"I'll have to find out. Dad says it's big. Music. How does that sound? Haydn's Twenty-Eighth Symphony. Our favourite. Forget the packing. Come and enjoy your coffee. And I've cleaned down the window. Don't ever say I'm not a good househusband. That's better. You're laughing. The only thing better than the sound of your laughing wife is the sound of your laughing child. The happy laugh of a child. That's perfection."

Letting her coffee go cold Martha finished packing, the chatter from Phillip calming her nerves, the music playing gently, the noise of New York not part of her consciousness. When she walked back into the living room she was feeling better, her mind and body free from the pain.

"Your coffee is cold. Come and sit next to me. The important thing for you to do is relax. Last time your work was full of stress and you were drinking. Relax, Martha. Forget work and all those people. Wasn't that Haydn symphony beautiful? I never grow tired of listening to that music. Must have heard it a hundred times. Can't watch the same movie or read the same book a hundred times. What are we going to do tonight? I could take you out to dinner."

"I can't drink. What's the point?"

"Exactly. Maybe a little Mozart and we'll both read our books. I'll put your coffee in the microwave. What would we all do without modern technology? We're all going to have the perfect life. Maybe I'll open myself a nice bottle of wine. It's only another four months to our baby and then we can drink together. Now, let me tell you..."

Smiling, settling back on the couch, she listened to her Phillip. He was right. Everything in the future was going to be perfect. Linda, thought Martha. I wonder what happened to the violin player's Linda? There was always a Linda. Or a Phillip. In all of their lives. And she was lucky. She still had her Phillip, with an open bottle of the best South African wine in front of him, a flared glass flush with red liquid.

"Cheers, Martha. To life."

"Thank you, Phillip. For everything. I don't know what I would do without you."

"To Martha and Phillip. The easy-going couple. That's better. You're giggling. You don't have to live in the African bush to be easygoing. You can do it right here in New York on the forty-ninth floor. Just listen to the music. Mozart. Beautiful Mozart. Oh, and to our trip to England. Cheers again."

"You're nuts."

"Probably. Do you believe in heaven, Martha?"

"Of course I do. Don't you?"

"I'm never sure. I try to believe but I'm never certain. My school was run by a Church of England priest and all the boys but one in his house were confirmed into the Church of England. When my mother was killed and I asked him if I would ever see her again, the Very Reverend said he wasn't sure. I still respect that man to this day for not lying to suit the doctrine of his religion. The man did not say I would or would not see my mother. He told me he wasn't sure. It was all a matter of believing. We often say we believe something is right when we mean we're not sure. He eventually left the school and went on to be the Bishop of Dorchester. Men of such honesty are rare. I consider myself privileged to have had a headmaster who wouldn't lie to fulfil his calling. Are there any people left in this world we can trust, Martha? Priests and politicians operate much the same to suit their purpose. Religion and politics mingle. It's a dangerous world."

"Believe, Phillip. It's much easier. Have faith."

"I'll try. You have faith, Martha. I know the loss of our first baby haunts you. When I came home I saw it in your face. We go through our lives, the good and the bad. However much we believe or hope, nothing is perfect. You have to relax and take life as it comes. Stop worrying. You'll do yourself and the baby more harm by worrying."

"It's not so easy not to worry."

"Then believe. Blanket your mind. I'm here for you, Martha. You begged me in that letter to come back. None of us really know what life is all about. Whether it has a real purpose. Like religion, it's all about believing, about having faith. If we are being foolish by believing in whichever religion we believe in, it doesn't matter. The belief is all that matters. I respect that Very Reverend because the man could not lie. Both he and his religion were unable to lie to that small boy who had just lost his mother, a thing so devastating it is difficult to imagine."

"It's a lovely story."

"But, unlike most stories, it's true."

"Why are you standing up?"

"To drink a toast to an honest man. A man of truth. They are as rare as hen's teeth."

Feeling mentally queasy, Martha watched Phillip, standing to attention, drink from his glass, not sure if he was being serious. She was never quite sure when Phillip was being serious or just fooling around.

"Is it true? Did your headmaster really tell you he wasn't sure whether there is a God? If there is no heaven and an afterlife, then the rest of his religion is false. He did not believe in the Bible. Did not believe in God."

"I believe every word of the philosophy of Jesus Christ who was here with us on earth and try to live by his teachings. But I'm still not sure if he was the son of God. What about the heavens we look up to at night away from the lights of New York? Astronomers now tell us the heavens go on forever. Universe after universe. Galaxy after galaxy. We're just a minute part in the whole of it, but we think and say we are omnipotent. That we have a God. That we will live forever in heaven or in hell. Maybe life just comes and goes. Evolves as Darwin said. Who knows, Martha? Just don't worry about our baby and let the life inside you grow by itself. And if there is a God, by the grace of God."

"Sit down, Phillip."

"Yes, my lady."

"Give me a hug."

"I worry about you, Martha."

"You told me not to worry. You're contradicting yourself."

"Maybe I am. But you're my wife. There's no rule about not worrying about your wife. We are having this baby together. You and I, Martha. We're in it together. Despite you having to do all the work. We made the child together. That's how it works."

"What happened to the boy who was not confirmed into the Church of England?"

"He was Jewish. They allowed one Jew into each house. There were ten houses in my boarding school. Ten Jews. In the morning at line-up before walking to chapel, he was made to step forward out of the line. Not back. Forward. Exposed for everyone to see. I can still remember his name: Asher Hyatt. I still feel for his humiliation. Can you imagine what it must have been like to be humiliated twice a day before morning and evening service? And three times on Sundays, including the eleven o'clock service."

"Did this headmaster with so much integrity condone such behaviour?"

"I think he was given his instructions like everyone else associated with the church. He could tell the truth only in private."

"Why did they allow Jews into the school in the first place?"

"I have no idea. To prove a point? To humiliate them?"

"Why did his parents choose that school?"

"There weren't that many Jewish public school around in those days.

They were either Church of England or Roman Catholic. The boy needed a good education to compete. Maybe they thought they were doing those ten pupils a favour. Frankly, I don't think so. It was all part of a bigger plan to make the Christian religion dominant. Otherwise, they would have put the ten boys in the same house. The world of politics and religion works in mysterious ways."

"What happened to Asher Hyatt?"

"I have no idea. At school he kept to himself. A lone Jew in a sea of Christians. As boys, we had no idea what was going on. We were too busy playing rugby and cricket. Learning our lessons."

"Has England changed since those days?"

"Has the world? Probably not. They're all fighting for position using whatever means: religion, democracy, capitalism, communism, nationalism, racism, gender, the old class system. Whatever works. And then they back it with the military: with nuclear weapons; weapons of mass destruction. Nothing has really changed down the centuries. It's the same old quest for power and dominance by whatever means. Colonialism is taboo because it did not suit you Americans. Destroy the British Empire and communism and America will rule the world. No longer Rule Britannia but God Bless America. Or maybe America is just an extension of the old British Empire. Who knows what the buggers are up to anywhere in the world? Why I liked living in the Zambezi Valley, far away from the twists and turns, the perversions and manipulations of mankind. Who knows? One day soon they'll be throwing nuclear bombs at each other and life on this earth will be over. The whole game will be over. Man will have self-destructed. And maybe there is a God. Maybe he's had enough of all our filth and wants to get rid of us. Who knows? Who knows what happened to Linda? Who knows what happened to Asher Hyatt? Who knows what's going to happen to the world? But does it matter? One day we're all going to die. Then we'll find if it's lights-out or heaven or hell. There's no point in constantly thinking or you go round and round. There is only one certainty in life. That we shall die. And only then find out what it was all about. What we are all meant to be doing. What the purpose was in being alive. You see what's happening now? I'm going round in circles. And yes, I'll be happy when you can drink with me again. There's nothing worse than getting drunk on one's own."

"Are you getting drunk, Phillip?"

"Not yet. But I will if I drink this whole bottle of wine. Good. You're smiling."

"I'll make us sandwiches."

"That's my girl."

In the kitchen, making the sandwiches, Martha was not sure if she felt any better, the same pain of fear and loneliness surging over her. The music had stopped. When she looked through the open kitchen door, Phillip was standing at the plate-glass window just staring at the lights of New York. Martha shuddered and went back to finish making the sandwiches. Phillip's expression was gaunt, unhappy and bewildered. And he was right. Would they ever know what it was all about? At least she was pregnant. That much was certain. For the rest, she would just have to wait and see.

When they went to bed, Phillip was happily drunk. Physically and mentally exhausted, Martha fell asleep, sleeping right through the night without a dream. In the morning when she woke she was feeling better. There was nothing better than a good night's sleep to improve the temperament. When she dressed and slipped out of the apartment to go to work, Phillip was lying on his side in the big bed, dead to the world. She had put a cup of tea beside the bed with a saucer on top to keep it warm. Outside in the street, teeming with people, she hailed a cab. When she arrived at the office, Jack Webber had gone to deliver his presentation to Liberty Soups. Jaz had not come into the office. Franklyn's door was closed. She walked through to her office, passing Priscilla at reception, giving her a smile. All morning, Martha worked the phones, promoting her clients' business, all thought of herself and her pregnancy far from her mind.

An hour after lunch, a packed lunch brought to her by Priscilla from the vendor who worked the offices, she heard Jack Webber shout out with excitement. All three executive offices opened, everyone smiling, the whole staff on their feet.

"We got it, folks. We done it. We got Liberty Soups."

"Welcome, partner."

"Thank you, Franklyn."

"Tonight we shall celebrate. Well done. Ten million dollars. We're all on a roll. All it takes is hard work and dedication, everyone. Never forget. Everyone clap for Jack Webber and then back to your desks."

Smiling, confident and in control of herself, Martha walked back into her office, closing the door behind her. Today she was happy. For all of them. There was nothing better than a good night's sleep to remove the blues. For a while, she stood looking out of her office window. There was noise, bustle and people. Another day in the life of New York.

"Now, where was I?"

Picking up the phone, Martha went back to her work, the time flying, the day going by. At five she went home to bathe and dress for the party. It was going to be a celebration. One big company celebration.

"He got it, Phillip. It's Bowden, Crookshank, Fairbanks and Webber. How was your day, honey?"

"A perfect day of leisure."

"First we relax with some coffee and music and then get ready for the party. It was quite some day at the office. Give your wife a kiss. Tomorrow we leave for England. I'm on holiday, can you believe it?"

"I'm so glad you're happy."

"There's nothing nicer than feeling happy."

"Tell me. I love feeling happy. Today we are all happy: Jonathan; Volker; Angie; Mary and the cat. A perfect day."

"Did you drink your tea this morning?"

"I did. A little cold. No, it was stone cold. But I drank my morning cup of tea. It started my day in a good mood. All day the sun was shining. I've finished packing. All we have to do tomorrow is put our suitcases in the cab and drive to the airport. Have you finished your packing? That's my girl. Nothing better than being married to an organised woman."

"Didn't you go to Harry B's?"

"Not today. Today is Franklyn's party. We'll arrive at seven-thirty-five on the dot. Five minutes late for a party. Five minutes early for an appointment. What my father taught me. On the way, I'll stop the taxi at a florist so we can give Joanne a nice bunch of flowers. Another old English tradition. All about having good manners."

Smiling at the long-lost habits of the English, Martha decided to take a bath instead of a shower, the music playing a Beethoven symphony, while Phillip read his book. For half an hour, Martha soaked in the bath, intermittently turning on the tap to keep the water warm.

"You'd better get out the bath, Martha."

"Coming. Which one was that?"

"Beethoven's Seventh. I've finished my book. I hate it when I've finished a book. Takes a while to get into a new one. Never mind. I'll twiddle my thumbs."

Listening to Phillip's prattle, Martha got out of the bath onto the mat and dried herself, before walking naked past Phillip into their bedroom.

"Can you see anything?"

"Of course I can. It's a naked woman."

"Our baby, stupid."

"Either you're getting fat or it's the baby. I love your bottom. Come here."

"Don't be silly. We're going out to dinner. There's a time and a place for everything."

"There's always time for love."

"You're talking sex."

"Love and sex. They're the same thing when you're married."

"What are you talking about?"

"Does it matter?"

"Not really."

3

An hour and a half later, Phillip carrying a bunch of yellow roses, they knocked on the door of Franklyn's apartment. When the door opened, Phillip offered the flowers. They were the first guests to arrive.

"For you, Joanne. For all your hard work. Hello, Tildy. That dress is very pretty. Good evening, Clarence. How's university? Franklyn, my friend. Congratulations on the new partner."

"I'll put the roses in a vase. They're lovely, Phillip. Thank you so much."

"My pleasure. My goodness. Just look at everything. This is going to be some party."

"Marcin Galinski's coming."

"I believe he is, Tildy."

"He's the most handsome man I've ever seen."

"And the richest. Or will be, when we float the company on the stock exchange. How are you finding New York?"

"Best decision Dad ever made. School is much more exciting. The people are more exciting. I love New York... Another knock on the door. I'll get it."

"Go and finish laying the table. I'll answer the door."

"Yes, Mother. Anything you say, Mother."

"Don't be rude. Hello, Jack. Welcome and congratulations. This must be Tammy. Come in, both of you, and I'll introduce you to everyone. I like your dress."

"Thank you, Mrs Bowden."

"Call me Joanne. You must be so proud of Jack... Hello, Jaz. And, hello!

You must be the famous Marcin Galinski I've heard so much about. Come in. Let the party begin. The drinks are on the sideboard. Everyone help themselves. Whisky, brandy, gin. And whatever you want to go with it. The corks are out of the wine bottles. Put on the music, Clarry. Don't stand around. Tildy, stop gawping. Lovely to have you all in my home."

Martha watched the men help themselves and their partners, Phillip bringing her a glass of lemonade. Tildy was right. Marcin was a handsome man; tall, athletic, not an ounce of fat on his body; a man in his twenties at the peak of his looks; an infectious smile that drew all the women. Without a cent in his pocket, he would have had the women running after him. A half-smile, the knowing smile of an older woman on her face, Martha approached the genius. It had been a lucky day for all of them when her client told her about the young man looking for start-up money, connecting Marcin Galinski to her Phillip.

"How's the launch going, Marcin?"

"Brilliant. Utterly brilliant. Today alone, I've had twenty-seven requests from the media for interviews. Everyone wanting to know more about the software. All thanks to you my publicist, Martha. And without Phillip, we would not have got started. The office is in chaos, everyone laughing and smiling. Can't even imagine it going better, Martha. When do we go public, Phillip?"

"When you crack the hundred million paying customers."

"Take a while."

"I'll leave you two to talk business."

Watching Phillip return to the improvised bar on the sideboard, Martha turned back to Marcin.

"Congratulations, Marcin, on the baby."

"What baby, Martha?"

"The one growing in your lovely Jasmine's belly."

"You're pregnant! Why the hell didn't you tell me, Jaz?"

"I was waiting for the right moment."

"The right moment was when you found out you were pregnant."

"Don't get annoyed with me, Marcin."

"Of course I'm annoyed. You said you were on the pill. I'm far too young to be a father. For God's sake! What's the matter with you? Have you arranged for an abortion?"

"Of course not."

"I'm out of here. You conned me, Jaz. We live together because it's convenient. It's an affair. Not a marriage. You lied to me about birth control.

Are you out of your mind? I've got more than enough on my plate without some woman getting herself pregnant."

"I thought we loved each other, Marcin."

"Love! When did we mention love? I don't want marriage and children at my age. Let's go. We can sort this out in private."

"We can't leave the party. It's a launch celebration for your software."

"Are you coming with me or not?"

"I'm staying."

"Then to hell with you. And get your stuff out of my apartment. Pregnant! What are women going to get up to next? I suppose getting the Linguare account for your business was all part of the plan. I must be so naïve not to have seen it. Goodnight to you all. Goodbye to you all. Pregnant! That's all I needed. Get yourself an abortion, Jaz, and send me the bill."

Martha, having put her foot in it, looked from Marcin to Jaz and back again.

"Go with him, Jaz. I'm sorry. You said you'd told him. That you loved him. Go sort this out now for your own sake and the sake of your baby. Now, Jaz! Don't just stand there. You two live together. There must be more to it than lust. I'm sorry for putting my foot in it, Marcin. You two go off and talk. Forget the party. Your child is at stake. Off you go. And don't do anything either of you will later regret. And we did not con you at Bowden, Crookshank and Fairbanks, Marcin. We did a good job. The best job. You said so yourself. Those twenty-seven reporters would not have come anywhere near you without my help. Both of you go and calm down. You have a lot at stake, Marcin. People fight in relationships. Ask me and Phillip. We broke up after we lost our first baby. Now we're happy and having another baby. When the news has sunk in, think rationally and you'll work it all out. Be sensible, Marcin."

"How the hell is this meant to work now?"

"You make it work. Off you go, both of you. Talk to Aunty Martha when she comes back from England... Now, everyone. Let's get back to our party and celebrate Jack's success. And Tildy, pull your face up from the floor. There we go. I'll open the front door for you, Marcin. It's called a lover's tiff. After you make love, it will all blow over. You'll have a lot of fun being a young father. You can teach him yourself to play baseball. Talk, you two. All you got to do is talk. And make love."

After watching Marcin stride away down the corridor followed by a terrified Jaz, Martha closed the front door and turned back to the party.

"That went well! Silly girl. Never lie about a pregnancy. If I wasn't pregnant myself, I'd have a double scotch. Stop gawping, everyone. It's over.

One way or another, it's over. I wonder how many times in our own ancestral history that's happened? The chance of life. How it happens. How we all got here. Right from the very beginning. By tomorrow, the thought of having a son will have sunk in and Marcin will be dancing on the moon. Part of human nature. Why we've survived. Sorry. I'm doing a Phillip. What's for supper, Joanne? Life. You never know what's coming next."

"Rack of lamb."

"One of my favourites. And Phillip's too. Any food is my favourite when I'm hungry. What a day. And tomorrow we fly to England. Holiday time. Holiday in September. Come and dance, Phillip. The night is young. You have a good taste in dance music, Clarence."

"You think she'll be all right?"

"Of course she will be, Phillip. Everything is going to work out just fine. Let's drink to that infinitesimal chance of life. The chance of happiness. Give me a splash of red wine in a glass and I'll give you the toast... Thank you, honey... To life, everyone. To life. To life, love, and happiness."

"And if it's a girl?"

"He'll be even happier."

"I don't think I want to be a fly on that wall tonight. For a moment I thought he was going to hit her. How people change. Never would have thought it with young Marcin. Maybe the pressure of business has got to him. Poor Jaz. Maybe that's why she was scared to tell him. There's another side to the genius we haven't seen. Charming when he gets what he wants, not so charming when he doesn't. And if he's got a temper like that I'd be better off with my money somewhere else. Oh, wow. Whatever happened to the peace of my African valley?... Dance, Martha. Don't just stand there."

"Poor Jasmine."

"We all feel sorry for the woman. But who's right? Maybe she deliberately got herself pregnant to nail down his money. Too much money can be deadly. Gets people killed. Some people will do anything to get their hands on money. Someone else's money."

"Not our Jaz."

"Of course not. What was I thinking?"

"And she's good at her job. She's done far more for Linguare than me. It's her account. Oh well, if we lose it there are always plenty more out there. She'll have to keep her wits about her tonight, our Jasmine. Funny how you suddenly go off people. Did you see that look on his face when I told him she was pregnant? If looks could kill. Shame on him. Thank goodness we're flying out tomorrow, honey. It's better to let people sort out their own problems instead of being dragged into the argument. You're very good at dancing, Phillip."

"Of course I am. Smile, Martha. Don't worry. It's their problem."

"I really put my foot in it."

"That you did. That's better. You're giggling. I love it when you giggle. Did that splash of wine taste nice?"

"You have no idea. Do I not love a good glass of wine?"

"When our baby is born, we'll put him or her in a crib in the evening, tuck him or her in, and crack a bottle or two of our favourite wine. If he or she wakes, you can breastfeed the little bugger while looking out of the plate-glass window. When he or she is two years old we'll take him or her on safari. Got it all planned. You can't worry about other people's problems, Martha. Doesn't work."

"Poor Jasmine. She'll never have an abortion."

"I'm sure she won't. What she'll need is a friend. All of us will be her friends. I can smell the lamb cooking. Smells good. Don't know about you but I'm hungry."

"Do you think I should phone her later?"

"Leave it, Martha. All will be revealed in the fullness of time. It always is. The good or the bad."

"It was my fault."

"No, it wasn't. It was nobody's fault. It was nature. How it works. How life works. You have sex and the girl gets pregnant. Why are you looking guilty?"

"That's what happened to me the first time."

"And look at us now. Happy as pigs in shit."

"I wouldn't have put it quite like that, Phillip."

"But you know what I mean. Here we are. Dancing cheek to cheek."

"I love you, Phillip."

"Of course you do. And I love you, Martha. Gave young Tildy a fright. Did you see her face? Oh, well. What can you do?"

"You're prattling, again."

"You love it."

"I know I do. Prattling is part of the lovely gentle side of life. A soft breeze that blows over you, making you content. Two people who get on with each other, content with their world. We're lucky, Phillip. We have a beautiful apartment with the best view in the world. We both have money which prevents any thought of either of us using the other. We're equals. And we are about to have our own family. What more can you want in this crazy world? I feel sorry for Marcin. All that money and good looks, the ability to play sport, and if he isn't careful he'll blow it all out of the window. Whatever he says or thinks, that baby inside Jaz is his. Killing your own baby by having an abortion is the same as killing yourself. You live on in your children. I'm not sure if I like our Marcin anymore."

"Wasn't Jaz trying to trap him?"

"Does it matter if you and your partner are going to have a baby? The chance of life is so small. The chance of who we are. Which sperm fertilises which egg, the chance so small it's infinitesimal. And when we get the chance of life on this earth we must do the best we can. That baby is the lucky one. A life is growing in Jasmine's belly in the same way it is growing in mine. All four of us have a chance of leaving part of ourselves behind, giving our lives a true purpose. There's more to life than making yourself rich. We've both said the good life is about having our own family, passing on our parents' lives to our children. I know your mother died young in a terrible accident but she lives on in you and Randall, in Randall's sons.. In the baby inside my stomach... Now the music has stopped. I think it must be supper time. Poor Jaz. Poor Marcin. Poor baby. Let's hope for all of them he will come to his senses... Just look at that rack of lamb. I'm hungry. I've been eating more and more ever since you got me pregnant. What a world, Phillip. What a life. Let's just hope the two of them work it out. For the sake of the baby, if not for themselves... Do you need any help, Franklyn, with the food?"

"You think we'll lose the Linguare account?" The worried look on Franklyn's face made Martha look straight into his eyes.

"Who knows? Who cares? What I care about is that poor, innocent baby."

"Of course. I was thinking selfishly."

"Let the party go on."

"You think Jaz will come back again?"

"If she's got any sense she'll screw his brains out first. If he's got any. You can make a pile of money in this life and still not have any brains. But he's young. They'll work it out. How life goes on, Franklyn. That food looks perfectly delicious, Joanne. All your own hard work. Much appreciated. There's nothing better than good home cooking. Let's eat, everyone. My mouth is watering at the very look of it. And if he takes the account away from us because of his argument with Jaz, it'll be his loss, not ours. We're good. Really good. Don't ever forget how good we are, everyone. You can't win 'em all. You can't help 'em all. Poor Jasmine. My poor friend, Jasmine... Ah, the music is back on again, thanks to Clarry."

"Are you looking forward to your trip to England tomorrow?"

"Never felt more like having a holiday, Joanne. After that little balls-up. I really put my foot in it. Fly, fly away. It's a strange old world, everyone. Make the best of it. And don't forget, today Jack landed us Liberty Soups. Well done, partner. Let's all enjoy ourselves. I'm going to have a baby. And so is Jaz."

After everyone had served themselves, they all sat in silence looking down at their plates, no one sure what to talk about. Franklyn walked around pouring wine into their crystal glasses, all except Martha's. Marcin had knocked the stuffing out of the party. When Franklyn sat down at the head of his table they all began to eat. With the wine, the smiles came back on their faces, along with the chatter. The party broke up soon after they had eaten the pudding. Downstairs, Phillip hailed a taxi, opening the door for Martha, Martha feeling flat as a pancake.

"Are you going to offload your shares in Linguare, Phillip?"

"Some of them. I was going to do that anyway. When the value of a share goes up like that it's silly to be greedy and wait for the IPO. After all your successful publicity efforts, the shares are worth more and more. But what I saw tonight frightened me. He's too big for his boots. People like that make mistakes and we have no need to be part of it. I shall tell Franklyn. There are many investors out there who want to get in privately, before the company goes public, in expectation of the IPO. We three should all begin to disinvest. Jaz did us a favour tonight by not having told him she was carrying his baby. Tonight I saw another Marcin Galinski, a Marcin I do not like. We carry on as if nothing happened while quietly off-loading our shares."

"And if the shares double at the IPO?"

"Then we will have done a favour to the people who buy our shares. In and out is the right way to be a successful venture capitalist. Put in the start-up money, get the company going, and get out. I have never had any control over the running of the company despite having put up the initial capital. For no other reason than not knowing the first thing about computer software. Go with your gut, Martha. That's my philosophy. What I've done all my life. And tonight, after thinking it through at Joanne's lovely dinner, my gut tells me to get out of Linguare.com."

"You're good at business, Phillip."

"I know nothing about business. What I'm saying now is plain common sense, something my stepmother, Bergit, told me to listen to ever since I was a child. If doing good business is using one's common sense, then I'm a good businessman. Anyway, tonight's over. We're going straight to bed when we get home. Tomorrow is a long day. A good sleep will do us both the power of good."

"What's she going to do if he dumps her?"

"Have a baby. What pregnant women do. Even if you lose the Linguare account, she's not going to lose her job. She's good at the business of advertising, as are you, Jack and Franklyn. The business will survive. My guess is he'll come crawling back. He needs you more than you need him. There are plenty of single mothers in America. Jaz will just be one of them. But who knows? We'll find out more when we get back from England... Here we are. We're home. Mine, yours and our baby's. Let the game go on."

"What game, Phillip?"

"The game of life, Martha. The game of life."

PART 5

SEPTEMBER TO OCTOBER 1994 — "JUST A LINK IN THE CHAIN"

1

The plane took off at seven o'clock in the morning. After the rush to the airport, Phillip was able to relax, idly looking out of the small window, his mind far away. He was thinking about his family, and the wonderful times he had had with Randall growing up on World's View, the two of them helping each other through the trauma of losing their mother. Randall remembered nothing of their mother, Phillip remembered little. He knew her grave at the top of the two-thousand-foot escarpment overlooking the Zambezi Valley where his father had planted the wooden cross with the words 'Go well, my darling' burned into the horizontal crosspiece. Thinking of the lonely cross in the great silence of Africa made the tears come to his eyes. When all the other English were kicked out of Zimbabwe, her bones would be all that was left.

"Why are you crying, Phillip?"

"Am I? I'm sorry. I was thinking of the grave of my mother, a mother who will never see her grandchildren. It's all so far, far away. Another life. A life forgotten, and not just the life of my mother. The life of the old, colonial Rhodesia. Never mind. When we come back from England we should take a side trip and visit your mother in Kansas City. Give her a surprise. You can extend your holiday by a couple of days. Part of being your own boss. You can do what you like. Five more hours, Martha, then the family fun begins. I miss my family. Always have done. We were all so much part of each other's lives on the farm. Now, look. Here comes our breakfast on a trolley. Thank you, kind lady. Eggs, sausage and whatever for both of us. And tea for me.

Coffee for my wife. We're on our way to England, but you know that... There we are, Martha. Breakfast on our laps."

"If it's a girl, why don't we call her Carmen? In memory of your mother."

"What a wonderful idea. She'll live again through our child. Would you mind?"

"You were crying... How's your breakfast?"

"Not quite like breakfast on the farm. But it will do... Carmen. Our child is going to be Carmen."

Trying to imagine his mother made Phillip think of his grandfather, Ben Crossley, Carmen's father, the man who had left him all the money, some of which he had used for the start-up capital he had invested in Marcin Galinski. The world indeed went round in strange circles: from the glamour of Hollywood to a lonely grave at the top of an escarpment, to a company building its fortune on computer technology. Would Phillip's great-grandparents have ever imagined that future for their descendants? And what was the future a few more generations down the line? Where would the world be, if it hadn't blown itself to pieces? It all made Phillip think as he sat, his head turned sideways to the small, round window, as the plane droned on and on, further away from the new America, nearer to the old England, an empire beginning, an empire lost forever. Despite the good sleep from the previous night, Phillip fell into his dreams, a small boy running through the wilds looking for his mother and shouting 'where are you, Mother', the tears down his face, the feeling of loss excruciating. In his dream, Phillip reached the grave of his mother, the cross bent back at an angle, Phillip screaming in his nightmare.

"What's the matter, honey?"

"I was dreaming."

"You were jerking in your seat. Must have been a horrible dream."

"It was. How long before we land?"

"A couple of hours."

"Did I sleep that long? How lucky. Flying is boring. Sitting for hours wedged in the same seat. I hate travelling on aeroplanes."

"Gets you there a whole lot quicker than in a sailing ship. Can you imagine relying on the wind to blow you back to England? Or blow you anywhere?"

"Must have been a whole lot of fun."

"What were you dreaming about?"

"My birth-mother."

"Poor Phillip. Must be terrible to have never known your mother. Poor Jaz. Poor Marcin. Life can be such a mess."

Two hours later, when the plane began its descent, the excitement came back. He wasn't home, because his home was in Africa, but it was the next best thing.

"Let the holiday begin, Martha. Here we are. Good old England."

An hour later, Phillip was shaking the hand of his father, kissing his stepmother, Bergit, shaking the hand of his half-brother Craig, holding his nephew Harold, and smiling at Jojo who couldn't stop smiling.

"Where's Randall, Dad?"

"On the Isle of Man. You're booked to fly to Douglas on Wednesday. Give me your suitcases. Good to see you, son. Well, here we are. Three families of Crookshanks. Let's go. It's eight o'clock in London. Another hour before we get to Chelsea. Did you have supper on the plane?"

"Breakfast and lunch. It's the time difference."

"Of course. I hate airports. Too many damn people."

"Thanks for coming, Dad."

"My pleasure. What else are fathers for than picking up their son at the airport? You look happy, Martha. How's my new grandson coming along?"

"Just fine. Everything is good."

"I'm so happy for both of you. We've got a couple of bottles of French champagne on ice back at the flat. I know you don't drink at the moment, Martha, but we'll all drink a glass to you and each other. I miss my sons. All of them. As I miss Myra. You have your kids and then they fly the nest. Such a shame."

"How it works."

"Of course it is, Phillip. The car's in the parking lot. September. Such a lovely month is September."

"It's Martha's favourite... Now, where do I begin?"

"At the beginning, Phillip. At the beginning. We want to hear all your news. When Bergit and I have pumped you dry you can go and relax with your brother on that nice island in the Irish Sea."

"What's he doing now?"

"Writing. They're both writing, hidden away on their small farm among chickens and the dog. They had two border collies but gave them to the neighbouring farm. The two little sods were always escaping and rounding up their sheep. Farmer was happy to take them over."

"Is London getting any better for you?"

"Too many people. Too much noise. Everyone wants to know your business. I miss the solitude of the farm where a man can think in peace. And everything you do in London costs money. How's New York?"

"The apartment looks out from the forty-ninth floor right over New York, buildings as far as you can see. If it's a girl, Martha wants to call her Carmen."

Crammed into the car, the luggage in the boot, the journey from the Heathrow Airport to Chelsea began, Phillip's father concentrating on the early evening traffic. With the mention of Carmen, the family, all except ten-month-old Harold, had gone silent, no one knowing what to say. In his small, pudgy hand, Harold held a miniature toy trumpet which he blew into regularly, making a noise more like the sound of a squeaking flute, while he bounced on his mother's knee.

"Have you heard from your father in Zimbabwe, Jojo?"

"Not a thing, Phillip. I doubt they even talk about us. We don't exist. What happens when you don't marry who you are told to marry and stay in the tribe. Never mind. They have their lives. We have ours. Doing charity work for an NGO, raising money for impoverished people, is highly satisfying for me and Craig. It also pays us a salary. And with young Harold, I don't have time to worry about my African family. I've joined a new tribe. The English. I like living in London. You can't get bored living in London. And we're happy. All that counts. He's going to be a musician when he grows up. The moment he's old enough, we're going to send him to singing classes. Have him taught to play the piano, the guitar, a trumpet. There's a place for Afro-Europeans in the music industry. Got to think ahead."

"So you're not going back to Zimbabwe?"

"Whatever for? If it weren't for charities, half the people in Mugabe's Zimbabwe would starve. Within a few years with all the farm expropriation, Zimbabwe will have to import most of its food. Which is where we come in. Despite what he says in public, Mugabe and his friends are not interested in the welfare of the people, they're only interested in building up money in their off-shore bank accounts."

"So what will happen?"

"There will be another revolution. Followed by another incompetent dictator. My father's life in a rural village doesn't require modern, competent management. The new cities are different. Why away from the suburbs of the elite politicians and their backers, the cities are turning into slums."

"Will it ever come right?"

"Of course. Someone else will run the place. This time it will be the Chinese. We Africans were not born to live in cities. We were born in happy villages and taught to feed ourselves, not to rely on other people. Cattle and crops. All you need for a happy life in rural Africa. Why my father's so annoyed with me for leaving the family and all our traditions."

"It's one big world these days, Jojo."

"Of course it is. One big, global village. Harold here will be fine. He's part of both worlds. Aren't you, my darling?"

"Your English has greatly improved."

"Should have done with all my reading. If you want to fit in to a new life, you've got to learn. Education. What Mugabe once preached, seeing he was a teacher. But that's all gone now. It's all about power. Holding onto power. The moment a dictator loses power, they kill him. Along with his rich cronies. Now Europe is trying to trace and freeze their offshore bank accounts. Makes me laugh. Oh, well. What can a girl like me do except look after my baby? When's your baby due, Martha?"

"Four months' time."

"I'm glad for you. We're all glad for you."

"Are you going to teach Harold Shona?"

"Probably not, Phillip. Shona won't be much good to him in the world of music. You got to think ahead. How it works."

"How everything works, Jojo. Why do you think the Chinese will take over?"

"They want the minerals. Whatever is in the ground. Forget the virtues of communism. And not just in my country. In the whole of Africa. The whole of mineral-rich Africa. The Chinese are coming, Phillip. Once it was the British, the French, the Portuguese and the Belgians. Even a few countries in Africa were colonised by the Germans. They all wanted land and minerals. Cheap labour to grow their tobacco and send it back to England. Nothing changes. Before the European invasions, the tribes of Africa fought with each other over the land. The trick is to live in the moment, which is why we are in England away from all the uncertainty. Maybe one day we'll go back. Craig says you never know what's coming next in life."

"A glass of champagne by the sound of it."

"That will be nice. My little boy just loves playing that trumpet."

From Jojo to Craig to Bergit, Phillip listened to the prattle, not sure if it made any sense, not sure if life itself made sense. They were all chasing something. Phantoms in the sky. Dreams of the mind. Running from the fear of insecurity. Each trying to survive in the whirl, the greed and sometimes the nastiness of humanity, all going round and round. He was tired, exhausted from the stress of flying. Instead of worrying, he let his mind go blank. When they arrived at his father's Chelsea home he took the luggage out of the boot and followed his family inside the block of flats. Everything inside the flat was ready: the cold supper on the long table covered by a light white gauze, the champagne in the fridge, the fluted glasses waiting for them on the sideboard, the spare room ready for himself and Martha with sweets on the pillows to remind Phillip of his childhood. From the bedroom, putting down their suitcases, he heard the pop of the cork coming out of the champagne bottle. Back in the lounge, he was given a glass of champagne by his smiling father, the cloth over the food having been removed displaying the sliced cold beef and the pieces of chicken, Bergit mixing the salad dressing into the big, wooden salad bowl. They toasted the family reunion and sat down at the dining room table. From the couch behind Phillip, he could hear his nephew blowing his trumpet to get attention, only his mother taking any notice. By the end of the meal, and the second bottle of expensive champagne, they were all ready for bed, Jojo and Craig sleeping on the pull-out couch in the lounge. It was the end of Phillip's evening, the end of the journey that had taken him home to his family. For a long while, he lay awake next to the sleeping Martha, listening to the sounds of London: the sound of traffic, the hoot of a horn, the wind blowing over the Thames. In the quiet of the bedroom behind the drawn curtains, Phillip fell into his dreams.

2

The days of family went on through until Wednesday when the next journey to the Isle of Man began. It was the first week in October, the wind blustery, with dark clouds scurrying across the sky. When the plane landed at the small airport near the town of Douglas, Randall was waiting for his brother. They shook hands, smiles on their faces, the old, male English traditional greeting. In Phillip's upbringing, you shook a man's hand and kissed the cheek of a woman. No hugging as it was considered undignified by well-bred Englishmen, all part of the old vanishing class system.

"How are they?"

"Where's Meredith? They're fine. Jojo's just finished reading the entire works of Dickens. Can you believe it? To improve her English. That girl's got brains."

"She's near the end of her new children's book. Wanted to try and finish. It's a downhill race at the end."

"Sorry to interrupt."

"She's looking forward to some company. To some woman's talk with Martha... That's all you've got? Let's go. Good to see you, you old bastard. The weather's changing. The moment September goes out, the winter comes in. But we survive. Big log fires. Thick curtains over the windows. The perfect place to write. Never was able to write a book with people around. I'm going to enjoy this break. Every now and again you need a break from writing. A time to get back into your own mind instead of the minds of your characters. All this must sound like rubbish to you two. Martha, you look radiant. How's the great US of A? I avoid going over to see my publishers. All that media attention drives me crazy. Never understand it all. Why does a man need a publicist? No offence, Martha. My books should talk for themselves. Not me. They read my books, not me."

"How do you get them to pick up your book, Randall, if they've never heard of it? People have to be told what they want to read. Or the good book sits on the shelf."

"Word of mouth."

"They're too busy talking to each other about themselves. Advertising. That's the modern world."

"How's the new company coming along that Phillip told me about?"

"Apart from one of my business partners deliberately getting herself impregnated by the owner of our client without telling him, everything is good."

"Whoops. How old is she?"

"Young. They're both young."

"You see that mountain over there? The only mountain on the Isle of Man. That's Snaefell. The house is below the mountain, away from the sea. In winter you can see snow on top of that mountain. Peace and quiet. Just perfect for a couple of reclusive writers."

"Do you hate people?"

"Only sometimes, Martha. I've hated a few in New York when they tried to use me to get a story."

"You can't have it both ways. They either write about you and you sell your books, or your books stay in obscurity."

"You're probably right. Initially, I loved all the attention. When we get what we want we're inclined to be selfish."

"When are you coming over?"

"Soon. Or they won't publish my next book."

"Can't you introduce us to Villiers Publishing? Bowden, Crookshank, Fairbanks and Webber would have their advertising account."

"Aren't they a bit big for a company that has just got started?"

"Got to shoot for the moon, Randall."

"How's the baby?"

"Fine. Stopped drinking. Stopped worrying. And I leave the office at five o'clock in the evening. How's the little Douglas? Did you call him after Douglas the town?"

"We say it was a coincidence but it wasn't. He was born here in a clinic. He's fine."

"Are you going to have any more?"

"We hope so... There we are. One Land Rover. Luggage in the back. We can all sit up front. I'm going to drive round the coast. Show you the beauty of our little island."

"Do you ever go to Ireland?"

"Not yet. We're happy at home just writing our books."

"You're lucky, Randall."

"I know I am, Phillip. Next best thing to World's View."

"Do you have any friends in the Isle of Man?"

"None that we know of. We keep to ourselves. No one knows who we are. We're Randall and Meredith. Not those writers with the famous American publishers with millions of readers. Better to stay anonymous. Keeps everyone happy. We're just the couple with the kid on the next smallholding. How we all like it. Fame can be cruel, Phillip. Can crucify you. Kill you. As it has done a lot of other famous artists. Not worth it. I just like doing the writing. How it's going to stay."

"Until you get to New York."

"Until we get to New York. But there is there. And here is here. Never the twain to meet."

As they drove around the coast, Martha and Phillip looking out of the Land Rover's window, Randall concentrating on the road ahead, Phillip felt a shaft of jealousy for the perfection of his brother's life. Randall had something to do with his day. For Phillip, it was all about having something to do. A writer had an all-absorbing hobby that stopped the boredom of sitting alone in a swank New York apartment with only money and venture capitalism to think about, an old homeless violin player, an old woman with a stray cat, a bar called Harry B's. Randall had purpose. Phillip had none. Staring at the waves breaking on the shore, Phillip wondered if there was something wrong with him. Or had his life been too easy? Born into a family of wealth. Never once in his life having to worry about money; to never even imagine not having money in his bank account. It had all been too easy. For others, millions of others, even billions, every day was a physical grind to make enough money to pay the bills, to pay off the debt, to try and save for an uncertain future. What was life like in a permanent state of poverty, with no way out of the trap? And there he was with all the money in the world a man could ever need to satisfy materialism while often, alone, he was bored out of his mind. Life's ironies never failed to make Phillip wonder what life was meant to be all about. In his mind, he floated out of the car and hovered over the sea, a sea that rolled to the shore long before man had come to the tiny island that Randall now called home. A seagull spoke to Phillip, calling and calling, crying in the sky, mocking man and his worthless world that came for each of them and went without any purpose. Would his Carmen have a life? Would she find the answer and purpose for an existence? Sadly, floating with the gulls looking down, Phillip's imagination doubted it.

"You know, some people at our age are grandparents."

"What did you say, Randall? Why is the cry of a seagull so damn melancholic?"

"Some women get pregnant at sixteen. By the time they reach their middle thirties their daughter has had a kid. Happened a lot in the last century when men married very young girls. Getting married at seventeen was quite the norm for a girl. The perfect beauty of youth, I suppose. Easier for the father to trade. Then the poor girl had nine children. Can you even imagine all that work in the house? Even if you had servants... Seagulls like to cry when they're floating on the thermals. It's their way of talking to each other... You think us three will live long enough to become grandparents?"

"What's the new book about?"

"People. They're all about people."

"Do they enjoy their lives?"

"Some of them. Some of the time."

"Are you happy, Randall?"

"Of course I am, brother. I'm a married man with a son, a nice home and a book to write. What more could a man ask for from life? Are you happy, Phillip?"

"Of course I am... Do you get penguins in the Isle of Man?"

"Never seen one. We turn off the road here. Doesn't take long. It's just a little island. Welcome to Rabbit Farm."

"Why Rabbit Farm?"

"Plenty of wild rabbits. No foxes. We're having rabbit stew for supper tonight. There's Meredith and Douglas. Wave, everyone. Can you believe it? It isn't raining. Up closer, how do you like our mountain?"

"Have you climbed it?"

"Many times. Up one side and down the other. When the girls are nattering, we'll go for a climb. Here they are, darling. Straight from America. What's for lunch?"

"Ham, eggs and chips. Are you hungry?"

"I'm always hungry. How did it go?"

"Douglas woke up and broke my concentration. Kids can drive you nuts. Hello, Martha. Hello, Phillip. Welcome to the writers' nuthouse. All we do here is write stories down on paper... Tea or coffee? Douglas, this is your Uncle Phillip and your Aunty Martha. It's about to rain. Come in. I put on the kettle when I heard the car. Wow, this is fun. People. Other people. Come in. How do you like my house? Randall tells me you're pregnant. Congratulations. What life is all about. Having children. It's just so fulfilling. It's our little island set in a silver sea. I love plagiarising Shakespeare... The dog's name is Polar Bear. He's a white Alsatian. I'll introduce you to the cats later. Seven of them. Mother and her grown-up litter. I love animals. They never answer back, do you, Polar Bear? He has a bad habit of sitting on the lounge furniture. But what can you do? It's so nice to have company, isn't it, Randall? We've both been so looking forward to your visit. All we have here is the wind, the sea and the mountain. A world of our own... Tea or coffee, Martha? I don't have to ask Phillip. The Crookshanks all drink tea."

"I'm sorry to interrupt your writing. Coffee would be nice."

"Instant, I'm afraid... Don't worry. I'm probably just writing letters to myself. Villiers Publishing gave me a fifty-thousand dollar advance for *Talking to the Animals* but they still haven't published my book. We think the money was just encouragement to keep me writing and give me something to do so Randall can write his bestsellers and make Villiers Publishing all that money. And it worked. When we go over, we'll have another go at them. The new book is about cats. Six of them. From the same litter. They all talk, of course. The oldest male has perfect English. They all live here on Rabbit Farm. Sometimes I'm not sure if my own cats are real or part of my imagination. Do I sound crazy, Phillip?"

"Not at all. A short while back I was flying with the seagulls over the sea."

"Good for you. We're all out of our minds."

"What's it called?"

"*Party for Pussycats*. How does it sound? There you are, Martha. One cup of instant coffee. Let's go and sit in the lounge and let the tea brew in the pot for a moment. Tell me about the real world. What's been happening out there? We don't have television. Lots of music and books. Television distracts the mind. The news is always awful. Who's killing who at the moment. The news in the days when I had television was always negative. Or about some celebrity getting herself drunk. All about publicity, I suppose, Martha. All the same old game."

"Phillip calls it the game of life."

"Then I wasn't wrong. One day, when Douglas gets older, we'll have to rejoin the real world. For now, it's nice to live in peace... Polar Bear spread out on the couch. Look at the way he looks at me. One dog and seven cats on my couch. Mother and six children... What are we going to do today? Company. It's so exciting. Funny how you don't miss company until you have it. For a few days after you're both gone, it'll be lonely. Then you get used to it... Animals! Off the couch! There you go. Good as gold. Don't know what I'd do without my animals. Those over there, or the ones in my head. I'm going to light the fire now it's raining. When it doesn't rain, we go for our walks. Well, here's me doing all the chattering. What happens when you've been without company for so long. I have a bad habit of talking out loud to myself. You'll have to put up with me until I've talked too much. We all talk too much, I suppose. Just look at that rain coming down. You timed it perfectly. I'll stop jabbering and pour the tea. Milk in last. An old habit from my upbringing in Liverpool. My father has been with the same insurance company for over forty years. The Liverpool, London and Globe Insurance Company. Not that you want to know. Can you imagine working for the same company all those years? He'll retire soon with a nice pension and not a damn thing to do for the rest of his life. Would you like a biscuit with your tea, Phillip? Why are you laughing?"

"It all sounds just so familiar. When you've made everything or inherited everything, all you're left with is boredom."

"You can't be bored. You live in New York. You don't know how lucky you are."

"Would you like to live in New York, Meredith?"

"I'd love to. Except we wouldn't be able to write. You enjoy what you have in life. What's the secret? How's little Harold, Phillip?"

"He likes blowing his trumpet. Jojo's just finished reading the entire works of Dickens."

"My goodness. Do you want that biscuit?"

"I'd love one. I've got two cats on my lap."

"You're lucky you haven't got seven of them."

"Have they got fleas?"

"Not too many. I rub powder in their fur."

"Have you read Randall's new book?"

"He won't let me read anything until it's finished. Then I'll do the typing. We both write in longhand. Best way to go. Lets you concentrate better. We tried making Douglas's bedroom soundproof so we could work without interruption but it didn't work. I worried about him too much when I couldn't hear. Totally blocked my writing. Randall tried writing in the shed. Didn't like the place. Too cold. Couldn't get settled into the world of his book and drift away with his characters. I'm a mother, a typist and a writer who will most likely never publish a book. They tell you your book would be a bestseller if you had already published a bestseller. Makes sense. People read authors they know. Randall was lucky to get started. We shall just have to see. Hope springs eternal. We have our life which is a lot better than most people's. I'm trying to have another baby. My mother always says that if you're going to do a job, do it properly. Three kids. That's my aim... Biscuit, Martha? Help yourself from the tin. A biscuit tin. Relic from my grandmother. She always had her biscuit tin handy when we kids visited. You would have liked my grandmother. All my grandparents are dead. Sad, really. Life comes and goes. Nothing lasts forever. There's always a new generation to fight their way through the world. Fight their way through life... Before you go to bed, I'll light the fire in your bedroom if you like. There are fires in every room. If you're cold, that is. Got to look after our guests."

Listening to his sister-in-law spilling out words, Phillip's jealousy for Randall's way of life evaporated. Under the constant gush of words, he could see Meredith's unease. She was all on her own, however happy she thought she was being married with a son. A woman needed someone to talk to. Needed a friend. Randall had his imaginary friends that talked to him through writing his book. Idly, not hearing a word Meredith was talking about, he wondered if his brother's marriage really worked. Whether Randall put his books before his wife. An all-consuming passion that excluded everyone else from his life. It made Phillip think his life in New York wasn't so bad after all. Covered in cats, he drank his tea, keeping his thoughts to himself. The white dog, lying flat on its stomach on the floor in front of Phillip, head on its outstretched paws, was watching him, a knowing look twinkling in its eyes. Phillip leaned forward, forcing a cat off his lap, and stroked the top of the dog's head. It was so good to be back among animals, the thought sending a shaft of loss through his mind. Maybe the trick in life was to store up memories, relive his past life in the African bush through his memories. Not getting enough attention, the baby began to cry, kicking his feet against the base of the pushchair, pulling at the strap around his waist. Smiling to himself, Phillip watched his nephew take back the centre of attention, stopping his mother's flow of words. The rain outside had stopped as quickly as it had begun.

"You want to go for a walk, Randall? Let the girls talk. Wouldn't mind stretching my legs. My biggest fear when flying is getting the cramps."

"Let's go. Just like the old days. The Crookshank brothers on safari. We've had some pretty varied lives, brother."

"Don't tell me."

"Did you bring some boots? We're the same size so you can borrow a pair of mine. Boots and a raincoat. How it works on Rabbit Farm. When we get back from our walk, I'll open the bar. Sundowners, even if the sun doesn't set at six o'clock. They all drank too much in Rhodesia. Partly the war. Mostly something to do. Meredith and I open the bar every night. Probably not good for us but who cares? Got to enjoy yourself. See you later, girls. Have fun... Just look at my dog. You only have to mention going for a walk and that dog goes berserk... How were Dad and Bergit? You can tell me all about them. Is he miserable, stuck in a flat all day?"

"Probably. Tries to make the best of it. He's lucky. He's still got money. Many of those old Rhodesians living in England are broke. Living off the largesse of the British government and charity. All the hard work of their previous lives down the drain. Are you really going to stay here for the rest of your life?"

"When Douglas gets older, we'll have to move nearer to people. Life's a constant change, brother. Try these on. Grab that raincoat on the stand... Biscuits and tea. I like biscuits and tea."

Trying on the boots with the dog watching with explosive anticipation, Phillip got himself ready.

"Do you like walking in the rain, Randall?"

"You get used to it. You get used to anything in the end. Have a good natter, you two. See you later, alligator."

"In a while, crocodile."

Outside, beneath black clouds scudding in front of the wind, the brothers strode from the house.

"We all talk so much crap."

"But it's fun, Randall."

"I suppose it is. We'll walk to the mountain, or we can walk to the sea."

"Let's walk to the sea. We can climb Snaefell when the clouds aren't so threatening. Do you remember those early days on World's View when we used to get out of the house on our own and walk for hours? With a gun."

"Always with a gun. I remember them as if it was yesterday. All our yesterdays. Shakespeare wrote about it. 'When all our yesterdays have lighted fools the way to dusty death.'"

"Don't put that in your novel. Make the reader miserable."

"However true it is?"

"People want to be made happy."

"Of course they do. Listen to that. The girls are laughing. Sound travels far on a farm. Poor Meredith. What have I done to her? Can we stay with you when we come to New York?"

"Of course you can."

"She sounds happy. That's good... Look over there. Rabbits. The place is overrun by wild rabbits. Welcome to Rabbit Farm, my brother."

"Glad to be here."

"Let's make the best of it... 'Tomorrow and tomorrow and tomorrow, creeps in this petty pace, from day to day, to the last syllable of recorded time;, and all our yesterdays have lighted fools the way to dusty death.' William Shakespeare. Such insight. Such insight. Such extraordinary understanding of the human condition. My new book is to be called *All Our Yesterdays*."

"What's it about?"

"I told you. It's about people. All of us. A passage of life."

"Is it going to make your readers miserable?"

"I hope not. Life's not all bad. Just parts of it."

"Is she happy?"

"Is Martha happy? Who knows what other people really think? They say one thing and think another. Even our wives. And now we're bringing up children. Did you see the boredom in my son when no one was paying him attention? We're all a bit like that. We want to be told how nice we are. Constantly. When I'm writing or thinking about my writing which is most of the time, Meredith goes on the back burner. Only when I come out of my imaginary world do I give her the attention she wants. Relationships are difficult. I hoped her own writing would give her something to do. Give her satisfaction. That we would be two artists enjoying our work together. But you never know. In the evenings over drinks, we have fun. She misses having other people around."

"She should be so lucky. Too many people can drive a person crazy. Other people always want something from you: emotional, material, or just someone to talk to about their problems."

"Somewhere there's a happy mix of solitude and people. Company. Other people's thoughts. I do miss intelligent conversation. Meredith and I have said everything we have to say to each other. We bring up a subject and plough the same furrows. Martha goes to work and lives her business life, something she can talk about to you when she comes home at night. There is nothing different in our days, other than the content of our books, that neither of us like to talk about until the book is finished. And when a book is finished, that's it. It's finished. Other than reading the book there is nothing for us to talk about. You can't rewrite a book after it's finished. Unless you want to mess it up."

They walked on towards the distant sea, Phillip trying to think of something else to talk about.

"I have a new investment in a start-up. Getmethatbook.com. We're going to sell books online with software that enables readers to search and find the kind of book they like to read, instead of being submerged in all the celebrity publicity and end up reading rubbish. Serendipity making pleasant discoveries, though not by accident. It will enable individual readers to find their own tastes, subjects that interest them, and not have to read what is pumped at the masses. So often on television you watch a movie and turn it off halfway through because you didn't know enough about the film before you started watching. Our new online company is designed to give readers better choice. Their own choice, not the choice of the marketeers. There are millions of books out there. How do you find the ones you want to read? That's our new business. You're lucky, Randall. You've had a few million readers who know what to expect from a new Randall Holiday book. It's not so easy for an unknown author. Or a writer lost in the passage of time. Will it work? Make us the fortune we are about to make from Marcin Galinski's Linguare.com? Who knows? We hope it will. Why I invested some of my money in Perry Mance. What do you think, Randall?"

"If it works, you'll revolutionise the book industry. Put the big publishers out of business by selling a few copies of millions of titles instead of millions of copies of a few titles. There won't be a need for all the stunts and vast investment in advertising. You'll likely take readers from me. But if every reader gets what he wants to read instead of what he's told to read by the media, I'm all for it. I hope all my readers enjoy my books. That my characters communicate with them. That my books give my readers pleasure and satisfaction. The new world of internet technology is mind-boggling in its potential. If it works, you'll end up with the world's biggest bookshop. People will read by downloading books. You won't have to print. The savings from all that media advertising and running the printing presses will be passed on to the reader."

"When you come over to New York, I want you to meet Perry Mance. He's young and volatile. You can help him with ideas from the writer's perspective so he can use them to help people search for what they really want to read. Not just a load of light trivia. Look at that. Do you think Polar Bear will catch that rabbit?"

"Not a chance. The rabbit's playing with him. Why it keeps changing direction. It's a shame we humans like to eat meat. Like to eat animals. When

I'm having supper tonight, I'll try not to think of that rabbit... Polar Bear! Come here, boy... Shit, it's starting to rain. I loved Rhodesia. For six months of the year, we didn't get a drop of rain. Next time we walk to the sea we'll bring a fishing rod. Nothing better than eating one's own catch. How man used to live. Hunters and gatherers. No supermarkets. Nothing artificial. Just man and the wilds. I envy our prehistoric ancestors. Short, happy lives fending for themselves... That shower has passed over. Nothing wrong with a bit of rain on a man's face... What are we doing, Phillip?"

"What do you mean?"

"With our lives. What are we doing? One minute we're in Africa on a tobacco farm, the next in New York or an island in the Irish sea. Always chasing rainbows. I only go on writing because I have nothing else to do. And even for Meredith's sake, what's the point of partying with strangers? What are we all up to? I turn thirty-seven this year and running out of new ideas for things to do with my life. What do you do in life when you've accomplished what you set out to do? I'm going to run out of books to write unless I start writing all that fantasy crap for teenagers. I could live another fifty years. What the hell am I going to do for the next fifty years?"

"Go fishing."

"I'm serious."

"I know you are. Why I'm being ridiculous. I have no idea, to answer your question. I'm in exactly the same predicament. For Marcin Galinski and Perry Mance, both in their early twenties, everything is new. Everything a challenge. Everything exciting. They want to become rich. Think money will buy whatever they want from life. But it doesn't. Once you've been to half a dozen fancy Manhattan restaurants they become boring. You made it. Got the T-shirt. Life in the African bush was never boring. Or was it because I was still young in my mind? Enjoying something I knew Mugabe wanted to take away from me? You realise he hated us whites. No one likes a stranger to take over their country and tell them what to do. You know the whites are pouring out of South Africa? As they have out of Zimbabwe where the white population is now less than a quarter of what it was twenty years ago. Maybe that threat of losing it retains my interest. Maybe I owe Mugabe one for maintaining my passion for Africa. It's one big strange world that few of us have answers to. And when we get an answer it never lasts... They'll be talking their heads off back at the farmhouse. Natter, natter, natter. Do you love Meredith?"

"Do you love Martha? Do we ever love anyone? Or do we think we love when we want something? Or are scared of being left on our own? Why we have children. Someone to look after us in our old age. Doesn't work, of course. They just put us in old age homes and let someone else do the work. I don't think the human condition is as complex as we like to think it is. It's all simple survival. From one generation to the next."

"We need a drink to cheer ourselves up."

"Probably... Polar Bear! Where the hell's that dog? Ah, there he is. That dog's always happy. That's something. Tonight, we'll all get as pissed as newts."

"Martha can't drink."

"She can watch us. Tell us tomorrow how much crap we were talking. Good to see you, brother."

"Likewise. Now look at that. The sun's come out."

They walked and talked as the sun sank into the sea, the wind snatching at the top of waves. Closer to the shore, three fishing boats were making their way back to port. They turned back and quickened their pace as the sun fired a shaft of light at the darkening heavens. Over to the left, the mountain stood in all its lonely majesty, soaked in the last rays of the sun. The dog reached the beach and was chasing seagulls, the birds rising and falling back on the sand with the passage of the dog, the birds always at a safe distance. For Phillip, there was something lonely about seagulls on the shore. Just the sand and the birds, the wind and the waves, a place for the birds to scavenge for their food alone, the washed-up shellfish and debris from the deeper ocean. And across the sea was Ireland, another bed of hatred and argument with the British. Ignoring Polar Bear, who refused to come to Randall's calling, they made their way back to the house, the shadows long through the trees and farm buildings as Randall opened the front door. They could hear the girls talking to each other, neither girl getting a word in edgeways. Phillip went back to the open door to look for the dog, calling his name out into the dusk. Back inside, the fire was burning bright in the grate, the polished black beams of the ceiling reflecting the flickering light of the flames.

"Let's open the bar. What you want Phillip? Martha can have a cup of coffee. Leave the door open for the dog and get those cats off the sofa. How was your afternoon, girls? How's my son? We had a lovely walk even if we did get wet. You get used to walking in the rain in Britain. I need a beer. A couple of beers... Ah, there you are, Polar Bear. Go and have your supper in the kitchen. All that chasing rabbits and seagulls must have made you hungry, my dog... So, what did you girls talk about or is that a stupid question? A gin and tonic for my darling wife. It's sundowner time. Is the stew in the oven? Nothing more to be done with the food? Good. We can relax and have a drink. What's it going to be, Phillip?"

"I'll join you with a beer."

"Good lad. We can hit the whisky bottle later. A glass of wine or two with the stew. We're going to have a party. Sorry you can't drink, Martha, but well done. No more complications. Always best to be careful when you're having a baby. Life's about being organised. There we are, brother. Cheers. Cheers to all of you. Cheers to having you here. There's nothing better than a family reunion. Let there be many more of them. My, that fire looks good. There's nothing more welcoming than a fire. Don't worry. I'll close the door. Dogs and cats. This place is a madhouse. A lovely madhouse. To long life and happiness and Martha's new baby. Tastes good, brother. That first beer. Tastes good. What would we do without alcohol? And if it's a girl you're going to call her Carmen. A toast to our long-dead mother, Phillip. To our mother. Thank you for giving us both life, my mother. Giving Douglas life and all those to come. Without that link in the chain, we wouldn't be alive. All those links in the chain. All the way back to the start of humankind. Makes you think. The chance of life so slim. And here we are on Rabbit Farm. Cheers."

"Cheers!"

"Now we can really get started."

Phillip drank the first and second beer sitting in a comfortable armchair next to the fire with Randall sitting in a similar chair opposite to him on the other side of the flickering fire, the only electric light in the room a standard lamp behind Randall. The girls sat with the cats on the sofa that faced the fire. On Phillip's immediate right sat Meredith, on Randall's immediate left sat Martha. Polar Bear had crept in to lie flat on his side on the small carpet in front of the fire, and fallen asleep. There was no sound from Douglas in his cot in the bedroom. The girls kept talking to each other, Phillip smiling at his brother as they half-listened to the constant chatter. Phillip was hungry, thinking of the rabbit stew on a low heat in the oven. He could smell the food, making his mouth water. A rush of wind blew against the house, pushing air down the chimney, brushing the red-hot coals. Phillip could smell the fire from the grate as a dump of soot came down the old chimney onto the coals. The dog opened his eyes and shut them again. Randall opened the bottle of whisky and put it on the small side table next to his right elbow. Like the Scots to the north of them, they drank their thirty-year-old whisky neat. The whisky glasses were cut crystal and heavy. After the second tot of whisky, Phillip was not so hungry. They talked to each other across the fire and in front of their women, old reminiscences from their lives as boys growing up on their African farm. The dog's front paws jerked in his dreams. Phillip leaned forward and gently stroked the white fur of the dog's head.

"Still chasing rabbits in your sleep, Polar Bear?" Phillip smiled at the dog as he spoke, making Randall look at his wife.

"Rabbits. We'd better eat, Martha. It's good to have food in your stomach when you're drinking. I'll get the wine, you get the stew."

"Where do you want to eat?"

"On our laps in front of the fire as usual. Put the pot on the kitchen table and we'll help ourselves... Want another gin, Meredith?"

"Of course I do. Cats, a dog and company. It's such a lovely evening. Martha tells such lovely stories about New York. I'd so love to live in Manhattan, but then we couldn't write our books. Too many interruptions. Too much stuff in our heads. Randall says he can't write a novel if his brain is cluttered with anything else than a story. Pity. Shouldn't complain. We both love writing. A nice long visit. What Martha and I are planning. Forty-nine storeys up in the sky. The lights of New York. I can't wait. We've nearly finished our books. Then we'll go on a journey. I'm going to leave Douglas with my mother in Liverpool. She's always pestering me to look after her grandson. Give her something to do. My poor mother. She gets so bored. All she has is her daily routine. She says a mother gets lonely when her children have gone on their way. Let me go get the food. The meat's chopped up. We can eat from a bowl with a spoon. Use the ladle to help ourselves."

Martha looked at Meredith and smiled.

"I'm going to eat and go to bed. You don't mind? I'm thinking of my baby. You three can go on drinking together. When Meredith comes to New York we're going to go shopping. Really go shopping. No point in having all that money in the bank if we don't spend it. I'll take a couple of days off work... Rabbit stew. Can't remember the last time I ate rabbit stew. You want any help, Meredith?"

"You and Phillip sit where you are. We're the hosts. First I'll check on Douglas and then get the pot out of the oven. My, that wind is blowing. What's the matter with Polar Bear? Keeps jerking in his sleep. It's so lovely having company. Someone to talk to. Oh, well. Enjoy it while you have it. What my mother always said. Douglas will love living with his grandmother and all that attention."

Not sure if he hadn't broken his brother's life of tranquillity, Phillip finished his whisky while Randall went to get the red wine and the wine glasses.

"Come and get it."

Getting up from his comfortable chair, Phillip found the whisky had got to him, making him stumble. Martha gave him a look. He went into the kitchen and helped himself to a bowl of rabbit stew, taking the first spoonful standing up in the kitchen. The stew was delicious. And Randall was right. It was never good to drink on an empty stomach. Especially when his wife wasn't drinking.

"Are you all right?"

"Of course I am, Martha. You wouldn't have noticed when you were drinking."

"Probably not. Ironical, I suppose. I was as bad as the rest of you."

"Are we bad?"

"You're all drunk!"

"We're not drunk yet."

"But you will be. Bet my last dollar on it. Why I'm going to bed when I've eaten. Sober at a party. Horrible. Makes me realise how much nonsense I talk myself when I've been drinking. Nothing worse than a sober member of the party looking critical. Why do we always have to drink to enjoy ourselves? There I go. See what I mean?... My goodness. This stew is good. Good food and good company. What more can a girl want?"

After one glass of red wine with the stew, Phillip went back to the whisky. He had finished his stew. Martha got up.

"Don't get up. I'll see myself to bed. Enjoy the rest of the whisky. Thank you all for a lovely day."

Smiling, shaking her head, a sign of 'don't fall down drunk' on her face, Phillip watched Martha go off to bed.

"Don't I get a kiss?"

"Later."

"You should be so lucky."

"A girl can only hope. I'll light the fire in our bedroom. That wind is really howling. Why's that cat following me?"

"They like to sleep on my pillow. Close your door."

"Thank you, Meredith. Goodnight."

"Goodnight." After the 'goodnight' chorus, Randall got up from his chair with the whisky bottle and poured into their glasses.

"That's half a glass!"

"Are you complaining, brother? Now, where were we... Meredith, tell Randall about your family. All those siblings... Cheers again."

By the time the whisky bottle was finished they were all happily talking gibberish. Meredith got up and fell back onto the sofa, half sitting on one of the cats.

"You want some help?"

"I'm legless."

"Oh, my goodness."

"Don't just sit there, Randall. Help your wife."

"We can all slide out of our chairs and crawl to bed. Not a sound from Douglas. Sleeps like a baby. Well, he is a baby. We'd better try and go to bed. I've twice wrung the neck of the whisky bottle. Not a drop left. Don't think I'm going to do much writing tomorrow. Neither are you, my darling. The talking cats will have to wait. Can't write on a raging hangover. That's the one thing I hate about drinking. The morning after. No pleasure without pain. What they say... One, two, three. I'm up!"

"Come and help me."

"How's the cat?"

"I only sat on her tail."

"Give me your hand. Concentrate, Meredith. Stop giggling."

"Put the fender in front of the fire. Don't want to burn down the house."

"Always looking after me. Good thinking... There we are... One, two, three. Up you come. Can you get up, Phillip?"

"I hope so."

"See you tomorrow. Leave the lamp on. You do know which room you're in?"

"I hope so. Go to bed. I'm going to sit awhile. That wind can howl. I can almost feel those waves crashing on the shore. How far away are they?"

"A couple of miles. Sound travels far and loud at night."

After watching his brother and sister-in-law stumble off to bed, Phillip tried to get up. Like Meredith, he was legless. On the third attempt, holding the side of his armchair with both hands, Phillip made it up onto his feet and stumbled through the room to the closed door of their bedroom. The cats all stayed on the couch, not even looking at him. As quietly as he was able, Phillip opened the bedroom door. He was well and truly drunk. Inside, the fire was alight in the grate, the coals glowing red in the dark. By the light of the fire and holding the wooden foot of the bed with both of his hands, he made his way to his side of the bed where he sat down and took off Randall's boots. With more effort, he got out of his trousers and climbed into bed. Martha had not woken. Expecting to pass out when the back of his head hit the pillow, nothing happened. He was wide awake. He had a headache. He couldn't sleep. The rain was lashing at the outside of the windowpanes like some unseen giant. The waves crashed on the distant shore. Somewhere, a door was banging, a constant racket in the wind. For what seemed like hours, Phillip lay on his back as the alcohol he had drunk coursed through the blood in his body. There was no sound other than the wind and the rain and the banging of the door. Was drinking worth it? Phillip wasn't sure. The lucky one was Martha lying peacefully on her side next to him sound asleep. Phillip began to worry. He always worried when he couldn't sleep. There were always worries. There was no sound from little Douglas as the night went on and on, only the wind, the rain and the banging, and the waves crashing on the shore. When Phillip fell into a troubled sleep, his dreams were horrible.

3

In the morning, Phillip woke, his mouth tasting like the bottom of a parrot cage. His head ached. He felt nauseous. It wasn't worth it. Drinking just wasn't worth it.

"Morning, honey. Rise and shine. The rain has stopped."

"Don't shout!"

"I'm not shouting."

"You are. I've got the mother and father of a hangover."

"Poor Phillip."

"Don't even touch me... Why do we drink, Martha?"

"You tell me."

There was no sound coming from Randall and Meredith. The house was silent. Another day. Another hangover. Phillip thought back to the conversation with his brother. To the words of William Shakespeare: 'This petty pace from day to day.' Not sure what they were all up to, Phillip got out of bed and went to the bathroom where he stood and stood, emptying his bladder. A door opened, adding sound to the cascading piss going into the toilet. Life was all so fundamental, he told himself. You ate and crapped it out. You drank and pissed it out. One day you felt good. Another day you felt horrible... Blaming the booze for all his woes, Phillip flushed the toilet and went to the basin where he stood looking at himself in the mirror.

"Crookshank, Crookshank, where were you last night? You look disgusting."

With his face washed in cold water, his hair back in place, Phillip carefully let himself out of the bathroom. Outside the door, his brother was patiently waiting his turn, holding his crotch. Neither said a word as Randall pushed past to the toilet. In the lounge, the first thing Phillip saw was the empty whisky bottle lying on its side on the floor. Meredith came out of one of the rooms, gently closing the door behind her.

"He's still sleeping, thank goodness. How are you, Phillip?"

"Bloody horrible."

"You two really drank last night."

"How are you feeling, Meredith?"

"Felt better. No pleasure without pain. Didn't we have fun? I hope so. Martha's the happy one this morning. She's in the kitchen getting us breakfast. Do you know, last night we didn't even turn on the radio?"

"At least that was something. Did you drink when you were having Douglas?"

"All we do on Rabbit Farm for entertainment. No one told me not to. I got myself pregnant and had a baby. No problem."

"You were lucky."

"We never know when we are lucky, Phillip. There's aspirin in a bottle on the dining room table. Take a couple. Helps the headache."

"Where's the dog?"

"Outside with the cats. It's a lovely day. The sun is shining. You'll feel better after some breakfast."

"Are you going to write today?"

"Are you kidding! You and Randall are going to walk up one side of Snaefell and down the other."

"As a punishment?"

"As a therapy... Flush the toilet, Randall!"

"Sorry."

"He can't even think on a hangover. Martha and I are going to drive down to the sea and walk down the beach. Don't forget the aspirin."

"I won't. Good morning, Randall. How are you feeling?"

"Horrible. Plain horrible. Is drinking worth it?"

"What I was asking myself."

"And after a good long walk we'll come back and start all over again. We had a good chat."

"That we did. Life on the farm. *All Our Yesterdays*. I like your title."

"I can smell the bacon cooking in the kitchen. Nothing better than the smell of fried bacon. Another day. Another yesterday. Another tomorrow. How it goes, Phillip. On and on. And we all have a lovely life. Or we hope we do. Do you like living in Manhattan?"

"Not particularly. Not that it makes any difference."

"That's my point, brother. That's my point. You're as happy as you feel in yourself. Wherever you are. Let's go and find Polar Bear and then come back for our breakfast. Those aspirin will help. All you need is a little help from your friends. And that's the Beatles, not Shakespeare. What a life. You want a beer, Phillip?"

"Don't be bloody ridiculous!"

"Just kidding. Some say it helps."

"They're called drunks."

"Of course they are. How silly of me."

"Are you poking fun?"

"Probably. Never take life too seriously. Never helps. Nothing really ever helps... After you, Phillip."

"Thank you, Randall."

"My pleasure."

Breakfast was ready. They ate in the kitchen, no one wanting to talk. The parched taste in Phillip's mouth went away with the bacon and eggs. Martha had made them coffee. Good, strong American coffee. By the time they went with the dog to walk the mountain, Phillip was feeling better. For the first mile the brothers kept pace with each other, neither of them talking, a companionable silence, both of them enjoying the other's company. The climb up the side of the mountain made them concentrate, both of them labouring. At the top, they sat in the morning sunshine and looked around at the surrounding sea, no distant land to be seen, no England, no Ireland. Even Polar Bear had sat down.

"Beautiful. Plain beautiful. Nature at its best. Don't get a place of perfect peace like this in Manhattan."

"What would you like most to do with the rest of your life, Phillip?"

"First, I would like to get rid of all the politicians and live in peace in my Africa. Run my safari business. Live the winters in the Zambezi Valley. The hot summers in the Vumba cottage. Spend a life of peace without stress and worries with my wife and children. But like so many other things in life, it's a dream. There are always other people to shatter your dreams. And not all the customers are pleasant either. But that's life as part of the human race. Peace and solitude with those I love. That would be my dream. A bit like living here and writing books for a living."

"It's not going to last."

"It never does. We're never satisfied, even when we get what we think we want. Was there ever an answer to a perfect life? I don't think so... If there's no one on the beach can we skinny dip? I didn't bring a bathing costume. You remember skinny dipping in the Zambezi River?"

"And firing first into the water to scare off the crocodiles. Of course I do. Memories. That's what it's all about. Making memories... That was quite a climb. Not as fit as I used to be."

"We're not youngsters anymore. Even though we tell ourselves we are. What's it like being a father?"

"It's different. You have to learn to be responsible. Young Douglas is totally dependent on me and Meredith. Will be for years to come. I always think of Dad as a pillar. A great, strong pillar I can go to lean on when I get into trouble. He's always there for me. I want to be the same for Douglas."

"Have you been in trouble?"

"Not recently. Not since Grandfather Crossley left us all that money. Money helps keep us out of trouble."

"Why I want to get that legacy for Jonathan, my homeless violin player I met in the park. The security of having money. About all there is, I suppose. I've talked about Jonathan."

"We'd have made our own money."

"Probably. Having it helps me not worry when I invest in a start-up. Must help you as a writer in case you get writer's block and your publisher stops sending you your royalty money. You don't need a fortune in life. Just enough to be able to live without worrying. We've been lucky, Randall, to be born into a family with wealth. And given through our genes the ability to think. It's always difficult to imagine other people's lives. And what we have we take for granted."

"Did we take each other for granted?"

"We were there. Alone with Dad. And then we were lucky. Along came Bergit and, later, Craig and Myra."

"How is she?"

"Happily married."

"She's lucky."

"Julian hates all that Hollywood nonsense. He'd love this place. Right here on the top of a mountain. Bring Meredith over to Manhattan for a holiday and she'll go home content. A month or two in the Big Apple and she'll want to run for it. But who knows? We're all different. Shall we walk, brother?"

"Lead the way. The dog's up, ready to go. Shall we run down the mountain?"

"Don't be bloody silly. How's your hangover?"

"Much better, thank you."

"So's mine. Nothing like a bit of strenuous exercise to clear the head."

They walked down slowly enjoying the view. Polar Bear put up a pheasant that flew away down the slope making a loud calling noise, briefly disturbing their peace. Phillip watched the big bird drop back into the grass and disappear from sight.

"What's the meaning of life, Phillip? Why are we here? Some say if we behave ourselves we go to heaven. Priests. You go to a priest and ask God for forgiveness and all is well again. Is there a heaven, a future? Or is it another way to control us, to make us behave ourselves? No one really knows. I write about the meaning of life to try and find a purpose. But I never do. We just come and go and have done since the beginning of time. All this writing, your investing, the girls' desire for children, what is the purpose? All the kids do is start the whole process all over again. No one learns. No one finds out. No one can tell you the meaning of life. Look at that butterfly. That beautiful butterfly hovering over that flower, sucking out the nectar. Has that insect got a meaning? Are we any more important than a butterfly? And who is he, that one there? We don't know. Does he? Or is seeking nectar which also fertilises the seed of the flower and makes the plant grow again, the purpose of that butterfly? Or will we all just vanish in a new ice age or a catastrophic nuclear explosion that destroys the earth? Do we suddenly find ourselves in heaven with twenty vestal virgins or whatever else all those religions preach to us? Will that butterfly find itself in heaven for all eternity? Mostly the religious tell us only man goes to heaven if he behaves himself. Why just us? What's so special about mankind? That butterfly has life, just like you and me. Like Polar Bear. Like that squawking pheasant. What about all the unseen fish in the sea over there? None of it I really understand. Maybe I think too much instead of just getting on with it. A writer has to think. Maybe life is better when you just use your hands to work, and not this unseen part of us that's locked in our heads. And there goes a rabbit. And there goes Polar Bear. Is he after that poor bloody rabbit to eat or to chase and have fun with? We ate rabbit last night to give us the energy for our walk. What's the meaning of it all, Phillip?"

"I have no idea."

"And neither has anyone else if they're honest, despite all the talk."

"Is the water going to be cold?"

"The water of the Irish sea is always cold. But exhilarating. So far as I can see there's no one down there on the beach."

"Are you happy with your life, Randall?"

"Of course I am. What a bloody stupid question. Are you happy?"

"As a pig in shit."

"Pigs love shit."

"That's my point... Carmen. Her name's going to be Carmen. Our mother is going to live all over again."

"'To the last syllable of recorded time, when all our yesterdays have lighted fools the way to dusty death'... Life goes on, Phillip. How it works. All you need is a boy and a girl. The pollen in a flower and a passing butterfly. I love the way they keep opening and shutting their wings when they sit on a flower. As if they're enjoying themselves. Why don't we sit on that rock for a while and contemplate our navels."

"Did you hear about the chap who sat on a rock and put his thumb in his navel? When he'd finished contemplating he took out his thumb and there on the end of his thumb was his navel."

"What happened?"

"When he stood up his arse fell off."

"I was being serious about the meaning of life."

"I know you were, Randall. I was trying to lighten the mood."

"How did you sleep last night?"

"I had nightmares. My night was full of horrors. Faces without noses. Ugly people. Bangs among the pulsing shadows. A world full of fear. And all from drinking too much of your whisky, for which I thank you. Not the nightmares but the whisky."

For a long while, they sat in silence, contemplating the scenery. When Phillip stood up, his brother smiled at him.

"At least your arse didn't fall off."

When they reached the shore, the tide was going out as they walked along the waterline collecting shells like two small children on holiday. The sun was still shining, the waves rolling to the shore, no longer pounding. Phillip took off his clothes and ran into the sea.

"Come on, Randall. Get your gear off. That boat is too far away for anyone to see."

"Is it cold?"

"Of course it is. Run, brother. Dive into the wave. If this doesn't cure your hangover, nothing will. I feel so young. It's wonderful to feel so young. This is what life is all about. Having fun."

Randall came up with a mouthful of water which he squirted towards the distant merchant ship. They were both laughing like schoolchildren.

"Haven't enjoyed myself as much as this for ages."

"Neither have I. Race you down the beach to get warm."

"What about our clothes?"

"We'll come back for them. There's no one around. Run, brother. Run. This is life."

"You're nuts."

"What's wrong with being nuts?"

"Nothing. Sometimes I take life too seriously. We'd better circle back. People do come down to the beach. I love the Isle of Man. People are so few. I have my freedom. There's nothing better in life than not having to put up with people... You think the girls will be as happy as us?"

"By now, they'll have talked themselves to a happy standstill. Women love gossiping."

"What will they talk about?"

"You and me, Randall."

"Should we come before or after Martha has the baby?"

"As you wish. Finish your books and pay us a visit. We'll go to a concert. Go to the theatre. Listen to Jonathan playing the violin in the gardens of the park. He was once in the New York Philharmonic. Life with all its ups and downs. And now he's going to be rich."

"Will he be happier?"

"Who knows? Better than sleeping at night on a cold bench. And feeling hungry. Here we are. Clothes. Back to civilisation. Bare arse in the Irish Sea. That was fun."

"We'll walk straight back. I'm hungry... There we go. Normal people wearing clothes... Just look at him. I'm not sure which that dog enjoys most, chasing rabbits or seagulls."

"We're going to remember this day for the rest of our lives."

"Of course we are. There's nothing better in life than having a brother. Having fun with a brother. And finding the meaning of life."

"You'd heard my joke before?"

"Of course I had. It's as old as the hills. And the sun's still shining. What a day."

They walked and walked, at peace with their world, Phillip taking in the countryside. They passed a field with an old derelict house, its roof missing, the grass and bushes growing up to the crumbling walls.

"Why don't they knock down those old buildings?"

"Can't do that. They're the homes for the little people."

"Are you pulling my leg this time?"

"No, I'm not. It's old Manx folklore. When a farmhouse is left empty and the roof comes down the little people move in. Once the little people move in you can do nothing about it. You have to leave it. Superstition, Phillip. This little island all on its own is old. Very old. The Manx people go back further than the ancient Britons. No one knows how far back. No, those derelict buildings are part of their island's heritage. Deep in their island culture. If the little people are happy, so are the islanders."

"Must have seen six or seven of them."

"Roofless, derelict farmhouses are dotted all over the island. History. Ancient history. Passed from father to son, down all those thousands of generations from when man first found this island in the sea and made it home. Never upset the little people or you'll regret it."

"You are being serious?"

"If you don't believe what I say about the folklore, ask any Manxman."

"Who are the Manxmen?"

"Ancient Celts. They have their own language. We're foreigners, Phillip. Invaders of their island. All part of Britain and its history. After the Celts came Romans. Anglo-Saxons. Normans. And now, who knows. People coming from all over the old British Empire. Britain is becoming cosmopolitan. A mix of everyone on earth. But, whatever they do on this island, they don't want to touch those roofless, derelict houses or they'll regret it with their lives. The power of the little people."

"Do you really believe it?"

"Like you, Phillip, I'm not sure what I believe. But what I have learned in my life is to respect the beliefs of other people."

"Are you going to write about it?"

"Not today."

"It's not in my history books."

"Of course it isn't. It's superstition. The history books are full of conquests. Of war. Knights in their shining armour. They are the ones that we think make history. People like to read about action, not about ancient superstition. Unless it's part of their religion."

"Were our family descended from the Celts?"

"Probably. Somewhere. Somewhere way back, the genes of the Celts mingled with the genes of our ancestors. And here we are. But we don't know what made us. It's only the rare family, like the family of your homeless Jonathan, that can trace their lineage back more than five generations. Many can't even do that. Can't even trace their lineage as far back as their fathers. None of us know who we are. Or where we came from. Or where we're going. All part of the mystery of living. What you and I know for definite is that we are brothers. That Dad is our father. That our mother was Carmen. That is what's important to me. And if we are all going to heaven or hell we'll meet all our ancestors. All of them. Right back to the very beginning. Whatever was that beginning? In heaven or hell, we'll learn the truth about life. Until then, we just get on with it. Enjoy it. Have fun. The wind's coming up. We'd better hurry. Lunch. I want my lunch."

"What's for lunch?"

"We're about to find out. It's all basic, Phillip. 'A tale told by an idiot.'"

"Can you stop quoting Shakespeare?"

"How do you know it was Shakespeare? All writers write about what they heard. What was passed down. A writer's experience. And in bits and pieces, we all live similar experiences and hear old sayings. Usually, only the truth gets passed down. We learn from old experience. Or we try to. Until we go to war with each other again. Wars and revolutions are what make history. All that history you read about at Rhodes University. You'd think by now we'd have learned that stabbing each other with swords, or throwing bombs at each other, does more harm than good. To everyone. The victor or the loser. The Anglo-Boer war started the British rot. The First World War destroyed the best of the youth and with it the best of the genes: the average life of a second lieutenant in that war was ten days. And as if the British and Germans hadn't done enough to each other to destroy civilisation and intelligent thinking, twenty-one years later they started all over again, bringing Asia into the worthless carnage. And that world war only finished when the Americans dropped an atomic bomb on the Japanese. Since then it's been a host of petty wars across the planet. Civil wars among one's own people. Wars against neighbours. Wars in the name of religion. What a mess. Will it end? I doubt it. Not until we blow ourselves to pieces. You and I ran away. You ran to the Zambezi Valley. I ran to the Isle of Man. Follow, lead or get the hell out of the way. We chose the latter. Where I want to stay. Where you would like to go back to. But it doesn't work that way. The Marthas and Merediths want to be involved with other people. For the sake of their children, if not for the sake of themselves. Man and woman never really change. It's called life. Life in New York. Life at your university. Life on Rabbit Farm. And life goes on. For all of us. Until the day we are dead. How does that make you feel?"

"Miserable."

"Polar Bear! Come here, boy. Leave those poor rabbits alone."

They walked on slowly, both of them thinking. They walked on the narrow, winding tarred road to avoid the puddles on the pathway. As quickly as it came up, the wind went down, the sun came out warming Phillip and making him smile. There was no point in worrying where they came from. Or where they were going. Nothing was going to make any difference. Ahead, a big oak tree, rich in acorns, stood by the side of the old road. A wooden bench, a plank of wood on thick wooden sides, stood under the spreading tree. In the distance they could see the roof of the old house on Rabbit Farm, surrounded by its outbuildings. The two-plank bench looked comfortable. They were both tired from the climb and the walk.

"You want to sit?"

"Why not? Looks perfect. The sun is shining, the birds singing and those cows are enjoying the grass. Seems a million miles from New York and our apartment on the forty-ninth floor."

"Why is it families live so close and then so far apart? Dad in London. Craig in another part of London. Myra in California. You in the sky above the streets of New York. And me here. Occasionally to meet. Broken up families are sad. But that's the new world of fast aeroplanes and making our livings. In another time, your father had a business or a farm and you carried it on. Now nothing lasts longer than ten years. People buy and sell their businesses. Sell their houses to climb the ladder or downsize to save money, depending on their circumstances. Nothing is permanent. Even the countries we live in. And when you try and make it permanent like Dad on World's View, along comes a Mugabe and you have to go. Makes all our lives so uncertain… My goodness. Look at that. My dog's had enough of chasing rabbits. Sitting with his tongue hanging out, puffing away. Did you know dogs sweat through their tongues?"

"Are you going to have any more children?"

"Probably. Meredith wants to have three kids. To make a proper family. She found me when I was writing in a Welsh forest, far from the madding crowd. I opened the door and there she was. How life goes. She didn't even knock. You open the door and there's a young girl who becomes your wife and companion for life. Chance. Pure chance. Sometimes it works. Sometimes it doesn't. They say half of marriages end in divorce, like my first one. Why many people just live together. You know what I'm talking about. After Martha lost her baby you two split up."

"She tried to commit suicide by jumping off the balcony. Changed her mind at the last minute. An old lady across the way had waved at her. Told me to bugger off. And now we're doing it all over again."

"This time it will work. I know it will."

"Like me, you don't know. We hope it will. We don't know anything for certain."

"If we knew what was going to happen to us we'd all jump out of the window… How are my boots treating you?"

"I can feel my feet. Haven't walked so far and hard since those years growing up on our Rhodesian farm."

"Food calls. Let's go. Up we get. Oak trees are so beautiful. I love living in the country. And next time we meet, we'll meet in New York. I can see one big egg sandwich and a glass of beer."

"Shouldn't we wait until five o'clock before we drink?"

"Probably. Sundowners. Come on. Come on, Polar Bear. One last leg and we're home. Home. Beautiful home. The place we all hanker after."

Side by side, the dog in front, they walked back to Randall's home. The sandwiches were waiting. Phillip watched his brother lift his son from the cot and raise him high above his head, the child gurgling with excitement. The girls, deep in their girl chatter, barely stopped talking. At five, the beers came out and the drinking began again, the socialising, the banter and amusement. Another day for Martha on holiday.

On the Sunday it was time for Phillip to return to London and begin his quest to validate Jonathan Fernsby's ancestry to the British government. To prove Jonathan's heritage. Randall drove them to the small airport, leaving Meredith looking sad with her baby. The girl was lonely. She needed friends. Feeling sympathy for his sister-in-law, Phillip turned round in the back of Randall's car as they drove down the Rabbit Farm driveway and waved. Holding the baby in one arm, Meredith waved back, a forlorn picture of loneliness.

"You'd better hurry up and finish your books. She's lonely, Randall."

"Bored, more likely. I write each day for a lot longer than Meredith. She gets bored. All she has is the house to clean and the boy to look after. And when it comes to house cleaning I do my share. There's nothing worse in life than boredom. We're going to miss you two. Thanks for coming."

"It was our pleasure. See you in New York."

"Good luck with Jonathan Fernsby and all the bureaucracy. Getting that money from a man they think has no relatives will be like getting blood out of a stone. Even with all your birth certificates back to the first Fernsby to arrive in the great United States of America."

"They can't deny the truth."

"They'll avoid the truth. It's easier than making a decision. Civil servants hate making decisions. They like to be told what to do instead of making their own decision and if it's wrong, getting themselves into trouble. Doing nothing is always better. That old fortune of the Earl of Fernsby's is in the guardianship of the government. They won't give it up easily. Especially to some American. The money is safe where it is. That's how they'll look at it. Have fun, Phillip. You'll need an army of lawyers and years of time, if I'm not wrong."

"I've got a week. A working week. I start at the Home Office at nine o'clock tomorrow morning. Then the Treasury Department. St Catherine's House. They're all going to get copies of the documents my lawyers obtained in America. Facts and facts. He's the legitimate Eighteenth Earl of Fernsby. Heir to the throne, so to speak. The money belongs to the title, not some distant relative on the female side of the family. The title goes to a male heir or it becomes extinct. Only if a female member of the family can prove without doubt there are no male heirs alive can they lay claim to that inheritance. Probably why the Seventeenth Earl didn't make a will and died intestate. Hoped all that money would dig up a successor. Find the English earl."

"They'll want to know why your friend who plays for his supper with a begging bowl, hasn't come over himself to claim his title and his inheritance."

"He doesn't want the money. Doesn't want the responsibility and fuss that will come with it and the title."

"Better not tell that to the bureaucrats."

"How far are we from the airport?"

"Half an hour. The road is winding. Is Dad meeting you at the airport?"

"We're catching a cab to Chelsea."

"Give them both my love."

"They miss you."

"I miss them. Maybe it's good to tell people you miss them. You miss people you love. And dogs, of course. I love Polar Bear. I'll miss him when we go to America."

"And the cats?"

"And the cats. Life on Rabbit Farm."

"What are you going to do with the cats and dog when you come to America?"

"Put them in a cattery. The dog in a kennel. They'll hate it. There's a price to pay for everything. And not just for yourself."

4

On the following Friday morning, after a week of being sent from pillar to post, every civil servant Phillip approached with certified copies of Jonathan's documents passing the buck, he received a phone call from the Chancellor of the Exchequer's private secretary.

"Mr Crookshank, will it be convenient for you to meet the Chancellor at eleven o'clock this morning?"

"Am I at last getting somewhere?"

"Probably. Please don't be late. The Chancellor is extremely busy. Be five minutes early. Do you have a pen?"

"Of course."

With the time and address of the appointment written down carefully, Phillip looked up at his father with a smile. He had repeated the name, time and address to the private secretary to make certain it was correct.

"Just look at that, Dad."

"Some people are impressed with titles. Especially old ones with a history. Don't be late."

"What the man said."

At ten minutes to eleven, Phillip was sitting in a chair outside the Chancellor's office, having given his name to the receptionist at security. At eleven o'clock on the dot, he was ushered into the man's spacious office.

"I believe you grew up in Rhodesia, Mr Crookshank? Please sit down. I had a second cousin who farmed tobacco in Rhodesia. Like your family they lost everything. Now, where are we? The Eighteenth Earl of Fernsby. Do you by any chance have a photograph of him? The rest of the documents seem to be in order. I've authorised my department to break the trust and make all the funds available to the Earl. Pity he didn't come over himself... Is this a photograph of the Earl of Fernsby? My goodness. Looks down and out to me."

"He's homeless. When I met him in a small New York park he was playing a violin with only two strings. Begging for a living. He was homeless. I bought him that violin and took the photograph. In a better life, Jonathan played in the string section of the New York Philharmonic until arthritis in his hands prevented him from playing professionally. We became friends. Why I'm here. Jonathan preferred to stay in New York."

"You're a kind man."

"Thank you for doing something."

"The buck stops here, Mr Crookshank. I think it was President Truman who had a small wooden sign standing on his desk in the White House, with the words 'the buck stops here' painted on the wood so everyone could see. Maybe I should have one made for myself. A very good morning to you. Mrs Walsh will see you out... Homeless. Never met a homeless man in my life. Poor man. Life really can be strange."

"Thank you on behalf of Jonathan."

"My pleasure."

"How much money is in the trust?"

"Twenty-eight million, four hundred thousand, one hundred and seven pounds after all the legal and tax expenses. Does he have any children?"

"Not that I know of."

"Then he'll have to get busy."

The man smiled at Phillip, put on his reading glasses and looked down at the papers in front of him: the interview was over. Wanting to trip the light fantastic, Phillip left the office.

THE NEXT DAY they flew home. On the Monday, when Martha had gone to work, Phillip found Jonathan in the park, playing his violin. There were three dollars in the hat, the proverbial begging bowl. When Phillip gave him the news, Jonathan laughed, his eyes popping.

"What are you going to do with all that money, Jonathan?"

"Start my own orchestra. Publish my songs. Help young people who want to enter the music business."

"I didn't think you were going to be so happy."

"Didn't want to get my hopes up. It all seemed too good to be true. In my life, I've had too many let-downs. Didn't want another one. Money. I can't even imagine all that money. My word, I can afford to get a haircut. Give me a hug." The man was crying.

When Phillip walked home he was thinking of only one thing: would Jonathan be happier with all that money? Phillip wasn't sure. Only time would tell.

Back on the forty-ninth floor, Phillip stood alone staring out of the window. In the end it had all been so easy. All Jonathan had to do was provide the British consulate with his bank account details and all that wealth of centuries would be his. Phillip's lawyer, who had verified Jonathan's lineage, would confirm the validity of Jonathan's new bank account. From being a pauper, the man would be rich with one electronic transfer, faster than the blink of an eye. With over forty-five million dollars, instead of being ignored, the predators would target Jonathan: the investment managers, the so-called tax consultants, every charity, every conman in town, Jonathan the perfect target. And then would come the women, all of them smelling the rich scent of easy money. Would the money survive another three centuries? Would Jonathan go to live in England as the Eighteenth Earl of Fernsby? Would he buy himself a country estate? Employ servants? Live in luxury and forget about orchestras and struggling young musicians? Would he look back with regret at losing his life as a bum that came without a single responsibility? As Phillip stared unseeingly out of the window, high above the rat race of New York, he wasn't sure. For all his desire to do good, he had turned his violin-playing friend into a target. It was said a fool and his money were soon parted. Was Jonathan, the unshaven, long-haired, often hungry old man a fool? Phillip did not know. And now he wasn't sure if he had done the right thing. Mostly in life, it was better to mind one's own business instead of interfering in the lives of other people.

When Martha came home at nine o'clock, far later than Phillip had expected, he was sitting on the sofa listening to music, an unread novel opened upside down on his lap.

"You're late. What about the baby?"

"We had two weeks' holiday. Everything is fine. There was too much to catch up on in the office."

"What's happening with Jaz and Marcin?"

"She's moved back into her apartment in this building. Seeing Max to sooth her hurt feelings. She and Marcin are back to their old business relationship as if nothing happened. He doesn't want a kid. She doesn't want to lose our biggest client."

"Is she still pregnant?"

"Oh, yes. She's keeping the baby. When I asked her, she had a knowing smirk on her face."

"Was it love or money?"

"Money, Phillip. It's always money. When a healthy child is born she'll be able to prove by DNA that the genius is the child's father. Then we'll see what happens."

"Was the pregnancy luck or deliberate?"

"We'll never know. Better not to know... Have you eaten? Good. So have I. Did you find Jonathan?"

"His eyes nearly popped out of his head... How's business?"

"Two new clients while I was away. Everything is rosy in the Bowdens' garden. Are you going to make me some coffee?"

"At your service, my lady. Come and sit down. Relax. I'll turn on the television. Monday night on the forty-ninth floor."

"I don't want to watch television. It's all the same old story. The world news never changes. Just the places... Two million sample disks of the voice recognition software in the first two weeks, and the graph is rising sharply. You'll get your hundred million to go public, just a question of time. I'm exhausted. There's so much happening."

"Don't jeopardise your baby."

"It's a constant problem for working mothers. Before and after the baby. Can a girl do two things at once? I hope so. I'll be home by five tomorrow. Must stop getting excited."

"Did you get anything out of Randall in the Isle of Man to help you market getmethatbook.com?"

"Randall said he knows how to write books, not sell them. That's the publisher's job. Why the publisher makes most of the money. There was one snippet I passed on to Perry Mance and his team: if the website could somehow offer the reader free chapters of a book then he will know what he's getting before he pays for a book. Randall says you can see quite quickly if the book is worth reading. Getting a free chapter is easier for the reader than standing in a library or a bookshop flipping pages. A free chapter is like watching the trailer of a movie, something that doesn't happen these days on television. You get offered all these films and one-hour series with a couple of lines to tell you what it's all about. A drama or a comedy but little else. Why TV bores me so often. You watch for twenty minutes and change the channel."

"How is Perry doing?"

"If you ask me, it's going to work. At the moment, we're making sure the patents and copyrights are unbreakable. Don't want to get it right and have someone swipe the business. It's your money invested, Phillip."

"It is a rat race, isn't it?"

"Of course it is."

"I'm worried about Jonathan."

"Why?"

"Whether, with all that money, they'll rip him apart… What happened to our idea to call on your mother in Kansas City when we got back? We were going to extend our holiday."

"Franklyn's phone calls while we were on holiday. I'm a partner in the business, not just a salaried employee."

"Pity. She must get lonely."

"Priorities, Phillip."

"Of course. Priorities."

"Have you made the coffee?"

"Coming."

"Is the new book you're reading any good?"

"It's a load of crap."

"Why did you buy it?"

"The blurb looked good. The first page read well. There's just no story. Are you sure you don't want to watch television? When you've had the baby, we'll be able to relax with a drink."

"Did you go to Harry B's?"

"Not yet. Today was Jonathan Fernsby day. The soon not-to-be-homeless Eighteenth Earl of Fernsby… There we are, my lady. Coffee. Exactly as you like it. I'll put on some music."

PART 6

NOVEMBER TO DECEMBER 1994 — "LET THE BAG-LADY SING"

1

At the end of November, the winter came with a vengeance, Phillip walking the wet streets of New York with a thick coat and a scarf wrapped around his neck. It was the furthest away from Africa he could imagine. The leaves in the park had fallen, the wet wooden benches were free of people, no sign of the cat or Mary. No colour in what had been the flowerbeds. Pigeons sat on the bare branches looking cold, not a chirp from any of them. As expected, there was no sign of Jonathan, now a rich man with better things to do than beg for a living. In the month since the Monday after Phillip's return from England, there had been no word from Jonathan. Phillip had thought of calling the lawyer who was to verify Jonathan's bank details but decided he had done enough. People were strange. When they had what they wanted from you they left you alone. For Phillip, it would have been nice to receive a thank you. But that was how life worked. The satisfaction was in helping people, not in the praise. Or that was what he tried to tell himself.

On the last Friday in November, Christmas round the corner, Phillip walked from his apartment building to Harry B's. That morning he had received a letter from Randall saying they had finished their books and were coming to New York. Smiling at the old way of communicating, Phillip had phoned his brother to say a room in the flat was his whenever they wanted. They had chattered for half an hour on the phone. When Phillip walked into the familiar bar, Terry was behind the counter, no one around that Phillip recognised. New York was constantly changing. Phillip drank two beers and went home. There was no one to talk to. He had thought of going to the gym but given up the idea which had made him feel guilty. It was one of those days. He was bored. Nothing to do. At least Randall and Meredith would be staying with them for Christmas. He was sitting on the sofa twiddling his thumbs when the phone rang.

"Hello. Phillip Crookshank speaking."

"Have you heard from Jonathan Fernsby?"

"Hello, Andrew. How are you? How's the law business? No, not a word. Now he's rich he's probably got better things to do than talk to me. I'd remind him of when he was a beggar in a park."

"I don't think so. I've just had a phone call from the British consulate. You must have given them my number. I was to go with Jonathan to the consulate to confirm his credentials. To give them a sworn statement. They have not heard from Mr Fernsby, or whatever he calls himself these days. All that money is sitting unclaimed in the bank of London. I was looking forward to giving our friend Jonathan a nice little bill for my services."

"Send me the bill, Andrew."

"Do you know where to find Jonathan?"

"Not really. I could ask the hospice if he's stayed there recently. Call at the soup kitchen. I only met Jonathan in the park. No one does much in the park in winter."

"Check him out, Phillip. A man doesn't leave that kind of money lying around without a reason. Something must have happened to him."

"It never stops."

"What never stops?"

"Life, Andrew. Thanks for the call."

With several copies of Jonathan's photograph in his pocket, Phillip, feeling better with something to do, went down in the lift and found himself a taxi.

"Do you know the whereabouts of the nearest hospice? There may be more than one. And the local soup kitchens?"

"You don't look in need of shelter."

"It's not for me. Can you help me? We'll drive on round until I find the man I'm looking for."

"Give me a minute to think... Yes, I have the hospice. They'll tell us the address of the soup kitchens. Has someone stolen something from you?"

"Quite the reverse."

"Do you live here?"

"I own an apartment on the forty-ninth floor. Your taxi fare is quite safe."

"Just the mention of bums makes me cautious."

"Nothing wrong with being cautious."

"Where you from?"

"Zimbabwe, if you've ever heard of it. You must hear a host of different accents. My wife's American."

"I'm from Puerto Rico. You been to Puerto Rico?"

"Never heard of it... Just kidding."

"Where is this Zimbabwe?"

"Southern, central Africa."

"What you doing there?"

"Trying to avoid the world... Let's find that hospice."

It was always the same. Everyone wanted to know your business. Hoping the driver knew where he was going, Phillip sat back in his seat. He was likely on a wild goose chase, looking for a phantom. Looking for a homeless man without an address was going to be difficult. With all that money waiting, had Jonathan fallen sick? Life was full of irony. After twenty minutes, of what to Phillip seemed like driving in circles, the taxi stopped.

"That's your building. And that's the entrance. Don't drop too many people off at this address."

"Will you wait? Here's a hundred dollars in advance. If I find what I'm looking for there'll be a fifty-dollar tip."

"It's my lucky day."

"I hope it's mine. I won't be long. If they don't recognise the photograph we'll move on."

"Write down the addresses they give you."

"Of course, Mr Puerto Rico. There's a bum over there coming out of the entrance. You found the right place."

"The clock's still ticking."

"It always is. You'll get your taxi fare and the hundred dollars. Were you sure where you were going?"

"Not really. Been here once, a long time ago. When I first arrived from Puerto Rico."

"You stayed here?"

"For a couple of nights. Then I got a job as a cab driver."

Inside the run-down building, an old man sat reading a book behind the front desk, not bothering to look up at Phillip.

"Can you help me?"

"We're full for the night."

"I'm looking for someone."

"This isn't a hotel. They don't have room numbers. All the beds in the dormitory are full. They come in at night and go out in the morning."

"Would you be kind enough to stop reading and look up at me? Thank you. Have you seen this man?"

"Don't recognise him."

"He plays a violin."

"Oh, him. Some twerp bought him a new violin. All we got was what he called classical music. I hate classical music."

"That twerp was me. I'm urgently looking for Jonathan."

"What's he done now?"

"He inherited a little over forty-five million dollars."

"You've got to be kidding me?"

"When did you last see him?"

"A month ago. Must have got his money. Be nice if he'd given me something for all those times I let him in out of the cold."

"You'll get something from me if I find Jonathan. Here's my phone number. Can you write down the addresses of any other local hospices and all the soup kitchens? Here's ten dollars to start you off. Another hundred if you find him and let me know. Oh, good. I've got your attention."

"Damn right you have. Can you make the down payment fifty dollars?"

"Of course I can. Please hurry. There's a taxi waiting for me outside."

"This is the only hospice in this part of Manhattan Island. There are two soup kitchens close by. There you are. Help yourself."

"I'll leave you a photograph of Jonathan to remind you."

"A hundred dollars will remind me every morning."

At the two soup kitchens, Phillip drew a blank. To each of them, he gave his phone number and a photograph of Jonathan, with a promise of a hundred dollars to the person that found him.

"Do I get a good tip for trying? Where to now, Mr Zimbabwe?"

"Harry B's. I need a drink."

Outside Harry B's, standing on the sidewalk, Phillip gave the Puerto Rican his taxi fare and a fifty-dollar tip.

"You've been most helpful."

"That's my job. What the man who owns this cab told me. Always be helpful."

"A wise man."

Frustrated at getting nowhere, Phillip went inside and up to the bar, ordering himself a double whisky.

"Something wrong, Phillip?"

"There's always something wrong. I've lost the violin player. Thanks. Cheers. Or as my father says, down the hatch."

"Welcome to Harry B's."

In his whole life, Phillip had been lucky. As far back as he could trace his ancestors, none of them had ever had to make use of a hospice. Never had to beg. Never had to ask for charity. All they ever had to rely on was family. Hoping that Jonathan had not suffered a fatal heart attack from all the excitement, Phillip looked around the bar. The place was empty of familiar faces. After two double whiskies, Phillip went home. Ever since the phone call from Andrew he had got nowhere. The man had to be somewhere. The next job was to go to the police. Report him missing. Dead or alive, he'd show up somewhere. It was Martha's last month at the office. Or so she had promised. When she came home at five o'clock, Phillip gave her a hug. The baby was really showing. In two months' time, he was going to become a father.

"Can I feel him?"

"Of course you can. One nice big round stomach. And a slight backache. Not long now, honey. I need a drink."

"Not long to wait. That first drink after the baby is born is going to taste good... Jonathan has gone missing. The money hasn't been touched. The British consul phoned Andrew."

"He's made a run for it?"

"Not without his money. And at this time of the year, he can't make money in the park. Jonathan Fernsby has vanished with the money still in the London bank... How was your day?"

"Hectic as usual. Clients are always wanting something. We've hired an assistant at reception to help Priscilla. A general factotum. Everyone in the office can use him for all those odd jobs that take up so much time. Makes the trained staff more productive."

"There was a letter this morning from Randall. Called him on the phone. We have three more guests for Christmas."

"How long are they staying?"

"As long as they like. Tomorrow, I'm going to the police station to report Jonathan missing. Not that they'll be much interested in a homeless old man. He must be in trouble. No one leaves that kind of money lying around."

THE DAY after Phillip reported Jonathan missing to the police, the phone rang. Phillip picked up the phone and said hello. It was lunchtime. Outside it was raining.

"He's here now. Came in ten minutes ago."

"How is he?"

"Cold and wet."

"Is he sick?"

"Just hungry. Come over now and you can give me my hundred dollars."

"I'm on my way. Don't let him leave."

"We'll give him a second helping."

A taxi took Phillip straight to the soup kitchen. The tired old woman who had made the phone call smiled when he gave her the hundred dollars.

"Thank you. My husband's unemployed. Has been for years."

"Can't he find a job? The economy is booming."

"Prefers to wear his slippers and live off his wife. Your man is in the dining room with the rest of them. Why are some people so lazy?"

"Part of human nature. He's lucky to have a caring wife."

"He's better to have around than live on my own."

"How long have you been married?"

"Forty-two."

"Did he always wear slippers? Thanks for your help. I'll mention your predicament to Jonathan."

"Why would he care? Can't do anything about it."

"You just might get a nice surprise."

"Through the door. You can see in through the small round window."

Through the window, Phillip could see the hoboes seated on benches at the long wooden tables, heads down, shovelling food into their mouths. Running his eyes up and down the rows of people, Phillip caught sight of Jonathan feeding himself bent forward over the table. He pushed open the swing door. Inside, there was a hum of conversation, looks of satisfaction, smiles on people's faces. Next to Jonathan, deep in conversation between spoonfuls of food, was an old lady wearing more than one overcoat. Behind her, tied together so they would not be separated, were a pile of old carry-bags, all stuffed full. Phillip walked through to stand behind Jonathan, no one taking any notice. The old lady gave him an upward, sideways glance and looked back at her food.

"Why didn't you go to the British consulate?"

"Why, Phillip. Hello. Have you come for lunch? This is my old friend Jean. Jean, say hello to my friend Phillip. Jean's the proverbial bag-lady, aren't you, my darling? Across is George and Godfrey. Sid's on my left. All old friends. There's nothing better than old friends. Noah, can you move up a little so Phillip can squeeze in? If you take a plate and go to the kitchen window, they'll give you some lunch. Nothing tastes better than food when you're cold and hungry. Nice and warm in here."

"I'll just sit down. I ate breakfast."

"Now, aren't you lucky?"

"Aren't you going to tell me what's going on, Jonathan?"

"Nothing is going on. That's my point."

"When you've finished your food, I'd like you to come with me. You owe me that much."

"Everyone. Listen up. This is the man who gave me my new violin. Anyone want a concert? That's the stuff. Happy days are here again. When I've finished eating, I'm going to play and sing you my latest love song, dedicated to Jean. If you love it, shout, if you don't, boo. How did you find me, Phillip?"

"Aren't you going to the consulate?"

"I'm afraid not. I enjoy my life as it is. I have friends. Old friends like Jean who I have known for years. I can't even imagine that other life."

"Music! We want music!" The whole room had stopped eating as they all called for music, shouting in unison. They were all having fun.

"Are you crazy, Jonathan?"

"Not really. I don't have any family to worry about. My only friends are here. I'm happy, which is more than can be said for a lot of rich people. Why should I change my life?"

"It's freezing cold outside."

"But not in here. Have a forkful of my lunch. You'll love it."

"What about the charities?"

"I'll leave that to the British government."

"Your eyes nearly popped out of your head."

"And then I had time to think. You gave me all I wanted, Phillip. You gave me my violin."

"Music! Music!"

"See? Listen to them. Tell me this isn't fun. Why don't you stay and listen to the music?"

"What's the song called?"

"'All I Ever Want is a Friend.'"

"Do they know about it?"

"Of course they don't. And please don't tell them."

"I'm going to wait outside for you."

"You can wait as long as you like. But it won't change my mind."

"I'll be waiting at the desk. Nice meeting you, Jean."

"Who are you, may I ask?"

"Jonathan doesn't want you to know. We'll have to see."

"Don't trip over my bags."

"I'll try not to. Just one last conversation, Jonathan. And then I'm out of your life."

Phillip gave the old lady at the desk a smile and went outside to pay the taxi. Inside again he stood at the desk, nowhere to sit down. After ten minutes the noise inside quietened, and then there was silence, followed by the perfect sound of a violin, the melody flowing, the music catching the attention of the old lady behind the desk. Quietly, a female voice began to sing, the voice growing stronger as the singer got into her stride. Phillip walked across to the door and looked through the small round window. Everyone inside had stopped eating. Jonathan was standing up behind the bench next to the pile of bags, his feet splayed, his head down sideways to his violin. Next to him stood Jean the bag-lady singing Jonathan's song of friendship. When Jean finished the song, and Jonathan brought down his violin, the room erupted, everyone clapping and shouting their excitement. For half an hour, Jonathan and Jean gave them a concert, giving Phillip goose pimples. When the concert was over, the swing door opened, letting out the people. The last two to come out were Jonathan and Jean, Jean with her bags strung over her shoulders, Jonathan carrying the case with his violin.

"Where did you learn to sing like that, Jean? Your new song is perfect, Jonathan. They all loved it."

"Nothing more satisfying than a good audience."

"Would you like to come with me to the little Italian restaurant I go to close to the park where we met? We can take a cab."

"They wouldn't let us in. Jean and I would be an embarrassment, wouldn't we, Jean? Anyway, I don't like Italian restaurants. Haven't been in a restaurant for years. Why don't you walk back with us to our home?"

"You have a home?"

"An old building is going to be knocked down when the developers get rid of the last tenants. A few of us moved in. The developers say they don't mind, provided we get out with the last tenant. Not everyone treats us like shit."

"Can we talk privately?"

"As privately as you wish. Jean first sang in her school choir. I've been giving her voice training. As you heard in the park, I can write the music and the words for my songs, but I can't sing. Shall we walk? It's so nice to feel full. They really enjoyed Jean's singing. Playing and singing for our friends. Now that's enjoyment. We can use the toilet in the building. Even use one of the bathrooms. Unfortunately, there's no hot water. You know what I want right now, Phillip? To soak for an hour in a nice hot bath. But you can't have everything in this life."

"Isn't the building cold?"

"Freezing. At night, we huddle together on the floor, keeping each other warm, covered in blankets. If she had had the right training earlier, my Jean could have been an opera singer. Life with all its missed chances. But you know what they say: better late than never. When you and I have our little talk, we'll have it alone. I don't want to bother the others. Wow, that lunch was good. Should last a couple of days."

"Can I help you carry those bags, Jean?"

"I'm used to carrying my own. Makes me feel secure, having them close to me."

"How far away are we from your 'home'?"

"Half an hour. Jean and I walk slowly. I'm sixty-five next month. Jean is a little younger. You can carry the violin if you insist. I'm never sure how old I look with all this hair on my face. Not that it matters. Not long to go now, Phillip. Five more years. Maybe ten. Why I don't ever want to lose my friends. Friends look after each other. Don't they, Jean? 'All I Ever Want is a Friend.' She sings my song so beautifully. Makes my heart sing."

"How much longer have you got where you are?"

"Who knows, Phillip? Who knows? It's all in the lap of the gods. We go where the wind takes us. We never worry. We enjoy what we have. Why, beneath our appearance, we're happy. Not what you look like on the outside that's important, it's how you feel on the inside."

"They would have let you both into the restaurant. Angela the waitress and the Italian owners are nice people."

"They probably would. Not everyone you meet in life is bad. Just most of them for me, unfortunately. No, maybe that's not true. You often remember those in your life who did you a disservice and forget the nice people. The older I get, the more cynical I become. I miss the flowers in the park. Winter is so long."

"You could live in a warm climate."

"I could also be living in hell."

They trudged on, the old lady borne down by the bags she did not want to let out of her sight. It began to rain. They walked close to the buildings to keep out of the way of passing people. No one looked at Jonathan or Jean, averting their eyes. The traffic roared. The world went on. They turned down a side street and entered an old building, walking slowly up two flights of stairs. Phillip could see that Jean was exhausted. Some of the empty rooms had been gutted, the doors removed. There was one closed door. Behind the closed door, Phillip could hear the television. At the end of the corridor on the second floor, they entered one of the gutted apartments.

Three women and two men, all well past their prime, were sitting on the floor with their backs to the wall, each covered in an old blanket. It was cold in the room. They all smiled up at Jean and Jonathan, keeping their hands under the blankets. There was no furniture, or curtains over the windows. One of the old women was visibly shivering. Jean put down her bags, opened one of them and pulled out a grey blanket, huddling down with one of her friends against the wall. In the middle of the room, someone had placed a saucer with half a candle waiting to be lit. Jonathan nodded towards one of the doors inside the apartment. Phillip followed him into a bathroom, and Jonathan closed the door behind them.

"Keep your voice down, Phillip. My business is my business. You can sit on the edge of the bath. I'll put the lid down and sit on the toilet."

Behind Jonathan, another half-used candle stood on a saucer on top of the back of the toilet, an old cigarette lighter next to the saucer. Jonathan looked at Phillip and waited, neither of them saying anything.

"Why, Jonathan? Living like this is appalling. Had the others eaten? You could feed every homeless person in New York with all that money. All you have to do is go to the British consulate and give them proof of your identity. By the day after tomorrow, you can be out of all this shit. I don't understand you. What's the problem?"

"I'm not sure if I am able to change who I have become, and I don't want to become that other person. I'd lose my friends. People would say they like me for all the wrong reasons. I would spend the rest of my life being a person I am not. I didn't make that money. Neither did my father. Just the fluke of there being no other male members of the Fernsby family left me in line for the inheritance. My only passion in life has been music. You saw that again this afternoon. People clapped, genuinely, it wasn't just a bunch of people telling me how good I am in the hope they'll get something out of me. With forty-five million dollars, I'll be the perfect target, everyone wanting some of the pie. They won't want me, Phillip, they'll want my money."

"But you'll be living comfortably."

"Will I? Or will I constantly be protecting my back? I'm too old to be bothered with luxury. Too old to show off, too old to begin a successful foundation to give away my money to people who need it. I'm too old to defend myself, to defend that money from being stolen. And worst of all, I would not have a true friend left in the world. Would those people outside be genuine friends if I brought them into your world? I'd be hounded by everyone for my money. They wouldn't want me or my music. And there's another problem. Probably the biggest problem, the one I least want to face."

"What's that? Money can protect you from problems."

"But not from my sisters."

"You never mentioned you had family."

"I try not to even think of them, let alone bring them into a conversation. And, to answer your earlier question, my friends in the next room were all at the soup kitchen, eating and listening to our music. They've all been fed. We were lucky. The system we have works. Why must I change my life? If I do, both my sisters will demand their share of the family inheritance. Their children will demand it. They will go to lawyers to get what they consider their right. We're Americans. There's no male inheritance in America, the money and the title going only to the male. Women's liberation would challenge the Fernsby will in the courts. Oh, and don't look at me like that. You haven't met my sisters. When my hands developed arthritis and I lost my job in the orchestra, losing the only life I ever wanted in the process, all they could say to me was get another job. Do some work. Earn yourself a living. Stop being a bum. They didn't want anything to do with me. They didn't even invite me over for Christmas. I have had no contact with my sisters or my nieces and nephews for twenty-five years. And if I were rich, they'd be all over me and want to show me off to their friends. If, by then, they hadn't crucified me in those lovely American courts. What's the point in taking all that money if it's going to make me miserable? Does money make you happy, Phillip? It makes most people greedy. I'm too old to shave my beard and look at myself in a mirror in some fancy apartment surrounded by people only interested in my money... Do you want to test it now, Phillip? Then go outside and tell my friends that the day after tomorrow I'll be worth forty-five million dollars. You'll see an instant, horrible change in what is at this moment true friendship. And if I give each of them a pile of money, will it change their lives for the better?"

"Of course it will."

"Then go and tell them, Phillip. I challenge you. I appreciate your help. I greatly appreciate my new violin. Either go out there now and tell them or leave me alone. Next year, when the sun comes out, I'll see you in the park. I'll play you my music."

"So you don't wish to be rich?"

"No, I don't. I've been reading about the pursuit of wealth in all those discarded newspapers for years. And no one in that world ever seems to be content, let alone happy. It's a horrible world, the modern world of materialism. Leave me out. Let them tear themselves to pieces. Just leave me out of it, Phillip."

"I should have minded my own business."

"You tried to help. Nothing wrong with trying to help. Thank you again for my violin."

"Couldn't you have found some other kind of work? Another career? Arthritis only affected your hands. You were still young."

"All I know how to do is play a violin. My mind and body only work with music. I tried manual jobs and failed. Couldn't see the point. Started drinking. Whatever I earned as a daily wage, I drank. Became a bum. I hated my jobs. Why my sisters kept their distance. Now it's my turn to keep my distance."

"Maybe someone in the music industry will hear your songs and want to record them."

"They'll listen to a beggar on the street? I don't think so. They want a celebrity name. A good-looking man. A pretty woman. Not a down-and-out bum. How are they going to market a bum?"

"Make one hell of a story."

"No thank you. Let my friends hear my music. That's my satisfaction. That's all I want from my music."

"Wouldn't you like the whole world to hear your songs? Give millions of people pleasure?"

For a moment, Jonathan paused in his argument, looking up at the ceiling. "Maybe."

"There you are. There's hope. I'll leave you be, Jonathan."

"You're not going to tell Jean and the others?"

"Of course not. It's none of my business."

Phillip got up from his seat on the edge of the bath, put out his hand and shook Jonathan's hand, both of them looking at each other, both of them silent. Jonathan kept his seat on the lid of the toilet as Phillip walked out of the bathroom. The sleeping, well-fed old people, huddled close to each other under their blankets, took no notice. Phillip shook his head. They were worlds apart, Phillip no longer understanding what the world was all about.

When the taxi dropped him back at his apartment building it was still raining. Pushing himself through the revolving door, Phillip found the other world of warmth and materialism. Upstairs, Martha was home from work, sitting comfortably in front of the television watching an episode of *Cheers*.

"Thought you didn't like television?"

"Where have you been? Harry B's? This show is quite a giggle."

"I found Jonathan. He's got a girlfriend who sings like an angel. Doesn't want his money. I give up. Would your media friends be interested in a bag-lady singing a hobo's songs? The song was really good."

"Make one hell of a story."

"What I told Jonathan. I think his hidden ego would like his songs to become famous. Leave something behind. There's something in all of us that wants to leave something behind. Leave a legacy to show our lives have had some meaning."

"The fame would go to the bag-lady."

"Now that would suit Jonathan. Anyway, from now on its none of my business. Do you want to hear the rest of Jonathan's story?"

"Not really... Where did she perform his song?"

"At the soup kitchen."

"Interesting. Come and sit down. I'm sure the bar called Cheers is just as much fun as Harry B's."

"How's our baby?"

"Come and feel. She's kicking."

"Oh, my goodness. I can feel him."

"Give your wife a kiss."

"It was like an angel had come down from heaven. I was outside at reception waiting for Jonathan to come and talk to me in private. He didn't want his hobo friends to hear what I was going to say. Then the dining room went silent. Not a sound. Could have heard a pin drop. The violin began, the sound of a lovely melody. And then to cap this perfect melody the voice of an angel began to sing 'All I Ever Want is a Friend'. The angel voice was deep, the voice of an older woman. The lyrics were clear, with the violin weaving in and out of the singing. I had goosebumps. The old lady at reception had stopped doing her work, her attention was captured by the music. When the music stopped there was dead silence, followed by a wild burst of applause that went on and on. When the shouts and table-thumping stopped, another song began. And another. And another. I had heard one of the songs before in the park, sung by Jonathan. As I looked through the small round window in the door to the dining room I could see Jonathan and the old bag-lady standing, everyone else sitting at the long wooden tables. Jonathan had introduced her to me as Jean, his friend of many years. I was awestruck, watching her sing these songs. Later, when I asked Jonathan if he would mind his songs being played to the world, he wasn't so sure he wanted to keep them to himself. Maybe that's the way to help them. Instead of making him the wealthy Eighteenth Earl of Fernsby, we make his songs live forever. We make Jean the famous singer and let her do what she wants with the money."

"You haven't given me that kiss."

"Were you listening to me?"

"To every word. Can I mention the Earls of Fernsby?"

"I suppose so. He was the one who told me about his relationship to the English Fernsbys. How the whole thing came up in the first place."

"It makes a better story. After all my promoting of Marcin Galinski, I've got to know how the mind of the media works. Let me think about it. At the end of the month, I'll have nothing to do when I leave the office. I could make a few calls. Test the market. See if I get any reaction. We could find someone to start a new recording company. If I could put together the right publicity stunt you could have another start-up, Mr Venture Capitalist."

"I'm not trying to make money out of him."

"But you'd be in control. We wouldn't have some smart-ass recording company running off with most of Jean and Jonathan's money. In that business, how does the musician really know how many records are sold? He has to believe what the record company tells him. What the record company tells the artist's auditor. They pay the artist what suits them."

"Jonathan was going to form a charity to give away some of his inheritance. If we own the recording company we can channel a good portion of the profits to Jonathan's chosen charities. It's a win-win for Jonathan without the problems he fears from having all that money. He'll be in the background. You think you could do something, honey?"

"I can try... Now. Do I get that kiss? Thank you. There's nothing better than the perfect kiss... It'll give us something to do together while we're waiting for our baby."

"Maybe Perry Mance would be interested in promoting music. What's the difference between a book and a record? The online marketing system would be the same. In the end, getmethatbook.com will become an online publishing house, there won't be any more need for print publishers, the writers will go direct to getmethatbook.com. The same could be said for musicians. Writers need to vet their work and proofread the final copy. All a musician requires is a recording studio to record the music. There are plenty of independent recording studios who would record for a few thousand dollars. Where's the problem in Jonathan having to go to a recording studio?... I still don't understand why he hasn't gone to the British consulate to claim his inheritance. Am I meddling in his affairs again?"

"People need looking after, Phillip, even when they don't realise it. The man lives on the street. That can't be a life. It's right for you to help a man who's down and out. If you don't, it will be on your conscience."

"He thinks he'll lose his only true friends."

"People are all the same, rich or poor. Friends are all the same. We all like to believe we have friends. All musicians like the sound of applause. If his music and her singing are as good as you say, and the idea's building in my head for the publicity work, the applause will be deafening. There are only two ingredients that are important: the song and the publicity. If the music is so good and the singer so good, all you need to succeed is my publicity. In the end, most of today's success comes from good marketing. From companies like Bowden, Crookshank, Fairbanks and Webber. My job is to get the public's attention. When you get their attention with a good product all you then have to do is collect the money. Money today is made by the brain, not by the hands. It's mental, not physical. Yes, you need a singer but there's no singer without a song, a song that comes from inside Jonathan's head. Years ago you had to dig the ground and plant the seed to grow your food. Now you dig the mind. Don't worry about disturbing your violin player's life of a homeless man. When he hears all that applause you'll be the friend he really wanted. You see, life as a venture capitalist isn't as boring as you say. This one is going to be fun. And if we win, rewarding in more ways than one. You'll have created something, Phillip. Not just more boring money, as you call it. It will give you deep satisfaction. Leave it all to me. It's quite a story. Let my mind work on it. Why you think too much money is boring I never understand... Now, look at that. The show's over. I've missed the end of *Cheers*. You want to eat in or go out tonight?"

"You mind if I stand and stare out of the window for a few minutes?"

"Do what you like, honey."

"All those people out there. All with their little lives. What's it all about?"

"You tell me. Life in all its glory. Warts and all. Isn't that what you told me? He's going to love you if it works."

"You mean Jonathan?"

"No, silly. Perry Mance. He wants it all. We're going to lead him into the record business. Of course, he'll have to give us more shares in his company. Business is fun, Phillip. Stop staring with that gloomy look on your face. You'll be doing Jonathan a favour. We all need a little help in life, mark my words. I'll put on some nice music and let you stand and think. Not long now and there will be a third member of the family. Carmen. I'm sure it's going to be a girl."

"Your doctor still hasn't told you?"

"Haven't asked him. Would have told you if I had. I told him right at the beginning not to tell me until our baby is born. You think it will be all right this time? I worry all the time. I wish I had more faith. We'll go to church again on Sunday. Faith, hope and charity. Isn't that what it's all meant to be about? There we are. Haydn's Twenty-Eighth Symphony. Our favourite. What's wrong with that?"

As Phillip stared out of the big window at the skyscrapers of New York, he wasn't sure of anything. Were all those people down there burrowing away in the concrete jungle living little lives standing in their kitchens, sitting in their chairs, asleep in bed with their dreams? Or were most of them living big and exciting lives, the great future calling, life a constant adventure? Was his own life an adventure? He hoped so, but he wasn't sure. Poor Jonathan. Poor Jean. Or was it really poor Phillip with his fancy life on the forty-ninth floor hoping for a baby to give his life purpose. With his mind going round in circles he tried to listen to the music of Haydn while he thought back to his life in the African bush, to the glory of nature in all its perfection. Instead, all he could see was the world of people, the city of New York where the lights outshone the moon and the sun rarely penetrated.

"At least we can hear the music."

"What are you talking about?"

"It doesn't matter. Are you going to employ a nanny?"

"Of course I am. Who else is going to look after the baby when I'm at work? Unless you want to change the nappies. No, I didn't think so. We'll employ a live-in nanny who can live in the spare bedroom with the baby. That way my sleep won't be interrupted. My mind will be crystal clear every morning when I go to work. You got to have eight hours' good sleep to function properly. Or the mind gets muddled and makes mistakes. Can't afford to make mistakes when you're running a business. Franklyn agrees with me. Don't know about Jaz. She's too interested in men. What she's going to do as a single mother is beyond my comprehension. The world is nuts. She goes to meetings at Linguare, talks business half the morning to Marcin and neither mention their baby. Crazy. They're having a baby together, for goodness sake. Thank goodness for central heating. Must be bitterly cold outside where you're looking. Thank goodness for plate-glass windows. Draw the curtains, Phillip. I can't imagine what life must be like for Jonathan."

"He has his friends. Says he's happy."

"We all talk rubbish."

"Then why doesn't he collect his money?"

"You can't live other people's lives."

"But I'm trying to change his."

"Let's go out and have dinner in a restaurant with live music. Or we can go to a concert and eat afterwards. I love life in the city. There's so much to do. Are you happy, Phillip? You look so sad today."

"Of course I am. And I'm hungry. Let's go find ourselves a restaurant."

"Shouldn't we book?"

"Let's take our chances. Makes it all the more interesting."

Phillip smiled to himself. Life on the farm. Life on the banks of the Zambezi River. Life in New York City. In the end, it was all the same. It all came down to eating.

"I wouldn't mind a nice piece of fresh Zambezi bream."

"That you're not going to get. Put your coat on. It's cold outside. You haven't talked to me about Africa for a while. That's something."

"Don't you like me talking about Africa?"

"You have to go forwards in life, not backwards. The days of the white man in Africa are over. The British Empire is over, Phillip."

"You're probably right."

"I know I am."

"Why are women always right?"

"Are you arguing with me?"

"Of course not."

"We think practically. You have to be practical in life. And that includes your Jonathan Fernsby. His music is worthless until it's turned into something practical. Turned into money. Look at Randall. He turned his passion for writing books into money. Or rather his publisher turned it into money for him."

"Everything is commercial."

"Of course it is. We'll catch a cab and ask the cab driver. He'll know the new best restaurant. The taxi drivers of New York know everything... I've got a backache. The baby is getting heavy. Weeks now, honey. Weeks. Then we'll both have what we want. A family that will go on forever."

2

On Martha's last day at the office, Phillip took himself off to the pub. He had nothing to do. Nothing to think about. There had been no further mention of Perry Mance or Jonathan, Martha busy handing her accounts over to Jasmine for Martha's six-month sabbatical. Whether she'd last that long away from her work, Phillip found questionable. Once a healthy baby was born, a nanny employed, Martha would be itching to get back to work. Harry B's was packed. On the last working day of the month, everyone had been paid, everyone had money in their pockets. An extra barman Phillip didn't know was helping Terry behind the bar. She was young, pretty and smiled seductively at Phillip. Most married American men wore a wedding ring on the third finger of their left hand. Rhodesians rarely did. Phillip smiled back at the girl. It was all part of the pursuit of life. The quest for a husband. The quest for stability and security. With the glass and the full beer bottle in front of him, Phillip looked around. All the accents were American. Terry was running up and down his bar like a dog at a fair, filling his customers' orders, keeping them happy, getting as much money as possible from the best day of the month. Phillip poured his beer into the glass and took his first drink, the girl having gone to serve another impatient customer. The clock behind the bar between the bottles of whisky said five minutes to three. On Martha's last day, Phillip expected her home late. He had time to get happy. Time to get drunk. Wedged onto his barstool between two strangers, Phillip looked straight ahead at the rows of bottles and let the alcohol slowly take effect. It wasn't quite like the Centenary club back in his days on World's View but it did not matter. As people drank they became happy wherever they were. The second hand on the clock went round and round, the beer went down, pint after pint. It was a happy afternoon for Phillip.

"You going to work here permanently?" With the fourth beer down, Phillip had lost his inhibitions.

"I'm a friend of Terry's. Terry owns Harry B's. I help him out in emergencies. He tells me you're from Africa. That your wife is about to have a baby. Lucky you. Enjoy that beer."

"What do you do when you're not helping out, Terry?"

"I work in a sound recording studio. My ambition has always been to be in the music industry."

"Now that's a strange coincidence."

"How do you mean? Are you in music?"

"Maybe. Where's the studio?"

"Round the corner. Work was slack today. Competition is tough. Why my boss let me come help Terry."

"What's your name? I'm Phillip."

"Amelia. Terry says you're a venture capitalist. What's a venture capitalist?"

"You'd better go serve the customers. Everything on my tab?"

"Of course it is."

"Are the tips good?"

"Wouldn't be here if they weren't. Rents are high in New York."

"This time give me a single malt whisky before you go... What would your boss charge to record a medley of songs?"

"Depends on how long it takes to record and process. You got to get the bugs out. Why you ask?"

"I have a friend. Two friends, in fact. They are homeless down-and-outs."

"We'd need the money upfront. A session will cost you eight thousand dollars."

"That's a lot to record half a dozen songs."

"Good work doesn't come cheap."

"Of course it doesn't. How would I get hold of you?"

"Ask Terry... Hoboes. That's weird."

"We'll have to see."

"Pity you're married. I quite like older men. The young ones are all the same. All they want is to get into your pants."

"Life, Amelia. That's how it goes. Whatever we say or seem to say, we all want something. Are you looking for a husband?"

"A girl's got to start young if she wants to get the right man. Good opportunities don't crop up every day. You got to work on making yourself a good future. How long have you been married?"

"A couple of years. I left it late. Not too many girls live in a safari camp. What's the name of the recording studio?"

"Manley and Thombs. We're young, dynamic and know what we're doing."

"I'll remember that, Amelia. You'd better go. That man two down from me is waving his empty glass. When you've finished, bring me my bill. Got to go."

Downing the last of his beer, and topping it off with the whisky, Phillip eased himself off the barstool, the strangers on either side of him having not said a word all afternoon. Some talked. Some sat. It did not matter. Outside the rain had stopped, the street lights were on, people walking up and down the sidewalk on their way home from work, cars on the road impatiently hooting, the drivers frustrated by the traffic. Phillip decided to walk home, the only exercise he would have all day. Walking made the alcohol pass more quickly through his body, clearing his head. With the collar of his coat up to his ears, hands deep in his pockets, Phillip walked through the streets of the city.

Back home on the forty-ninth floor, to Phillip's surprise, he found they had company. Martha was sitting on the sofa entertaining a man. They were drinking coffee, Martha leaning back against the cushions, the round belly clearly visible. She was smiling, the conversation animated. With the beers and whisky partially walked off, Phillip smiled and sat down in his comfortable armchair, opposite Martha and the stranger.

"Thought you'd be home later on your last day at work."

"You been to Harry B's? I can smell the alcohol from here. This is Chad Fox, an old friend of mine from the *Herald*. One of the first to get a copy of Marcin's voice recognition software and write about it. He wants some help from you. You want some coffee? While you two have your talk I'm going to lie down. Having a baby at my age is tiring."

"What's it all about?"

"Jonathan. Chad sneaked into the soup kitchen dressed as a hobo. He hasn't shaved for a week. Look at him. He calls it going undercover. The old lady at reception you talked about with the unemployed, slipper-wearing husband phoned him when Jonathan came for his food carrying his violin, accompanied by the bag-lady. No one took any notice of Chad, he blended in so well. Journalists are sneaky when they're hunting for a good story. Chad says you were right, Phillip. The bag-lady sings like an angel. The concert went on for an hour. Sounds like Jonathan has written her more songs. With the concert in full swing and everyone's attention centred on Jonathan and Jean, Chad stood behind the seated hoboes and recorded the concert so he could show his boss what it was all about. They want to do a big piece on Jean and catch the public's attention and the rest of the media. I'll leave you two to talk."

When the bedroom door closed behind Martha, Chad, with a permanent smile on his unshaven face, sat there, his blue eyes sparkling with amusement. Phillip went to the cocktail cabinet and took out two glasses and a bottle of his favourite double malt whisky.

"You want a drink, Chad?"

"Thought you'd never ask."

"I've got a start on you. Had four beers and a whisky in the pub. What do you want from me?"

"An introduction to Jonathan. Martha says you know where he's squatting in an old building that's soon to be demolished. The weather forecast is rain tomorrow. He won't be walking the streets."

"How does that look?"

"Perfect. To your health, Phillip."

"To your wealth, Chad. I suppose I can take you around. I did promise Jonathan I wouldn't interfere in his life."

"At first I'll talk to Jean. Tell her how I heard her sing. All you have to do is introduce me to them. By the time I've written an article on Jean, CBS or any one of the TV channels will want to broadcast her singing. It's the most extraordinary experience. You can't imagine someone singing so well looking like that. Maybe they'll invite her to sing one of Jonathan's songs on a talent contest. Or a concert to raise money for the homeless. Every part of the media loves a good story. My boss is excited. Stories like Jean's catch people's attention. Makes them feel warm inside. From destitution, living on the streets of New York, to fame. Real fame. That woman can sing, Phillip. Never heard anything like it before. Her voice, backed by of all things a violin, is quite extraordinary."

"You're not going to write about Jonathan?"

"All depends what he says."

"Just don't bring me into it. He may like his songs to be heard. Just doesn't want the rest of it."

"Leave it to me. Shall we say ten o'clock tomorrow morning? I'll meet you here. If they're not in the old building we'll try again another day."

"Wear plenty of warm clothes. The building is freezing. What do I say to Jonathan?"

"Nothing. Leave it all to me. Getting information out of people is my profession. Oh, and your wife spoke to Perry Mance. He likes the idea of getting into the music business."

"I won't be doing this for myself."

"Of course you won't, Phillip. We're both just trying to help a pair of down-and-outers. But, oh, wow, can she sing. And the music. Close as I've heard to perfection in years... Tell me a bit about yourself, Phillip. I know you met Martha in Africa. That your grandfather was Ben Crossley."

"Are you going to write about me?"

"Isn't it all part of the same story? I like a good story. So do our readers. What keeps up the circulation. The bigger the circulation, the more we can charge for advertising. Keeps me in my job. And didn't I read somewhere your brother is Randall Holiday? Now he can write. If I could write a novel that good I wouldn't be sitting here looking for a good story and drinking your whisky. She's a lovely woman, Martha. And when it comes to publicity she's one of the best. This one is going to be big... You got more of that whisky?"

THE NEXT MORNING, feeling he was being led by the nose, Phillip showed Chad the old building the developers were going to tear down to make themselves a fortune. Chad was dressed like a hobo, his hair uncombed surrounding an unshaven face. Somehow, he had blacked out one of his front teeth. With nothing to do, Martha had stayed in bed.

"Why are you dressed like that, Chad?"

"Never look rich in a poor man's house. You got to blend in. Make the interviewee feel comfortable. The more they relax, the easier it is to wheedle out a story."

"They may not be here."

"Let's go in and see. When does your Harry B's open?"

"Eleven o'clock."

"Good, when we're done here I'll buy you a beer."

"You can't go to Harry B's looking like that."

"We'll see. I'll use my charm. Getting what you want is all about using your charm. When's this place coming down?"

"When the developers kick out the last tenant."

"Do they bribe the ones who don't want to leave?"

"Probably. We live in a wonderful world. It's all about money."

As they walked up the stairs they heard the violin, followed by the singing of Jean. They both stopped to listen.

"We're in luck, Phillip."

"Sounds like it. It's the same song I heard in the garden during the summer. Jonathan called the song 'The Last Time I Heard of Linda'. Jonathan was twenty years old when he last saw Linda. She was nineteen. He said you never forget your first love."

"This story gets better and better. Come on."

"Who do I say you are?"

"Chad Fox from the *Herald*, a big fan of their music."

Upstairs, the door hung open. Only Jonathan and Jean were standing, the others were huddled against the wall under their blankets, a small oil-burning heater in front of them. One of the windows had been knocked out. The room was as cold as charity. Jonathan was wearing mittens. When they saw Phillip the music stopped.

"What happened to the window?"

"They want us to get out. Yesterday, when we got back from the soup kitchen, the window had been broken open. To what do I owe this privilege, Phillip? You said you were going to leave me alone. Oh, now I get it. The same man who recorded our music at the soup kitchen."

"Meet Chad Fox from the *Herald*. He wants to promote Jean's singing. Asked me to introduce you. You said maybe you'd like the world to hear your songs. I'll leave you two to talk... I love that song. It's so nostalgic. Linda. 'The Last Time I Heard of Linda.' It's so young."

"Hi. I'm Chad Fox disguised as a hobo. Your lady can sing, Jonathan. Hello, Jean. You sing like an angel. I want to promote a concert to raise money for the homeless with you as the lead singer, Jean. Would you like that? I need lots of background information from both of you to get the story going. My, it's cold in here. Hello, everyone. I'm Chad. I'm here to help you all. Please carry on with the music. Do you mind if I make another recording? If I have my way, Jonathan Fernsby, your music will live forever through the singing of Jean. My newspaper will provide the backup. We will provide the rest of the players in the string quartet to give Jean's singing even more depth. Do you mind if I sit down next to your friends? You don't have to leave, Phillip... Oh, well... Now, where were we? Fernsby. That's an unusual surname. I know that name from somewhere. Isn't it English?... Please sing for us, Jean. The perfect sound of an angel. Where on earth did you find a voice like that? Give me the song of Linda again. I want the whole world to listen. Music. What would this world do without music? Where did you learn to play a violin like that, Jonathan?"

"In the New York Philharmonic."

"My goodness. The New York Philharmonic. Tell me more. Mind if I warm my hands over your little heater? When are they going to push you out? So, Jonathan, once upon a time you played in the most prestigious orchestra in the whole of America... Sing, Jean. Sing me a song. One day soon you're going to be famous... Goodbye, Phillip. See you in Harry B's."

Phillip left, trying to close the door properly behind him. Someone had bent the hinges to make that impossible, the developers taking no chances. Halfway down the stairs, the song of Linda began to play again. Phillip shook his head in amusement. Chad was good. Really good. Jean's face had lit up with a smile at the mention of fame. At least he had not stuck his nose in. What they told the newspaper about themselves was now up to Jonathan and Jean. Outside the old building, the cab driver was waiting, reading the morning *Herald* newspaper. Chad had promised him a good tip for waiting.

"He's going to be there a while. Drop me at a pub called Harry B's. I can give you the directions. Then come back again and wait for Chad."

"They were there?"

"Singing a song. All worked perfectly."

"Everything works in New York."

"I hope so. If the pub isn't open I'll find myself a café nearby. No problem."

"Isn't it a bit early to start drinking?"

"It's never too early to start drinking. I'll pay for this leg of the journey. It's nearly Christmas. Another month and it's Christmas. You go back the way we came earlier this morning. The pub is round the corner from my apartment. No hurry. The place opens at eleven. Why does everyone want to be famous? By now our Chad will have them eating out of his hand. Everyone telling their story. Poor Jonathan. Money. No one leaves you alone when you have money. Or the prospect of money. Or they think they can make you famous."

"What are you talking about?"

"A man's life. A life I promised to leave alone."

"What's wrong with being rich and famous?"

"It'll destroy them."

"Can't be doing too well squatting in that old building. You got to have money in New York. The only way to go. Ten years down the line I'll have a fleet of my own taxis, a fancy apartment and a wife twenty years younger than me that looks like a film star. Life's exciting. Got to have ambition."

"Maybe. Wish you luck... Anything worthwhile in the newspaper?"

"Nothing. Except the sports pages. You'd better pay me for this morning's leg of the journey in case your friend has left when I go back."

"No problem. He'll give you the big tip if you're there to pick him up."

When Phillip got out of the taxi and walked across the street to Harry B's, he found he was lucky. The door was closed, but through the window he could see Terry polishing glasses behind the bar, getting everything ready for another big day at the end of a month. Phillip tapped on the window, catching Terry's attention and bringing a smile to his face. Phillip stood back and waited.

"Why do I always talk to cab drivers? Makes no sense. Why would they be interested in my problems?... Good morning, Terry."

"My, you are early."

"Had a meeting that ended early for me. When Chad's finished getting his story, he's going to meet me here. He's a journalist. If he likes your place it'll be good for your business. Journalists drink together. It's cold today. Can I get a cup of coffee? It's too early to start drinking."

"How long will he be?"

"I have no idea. Could be ten minutes if they won't talk to him. A couple of hours if they do. Is Amelia working today?"

"She helps me when she can at the end of the month. Depends on what's happening at the studio. One coffee coming up."

"He's dressed like a hobo to get his latest story."

"Who?"

"Chad Fox. The man from the *Herald*. Be nice to him."

At eleven, when the bar officially opened, there was no sign of Chad. At one-thirty, when Phillip was on his third beer, deliberately taking it slowly, a beaming Chad walked into the bar. There was still no sign of Amelia. The bar was busy. Phillip introduced Chad to Terry.

"You don't mind?"

"Why should I? You're a journalist. At least you don't smell. That's a joke. What are you having?"

"Did you get your story? Give him a beer, Terry."

"It was like opening a floodgate. Why I've been so long."

"Was the cab driver waiting?"

"I had to walk two blocks in the rain to hail a cab. Cab drivers are not too keen to stop for a hobo. Nice bar… Once Jonathan heard his girlfriend's extraordinary story, he was happy to talk about himself in front of the others. My guess is he'll get his Fernsby money and pass most of it on to a foundation. I told him we can find the right people to run the Fernsby music foundation. There will be scholarships to Juilliard and other schools of music around the world. He had no idea Jean had been a professional musician back in the sixties. She's never heard the Earl of Fernsby story. They were too scared to bring back their past. They both wanted to live in the present. Give me half an hour while I sit here making my notes. I'm going to get a dozen articles out of this story, all thanks to your Martha. Good stories are difficult to find. I'll fill you in as I go along."

"Write your notes, drink your beer and when you're finished tell me the story of Jean. Was she famous in her youth?"

"She might have been if she hadn't got pregnant. The piano player who ran the band made her have an abortion. Broke up the band. Jean, a beautiful twenty-year-old Jean, hard now to imagine, went from band to band, gig to gig. She tells me the abortion made her drink, the only way she could forget killing her own son. When she was sober, the people loved her. Not so good when she drank. By the time she was thirty, she says she had lost most of her looks. Her voice had deteriorated. She was down the slippery slide, facing the abyss. By the time she was forty she was out on the streets, a foulmouthed bitter woman that hated everyone but mostly herself. She said by then she had slept with half the men in New York. The sixties and the seventies. The rock 'n' roll period. The Beatles. Elvis Presley. The pill to stop a girl getting pregnant. No HIV AIDS. A lot of young men and young women destroyed themselves in the sixties. Jean says most of them didn't care. And then she met Jonathan when she was fifty, himself a recovering alcoholic, and they became friends. Real friends. True friends. Why Jonathan didn't want to change his life by telling Jean he was going to be rich. They haven't had a drink in all the seven years they've been together."

"Are they lovers?"

"No. Just friends. They love each other but they are not lovers."

"Does she want to be famous?"

"Oh, yes. And with the voice training she has had from Jonathan, and now his glorious music, she has every chance of being famous. She wants to come out and tell people about the abortion, about killing her child. She wants all those pregnant unmarried girls to hear her story. The anti-abortion lobby will love it. She wants to sing for her kid. For the life that never was. And Jonathan wants to help her. Give me a while to write down the keywords that will jolt my memory. I have a system so I don't forget anything, and when I write, the story flows. I like to write my articles so they run uninterrupted. The way your brother writes his novels. Booze, Phillip. Be warned. We all have to control our drinking if we don't want to end up down the plughole."

"What did the other hoboes think of Jonathan's story?"

"Their eyes lit up. Jonathan has promised to create a trust in which each of his friends will be a beneficiary. They won't get their hands on the capital. Just a monthly, liveable income."

"Will Jean and Jonathan still be happy?"

"Only time will tell. Can't be any worse than the way they are living. As I was leaving, the developer arrived to kick them out of the building."

"What name is she going to sing under?"

"The Bag-Lady, of course. Maybe later, if it works, she'll go back to Jean."

"What's her surname?"

"She hasn't told me yet. There's a lot more story to come."

"How are you going to stay in contact?"

"I gave Jonathan a mobile phone."

"What was the name of the father of the aborted child?"

"Vasco Henriques."

"I know that name."

"Of course you do. He's famous. Sold millions of copies of his records. He didn't just play the piano behind Jean, he sang with her. If they hadn't fallen out over the baby, they would have become famous together."

"Does she still hate him?"

"She still loves him. Her one and only love. A bit like Jonathan's Linda."

"What was Jonathan's reaction to Jean's promiscuity?"

"He gave her a tired look and walked over to stare out of the shattered window. In our minds, we make our friends who we want them to be, not who they are. We all carry our own garbage. Nobody is perfect. When he looked back at her the way he looked had changed, she was no longer his perfect dream. Now they've both come clean with each other, their relationship will likely change."

"Why Jonathan didn't want his money. How did Jean react to her hobo friend becoming the Eighteenth Earl of Fernsby with forty-five million in the bank?"

"Astonishment, followed by a look of speculation. It made her think. Made all of them sit up and think."

"We've destroyed their lives."

"Wasn't much to destroy."

"Their happiness. Their friendship. Their emotional support of each other. Damn. I knew it was wrong to poke my nose into other people's affairs. Poor Jean. Must be terrible to kill your child and then end up with nobody. What happened to Vasco Henriques? Haven't seen his name in the news for a while. He was the same period as Frank Sinatra's Rat Pack. Dean Martin. The era of singing when you could understand the words they sang. Now it's all banging and noise."

"You can hear every word Jean sings as she sails up and down all those octaves. Why we'll quickly make her a celebrity."

"Will they ever be happy again together?"

"She'll love trumping the man who made her kill their child."

"But you say she still loves him?"

"Love can be complicated."

"Don't tell me... Where are they staying tonight?"

"Somewhere in the gutter. You're too much of a romantic, Phillip. You got to be practical. Once he claims his money, he'll be able to look after all of them."

"And then come the predators... Or have they arrived?"

"Are you referring to me? For goodness sake, Phillip. I'm doing them a favour. There's nothing wrong with living in comfort, not having to worry about money. Life goes forward until the day we die. I'm going to give them a new chapter that's worth living. Did you see them huddled against that wall?"

"I should never have left Africa."

"But you did. You're going to now have a child to be part of the rest of your life. Oh, and I'd like you to tell me more of that African story. I want you to give me an insight into your brother and Ben Crossley. What it was like growing up with a famous grandfather."

"Only met him for the first time when I was thirty-one. He broke up with my grandmother shortly before I was born and went to America. But he left me and Randall all his money, or I'd still be running my safari camp on the banks of the Zambezi River."

"How did you meet my friend, Martha?"

"She had organised a tour for singles to go on safari. We had a one-night stand. She got pregnant... You go over to one of these tables and write your notes, Chad. Ah, here comes Amelia... How was the music business today, Amelia?"

"Quiet as a mouse."

"We've got some business coming your way."

"Why do you look so sad?"

"I've just ruined the life of a good friend of mine. The one whose music you're going to record."

"Who's that man you were talking to now sitting at the table? We don't allow down-and-outs in Harry B's."

"He's a top journalist at the *Herald*. Been undercover getting a story. When he's finished writing his notes he'll be up here at the bar. Cleared his disguise with Terry. Treat Chad Fox lightly and he'll bring in the rest of his journalist friends."

"Is he married?"

"I have no idea."

"He's not wearing a wedding ring."

"Neither am I. And hoboes don't wear wedding rings."

When Chad stood up, putting his notebook and pen in the back pocket of his trousers, he walked across to the door of the men's toilet and went inside. When he came out and joined Phillip at the bar he had combed his long hair and tied it at the back into a ponytail. When he grinned at Phillip the black tooth had gone.

"You almost look presentable, Chad."

"Now we can drink. We're all organised. Tell me more about Phillip Crookshank."

"Amelia, that pretty girl over there behind the bar, wants to know if you're married."

"Once. Lasted a couple of years. There's too much female distraction for a journalist in New York."

"How old are you?"

"Thirty-five. The thirties are a man's best hunting years. You still have your looks if you ever had any and you have money. A journo's expense account can pay for a night out with a good-looking girl. Women like to be spoiled, Phillip. A good meal in a posh restaurant with a fancy bottle of wine is all it takes... She's nice. Just my type."

"She's looking for a husband."

"They all are. All part of the fun. We all want something. Wine, women and song... Hello, pretty lady. I'm Chad. Give me a beer. The same beer as my friend. What's your name?"

"Amelia. I work here part-time. During the day I work in a recording studio."

"Now that's a nice coincidence. When you've finished tonight, why don't we have dinner?"

"Dressed like that?"

"Maybe tomorrow."

Amelia bent down to get his beer out of the fridge with a smirk on her face.

"There you are, Chad. Drink your beer."

"Put it on the tab. I like this bar. Right. Where were we before I was so sweetly distracted? So there we have it, Phillip. The bag-lady is in the bag. They're going to love her story. A voice that goes all the way to heaven. Let's have some fun. Let's get drunk. To hell with the consequences. When am I going to get to meet your brother, Randall Holiday?"

"He'll be in New York for Christmas with Meredith and Douglas. They're coming over from the Isle of Man for a holiday, and for my brother to see his publisher. I'll introduce you. Oh, and this is my last drink. My wife is pregnant. She can't drink and needs my company. What happened to your wife?"

"She ran off with an old man who had lots of money. She'll now have money for the rest of her life."

"Any kids?"

"No, thank goodness. Don't worry. I'll find someone else in the bar to drink with while I wait for Amelia. She's smiling at me. That lovely, sweet, seductive smile of a woman on the hunt."

"What's your next trick?"

"With Amelia? Oh, the story. After I've written the most heart-rending story of what it's like living in the gutter while singing like an angel, I'll send my two recordings of Jean singing to CBS and suggest they broadcast them to fundraise for the homeless. They're a news channel. They'll love it. Corporate America loves to make itself look good. Once we have the public's attention, I'll break the story of the Eighteenth Earl of Fernsby. The story of you, Phillip, a man of considerable means helping a beggar playing a violin with two strings missing. You bought him a new violin. How this all started. Your brother will come into your story, a name the public know. Your grandfather. My readers will gobble it up. My editor will smile. Everyone will smile. This is America, Phillip. In America, everyone wins. Or at least that's the story. Make my readers feel good. Rich people like to be seen doing good, makes them feel less guilty for having all that money... Why are you shaking your head?"

"With Jean and Jonathan famous, the whole world is going to want a piece of them. What a lovely world."

"What's wrong with wanting a piece? In my story, everyone wins. Up goes the circulation of the *Herald*. Up goes CBS ratings. The public donate to a good cause and feel good. Jean sings her heart out to an adoring audience. Jonathan gives music scholarships to impoverished students. His hobo friends live in comfort. And it won't do any harm to the business of a venture capitalist, or his publicist wife. What's wrong with it, Phillip? Everyone wins... Have another drink."

"Just one."

"That's my boy. Those two will be happier with money."

"I hope so. Is your ex-wife happy?"

"She's rich. Always will be. In this material world, nothing else matters. Long live America. The American dream. And it works. This is the best damn country in the whole wide world. Let us lift our glasses to fame and fortune. The dream that lives in everyone."

"Did Jonathan tell you what he was going to call the foundation?"

"The Earls of Fernsby Foundation, in memory of the relatives who accumulated all that wealth."

3

Outside the rain had stopped. Phillip walked away with his collar up, not sure what to think of the world and his place in it. He walked home slowly, despondent. Inside the apartment, everything was quiet: no music, no television, just the constant sounds of traffic coming from outside the window. In the lounge, Martha was sitting uncomfortably on the couch. She looked terrible.

"What's the matter, Martha?"

"I feel awful. Have done all afternoon. Pains in my chest. Rumblings in my belly."

"Are you going to have the baby?"

"I don't know, Phillip. Help me. I'm so frightened."

"What kind of chest pains?"

"I don't know. It's horrible. My poor baby."

"Should we go to the hospital?"

"You can drive my car."

"I can't. I've had too many drinks with Chad. I'll call an ambulance."

"Do you have the number?"

"Of course. Always be prepared. You're as white as a sheet."

Trying not to panic, Phillip dialled the emergency number. The call was answered immediately. Phillip gave the man the address.

Half an hour later they were on their way, the panic terrifying both of them. At the hospital they took Martha away, leaving Phillip to sweat it out alone in the waiting room. It was all happening again. As the hand of the clock on the wall above the reception desk went round and round, Phillip's panic increased. When a doctor appeared asking for Phillip, the young man was smiling.

"Your wife is suffering from acute indigestion."

"She lost the last baby. We panicked."

"I believe so. You were right to bring her to the hospital. I have given her a large dose of medication and checked everything. The scans show your daughter is healthy and will join the world in six to eight weeks' time. Everything is normal."

"Is she feeling better?"

"A large burp and the chest pains are subsiding. They were caused by a combination of stomach gas and the weight of the baby pushing air up into your wife's chest."

"So, it's a girl?"

"Didn't you know? My goodness. Have a nice day, Mr Crookshank. You can take your wife home now."

"Why are you smiling so much?"

"That dose of antacid is going to be the most expensive bottle of antacid in history. You can pay for me, the hospital and the ambulance at the desk before you leave."

"Better to be sure than sorry."

"Of course it is."

"Did you tell my wife it's a girl? She didn't want to chance her luck by asking her doctor if it was a boy or a girl."

"You can tell her yourself."

Mumbling about people with too much money and chuckling to himself, the doctor walked back down the corridor. When Phillip was given the bill it blew his mind. He gave the girl his debit card, mentally thanking his grandfather for the money. It made him feel better about Jonathan and Jean. Having money wasn't so bad after all.

"Indigestion, honey. Can you believe it?"

"It's a girl. The doctor told me. Carmen. A second life for my mother through her granddaughter. I've never felt more relieved in my whole damn life. Give me a hug. All's well. How are you feeling?"

"Much better. He gave me a bottle of antacid to take home."

"I'll bet he did."

They went home, Phillip holding Martha's hand in the back of the taxi. They were both quiet, relaxed and happy. Back on the forty-ninth floor, Phillip put on the music and drew the big curtains across the tall plate-glass window. With only the standard lamp on, they settled back comfortably on the couch listening to Mahler's Fourth Symphony.

"How's the chest?"

"Gone with the wind, now I'm relaxed. How much did it cost?"

"You don't want to know. We're lucky we don't have to worry about money."

"Something good did come out of it... Did you ever see *Gone with the Wind*?"

"Who hasn't? What's the good news?"

"I told that nice young doctor I hadn't had a drink since I fell pregnant. He said two glasses of red wine are good for me now and again. Good for my indigestion. That a drink will help me to relax. Let's you and I open a nice bottle of your South African red wine and celebrate. I told you it was going to be a girl, honey. I've been dying for a drink for months. Mahler and a glass of Nederburg Cabernet. A little of last night's leftover curry and rice. You can heat it up for us. A perfect evening. From panic and fear to a perfect evening with my honey."

Phillip pulled out the cork with a resounding pop, poured out two glasses of wine, and turned back to Martha. Her eyes were smiling. They both raised their glasses to heaven and took their first sip, Martha rolling the wine round in her mouth before she swallowed.

"Nectar of the gods. Oh, does that just taste so good. Life in New York City. Everything close by. Everyone doing their jobs efficiently, from the ambulance driver to the young nurse and the young doctor. We're going to be all right, Phillip. He said everything inside me looks perfect. I'm so happy. Just look at us. A beautiful apartment, beautiful music and a glass of the best red wine. And we have each other. Soon to have our baby. What more could we ever want?"

The front doorbell rang halfway through the bottle of wine.

"Who's that?"

"Probably the ambulance driver come for a tip. You stay put. Enjoy your second glass of wine in seven months... Hello, Jasmine. Come in. To what do we owe the honour of your visit? Will you join us for a glass of wine? Martha, it's Jaz."

"I've found a nanny for you... Hello, Martha. Her name is Ivy. She's from South Africa, studying for a degree in ecology by correspondence. Twenty years old. Intelligent. Bright. She can study and look after your baby at the same time. Met her through Max. She has a five-year-old sister she adores. Loves children."

"You want a glass of wine?"

"Just the one, Phillip."

"We're having leftovers for supper."

"You keep the leftovers?"

"Phillip does. Says what the Americans throw away would feed half the starving on the planet. Anyway, it makes cooking easy. All we have to do is heat it up. Curry and rice tonight... I hope you've forgiven me for telling Marcin you were pregnant. Had no idea. Thought you loved each other. How are you doing handling my accounts as well as yours? Phillip, you'd better open us another bottle of wine... Tell me more about this Ivy. Oh, of course. You want me back in the office as soon as possible. What's a South African doing in New York? Two pregnant girls. Come and sit next to me. It's Mahler's Fourth Symphony."

"Ivy says a lot of young whites with good educations are leaving the new South Africa. Going to Australia. England. America. Anywhere they can get in. She was lucky to get a student visa. In the years to come, despite the great Nelson Mandela, she thinks there will be retribution, the way it is happening in Zimbabwe. She wants a life without worry. When I told her she could live in and earn a salary she said looking after your baby would be just perfect... Thank you, Phillip. Cheers, everyone... You might have done me a favour, Martha. I'd been building up to telling Marcin for days. Men. Sorry, Phillip. All they want is a screw. They say they love you and screw you. In more ways than one."

"Have you talked about the baby since you stopped living with him?"

"Not a word. It's all business. At least the account is safe. Later, it will be my turn. Does anyone care about anything other than themselves? But, oh, is he going to be rich. The new ideas coming out of that office are positively mind-boggling. Their minds never stop thinking. Leaping forward, one well-planned step at a time. Bouncing the ideas off each other's brains. And the little bugger inside my belly is going to have a nice big piece of the pie."

"Are you going to get back together?"

"Who knows, Martha?"

"How are you going to look after the kid as a single mother?"

"Same way as you. Employ a nanny. Get a bigger apartment. Ask the partnership to give me an increase in salary if the genius doesn't come forward with child support. I mean, we can't afford to lose his account, can we darling? And Marcin's got that look back in his eyes. Lust. Pure lust. Life is fun. It's so convenient living in the same building, Martha."

"How's Max?"

"Max, the good-looking janitor? He's fine. So, what's new?"

"The price of a bottle of antacid. Tell her, Phillip, how much it just cost us for a bottle of antacid."

By the time they were ready to eat, they had started the second bottle of wine. They were having a giggle. They were happy. Playing the confident words of the young doctor through his mind, Phillip stopped worrying. He was thinking positive. For himself and Martha. For Jaz and Marcin. For Jonathan and Jean. He began to wonder whether he hadn't been overhasty in thinking about off-loading his Linguare shares. As long as the lovers could work together, keeping things civilised, maybe all their investments would be safe after all? In the background, Mahler's symphony was still playing. With the girls talking babies, Phillip kept quiet, enjoying his wine. What a day. From listening to Chad playing his media barrage. To ripping his stomach in panic. To relaxation in the comfort of his own home listening to Mahler, looking from Jaz to Martha and back again. And inside both of them was the next generation about to join the world. Would his daughter enjoy her life? He hoped so. Would the child inside Jasmine ever get to know her father? He hoped so. Would Jonathan and Jean end unhappy in their new world of wealth and fame? Of that Phillip was not so confident. And it was all his fault. The baby inside Martha. Jaz meeting Marcin through his investment in Linguare.com. His meddling in a homeless man's affairs. If he had stayed in Africa, none of it would have happened.

Leaving them to talk he went into the kitchen, taking the leftovers out of the fridge, mixing the rice with the curry in one pot and putting it on the stove. The world was so full of the influences of other people. If the country he had once called Rhodesia had not been changed by the force of politics to Zimbabwe, his whole family would still be living in Africa. And where was the future for Carmen? Would America prosper? Would the economy carry on growing, making everyone richer? Or would something like a war or a financial collapse throw everyone into Jonathan's gutter, everyone ripping out each other's throats? Would democracy, with everyone wanting something for free, end up being successful? Or would all the benefits given to the people by politicians in their pursuit of power end in a mountain of debt for the next generation? Every democracy in the world going bankrupt? Thinking of his child, Phillip stirred the pot before putting the plates on the table. The music had stopped. The girls were now talking about their company business. Phillip found Mahler's Eighth Symphony and let it play, neither girl taking any notice.

"Food, my ladies, is about to be served. Please come to the table. And bring your glasses. This one is a choral symphony. How can so much everlasting beauty come out of a human mind? Let me help my wife up from the couch. What a day. And now everything is perfect. Let me go stir the pot before I burn the bottom of the pan... So, this Ivy thinks the blacks in South Africa will want their retribution for apartheid? And why shouldn't they? The trouble is, in the process of getting their own back they'll repeat what happened in Zimbabwe and crash the economy, sending the whole country, apart from the political elite, into poverty. If all the best brains leave there will be no one left to run the economy and employ the people. Kind of ironical. I've heard the whites in South Africa are leaving in droves. Zimbabwe has lost most of its white population. Funny. All that moral grandstanding has done more harm than good for the ordinary folk it was meant to help. Oh, dear. I'm talking politics. How boring. No wonder neither of you are listening. Come and eat your suppers... Once upon a time in England, there were three estates that ran the country: the King, Parliament and the Clergy. Then came the fourth estate: Chad's media. Now we have a fifth estate: the financial markets. Fun and games for everyone. In the end, I just wonder who will be more powerful: the President, the Senate and Congress, the Media or the Markets?"

"What are you talking about, Phillip?"

"I have no idea, Martha. How's the wine going down?"

"Delicious."

"And your chest?"

"Gone with the wind."

By the time Jasmine left to go down to her own apartment, they were all a little tiddly, Martha having drunk more than she should have. In bed, neither of them wanted to go to sleep. There was nothing much for them to do in the morning.

"How's the chest pains?"

"Not a thing. Oh, Phillip, I'm so happy. Do you think I drank too much wine? From now on I'm going to stop worrying. I feel a bit guilty but the doctor said I'd be all right. When shall we ask Ivy to move into the third bedroom? Do we wait until the baby is born? We can all get to know each other. That way, when I leave her with Carmen and go back to the office, I won't be worried. I won't have to be away from work for six months."

"We'd better try and get some sleep. That was quite a day."

"When's Chad's first article due to come out?"

"Monday. Journalists don't wait around when they think they have a good story. He says it's going to be on the front page. An eye-catcher."

"How they sell newspapers. Goodnight, honey. Sweet dreams. Turn the lights out."

Within a minute Phillip was fast asleep. When he woke from his untroubled dreams it was already morning, the light of day filtering through the heavy bedroom curtains. Getting up surprisingly free of hangover he went to the window and pulled back the curtains. Outside, the rain was pelting down on the city, Phillip glad for the warmth of their central heating. When he turned back to the bed, Martha was smiling at him, not saying a word.

"Are we going to church? It's Sunday. You want some coffee? Must be real cold outside. Can you still taste the wine in your mouth? What are you smiling about? You've got that look that says you're up to something. It's so nice to sleep right through the night without waking. Yesterday was quite a day. Come on, what's that smile, Martha?"

"I'm going to get hold of Ivy straight away, and if we like her, have her move in. I want to be sure I can trust her with my baby before I leave them on their own."

"There's more to that look than employing a nanny."

"Come back to bed. I want to make love."

"When do pregnant women stop wanting sex?"

"They never do, honey. We can do it the new way, the other way round... You know, you've still got the last traces of a tan."

"I'll go make the coffee."

"No, you won't... Why do you always sleep in your underpants?"

"We never had pyjamas in Africa. Most of my male friends said they slept stark bollock naked."

"Oh, just look at that, Phillip. You want it as much as me... There you are. This is what marriage is all about. Get in, Phillip. Get really in... That's my honey... Oh. Yes... That's it."

For a while they lay on their backs, neither of them speaking.

"It was all over too quickly."

"Stop complaining, honey. We can always do it again. Love in the morning. All right. Get up. Go make the tea. Let's spend the day in bed. We'll go to church next Sunday. Make some toast with the tea and coffee."

"At your service, my lady... The rain's still coming down in buckets... What's Carmen going to do on the forty-ninth floor of a block of apartments? There will be no cats and dogs to play with. No river to walk to through the long grass. You can't play catch in an apartment. The poor child is going to be locked up between four walls. I remember my own childhood on World's View so vividly. The sun was always shining. There was always something to do. In the night during the curing season when Dad got up to go down and check the barn temperatures, Randall and I used to go with him. To cure the tobacco just right he changed the temperatures in the barns twice a day. There were forty of them. Each high as a two-storey building. Dad said attention to detail was the core of success in any venture or business. There was a barn boy on night duty who fed wood into the forty furnaces but Dad had to check the tobacco inside the barns and make the decisions. The barn boy stoked the fires at the bottom of each barn to maintain the temperatures. He was my friend. I played football in the compound with his kids. Life on World's View was one big family. In the compound, they had a football field and a beer hall. The thatched houses stretched along the river. There was a school paid for by the farm that taught the kids. Not a bad life. Now it's all ending. Nothing in life stays the same."

"Go and make us breakfast. You're getting nostalgic."

"You grew up on a farm. What's Carmen going to do in a city?"

"Play with her toys and gadgets. Have friends to stay. There's so much for everyone to do in a city. Didn't you and Randall get bored on your own? The same old routine day after day?"

"I never knew the meaning of boredom until I came to live in a city."

"Are you bored in New York?"

"I was when you went to work. Don't worry. I'm getting used to the change. It's called life's evolution. Life's progression... What you want on your toast?"

"Lots of butter and lots of marmalade. Leave the door open. We can still talk. I love our chats in the morning. Thanks to that young doctor that wine last night was just about perfect. A party for three. I've got a nice feeling they will get back together again."

"And live happily ever after."

"Something like that. A few bumps on the way, perhaps. Nothing ever stays perfect. You have to work at life. As we have."

"Did Jaz leave you Ivy's phone number?"

"I wrote it down while you were in the kitchen heating up the supper. We should go to church."

"Too late. We've missed the eleven o'clock service."

"Time goes so quickly when you're happy."

"I wonder what happened to all those kids when they were tossed off the farm? Everyone went. Our family and the families of the labour force. Many of them from Malawi and Mozambique. Had to make way for Mugabe supporters and the supporters of his cronies. Politics stinks. Politicians only think of themselves wherever they are... Tea, coffee and toast coming up. Glad we're not going out. It's still pelting down with rain outside. Just look at it."

"You'd better put on your underpants."

"Now she tells me. If we bring Ivy into the apartment before Christmas there won't be a room for your mother. Randall, Meredith and Douglas can stay in one room. But what about your mother? She is coming for Christmas with Mabel Crabshaw?"

"Mum's coming. Don't know about Mabel. You're right. Mother comes first. How long are Randall and Meredith staying?"

"He'll soon get bored not being able to write. Too much shit in his head. Too much noise. Why real artists live in the country. Let's meet Ivy but not set a date. A South African and a Zimbabwean in New York. Now that's interesting. Make the call. Bring her round. When do we pick up our Christmas tree? Got to have a Christmas tree. This year is going to be family. How Christmas should be. Do these skyscrapers blow over in the wind? How many pieces of toast? When the wind blows I like to have my feet firmly on the ground."

"None have blown over so far."

"That's comforting."

"Two pieces of nice toast. I'm so happy, Phillip. I'm just so happy. Yesterday was a right royal fright as the English say. Now it's all such a relief. My baby. I can't wait to see my baby. Put on some nice music. Songs. Lots of songs. I want to be sung to. Was Jean really that good?"

"I could not believe what I was hearing in the soup kitchen reception waiting for Jonathan. If Chad gets CBS to broadcast that recording he made when he sneaked into the dining room it will become a sensation. First, he's going to wind up the reading public with his bleeding-heart article. Then we'll see the reaction."

"It's all about marketing, Phillip."

"How silly of me. I was preaching to the converted."

"We must bring Perry Mance into the picture right at the start."

"Is Chad any good at writing?"

"The best. A publicist only goes to the best. You'll see that tomorrow morning when you read the *Herald*."

"There we are. Food! Now, do you want me to put on some clothes?"

"Maybe not. It's nice and warm under the cover. What are we going to have for lunch?"

"First eat your breakfast."

"Do you think she's happy? She's come a long way in business in so short a time. I worry about Jaz. People have burnouts when they get what they want too early in life."

"How old is Jasmine?"

"She turned twenty-six in August. Two years older than the genius."

"How's the toast?"

"It's so nice to be loved and looked after. Maybe they'll marry, have five kids and all live happily ever after with all that money. Money. That's the word. The driving force for everyone."

"You can make it or steal it, Martha. Or manipulate the markets. Work around the laws of a country to maximise profit. Nothing is straight anymore. When it comes to making money, morals flew out of the window years ago. If they can get away with it, they do it. A man of honour. When did you last hear that expression?"

"Or, like Marcin, you can invent a legitimate product."

"And have a host of copycats going round your copyright."

"Why he has to constantly invent new products. You have to have brains to invent a good new product."

"And not many of us have those kind of brains."

"For decades, America has attracted the best brains in the world in pursuit of the great American dream."

"Greed."

"It's not greed. It's progress. The country and the world get richer. Everyone wins in a world driven by brains in pursuit of money that brings comfort. Don't knock the American dream."

"You're thinking of Jonathan and Jean and the rest of their hobo friends."

"If she can sing as well as you and Chad say, the world should hear her voice. Yes, money will be made. You have to pay for anything good in this world we live in. You get nothing for free."

"Except love."

"Love has a lot of meanings. We like to talk about loving each other, you and I. And we do. But what is that thing called love? Do we love how we look? Yes, you're an attractive, good-looking man. Do we love each other's minds? Yes, I could never live with a fool. Do we love how we treat each other? Of course we do. If we argued instead of having tea and toast in bed it would be most unpleasant. Do we love companionship? The joy of telling a soul mate how you feel? Of being looked after in an emergency like the one yesterday? No one likes to be on their own. They want to share their joy and their pain. Love is the combination of living. Of living happily. And then there's making love. And that's sex. Good sex like you and me, honey. I love you, Phillip, and hope I will be able to love you for the rest of my life, giving my life a true meaning. I want a home full of love for Carmen. Love is all the things in life that make it worth living... Where are you going?"

"To play those songs you want to have sung to you. Love songs. Then we'll take a nap, and after the nap, we'll make ourselves some lunch. Love on the forty-ninth floor."

"And you won't go all nostalgic on me?"

"It's not only nostalgia. It's my history. My memories. You must tell me more about you and your brothers growing up on your father's farm. I want to know everything about you, Martha. Every little detail. That way we'll become one person living our lives together in harmony."

"Well, let me think. Ford and Hugo. There was a time in summer when I was five years old. The first real story I remember. It all started early one morning on the farm..."

Smiling, happy to have got her talking, Phillip got back into bed and snuggled down under the cover, listening to Martha's story, the pelting rain and the traffic noise outside no longer in his consciousness. When the long story finished he got out of bed, went into the lounge, selected a programme on the music channel called 'love songs' and went back to the comfort of their bed. Within minutes, with the music playing, Martha was off on another story, Phillip happily listening. And the day went on. Another cup of tea. A sandwich lunch served in bed. A day of happiness for both of them they both hoped would never end.

After supper in the lounge with the curtains drawn, they drank a glass of wine, watched a romantic comedy on television, and went to bed where they slept, as comfortable as bugs in a rug, their dreams happy, neither of them waking until morning.

4

Beyond the bedroom curtains the sun was shining. Later, Philip told himself, he would go to Stigley's gym and afterwards pick up the morning newspaper while Martha stayed comfortably in bed reading her novel, a sweet novel of love and happiness that every one of them so wanted... Or was he kidding himself about life? Phillip was never quite sure. Were they saying to each other what the other one wanted to hear to make their own life more pleasant? Was there ever love and happiness? He hoped so. Even if it came and went, and hopefully came back again. In Phillip's mind, it was all about making life worth the living. Being pleasant to people. Thinking positively.

"Bacon and eggs? The usual?"

"Sounds good to me. And today I don't have to go to work. Breakfast in bed on a Monday. Poor Jaz. She'll have so much work to do. I'm sure Franklyn and Jack will help."

After breakfast, Phillip packed his gym bag, kissed Martha on the forehead and left her in bed absorbed in her novel. With the sun shining outside, he walked to the gym. Volker greeted him from where he was standing working a young girl. Apart from the girl, the gym was empty. For two hours Phillip exercised, building up a good sweat. At the newsstand down the sidewalk from the gym after showering and changing, he bought the morning *Herald*. And there they were, the two of them on the bottom of the front page below the headline: 'Do You Want to Hear the Bag-lady Sing?' Standing on the sidewalk next to a building, Phillip began to read Chad's article in praise of the most beautiful singing voice he claimed to have ever heard. It was all there, one punchline after another: the killing of her baby at the insistence of Vasco Henriques; the spiral through alcohol into the gutter; in old age, meeting her soul mate, a hobo like herself down and out on the streets of New York who brought back her passion to sing; a voice Chad shouted to the people of New York they must ask to hear by emailing the *Herald* newspaper; pull this woman out of the gutter; make a life worth the living and hear the perfection of music; do yourself a favour, reader, make her sing to you and hear the voice of an angel; and the man playing the violin next to her, the man who made a bag-lady happy? Tomorrow, readers, tomorrow I'll tell you the story of the Eighteenth Earl of Fernsby. But first, send us your emails and let the angel sing; send a donation to our fund for the homeless.

When Phillip finished reading the article he had a broad smile on his face. With the newspaper folded and tucked under his left arm, he picked up his gym bag and walked briskly away down the street. By the time he reached Harry B's, the pub was open, Terry alone behind the bar.

"Can you do me a favour, Terry?"

"Depends what it is."

"Read the article on the front page by Chad Fox."

"Oh, the reporter who went off with Amelia on Saturday night. What's it about?"

"A bag-lady. I want to know if the article gets to you enough to want to send the paper an email. Or Donate to a charity for the homeless."

"You want a drink?"

"A bit early. But I'll have a beer. The place is empty."

"Most get paid on the twenty-fifth of the month. By now they've paid their bills and most of it's gone. Anyway, it's Monday morning... One beer, Phillip. There you go. Now, what's this all about?"

"Have you heard of Vasco Henriques?"

"The singer? Of course I have. He's famous. Enjoy your first beer."

Not sure what to expect, Phillip watched Terry read the Chad Fox article. No one came into the bar. They were alone.

"Makes you think. Makes me realise how lucky I am having my own pub with regular customers like you, Phillip. Poor woman. Killing her own baby. But what does a young girl do if the man isn't interested? She can have an abortion like the woman in the article, or take the baby to term and give it away. A girl doing gigs in a band can't look after a child. I wonder what's worse: killing your own child before it's born or giving it away. No wonder the woman became an alcoholic. And in the end, she ends up an old bag-lady on her own. No family. No friends other than homeless poor sods. This article won't do the reputation of Vasco Henriques any good. But back then, what was he to do? He didn't want to tie himself down. Why wasn't the girl looking after herself? Was it really his baby? How many other men had she slept with? Maybe he paid for the abortion. And then there's the other side of the story: many young girls deliberately get themselves pregnant to catch a husband. What was the truth back then? Catholics see contraception as a sin. In principle, is there any difference between contraception and abortion? They both prevent the birth of a child. I don't think I could abort my own child but I didn't face the problem when I was in my early twenties and forced to make a decision. And isn't the world grossly overpopulated? The cause of all this global warming? That poor woman. And it's haunted her, her entire life... That reporter can write. I'll be thinking about that conundrum for days. What should she have done? What would have been right? Abort, give it away, or be unable to properly look after her own baby? It's easy to criticise other people when you haven't been through it yourself."

"Do you want to hear her sing?"

"If it helps. Up until now, she hasn't had a life."

"Are you going to send them money?"

"I'll send them an email that will hopefully help to make the poor woman rich and famous. The article says she wants to atone for her sin. Let's give her a chance. Some people's lives. What a mess. My church always tells us to count our blessings and not moan about the rest. Can she really sing?"

"Oh, yes. And if enough people follow your path they'll all be able to hear the bag-lady sing... You've got another customer. Can I have my paper back?"

"Sorry. I was too absorbed in my thinking."

"How much are you going to send them?"

"Fifty bucks. After reading that article it will make me feel better... Yes, sir. What can I get you on a bright and sunny Monday morning?"

"A shot of whisky and your newspaper. That article sounds interesting. Many years ago, I once told a girl to have an abortion. I still think of it. The kid would now be older than you."

"Do you mind, Phillip?"

"My pleasure. Was it a boy or a girl?"

"I don't know. I've never told my wife or my children. Make that whisky a double. You mind if I move up the bar? My name is Sam."

"Phillip Crookshank. Pleased to meet you."

"Do you have children?"

"Not yet. My wife is seven months pregnant. She lost our last baby at term and wanted to commit suicide."

"She's an older woman?"

"My age. And she doesn't have children. We had a one-night stand on the banks of the Zambezi River. I followed her to America. Enjoy reading my friend's article."

"Did your wife ever have an abortion?"

"If she did, she never told me. Said she didn't think she could have children. Why she hadn't taken precautions that night on the banks of the river. She was married twice before I got her pregnant. The husbands were infertile, or so they thought. No kids, no lasting marriage. How it works."

"Tell me more."

"First read the article and tell me what you think... Did you ever see the girl again? What happened to her?"

"I have no idea. I was a student, studying at an agricultural college in England. Soon after the abortion, I came back to America."

"Can you remember her name?"

"Oh, yes. I can remember her name. Guilt like that never leaves you."

Phillip sipped at his beer while Sam read Chad's article. Down the bar, Terry was using his computer to send the *Herald* his email asking to hear the bag-lady sing. When Sam gave back the newspaper to Phillip his jaw was locked, his eyes intense. His hand was shaking. He drank down the double shot of whisky and banged the shot glass back on the bar counter.

"Same again, Mr Barman."

"Are you going to send them an email?"

"Poor, bloody woman. Could have been the girl I got pregnant at ag college. I must have destroyed her life. I never dared go back to England to find out. It was a casual affair. Like so many casual affairs in the sixties. In the sixties, it was all about free love. Men getting what they wanted. Rock and roll. All of us selfish. That article has stabbed me in the gut."

"You'd better send the newspaper a large donation and tell them you want to hear the bag-lady sing."

"And hope that will make me feel better? I doubt it. Until now, I've never told anyone."

"Why don't you trace the girl you impregnated and find out if she needs your help?"

"And hurt my wife? I should but I won't. I'm far too much of a coward."

Terry put the full shot glass on the bar in front of Sam, giving him a twisted smile.

"Double shot, Sam. Don't worry. We all make mistakes when we're young. It was as much the girl's decision as yours. We all live with things we'd rather forget. Let's all hear the bag-lady sing. Send them your email. Life is what we make of it."

"And if your mother and father had decided to abort you, you wouldn't be here."

"Phillip here has a quip: if in some year when the human race was in its infancy, if you'll forgive the pun, someone had said 'not tonight thank you darling', neither would any of us. The world would be full of different people. Life is one big game of chance. Don't worry your guts about it, Sam. We all try to do our best, even when we fail."

"What would we do without bars?"

"What they're for. To let people talk to each other. Drink your whisky, Sam. You want another beer, Phillip?... Ah, more customers."

"Give me another beer when you come back."

For a long while, Sam sat silently looking at the full shot glass in front of him. Phillip waited, not wanting to break the silence. Despite being a Monday, the bar began to fill up. Amid the rush, Terry slid a full bottle of beer in front of Phillip. Carefully folding the newspaper, he stuffed it in his pocket making Sam drink down his whisky. Without another word, the man turned, got off his barstool and walked out of the bar. At the door, he turned and came back and put a twenty-dollar bill on the bar. He had not paid his bill.

"Forgot to pay my tab. And if I give a fat donation to their charity, do you think that will help? Do you think singing on television will help that pathetic old lady? When we sin like that we take the burden to our graves and most likely end up in hell. And what are these charities anyway? How much of what you give them goes to the homeless? The people who run those charities and NGOs don't work for nothing. It's a business like everything else."

"Let me buy you a drink, Sam. You can't change the past."

"You're right. Thanks. A beer. She's likely happily married with three grown-up kids and wouldn't want to hear from me in a fit. The man that wrote that article knows how to get at you."

"Are you a farmer?"

"No. I'm a teacher. I teach students from all over the world how to farm. Hopefully. Successful farming relies on the weather as much as anything. Well, maybe not with all these new genetically modified seeds the seed producers make so much money out of. They're the ones that make the money. In the old days, a farmer reaped his own seed for next year's crop. Not anymore. Good old America. We've got the world by the balls. The seed of a crop grown from genetically modified seed doesn't reproduce. You know anything about farming?"

"I grew up on a farm as did my wife. You want that drink?"

"Why not? I'm on vacation. They've all gone home. Tell me about your life back on the farm. You know, that genetically modified seed increases the crop by at least thirty per cent, making the farmer far more than he pays for the seed. When everyone in the world uses our modified seed there will be no other way to grow a crop. America will be in control of the world's food production unless someone breaks the seed producer's patent. Another way to control your enemies. Another way of waging war. And, of course, another way of making lots and lots of money out of other people's hard work. You can do without most things in life, including a home, but you can't live without food. And if someone hadn't impregnated his wife all those millennia ago we wouldn't be talking to each other. Makes you think. My kids are all so different, despite having the same mother and father. They're just the luck of my sperm fertilising that particular egg. So you think we're all related? The whole world distant cousins of each other?"

"The story goes, man originated in Africa, migrating into Europe. The world population has been migrating forever. We migrated to America. Africa migrated to America because they were forced into slavery. Now Africa is coming back to Europe and the merry-go-round continues. If we all stayed where we were in the first place we would have met and married different people. The chance of being alive are odds that boggle the mind."

"So I shouldn't be worried about my aborted child?"

"He or she isn't worried. And is life so exciting? Conscience, guilt, call it what you will, are good. Makes us hopefully behave ourselves. Provided there's a new crop every year, the world goes on. Modified or organic... Ah, there you are, Terry. Give us both a beer. That twenty-dollar bill on the counter is to pay for Sam's whiskies. After this beer, I must go home to my pregnant wife. Maybe we'll meet again tomorrow after I buy tomorrow's edition of the *Herald*."

"Do you have a job?"

"Sort of. It's a long story. Don't worry, Sam. You've done the best you can with your life. The way we all try to do. Thank you, Terry. Put the beers on my tab."

"So you think we are all Africans?"

"Probably."

"Why do we look so different?"

"The sun. It was hot in my Africa back on the farm. Probably why I still love my Africa. Why I have the never-ending passion to return. It's the home of my first ancestors. Where it all began on a Saturday night when she said 'please, darling. I want to make love'."

"You're telling a story."

"Am I? Who knows? Take it as it comes, Sam. Cheers. Your good health. And don't forget to send the bag-lady an email. She wants to sing. Let her sing. And it's all my fault."

On Wednesday afternoon, after Chad's phone call, Phillip went back to Harry B's. There was no sign of Sam or Chad when he walked into the bar with the morning copy of the *Herald* newspaper tucked under his arm. At the bottom of the page, under the heading 'The Bag-lady's Mentor' was his own story and how he had found the bag-lady and the Eighteenth Earl of Fernsby and given a homeless old man a new violin. The previous day's *Herald*, which Phillip had read at home, had told the story of a hobo who became an English peer and inherited a fortune. Looking around the familiar bar there was no one he recognised. Quietly, Phillip sat away from the bar and read the article, before going up to sit at the bar.

"Did Sam come in yesterday, Terry?"

"Not a sign of him. The man from the *Herald* has just walked in."

Phillip turned and smiled at a well-shaven Chad.

"I'm late."

"You're not. I'm five minutes early. What can I do for you, Chad? You do look smart today. Well-shaven. Wearing an expensive jacket. And just look at those shoes."

"The story of the bag-lady has blown up. She's the talk of the town. Give us a couple of beers, Terry. No sign of Amelia. Not surprised. They're getting a band together to back the bag-lady and the Earl of Fernsby. CBS liked the recording I made in the soup kitchen so they went back to make a proper film of them performing which they're broadcasting tonight. Amelia knows you and Martha have a company ready to promote a bag-lady album. Nothing wrong with being prepared. You can't believe the number of emails. And the donations for the homeless are flooding in. I must have tugged at their heartstrings. Today, Phillip, the drinks are on the *Herald*. You gave me a big one... Ah, you have today's paper. How do you like being famous?"

"Fortunately, the story is mostly about a bag-lady. I'm just a follow-up story to keep her on your front page. You didn't mention Martha."

"We'll talk about your wife later when she makes the bag-lady even more famous... Thank you, Terry."

"Why am I here, Chad?"

"For Amelia's sake, I want to make sure her recording studio makes the bag-lady's first album, with your friend Perry Mance picking up the tab, and your wife publicising the album. Even my boss was smiling at me by yesterday morning. Which is something. There's nothing better in the newspaper business than a stunt that works. To write well, you have to have a good story that appeals to the general public. Thank you, Phillip. Let's drink to an old lady who is now famous thanks to you."

"Is she happy about it?"

"Haven't spoken a word to either of them. Amelia wants you to bring them to the recording studio tomorrow afternoon. I can phone Jonathan on the mobile I gave him if you don't have time. Cheers. What a lovely week it's been. I just love life when it works. Happy days are here again. You should have seen my boss's face when those emails began pouring in."'

"Who's running the fund for the homeless?"

"I have no idea. My job is to find the story and write the articles."

"Well, if it isn't Sam. Sam, meet my friend Chad Fox, the journalist who wrote the article on the bag-lady. Come and join us. The drinks are on the *Herald*... Is Jonathan going to be in the band Amelia's putting together, Chad? A violin in a band? I'd imagined a string quartet."

"If he wants to he can play. If his arthritis is a problem Amelia says they can take out any false notes. Anyway, isn't it his composition, his songs he wants to live forever? He had his day as a performing artist. I don't know enough about music to know a false note when I hear one. But it has to be a band. A string quartet would be far too snooty. Got to appeal to the masses. So, are we agreed? We'll all meet at Manley and Thombs at three o'clock tomorrow afternoon."

"I don't even know where to find Jean and Jonathan."

"Then leave it to me. But join us at the studio tomorrow. I'll write down the address."

"How was your date with Amelia?"

"Perfect. Lust at first sight... So, Sam. What's your story? That's the trouble with being a journalist. We're always looking for a new story."

"What time are CBS broadcasting Jean singing 'All I Ever Want is a Friend'?"

"There are two songs, Phillip. That one and 'The Last Time I Heard of Linda'. Nine-fifteen. After the news. She'll break everyone's hearts. A bag-lady singing like an angel. A hobo playing your violin. A hobo who thanks to your investigating lawyer has now received the kind of legacy all of us can only dream about. Both of you must watch CBS tonight. It's going to be awesome... How's your beer going down, Phillip? Sam. Is it Sam? What's your poison?"

"I read your article on Monday."

"And what did you think of it?"

"Stabbed me right in my guilty gut. But I'm getting over it. Make mine a shot of whisky."

"Oh, you as well? My first abortion, I was eighteen. My father paid for it. With the story in the news, it's amazing how many of us have come out of the closet. Look at it as a catharsis. We all make our mistakes, Sam. A few drinks, jump into bed, and wham. How it works. Terry, give my new friend a double shot of whisky for stabbing him in the gut. And have one for yourself. Today, everything is on the *Herald*. Let's have a party."

Phillip, trying to keep his drinking under control, not wishing to end up an alcoholic, finished his drink and went home. Martha was in the lounge reading a book.

"How's my pregnant wife? How many times have I stared out of this window? The next stage in the Perry Mance saga is all happening. In addition to getmethatbook.com, there'll be a getmethatsong.com. The value of my investment will likely go through the roof. It's so ridiculous making money you don't need. I have the perfect cottage in the Vumba where we can live in peace and solitude, and here I am in New York making more money than I could ever spend, looking out of a forty-ninth-floor window at all of this. Can you even imagine all the shit in people's heads down there? Millions of them. All with the same ambition. To make as much money as possible. I don't get it. Chad wants us all at Amelia's recording studio tomorrow. The two are lovers. He wants to help her career. Progress in the Big Apple. What a world."

"What time is it?"

"Five o'clock. Or thereabouts. Why don't you want to live in the Vumba?"

"Don't be ridiculous. How many drinks did you have?"

"As few as possible."

"What's on tonight's agenda?"

"At nine-fifteen after the news, we're both going to hear the bag-lady sing, accompanied by a nice bottle of red wine. I'm going to open the bottle now, to let it breathe."

"You're going to turn into an alcoholic."

"What I'm worried about. But what else do you do in a city other than meet friends, have a drink with them, go home to your pregnant wife and open a bottle of wine? What's for supper?"

"Beef casserole."

"Oh, goody."

"Can I have a kiss?"

"Of course you can. You're my wife."

AT A QUARTER past nine with the ads rolling, Phillip brought the bottle of wine out of the kitchen with two glasses, putting them on the low table in front of the television. A newscaster announced that CBS was promoting a charity for the homeless that he hoped listeners would subscribe to after they had seen and heard the bag-lady sing, a poor homeless soul singing to the homeless in a soup kitchen with her friend playing a violin.

"Ladies and gentlemen. Kind and generous listeners. Be prepared to hear the bag-lady sing."

As Martha and Phillip sat drinking their glass of wine in front of the television, the picture of destitution in the soup kitchen went out across America. After the second song, Martha was crying tears.

"I'm not sure if I'm crying with happiness for her or out of misery for those poor people. Why on earth didn't Jonathan go get his money at the first opportunity? How do people live who look like that, always dependent on charity? Nothing on television has ever touched me like this. Oh, Phillip, she does sing like an angel. You're so good and clever to have helped them. I can't even imagine living their kind of lives. Give me another glass of wine and let me drown their sorrows."

"Am I?"

"What do you mean?"

"Good and clever. In that clip, they both look so happy. The hoboes roaring approval and thumping the table look so happy. We'll have to see how Jean and Jonathan behave at the studio tomorrow now their lives have been shattered."

"But they're going to be rich."

"I know they are, Martha. But are they going to be happy? As she said in her song, all you need is a friend. They both have friends. Now they will have to make new ones in a world rife with manipulating people. With people befriending them because of her fame and because of his money. Never sure of the truth. Never certain of who is being genuine. Never believing a word anyone says to you."

"You're talking absolute rubbish."

"Probably. You're right. It's all about the American dream, of owning one's own home and having lots of lovely money. I must get that cottage in the sticks out of my mind."

"You still had to pay for it. What's the difference? You still need money wherever you hide. And with our money, our child is never going to want for anything."

"Let's drink to Carmen."

"And our beautiful lives together. We have the ultimate American dream. And there's nothing better, honey."

"To happiness. Wherever you find it."

"To happiness. This wine is just so good. Nectar of the gods. Thank you, Phillip, for coming into my life. When she's maybe five years old we can take her to Africa and show Carmen where you grew up. When we want a holiday away from the cold of winter, we can go to your Africa. On an aeroplane, we're only half a day away. Good. Now you're smiling. Beef casserole with mashed potatoes followed by a glass of wine. Now, isn't that perfection? Love, good food, and a glass of wine."

"Can I turn off the television and play us some music? I'm sick of the media. Does CBS care more about its ratings than it does about the homeless? Of course it does, despite all those looks of concern and sympathy from their newscaster. People are two-faced. Does he care a damn about Jean and the rest of those hoboes? The mass media. How they work. Exploiting every story to their own benefit."

"I phoned Ivy while you were out."

"You're changing the subject."

"Of course I am. Does it matter Chad's or CBS's motive if they raise good money for the homeless, make a career for Jean and give food to people who are hungry? They need to pull on the heartstrings to make us open our purse strings. Put on the pop music channel. I don't want to listen to serious music. Not tonight."

"Any signs of your chest pains?"

"Nothing a dose of antacid won't sort out. She sounded lovely on the phone, with an accent just like my Phillip."

"What's her surname?"

"Hartley. Ivy Hartley. She wants to come and meet us tomorrow after she finishes her studies. She was so happy Jasmine had recommended her for the job."

"Hartley. That's interesting for a girl from Africa. There were three famous white hunters in what was to become Rhodesia. Back in the nineteenth century. Selous, Hartley and Brigandshaw. My Aunty Beth was a Brigandshaw before she married my father's brother and became a Crookshank. Her grandfather was Sebastian Brigandshaw, the white hunter. In those days people weren't so paranoid about shooting an elephant for its ivory. Yet now when they eat a nice piece of steak in a fancy restaurant they don't think of the poor cow. Did we think of the cow when we were eating our casserole tonight? I didn't. Anyway, in those days of Selous, Hartley and Brigandshaw there were more elephant in the bush than people. Everyone back home in England wanted something made from ivory. How the morals of people change... When's she going to move in? I've got to go to Amelia's recording studio tomorrow afternoon. I'll leave Ivy to you... Now, is that the music you want to hear? Songs from the rock and roll seventies."

"She's going to be famous."

"I know she is. And we'll make a bundle of money through our investment in Perry Mance. Lovely. Exploit the homeless. Don't shoot the elephants."

"Drink your wine, Phillip. You're beginning to bore me. You've never been homeless. For generations, your family have had money. Jean and Jonathan are about to have a life. A life that's worth the living. How would you like to sleep in a doorway tonight? Or under a bridge? It's snowing outside. Stop worrying about interfering in their lives. You did good, honey. As Chad said in his article, you did good. As will all those tonight donating to the homeless. I know Jonathan told you he was scared of the consequences of inheriting all that money. Likely, he just didn't think it was going to happen and was preparing himself for a let-down. I'll ask Ivy if she is related to the elephant hunter. Now fill up my glass. And despite the poor bloody cow, that casserole tonight was as good as it gets. Smile, Phillip. We have the perfect life."

Thinking of Jonathan once having had the money and fame in the New York Philharmonic, and not wanting to repeat it, Phillip sipped his wine and stopped talking. She was probably right. Money provided comfort. He was being silly. Jonathan and Jean were going to enjoy their new lives without having to worry about where their next meal was coming from. They would still have their friends. And Jonathan would have the satisfaction in life from helping other people. But like everything in Phillip's life, he told himself, only time would tell.

The next day, when Phillip walked into the recording studio of Manley and Thombs there was no sign of Jonathan. Jean was sitting on a stool looking like the Queen Bee, surrounded by long-haired young men. The five men were dressed in weird, coloured shirts, earrings in their ears, studs in their noses. For the first time since he had met Jean, there was no sign of her bags. The fear of losing her only possessions had gone. The drummer was setting up his drums, banging them with sticks, his bottom on the drummer's chair, his feet splayed, his hair falling over his face. Amelia was positioning a microphone in front of Jean. A young man Phillip had never seen before was talking to Chad.

"Ah, the money man. Come and meet Bruce Manley, Phillip. He needs eight thousand dollars."

"What are those weird animals on the front of their shirts?"

"Lizards. The band is called The Lizards. Bruce needs the money now."

"Where's Jonathan, Chad?"

"He didn't want to come."

"Has he given the British consul his bank account details?"

"I don't think so. Jean says when he found a copy of Tuesday's *Herald* in the new place where he and his friends are squatting, he read my article on the Earl of Fernsby, threw the paper on the floor and walked out of the old building. So much for my good journalism. First man to throw an article of mine on the floor in disgust. Now, can Bruce have his eight thousand dollars?"

"Of course. How silly of me. Money first. Way to go. I'll give you my debit card and get the money back from Perry Mance when we set up getmethatsong.com. Amelia, how are you? What music are you going to play? Hello, Jean. You have the most beautiful smile on your face. Are you going to record only the songs of Jonathan? Never mind. Just tell me where I can find Jonathan. Where are the new digs? You made my wife cry last night when she saw you singing on television. Where are your bags? Have you found yourself an agent? My Martha would love to act as your publicist. She's a little handicapped right now. She's having a baby next month. Silly of me to mention it. Have you heard from Vasco Henriques? Will Jonathan have to wear a lizard suit if he plays with the band? Oh, that should be fun. Now, where is he? Of course, Chad. Give Bruce my debit card. There you are, sir. Eight thousand US dollars. Now, is everything set? Good. Enjoy yourselves. Ah, thank you, Jean. So this is your new address. When are they going to give you some money? Signed on the dotted line, Bruce. Everything is about money. I'll be seeing you all. Good to see you looking so happy, Jean. Where do you think he went?"

"I don't know. Where do you want me to stand, Amelia?"

"Have a nice day."

"You can't go now, Phillip."

"I can, Chad. You've got my money. Now let me go look for my friend. For once in the winter, the sun is shining. Last night's snow has melted. He'll be in the park. Where we met. Enjoy making your record. Perry Mance is going to sell a million copies standing on his head with all the new media ways of advertising. Last night was quite some start. Let the bag-lady sing. Good luck to you all."

Phillip turned and left the room, no one bothering to look at him. They had what they wanted: the bag-lady, and his money. After finding Jonathan, his next job would be bringing Perry Mance into the picture. Anyway, what was eight thousand dollars? With his coat collar up despite the intermittent sunshine coming onto the street through the gaps in the buildings, his hands deep in his pockets, Phillip began his walk to the park. At least the bag-lady was smiling.

When Phillip reached the park, Mary, the old lady, was sitting on her favourite bench under the leafless trees, the stray cat on her lap. Jonathan was standing with his feet splayed on the grass some way from the bench, his begging hat on the grass in front of him. A few people were walking through the gardens. Sitting down next to Mary, Phillip looked across at Jonathan, unable to catch his attention. The violin began to play, Jonathan struggling with his arthritic hands in the cold. An old man passing by put a coin in the hat, smiling at an unhappy Jonathan.

"How are you, Mary?"

"A little cold. There's no warmth in the sun. No flowers in the flowerbeds."

"Have you fed the cat?"

"I always feed the cat... He's having trouble playing his violin... There. Someone else has given him money. It's difficult begging in winter. Poor man. There he goes again. That's better... The cat's fed. Can't sit too long in the cold."

When Jonathan put the violin back in its case half an hour later, a few notes and coins in the hat, Phillip got up from the empty bench and walked across the grass.

"Can't move my fingers when I want to. My arthritis is terrible today. At least the sun is shining. How are you, Phillip?"

"Why didn't you go with Jean?"

"I can't play, Phillip. Just look at my hands. I can barely bend the fingers."

"Haven't you opened an account with a bank?"

"I wrote out the music and words of my songs. Can a band read sheet music? Oh, well. Jean's happy."

"Are you going to open a bank account? The British can't send you the money until they have a verified bank account number. Do you want my help? Come on. Let's go to the bank. You've got to start helping people like those who put money in your hat."

"All they talk about now is my money. When they are going to get their allowance. They're like a hungry pack of dogs. They don't really like me anymore now I'm different. They only like my money. How did you find me?"

"A good guess."

"The little bit of fun I had in my life has gone. Even Jean's lost interest in me now she's the centre of all the attention. Will the studio give her money?"

"I'm sure they will. Are you coming to the bank?"

"I want to run away. The thought of all that new life is terrifying me. I've forgotten how it works. We found a new building to squat in. Being renovated. They left the door open."

"Do you have an identity document?"

"Not a thing. How do I prove to the bank who I am?"

"My lawyer has proof. All we need is for you to give the bank your signature and my lawyer will do the rest."

"Are you sure?"

"Try me. Come on. Pick up your hat. Once the money is deposited, we'll go and look for an apartment. I started the shit, Jonathan. Let me help you go forward into your new life the way Jean is going forward into hers. Change is never easy. Even change for the better. My wife is certain the change for you will be for the better. And all those students going to the Royal Academy of Music and the Juilliard School of Music. Think of them. Think of your friends living comfortably in a room in the winter that is heated. You're the Eighteenth Earl of Fernsby, even if you can't use your title in America. Let me help you, Jonathan. Let me finish what I started and hope it all did some good. Don't throw it away. Too many people can now rely upon you for help. The way you just relied upon the passers-by to drop money in your hat. By Christmas, you're going to have a warm home of your own and Jean's going to have made her first record. The world's going to hear your compositions, even if they don't hear your violin. Trust me, Jonathan."

"Can you trust anyone?"

"I like to think so. Have you eaten anything today? Right. First, we'll go to a burger joint and then we'll open your bank account. And it all happened right here in the park. Because of your music, forty-five million dollars are going to land in that hat. Smile, Jonathan. You still have lots of living to do. You and Jean. Jean the famous singer. Jonathan, the Eighteenth Earl of Fernsby. And it's all my fault. Good, now you're laughing. Put that money in your pocket, the hat on your head and I'll carry the violin."

"Thank you, Phillip. You've been good to me."

"I hope so. I really hope so."

"She can sing, can't she?"

"Oh, yes. She can sing. And you can write songs. Even if you can't play the violin, you will always be able to write your songs, the songs the whole world is going to enjoy. If we hurry, the bank will still be open. We can go to my bank around the corner."

"Is she really happy?"

"She's the Queen Bee. Atonement. She's going to atone for aborting her child."

"Poor Jean."

"Poor all of us. But life goes on."

"Not for her child."

They walked out of the park in silence to the burger joint. Afterwards, at the bank, they were shown into the bank manager's office. In an hour it was all over.

"You can draw money now if you so wish, Mr Fernsby. I read the article in the *Herald*. And your lawyer has confirmed your identity. Thank you for using our bank. Come with me to the teller. How much of an advance would you like?"

"Five hundred dollars."

"Splendid. When the transfer comes through from the British government, we will talk investments. The bank has all the facilities. Global equity funds, property funds. A complete investment portfolio... The Earl of Fernsby. My goodness gracious me."

Ushered out of the bank by a smiling bank manager, they stood for a moment in the sun.

"All we have to do now, Jonathan, is take a cab to the British consulate and ask them to transfer the money. Welcome to your old world. There's no looking back."

EPILOGUE

JANUARY 1995 —"BORN IN AMERICA"

Three weeks after Christmas, a week before the baby was due to be born, Ivy Hartley moved into the new nursery on the forty-ninth floor, a fantasy world for Carmen painted on the walls and ceiling. For weeks, Martha had worked on the perfect nursery, a permanent smile on her face. The wardrobe was neatly stacked with baby clothes. The cot with the droppable front nicely placed at the bottom of the single bed. Toys on all the little tables. Coloured lights that dimmed. The perfect home for a baby to lie on its back in the cot and see the world and hear the sounds of music, the low voices of her parents. To feel the care of the nurse who had come all the way from Africa to look after her, to love and be loved in a perfect world.

The day before Ivy moved her things into the nursery with Phillip's help, Randall, Meredith and Douglas had moved into their new apartment on the thirty-first floor, Max having introduced Randall to the realtor and taken his commission, their home on the Isle of Man put on hold to please Meredith, the cats and Polar Bear still left in the cattery and the kennels while Randall worked out what to do with them. Aggie had gone back to Kansas City with Mabel Crabshaw a week after Christmas, the two old ladies sharing the unfolding nursery as Martha pursued her passion for all the decorations, both Aggie and Mabel helping with the excitement.

Despite Marcin Galinski's pleading, Jasmine was still living in her rented apartment in the same building as Martha and Phillip, telling Marcin the only way he was ever again going to have sex with her was if he married her and made their baby legitimate, her sexual frustration happily taken out on Max, the obliging, good-looking young janitor.

Through the marketing genius of Perry Mance, getmethatsong.com had sent the bag-lady's first album of Jonathan Fernsby's songs halfway up the charts, everyone who had heard her sing and seen the advertising going to the shops to buy her music, the speed with which Perry had taken the recordings of Bruce Manley and outsourced their manufacture into CDs taking Phillip's breath away. In weeks, the sales had turned Jean from a bag-lady to a rich lady with a permanent smirk on her face, Jonathan no longer the centre of attention as she moved from poverty to a life of joyful comfort.

For Jonathan, life had not been so easy despite all the money now in his possession. From an obscure hobo on the streets of New York, he had become the target of people's attention, from the financiers wanting to handle his money, to the realtors wanting to sell him a home, to his two now cloying and gushing sisters and the entire pack made up of their children insinuating they had a right, if only a moral right, to some of the Fernsby money. For Phillip, it was a new, unrecognisable Jonathan: shaven, hair perfectly cut, clean new clothes, a bath every morning, his life a constant battle to keep all the people away from his money and create the Earls of Fernsby Foundation. With their new monthly allowances paid into their new bank accounts, his old hobo friends had lost interest in each other, no longer needing each other's help. Jonathan was just another old rich man, not a true friend in the world, using money to try and make himself happy, and knowing that all other people wanted from him was his money, all the false smiles and laughter sinking Jonathan into a permanent state of inner misery he only talked about with Phillip, both of them commiserating with each other at how hollow life can become. Even his songs being played to the world were an anti-climax, as they were gone, no longer his. However much money in royalties he was going to receive from getmethatsong.com, the story of Linda, the story of friends had gone forever, commercialised into popular music. The final stab in Phillip's feeling of guilt was Jonathan telling him he had never felt so lost and lonely in his life. The eyes of the newly shaven face were cold, the old smile in the park as he played the new violin no longer there. Trying to forget what he had done by interfering in other people's business, Phillip tried to concentrate on helping Ivy move into the apartment.

"So, are you related to Hartley the ivory hunter? Where do you want this suitcase? Two Africans lost in New York. Makes quite a story."

"So far as we know, he was no relation. Why do you ask?"

"My family have a connection going back to Sebastian Brigandshaw in the days of Selous, Hartley and Brigandshaw."

"This room is so cute. Thanks for giving me a desk under the window. The perfect spot to study. All we can do in the turmoil of Africa to protect our future is teach ourselves a profession."

"You know that old saying: he can take away your land as they did my father's farm. They can take away your money as happened to many in the Great Depression. But they can't take away what's inside your head. Welcome to the forty-ninth floor, Ivy. All we're waiting for now is baby Carmen. I'll leave you to unpack. Dinner's at seven. You have your own TV. Your own privacy. I'm sure it's going to work, thanks to Max and Jasmine."

"I think he's gorgeous."

"Careful. That's Jasmine's territory."

"I didn't know. Is the baby his? I thought the father was Marcin Galinski."

"There's another saying among the worldly. You are sure who your mother is as you came out of her womb. Your father is never quite so certain."

"That's terrible."

"How the world goes round. But as far as Jaz is concerned, I'm certain the father of her baby is the genius. Our Jaz has a way of doing things. She always says a girl has to look after herself in this world... Another week and my daughter will be lying in that cot at the foot of your bed. I'm going to be a father."

"Do you miss Africa?"

"Every day of my life."

"Do you think the whites will be allowed to stay in Africa?"

"Only time will tell. What politicians say and what they do are two different things. Today, reconciliation. Tomorrow, get the hell off my land. And would you blame them? Colonialism and the British Empire are as dead as the dodo. Life goes on. Today people are far more mobile. We're citizens of one big world. We come and go. Have done, I suppose, right down the centuries. Enjoy your studies and looking after Carmen."

"Are we going to eat together?"

"As you wish. The kitchen is yours. It'll all work out. Just keep a close eye on Martha until the baby is born. Especially when I'm not in the apartment. This time, so far so good. New life is in the making. A new generation of Crookshanks."

"Do you have a degree?"

"I do, in history. And history has a bad habit of repeating itself. Like in Zimbabwe, my guess is that in a few more years, when they've got a handle on the government, the whites won't be welcome in South Africa. Be prepared, Ivy. Always think ahead. If people can take something from you without paying for it they will. Call it thievery. Or politics. They say the land belongs to the African. And maybe it does. They'll get back their own. The whites will move on. In history, nothing stays the same, and nothing changes. We're an animal species. Just like the others."

"Where are you, Phillip?"

"Coming, Martha. Are your waters breaking?"

"Not yet. But it's near. I can feel the change coming. Does Ivy want a drink?"

"I'll ask her... Ivy, do you want a drink? It's sundowner time in New York... Good. You'll have a drink when you've finished unpacking... Coming, Martha."

In the lounge, Martha was sitting on the sofa, holding her bulging stomach with both hands.

"Why are you putting on your overcoat, Phillip?"

"Because it's cold outside. I'm going to the pub."

"When are you coming back?"

"When Randall and I have finished drinking. Make yourself a cup of tea and give Ivy a drink. If you need me, call my mobile."

"Is Meredith going with you?"

"I don't think so. Who's going to look after Douglas?"

Outside, having collected Randall on the way down, Phillip hailed a cab.

"Why don't we walk, Phillip?"

"Because it's raining. Come on. Get in. Let's do some drinking. With Ivy in the apartment, I don't have to worry about leaving Martha on her own. It's pub night. All the regulars I want to introduce you to. Are you going to live permanently in New York, or is the flat an investment? Women. They never know what they want. What are you going to do with Polar Bear? You can't bring the dog to New York. And the cats? Who'll look after Rabbit Farm?"

"Shut up, Phillip."

"I'm so sorry. How's the writing going?"

"Haven't written a word since I left the Isle of Man. Probably never will. What do you do in life when you've done it? Meredith likes all the attention. I hate it."

"Are they publishing her children's book?"

"They keep prevaricating. It's me they were after... What are you going to do with the rest of your life, Phillip?"

"Get drunk with my brother for starters."

"What's she like?"

"Who?"

"The nanny."

"Pretty in a way. Wears glasses. Bookish. A serious girl."

"Not your type. Of course, she's not a sexpot. Your wife chose the nanny."

"She'll be perfect for Carmen for the next three years. What do you do all day now you're not writing?"

"I sit and think. Sometimes I just sit."

"What do you think about when you manage to think?"

"Africa. Always Africa. I imagine myself back on World's View... Why are we stopping?"

"The pub is across the road. Welcome to Harry B's."

"What the hell are we doing in New York?"

"I have absolutely no idea. Ask the women. It's called married life, Randall. You do what they want. Women get bored without company. Anyway, we have to think of our children. Come on. The pub's up the stairs. At least we have a pub within walking distance even though we caught a cab. It's not all bad... What's Meredith doing?"

"Watching television. Some American sitcom."

"Is she happy?"

"As a cricket. Ever since I bought the apartment... These stairs are steep. We'll have a job walking down them when we're drunk... Hey. Look at this place. It's full of people."

"You see the guy with his arse flowing over both sides of the barstool? That's my friend Spence. Spence Meyer. Introduced me to Perry Mance through his son, Spence Junior. They were at New York University together before Perry started getmethatbook.com with my money... Hello, Spence."

"How's my investment going?"

"You didn't invest, Spence. You were given shares for introducing me to Perry Mance. How's Spence Junior? This is my brother Randall."

"The writer. I'm impressed. My son is getting drunk with a new group of fraternity friends. All they do. Work at their studies and drink. Chase women. Have fun. What I wouldn't do to be young again."

"And you still haven't been to Stigley's gym?"

"Don't be bloody silly. I'm fat, Phillip. Look at me. How am I going to exercise with a carcase this size? Have a drink. What are you both having? Terry, this is Phillip's brother. The famous author, Randall Holiday. The first round is on me. Now we can get started. And the good news, Phillip, is I have another potential start-up for you. Another friend of Spence Junior."

"How's the world of investment banking?"

"Pays a good salary. The bonus is good. Life in New York, the home of money. Now isn't that nice? The man next to me has moved down the bar. Now my friends can sit next to me. So, what are you writing, Randall?"

"Have you read one of my books?"

"Not yet. But I've heard of you. You're famous... What's it to be?"

"A beer. Whatever beer my brother drinks."

"And where are you from? Of course. Africa. Give them a beer, Terry. Let's get started."

By the second round, paid for by Phillip, Spence had turned to the man on his right, leaving Phillip to have a conversation with his brother. Spence and the man were talking about the commodity and stock markets.

"Why is it always about making money? The markets go up. They come down. I check my portfolio once a year and hope that trust managers have done their job with Grandfather's money. For others, like your friend Spence, talking money is their lifeblood."

"Keep your voice down, Randall."

"He can't hear me. I'm talking into your left ear... I'm going to ask the family on the farm next to Rabbit Farm to look after Polar Bear and the cats. Not the ones who took the two Collies. They're short of money. I'll pay them. Subsistence farming is what it says. You subsist. Unless you have a six-thousand-acre tobacco farm, you can't make money out of farming. Only big farms make money."

"Are you going back?"

"Who knows? We don't have permanent residence in America. But I expect the Americans would like the tax on my royalty cheques. You want another drink? My round... Who knows? She may get bored with New York if she doesn't make any friends."

"The wife of a famous author? Of course she'll make friends. Everyone in America likes a celebrity. Especially one to count as a friend. Most important, what are you going to do stuck on the thirty-first floor?"

"How's your safari business?"

"Nothing like changing the subject... I hear from Jacques every now and again. I still have the cottage in the Vumba. In this crazy world, you never know when you're going to need sanctuary. The safari business in Zim is good. There aren't too many places left on this planet like the Zambezi Valley. The world population has tripled in Dad's lifetime. Have you heard from them? It's not the same, talking on the phone."

"He hates living back in England."

"I know he does. But he's safe. The white farmers in Zimbabwe aren't safe. Mugabe's encouraging the war veterans to intimidate the farmers who haven't left. The farms are basically worthless if you want to sell them. No, our father is better off in Chelsea beside the River Thames. We don't have to worry about them."

"Do you think we'll ever be able to go home? Can you imagine living again in a warm climate without people on top of you? Rabbit Farm is beautiful, but most of the year it's bloody cold. Oh, well. I've run out of stories. They say a novel writer only has a few good books in his head. After that, you start to repeat yourself. When Hemingway ran out of story, he shot himself."

"Please don't do that, Randall. It's so messy. You want to switch to whisky? The guy next to Spence has bought him a drink. We're on our own."

"Have been ever since we lost our mother. You and me, Phillip. Just you and me. You know the best thing in life? Having your brother as your best friend."

"I'll drink to that... Terry, give us each a double shot of single malt whisky. The bar's nicely full."

"Coming up."

"And no, Randall. Not you and me. We'll never be able to go home. Can you imagine Martha and Meredith wanting to shut themselves away in the wilds of Africa? Most people seem to like living in the cities. So, we either have families or we go home and live on our own... That was quick, Terry... Cheers, Randall. To our families. To our kids. To their future. The past is the past. Best we leave it there except in your books. I wish I had something else to do other than be a venture capitalist. What's the point in making more and more money when you've got enough? I don't understand other people. When they've got a million, they want a billion. The money culture. Welcome to New York. I feel like getting drunk for a change. We haven't been drunk together for ages. Get pissed and talk rubbish."

"What about Meredith on her own, the second night in our Manhattan apartment? After this one, we'd better go back to my new place and get ourselves drunk."

"Of course. I was only thinking of myself. Martha can't drink until after the baby is born. The odd glass of red wine. But she can't drink the way I want to drink tonight in the company of my brother. Hang on. I've got a better idea. Why don't you phone Meredith and tell her to take Douglas up to the forty-ninth floor? Better still, I'll phone Martha and suggest she invites Meredith up for a drink. With the baby about to pop she won't drink. Meredith can drink with Ivy. Everyone is happy. The Crookshank brothers get drunk in the pub. The women get to chatter... What's a derivative? Spence is telling his new friend the bank is selling derivatives. You were in finance before the writing bug got hold of you. That must have been some effort working for the Brigandshaw group in London and getting your degree in economics at night school at the London School of Economics."

"If you want to survive comfortably you have to work. Derivatives are a way for banks to bundle their mortgages and sell them off to ignorant buyers. The buyer has no idea of the underlying risk. But the return is good. The buyer thinks he's getting a higher income. The banks palm off their liability."

"I don't understand."

"No one does really. That's the problem. Why they call themselves investment bankers and not mortgage lenders. It's a crooked world. Always has been. You have to keep your wits about you and question what you're being told. There's nothing better for a banker than palming off his liability. He gives five per cent to the bank depositor, charges ten per cent for the mortgage. Combines all the mortgages into a derivative and offers seven per cent interest, collecting the three per cent difference without leaving himself with a risk. Everything is fine, provided the chaps with the mortgages make their monthly mortgage payments."

"It's more complicated than that, Mr Writer."

"I'll bet it is, Spence. Sorry to listen to your conversation. You want a drink? Where is your friend going?"

"Home to his wife."

"What are you doing, Phillip?"

"Phoning Martha, brother... Hello. It's me. Randall wants you to invite Meredith up for a drink. We'll be home when we're drunk. Spence is with us. Has a new venture to talk about. How's our baby?... Good. Enjoy your natter with Meredith... That worked, Randall. Now, where were we? Derivatives. Bankers. The world of money. Welcome to New York, brother. Mine's a single whisky. Tonight we're going to enjoy ourselves. As are our wives... And then came Carmen. Welcome to a new generation, born in America. We're all over the world now, Randall. All over the world. I wonder what happened? In the old days, families stayed in the same place for generation after generation. I think it's sad. I wonder where Carmen will end up living her life? From Africa to Rabbit Farm, to New York. Thank you, Terry. Give us a round. Make the shots of whisky singles... Poor Jonathan. I wonder what the violin player is doing with himself tonight. Anyway, they are playing the bag-lady's songs, and you and I, Spence, through getmethatsong.com, are making money out of it. The world's only tangible product. Money."

"Let's drink to money."

"Of course, Spence. Let's drink to money."

. . .

When they went home they were both happily drunk. The three women were sitting in the lounge, the television on, no one paying any attention.

"Where's my nephew Douglas?"

"In the nursery fast asleep. How was the boys' night out?"

"Splendid. We had too much to drink and talked a load of crap. How are you enjoying America, Meredith? Don't you miss your animals?"

"Please don't trip over the furniture."

"Sorry, Martha. Are we all having another drink? Ivy, meet my brother, Randall. If you're not watching the TV, why not turn it off? What's the matter, Martha? Are you all right?"

"My waters are breaking. Get me to the hospital... Now, Phillip! I'm going to have a baby!"

"Can't drive. We're drunk."

"Call a bloody cab."

"Of course. As you wish. A taxi. Can you drive, Ivy? Of course, you don't have an American licence. How many drinks you had with Meredith?"

"Hurry, Phillip."

"I'm trying to think. Stop giggling, Randall."

Meredith looked from Phillip to Randall, both of them happily drunk, and shook her head.

"You two are nicely drunk. I'll go downstairs and hail a taxi while Ivy helps Martha get ready."

"What happens when your waters break, Meredith?"

"You have a baby. Stop laughing, Randall. Why are men so stupid? Come on, Martha. Let Ivy help you pack a bag. Do you want to give your doctor a ring?"

"They'll do that when I get to the hospital. I'm so frightened."

"Everything is going to turn out just fine. Relax. When I had Douglas, it was exactly the same. You two men stay where you are. They don't want drunks in the hospital. Ivy and I will go with Martha. You can come to the hospital when you're sober. And stop giggling, both of you."

"We're coming with you. All I need is a pee."

Seventeen hours later, with Ivy back at the apartment looking after Douglas, Phillip completely sober, Martha was still in labour, the fear in Phillip's stomach consuming him. The three of them were sitting in the room next to where Martha was trying to have her baby, Meredith lying on the bench fast asleep. Next to Meredith, Randall sat waiting. The single cry of the newborn baby lifted the fear from Phillip as the smiles broke out on their faces.

"What's happening? Have I been asleep?"

"She's had the baby. Carmen's been born. I'm a father, Meredith."

As Meredith sat up, a man walked through from the delivery room.

"Mr Crookshank? Your wife has had a healthy baby girl. Do you have a name for your daughter?"

"Carmen. After my late mother. Is everything good?"

"Everything is fine. Mother and daughter are doing fine. I want your wife and baby to stay the night in the hospital. I suggest all of you go home and get some sleep. Congratulations, Mr Crookshank."

"Can I see them?"

"Of course you can."

When Phillip walked into the delivery room the smile on Martha's face made Phillip's heart rise all the way to heaven. She was propped up on the bed, the baby cradled in her arm. The nurse was smiling. The doctor was smiling.

"Do you want to hold our baby?"

"I might drop her in my excitement."

"Don't be silly. Carmen, this is your father. Isn't she pretty?"

"I have never seen anything more beautiful."

"The doctor says you must go home. He wants us to stay the night. Go home, honey. Get some sleep. There you are."

"She's so tiny."

"What are you doing?"

"Counting her fingers and toes."

"Come here and give me a kiss. All's well that ends well. I'm so happy, I think I'm going to burst."

"I'm going to sleep the night in a chair. The others can go home. And you're right. All's well that ends well. Wasn't that Shakespeare?"

"I think so. You can lie next to me on the bed. When they move us from the delivery room the nurse will put Carmen in a crib, or we can all sleep in the same bed together. Thank you, Phillip. Thank you so much for my baby."

"Our baby."

"Of course. All my fear has gone. Gone forever. The three of us are going to be happy together for the rest of our lives. I'm a mother, Phillip. Being a mother is the most wonderful feeling in the world."

"Can the others come in to see the baby?"

"Of course they can. My life is fulfilled. Just look at little Carmen. Isn't she cute?"

A new life had come into the world making Phillip wonder what it would bring. Once upon a time, they had all been just as tiny, little humans lying in the arms of their mothers. Did the child know where she was? What it was? What it was to be alive? To have seventy, or eighty, or maybe a hundred years ahead of her like Mabel Crabshaw, all those years to be lived? Would the world be around for Carmen in a hundred years' time? How many children would Carmen have, how many grandchildren? Would his seed go on and on, the only reason for Phillip having existed? Or would she die like his mother, attacked by a pride of lions in the wilds of Africa? What did the child he was looking at have for a future? Would she be happy? That Phillip hoped more than anything else. He wanted that little face he was looking at to be happy for the rest of her life. A hope that seemed somewhat forlorn in the face of the world she had entered. Phillip kissed his newborn daughter on her tiny forehead. She was alive. They were alive. Life for the new. Life for the old. The purpose of his life, like the purpose of Martha's, had been fulfilled. His world would go on to the end of time, day by day, year by year. For Phillip, the world now had a future to be lived in whatever happened to him. For all the eternal centuries there would be a chance for happiness, a chance for living peacefully among people in joy, a better world, always a better world without so much of its present misery.

Putting the baby back in her mother's arms, Phillip left the delivery room in a strange mood, a mixture of premonition, exultation, fear and hope.

"You can both go in and see the baby. I'm staying the night with Carmen and Martha."

"You look far away, brother."

"I am, Randall. Far away in future history. In a world only my descendants will see. I have a child, and it feels so strange and exulting I don't know what it all means. My life has changed. Did you feel the same when Douglas was born? Is it just a moment? I feel strange. Transported. It's brought my own life into perspective. Given it meaning. Even understanding. Thank you both for being with me on this, the most understanding day of my life. For a brief flash, I think I can see what life is all about. I hope so. It makes my life have a meaning. For a moment, the mundane, the trivial has gone. I can see life's purpose far into the future... Through my daughter, my mother is alive again. Her life had purpose. Our mother's life, Randall, wasn't wasted. Our mother has been born again and is lying with Martha in the delivery room. Go say hello to her... Give me a hug, brother. I'm going to cry."

PRINCIPAL CHARACTERS

The Crookshanks
Craig Crookshank — Phillip and Randall's younger half-brother
Douglas Crookshank — Randall and Meredith's baby son
Harold Crookshank — Craig and JoJo's baby son
Jeremy and Bergit Crookshank — Phillip, Randall, Craig and Myra's parents
Jojo Tafara — Craig's Shona girlfriend
Martha Crookshank — Phillip's wife and Aggie's daughter
Myra Becker — Phillip and Randall's half-sister and wife of Julian Becker
Phillip Crookshank — Central character of *Scattered to the Wind*
Randall Crookshank— Phillip's brother

The Polands
Agnes (Aggie) Poland — Martha Poland's mother
Ford and Hugo Poland — Martha's brothers

Other Principal Characters
Amelia — Bar lady at Harry B's
Angela (Angie) — A student waitress who works in an Italian restaurant
Bruce Manley — Owner of Manley and Thombs music studio
Chad Fox — Journalist from the *Herald*, New York

Franklyn Bowden — Martha's manager at Horst and Maples advertising agency
Fred and Tinkerbell Mance — Perry Mance's mother and father
Gerta — Martha's assistant at Bowden, Crookshank and Fairbanks
Godfrey — Renée's husband
Gordon Blake — A salesman who Phillip met in Solly's Saloon, now working for Linguare.com
Grant Howard — An out-of-work New York chef
Hilda — Franklyn's assistant at Bowden, Crookshank and Fairbanks
Ivy Hartley — A South African student living in America
Jack Webber — An out-of-work advertising consultant from New York
Jacques Oosthuizen — Phillip Crookshank's safari business partner and distant cousin to Barend Oosthuizen
Jasmine (Jaz) Fairbanks — Martha's advertising assistant
Jean — The bag-lady and Jonathan's hobo friend
Jim — Perry Mance's uncle
Joanne Bowden — Franklyn's wife
Jonathan Wesley Harnsford Fernsby — An old violinist Phillip meets in a New York public garden
Larry and Tony — Perry's university friends
Mabel Crabshaw — An elderly friend of Agnes Poland
Marcin Galinski — A Yale graduate and owner of Linguare.com
Mary — Elderly English lady Phillip meets in a New York public garden
Max — Janitor of a high-rise apartment block in Manhattan
Munya — Sedgewick's assistant
Noah Hughes — Jasmine's boyfriend
Ollie Leftwich — A regular of Harry B's where Phillip meets him
Penny, Larry and Hank — Computer engineers who work for Linguare.com
Perry Mance — A young entrepreneur who Phillip invests money with
Priscilla — Receptionist at Bowden, Crookshank and Fairbanks
Renée — Jacques Oosthuizen's sister who lives in England
Robert — Jaz's assistant at Bowden, Crookshank and Fairbanks
Sedgewick — Phillip's safari driver and assistant
Spence Junior — Spence Meyer's son
Spence Meyer — A Jewish investment banker Phillip meets in Harry B's
Terry — The bar owner of Harry B's in New York
Tildy and Clarry Bowden — Franklyn's children
Volker — Gym instructor at Stigley's fitness club

DEAR READER

~

Reviews are the most powerful tools in our kitty when it comes to getting attention for Peter's books. This is where you can come in, as by providing an honest review you will help bring them to the attention of other readers.

If you enjoyed reading *Scattered to the Wind*, and have five minutes to spare, we would really appreciate a review (it can be as short as you like). Your help in spreading the word and keeping Peter's work alive is gratefully received. Please post your review on the retailer site where you purchased this book.

Thank you so much.
Heather Stretch (Peter's daughter)

ACKNOWLEDGEMENTS

~

Our grateful thanks go to our *VIP First Readers* for reading *Scattered to the Wind* prior to its official launch date. They have been fabulous in picking up errors and typos helping us to ensure that your own reading experience of *Scattered to the Wind* has been the best possible. Their time and commitment is particularly appreciated.

Agnes Mihalyfy (United Kingdom)
Daphne Rieck (Australia)
Hilary Jenkins (South Africa)

Thank you.
Kamba Publishing

WHEN FRIENDS BECOME LOVERS

BOOK FIFTEEN

~

Randall Crookshank has a lifestyle most would envy. A celebrity with a young wife, child, and pots of money. But he's desperately unhappy...

Living on the thirty-first floor of a New York apartment, Randall is bored stiff. And also, he cannot write and longs for the peace of his African roots. But Meredith is perfectly content, enjoying the company of her artist friends, including Clint...

Relying on Harry B's bar for friendship, Randall drowns his sorrow in alcohol. He hates his publishing commitments, wanting nothing to do with them. And meantime his marriage is crumbling.

It's not long after that Randall's life completely breaks down and he finds himself back in the snowy mountains of the Isle of Man, questioning his purpose in life. Alcohol seems the only way out of his misery, whilst he frantically tries to find his way back to his one true love. Yet, hope is fading...

When Friends Become Lovers is the fifteenth novel in the Brigandshaw Chronicles – a multigenerational saga, of passionate people living through the rise and fall of the Anglo-Saxon Empire.

Printed in Great Britain
by Amazon